PROPHET

NFINITE #1 ✦ ——————

PROPHET

R.J. LARSON

BETHANYHOUSE

a division of Baker Publishing Group
www.BethanyHouse.com

© 2012 by R. J. Larson

Published by Bethany House Publishers
11400 Hampshire Avenue South
Bloomington, Minnesota 55438
www.bethanyhouse.com

Bethany House Publishers is a division of
Baker Publishing Group, Grand Rapids, Michigan

Printed in the United States of America

Library of Congress Cataloging-in-Publication Data is available for this title.
Larson, R. J.
    Prophet / R.J. Larson.
        p.   cm. — (Books of the infinite ; 1)
    ISBN 978-0-7642-0971-0 (pbk.)
    I. Title.
PS3602.A8343P76 2012
813'.6—dc23   2011044912

Cover design by Wes Youssi/M80 Design
Cover photography by Steve Gardner, PixelWorks Studio

12   13   14   15   16   17   18   7   6   5   4   3   2   1

To Jerry
Your steadfast faith and encouragement
never cease to amaze me.

CHARACTER LIST

Ela Roeh \El-ah **Roe**-eh\ Prophet of Parne

Kalme Roeh **Call**-may **Roe**-eh\ Ela's mother

Dan Roeh \Dan **Roe**-eh\ Ela's father

Tzana Roeh **Tsaw**-nah **Roe**-eh\ Ela's sister

Kien Lantec (Lan Tek) **Kee**-en **Lan**-tek\ Ambassador from the Tracelands

Tek An \Tek **An**\ King of Istgard

Tek Lara \Tek **Lar**-ah\ A cousin to the king of Istgard

Tsir Aun \Sir **Awn**\ Istgardian commander

Ket Behl \Ket **Bell**\ Istgardian judge

Piln \Pilln\ Istgardian clerk

Ter \Ter, as in *Grrr!*\ Warden

Syb \Sib\ Warden's wife

Tek Sia \Tek **See**-ah\ King Tek An's sister

Jon Thel \Jon Thell\ A Traceland commander

Beka Thel **Bek**-ah Thell\ Jon Thel's wife, Kien's sister

Rade Lantec \Raid **Lan**-tek\ Kien's father

Ara Lantec **Are**-ah **Lan**-tek\ Rade Lantec's wife, Kien's mother

✦ I ✦

Tarnished snow sifted through the air, clinging to Ela Roeh's skin the instant she stepped outside. Warm snow. Impossible.

She rubbed at the flakes on her bare forearm and watched them smear across her brown flesh like menacing shadows. Ashes. What was burning?

Unnerved, Ela scanned the plain mud-plastered stone houses honeycombed around the wide public square. Houses built one atop another within a vast, irregular, protective curtain wall, sheltering the city of Parne. Mud and stone wouldn't burn, but the timbered interiors could. She'd seen it happen before, the thick dark smoke suffocating its helpless victims.

No, none of the houses were smoldering. Nor was Parne's crown, the temple. Good. A blessing.

A gust of wind brushed her face with more ashes. Ela tasted the harsh metallic bitterness and frowned. If none of Parne's homes were burning, then the ashes were puzzling indeed, because they must have come from a great distance. Parne, Ela remained convinced, was the most isolated city-state in existence. "Infinite . . ."

She stopped. Why pray about ashes without first learning their source? But perhaps she shouldn't wait, especially when those ashes were interfering with little things, like her ability to see and breathe. Really, she needed to cover herself. The ashes were clinging to her like living creatures, scuttling bugs determined to cause misery. Ela shuddered, imagining insects scurrying over her skin. Why hadn't she grabbed her mantle before deciding to take a walk?

Ela stepped back inside her family's home, a stark uneven box of a residence, exactly like every other home in Parne. Useful. Basic. Never changing from one generation to the next. Just like Parne's citizens. She snatched her thin brown mantle and called to her mother, "I'm going up to the wall! It's snowing ashes."

"What?" One dark eyebrow raised in disbelief, Kalme looked up from her work space by the low-domed plastered oven, but she continued to fan the oven's coals to a sullen red glow.

"It's snowing ashes," Ela repeated. "I'm going up to the wall to look for the fire."

"A house is on fire?" Kalme's eyes widened with the question, and she lowered her fan.

"No. The fire isn't here in Parne. But it must be huge if ashes are falling from so far away."

Kalme exhaled and resumed fanning. "Find your father and Tzana," she ordered. "Don't visit with Amar and his friends."

Don't create a scandal, Ela. She could almost hear the unspoken words.

"I won't," she promised her mother. Actually, Amar hadn't even been in her thoughts until Kalme mentioned his name. Why think of Amar at all? Ela was only *supposed* to marry him. Eventually.

Sarcasm helped nothing, Ela reminded herself. At least she hadn't snapped back at Kalme disrespectfully. Surely this was a sign of her growing maturity. Perhaps.

"Oh!" Kalme called out a parting order. "Bring more vinewood for the oven when you return. I'm running low."

"Yes, Mother." Ela took a deep breath, pulled the corner of her mantle across her nose and mouth, and then stepped out into the ash-laden public square. By now the dark flakes were descending thick and fast. Eyes stinging, Ela squinted and padded toward the stone steps built into the city's converged walls, leading up to Parne's rooftops, which rimmed the city's protective outer wall. There would be no running up these steps today. The ashes powdered the stones and her bare feet, denying her steady footing on the steps' surfaces.

"Ela!" a husky voice hailed her, then coughed. Amar.

Though tall, lanky, and dark-curled, like every other young man in Parne, Amar still managed to make her insides flutter. Just a little. Shielding his face with the corner of his cloak, Amar charged up the steps, slipped, and hammered a knee on the stones. Ela winced, but Amar shrugged off the injury, ignoring the shreds of dangling flesh and the blood oozing from a blackened scrape just below his kneecap. "Are you going up to the wall?"

"I'm not supposed to speak to you," she told him through the edge of her mantle.

"Good. I'm not supposed to acknowledge that you even breathe." His brown eyes crinkled with a cloak-concealed grin, and he took the last few steps up to meet her. Face to face now, he murmured through the fabric, "But I'm ignoring the rules today. I want to become acquainted with my wife."

Amar was the sort who needed a bit of a challenge. And right now, Ela was impatient enough to offer him one. "Wife? We're not even betrothed. So you mustn't presume my time is yours."

"That'll change in two weeks. Until then . . ." He slid his free hand inside Ela's mantle. His fingertips glided up her bare arm, making her shiver.

Ela shook him off and hurried up the steps to the rooftops. Stone pavings traced the sturdiest and least obtrusive public paths across Parne's terraced roofs. Mindful of her duty to evade Amar, Ela chose the most direct path to the city's broad wall walk. The ashfall was more scattered here, but new flakes clung to Ela, seeming to seek her deliberately.

Of course, she was entirely too fanciful. Why would ash flakes seek her deliberately? If Father could hear her thoughts, he would point out that ashes were without reason and unable to recognize her, or anyone else.

11

But where was Father? And Tzana? Ela stepped onto the wall walk, scanning its uneven contours and landings, hoping to see her father. There. Beside the northern lookout's shelter—a slender stone cupola wide enough for only one man, the lookout, who was sensibly sheltered inside.

"Father!" Ela's voice was so muffled beneath the ash-laden folds of her mantle that she doubted he would hear. But Dan Roeh was nothing if not acute. He turned immediately, his thin tanned face weathered, his expression grim. Nestled in the crook of his arm, Ela's fragile little sister, Tzana, peered at Ela over the edge of their father's patriarchal cloak.

Ashes crowned Tzana's wisp-thin black curls like a bleak benediction, muting their normal shimmer and wringing Ela's heart. Tzana looked like a tiny, dark, wrinkle-faced lamb, hushed with fear. What had the men been saying to frighten her? Squinting, Ela faced north and saw the source of the ashes. Smoke towered black above the crests of the wild borderlands that separated Parne from its neighboring countries. Surely an entire city had to be ablaze to create such massive billows above the clouds.

"Infinite," she murmured, "what is happening?"

Ela's question was rhetorical, no answer expected. But a whisper permeated her thoughts.

Close your eyes.

"What?" She gasped through her mantle, captivated, recognizing the Infinite's voice—hearing it as if He'd leaned over her shoulder and whispered into her ear.

Close your eyes and you will see.

She obeyed.

A vision slammed into Ela's mind. She reeled through the image against her will, comprehending the scene as if she stood in the midst of it. Countless homes ablaze, crackling with heat. Children wailing. Women kneeling on bloodied soil, screaming as their husbands fought for their lives, hopelessly outmatched by soldiers clad in thick square-plated armor. Soldiers who wielded

12

gigantic swords. Ela inhaled, almost gagging at the stench of burning flesh as soldiers set fire to screaming, dying men.

Helpless as any of the wailing women, Ela watched one of the bleeding men collapse. She felt his anguish for his family, his terror as the malevolent grinning soldier raised his killing sword one last time.

This is butchery, dishonorable and unjustified.... As the Infinite's voice whispered through the vision, Ela gripped her head and cried out in agony. The combined force of the words, the odors, the image, and its torrents of emotion were overwhelming her senses. "Stop!"

"Ela!"

Someone was shaking her. She returned to herself, shocked to realize she was sprawled on the ash-strewn walkway. Still alive. But her head hurt so badly she wanted to retch. Dry-mouthed, she shut her eyes again and whispered, "Infinite, what was that? No, please! Don't answer!" She recoiled at her stupidity and trembled, scared the answer's force would destroy her.

No answer. Tranquil darkness enveloped her instead—a blessed relief. Ela went limp on the stones.

✦ ✦ ✦

Someone shook Ela again. She finally opened her eyes and looked up into her father's face. Dan Roeh was staring at her, openmouthed, his expression a mix of fear and outrage. "What is wrong with you?" he demanded. "Get up!"

"Yes, sir." He was yelling at her because she had collapsed? Could she stand? Ela hardly knew. And by the look on her father's face, she could only presume she'd gone mad. Or . . . at least she must seem mad. But she couldn't be mad because the vision, the voice, and the emotions had been horribly real.

So agonizing that she didn't want to experience them again. Please, no.

Her father hesitated, then blurted the question Ela wished he'd asked first. "Are you well?"

"Yes." Now that the voice, the storm of emotions, and the vision had ceased, yes. She was only dazed. And alarmingly queasy. "Sorry. I don't quite know what happened." It was the truth. And she was afraid to petition the Infinite for details. Grit scraped between her teeth as she spoke. She longed to spit. She needed a drink of water.

"Ela? Are you listening to me? Take your sister home."

Ela pushed herself to her knees, eye to eye with Tzana, who now stood on the walkway, her small face puckered with old-woman concern.

"Want me to help you up?" Tzana squeaked, offering a tiny arthritic hand.

"Thank you," Ela mumbled, giving her little sister two fingers to hold, then dragging herself to her feet on her own wavering strength. She dared to look at her father again. He turned away. Amar, however, was staring at her oddly. Ela gave him an embarrassed half smile, then headed for the roof paths with Tzana skittering ahead of her, showing unusual liveliness. "Tzana, slow down. You'll slip in the ashes and break a bone."

"I won't," Tzana called back over her shoulder, not arguing but stating something she clearly regarded to be a fact.

Still dazed, Ela forced down her nausea and tried to gather her fragmented thoughts. Those poor families in her vision. She wished she could have saved those dying men. She longed to hold the children. To console their mothers. Tears slid down Ela's face, dripping black with ashes as she grieved. What had happened to those women and children?

They are now prisoners, the Infinite informed her. *Those who have survived are slaves.*

Dreading the impact of another vision, Ela braced herself and waited. But only the voice permeated her thoughts this time. And the voice was tolerable. More than tolerable. The Infinite's voice was compelling beyond any she'd ever heard. As it should be. Could she expect anything less from the Creator? No. And yet. And yet . . .

14

Why should she expect anything from Him at all?

She yanked the edge of her mantle over her nose and mouth again, then whispered, "Infinite? I'm no one special. Why are you telling me this?"

Because I know you will listen. Now follow your sister.

Tzana? Ela looked around, suddenly realizing she had stopped halfway down the stone steps. How had that happened? She didn't even remember leaving the terraces. "Tzana!"

The ashes were thinning now, but Ela still had to squint to see, her eyes felt so raw. Tzana was already at the base of the steps, poised in the open public square like a tiny dark-feathered bird. A listening bird. "Tzana!"

Tzana fluttered a hand at her. But instead of waiting for Ela, she crossed a corner of the public square and stopped before an ancient stone house. A tomb house.

What did Tzana think she was doing?

Deliberately, Tzana placed both hands on the tomb house's door and leaned forward, pushing it open.

"No! Tzana, stop!" Ela hurried down the remaining steps as quickly as the ashes and her own wobbly legs allowed. Tzana knew better than to violate the sanctity of a tomb house, didn't she? Tomb houses were dead. Plastered memorials honoring the names of the families who had once inhabited them. But sacrilege wasn't the worst part of Tzana's offense.

This wasn't an ordinary tomb house.

By now, other citizens of Parne were stopping to stare in obvious shock as Tzana scooted through the door, which should not have opened so easily. The traditional plastered seals alone should have been too hard for Tzana to force apart. "Tzana!"

Ela reached the doorway and paused, summoning her courage. This was the tomb of Parne's last prophet, Eshtmoh. Inspiration for countless terrors whispered by the children of Parne for more than seventy years. Eshtmoh the prophet had defeated monsters with mere words. Had foretold catastrophic droughts. Predicted assassinations, diseases, disasters of every kind. An Istgardian king had died of terror at the sight of him, and it had taken an entire army to finally bring Eshtmoh down to an early grave.

All true prophets died young. This was fact. Parne's elders could recite the name of each ancient prophet and the gruesome details of his death. At the end of a traditional recitation, the elder would shake his head, looking wise, saying, "A silver-haired prophet has failed."

"You'd best get that imp outta there!" someone scolded.

Matron Prill, a neighbor whose home rested above the Roehs' to the east, was shaking her ash-dusted topknotted head, her fists on her hips. "Wait until I tell your parents."

"I'll tell them first." Ela stepped into the broken doorway. How dare Matron Prill call Tzana an imp! Didn't she have a speck of compassion for Tzana's incurable aging condition? Why couldn't she, and everyone else in Parne, realize that Tzana was a blessing, not a sign that the Roehs were cursed? Poor Tzana—a tiny, wispy-haired old woman-girl before age ten.

An old woman-girl who was breaking down doors.

Ela stared at the door's timbers, wondering how her little sister had managed to demolish them. The door's wood was obviously still sound, yet Tzana was so fragile she often had to be carried through the city. "Infinite . . . ?" No. Please don't answer.

But how, as she lived and breathed, had Tzana managed such a feat?

Ela forced herself to call into the shadows. Her voice came out in a mere squeak. "Tzana?"

"Here!" Tzana sounded breathless. Thrilled.

Moving forward, her eyes adjusting to the gloom, Ela saw her little sister standing beside a massive clay rectangle plastered to the floor. Was that the prophet's sarcophagus? Ela stepped closer. Vinewood had grown up through the stone floor, twining thick over the tomb, as if protecting Eshtmoh's resting place. One particular branch of the vinewood was paler than the others. A bit straighter. It glowed oddly in the darkness, and Tzana clasped it in her small hands. Lifting it.

16

"Tzana, what are you doing? We have to leave *now*. Put that down!"

"But it's not mine," Tzana protested, her innocent voice filling the stark tomb house. She faced the doorway's slanting light and smiled at Ela. "It's for you."

The Infinite's voice whispered, *Will you accept?*

Accept?

The prophet's branch.

The Infinite was asking her . . .

Will you be My prophet?

Trembling, Ela quoted the ancient saying, unable to stop herself. " 'A silver-haired prophet has failed.' Is it true?"

Yes.

"If I accept will I die silver-haired?"

No.

Ela swallowed. Her hair would remain black. She would die young.

Will you accept?

✦ 2 ✦

Ela knelt and stared at the gleaming vinewood branch in Tzana's tiny gnarled hands, knowing she could refuse it. With her entire being, she felt . . . knew . . . the Infinite offered her a genuine choice. His patience settled her, even as she hesitated.

Tzana too waited patiently, holding Ela's death sentence. Still smiling.

"Tzana, what have you done?" Even as she spoke, Ela regretted the words. This was not Tzana's doing at all. The Infinite knew, of course, that fear for Tzana's safety was the only lure powerful enough to bring Ela to this place. To this decision.

Tzana's smile faded and her dark eyes glistened, brimming with unshed tears. "I thought this would make you happy," she pleaded. "It's a gift from the Infinite."

A gift. Was it? Ela hunched over and hid her face in her ash-smeared hands, resisting the impulse to bang her forehead on the aged stone floor. And yet . . . and yet . . . if she refused, would she ever hear His voice again?

"Infinite?" Ela sent up the plea and listened hard. Craving an answer.

Silence.

This was so unfair! Would He expect her to live the remainder of her life, enduring such unbearable silence? Already, her soul thirsted for His voice. "Infinite," Ela babbled into her cupped hands, "here I am—and I don't know why! Who has ever heard of a girl becoming a prophet? I'm clumsy and insignificant. No one will listen to me. And I dropped like a stone when You shared a vision with me. I'm not going to be of any use to You at all!"

You will. If you accept.

She drank in the words and sat up, thinking hard. She had two choices. Live to be old, silver-haired, and full of dry regrets, or accept this "gift" with all its uncertainties. Listening to the Infinite.

Tzana shifted slightly, clutching the prophet's branch a bit closer to her frail body. Ela pondered. Would this decision fall to someone else if she refused? And what would happen to those widows and orphans who suffered in the vision? Slaves, the Infinite had said.

Could she help them?

How could she not?

Despite her apprehension, Ela held out her hands, smiling at her little sister. "Thank you. I'm sorry I scolded you."

"I know." Tzana rested the branch on Ela's palms.

The branch was so light. And surprisingly warm. "Thank You, Infinite. I accept." But she was quivering inside. She leaned against Tzana and hugged her gently. "Help me up."

Beaming, Tzana tugged Ela's arm upward. Ela stood and paused to study the gap in the vinewood on the prophet's sarcophagus. Had Eshtmoh carried a forerunner of this same branch? What had he suffered during his time as a prophet? Were the stories about him exaggerations? And how old was he when he died?

No. She must not consider his death. Or her own. The fear would be too much. Breathe. Be calm. Steadier, she asked aloud, "Infinite? What now?"

Go outside. They are waiting for you.

They. Her neighbors, who couldn't be happy. Ela and Tzana had just violated one of Parne's most sacred sites. To Ela's knowledge, no one had ever broken into a tomb house before. What was the sentence for such a crime? A beating? Prison? A forced jump from the rooftops? Well, best to face everyone and endure the consequences with dignity. Chin up, shoulders back, Ela motioned Tzana toward the doorway. Dust motes and ashes mingled in the entry's slanting light, oddly peaceful.

Unlike the neighbors.

Even as Tzana stepped over the threshold into the ash-filtered sunlight beyond, Ela heard Matron Prill's scolding. "Look what you've done! How do you plan to repair that door? And the seals? Ela, you'll have to speak to the priests about those!"

"Take us to the priests," Ela commanded the outraged matron. "Immediately, please."

✦ ✦ ✦

Standing before the priests' council in their high stone chamber, with Tzana at her side, Ela told everything. Somewhere between her explanation of the Infinite sharing His overwhelming vision on Parne's wall walk and Ela's questioning Him about silver-haired prophets and dying young, the mood in the stone chamber darkened. All the idle whispers and chuckling among the priests hushed. Zade Chacen, Parne's imposing gold-and-blue-clad chief priest, backed away from Ela. Tiny edging steps, as if he feared she might notice.

Or as if he simply feared.

One of the chief priest's assistants spoke coldly. "How do we know you are truly the next prophet? Parne has not seen a prophet for seventy years. Furthermore, none of the prophets were girls!"

Ela almost argued that she was nearly eighteen, and—female or not—she hadn't chosen this role. Before she could speak, her scalp tingled. The branch warmed against her palm, its sheen intensifying almost unbearably, brilliant as lightning within her fingers.

Shielding his eyes with both hands, the doubter retreated. His long hair stood on end, and he gasped. "Forgive me! O Infinite, forgive me!" He dropped to his knees, cowering, as if he feared a blow from his Creator.

Ela forced herself to look away from the terrified man, toward the other priests in the stone chamber. "You—all of you—know this is truly the prophet's branch. I was asked to accept it, but I will gladly give this branch to one of you. Gladly. If you have been invited by the Infinite to accept it, *please* step forward."

No one moved and the chamber remained silent. Until the chief priest cleared his throat. "We will repair the doorway," he soothed, as the other priests nodded, their multiple gazes fixed on the branch glowing in her hands. "You must not worry. We understand the Infinite's own Spirit led you into this situation. When will you leave Parne?"

Leaving her birthplace hadn't occurred to Ela. But even as the chief priest was forming his question, she realized the answer. "I leave at dawn."

The branch glistened, and its sheen softened, becoming metallic. Mesmerized, Ela paused, studying it and listening to Him. It was her turn to clear her throat. Her first duty as a prophet was beyond uncomfortable. Trying not to squirm, she looked the chief priest in his eyes. "Zade Chacen, your Creator sees your heart. He knows what you cannot admit to yourself. You have become faithless and cold, never studying His words, never seeking His will. Never sharing His visions."

The chief priest's face slackened. "I . . . how . . . ?" He composed himself and stared over her head as if she didn't exist.

Miserable, Ela continued, "Your sons refuse to even acknowledge the Infinite, yet you favor them over Him. Therefore, you are removed from your place of power. As a sign to you, your sons will die on the same day, during a terrible calamity. Your descendants will never be priests again—though they will beg for the lowest priestly office, asking for nothing but bread to eat."

Most of the white-robed lesser priests were retreating now, avoiding Ela's gaze. She lifted the branch. "Wait." Everyone froze. "Where is Ishvah Nesac?"

One of the youngest priests—until now an onlooker from a shadowed corner—came forward. Reed-thin and slightly awkward, he knelt before Ela and shut his eyes, clearly expecting to be cursed. She'd never seen Ishvah Nesac before. She'd never heard the Nesac name. Yet now, through the Infinite's will, she recognized this young man. "Ishvah Nesac, you have been found faithful. Serve your Creator, seeking His words, His will, and His visions. He will honor you as His chief priest."

Clearly overcome, the new chief priest collapsed, whispering prayers into his hands.

Zade Chacen threw his priestly gold in a clattering heap at Ela's feet and fled the council chamber. Two handsomely clothed young men followed him, glaring silent threats at Ela as they passed. Chacen's sons, Ela knew. They looked so much like him.

Tzana hopped backward as if alarmed. Ela caught her tiny sister by one hand and steadied her. Nearby, Ela's erstwhile doubter stirred, tentatively, as if he still feared the Infinite's displeasure. Ela prayed for the man. How could she be angry with him if she had so many doubts herself? The branch cooled in Ela's grasp—ordinary vinewood now. "Come," she murmured to Tzana. "We're finished here. Let's go home."

Would this be the last time she saw her home?

Hand in hand, Ela and Tzana left the chamber. The ashfall had finally stopped. The air was clear, and Ela could almost pretend nothing had happened today. Except that Matron Prill was waiting in the courtyard below, watching Father, who was being jostled by Zade Chacen's irate sons.

"Leave him alone!" Ela released Tzana and stormed down the broad ash-dusted steps, so indignant that the two young men could have been giants and it wouldn't have mattered. "You've caused trouble enough for yourselves—why are you inviting more? You should be praying to the Infinite for mercy! Humble yourselves and He might forgive you even now—after all you've done!"

The two young men retreated, sullen, but visibly intimidated. Ela stared after them until they climbed a set of steps up to a terrace path and finally descended through a sheltered roof door.

"Ela, what's happened to you?" Dan Roeh put out one wide hand, then lowered it as if he'd wanted to shake Ela, but resisted. "First you have a fit up on the wall, then you break into Eshtmoh's tomb, and now you're screaming at Chief Priest Chacen's sons. I don't want them as enemies. When we return home, I expect an explanation." He bent and picked up Tzana, who had crept down the stairs, her movements slowed as if the effort pained her.

Matron Prill approached now, her expression pinched and disapproving as she eyed Ela. "I saw Chief Priest Chacen leave. You've been released?"

"Yes. The council agreed we've done nothing wrong."

"*That* is what's wrong with the priests' council," the matron huffed. "Those greedy men have forgotten how to punish anyone. Chacen's sons accept bribes instead!" She stomped away. Ela let her depart. Time was too precious to argue with self-certain neighbors.

Now, how could she tell her parents she was a prophet? She hardly believed it herself.

✦ ✦ ✦

Father listened in silence, but Mother began to sob and rock back and forth on her floor cushion. "This is my fault!" Kalme cried. Her sobs lifted to a full-throated wail, and she clutched her head, tearing at her smoothly coiled brown hair until it slid down past her shoulders. "He's taking you because I was afraid!"

Kalme tried to pull the branch from Ela's hands, but her fingers passed through the vinewood as if through air. "No! Ela, this is my fault! Mine! You should have refused!"

"Mother, this had nothing to do with you. It was my decision."

"I was your a-age," Kalme sobbed. "Before I m-married your father, the Infinite spoke to me in a vision. I longed to become His prophet, but I was afraid!"

Ela stared at her mother, speechless. Was this true?

Yes.

Infinite! Ela's heart bounded at His voice. He would know how to comfort Kalme. He . . .

Comfort her with the truth. Tell her.

"Mother." The woven floor mats crackled beneath Ela's feet as she crossed the room. She sat beside Kalme and placed the branch on the mat before them. Cautious, she hugged her mother. "You mustn't cry. Shh . . ." When her mother finally hushed, Ela said, "Your Creator has remembered you, and you must not blame yourself for my situation, because He doesn't blame you for refusing to become a prophet."

"But He's taken you," Kalme wept. "It's my fault!"

"He hasn't 'taken' me. I accepted His offer," Ela pointed out. "Equally important, if you had accepted the branch, I would never have existed. And I promise you, Mother, I'm glad I exist."

"Even now?" Kalme's slender body stiffened, and she looked Ela in the eyes. "Tell me you're not afraid."

"I am afraid. More than that, I feel unworthy and foolish and too young . . ." Ela cut her list short. She was filling herself with new doubts just by naming the ones she'd already acknowledged. Better to change the subject. "Mother, listen. I'm about to tell you something that you must tell everyone tomorrow after I leave."

"A prophecy," Kalme sniffed.

"Yes, Mother. Now, don't say anything foolish, or the Infinite will scold you and I'm the one who'll have to deliver your disciplining."

Kalme sobered and wiped her tears. "Tell me."

Joy mingling with her forlorn wish to meet this prophecy's fulfillment, Ela said, "You're three days pregnant. With a son. His name is Jess."

Seated opposite them, Dan Roeh gasped. He released Tzana, his pet, and she immediately tottered across the mat to Ela. Dan sucked in a thin breath and rasped, "A son?"

"Jess," Ela repeated, smiling, though the knowledge was bittersweet. "He will delight you both."

By now, Tzana was patting Ela's arm for attention. "I'm going with you."

"No you're not!" Ela shook her head, horrified by the thought of putting her little sister in any sort of danger—leading her into a world of fire.

Yes, the Infinite corrected Ela. *She is.*

Beside them, Kalme cried, "No, I want you here—my girls!" She sobbed again but at last she mopped her face. "There's no help for it, is there? I'm going to lose you." Kalme gave Ela a mournful look, then frowned. "How did you manage to smear yourself so badly with ashes? Let's wash those off."

Ela stopped her. "No. I was anointed with ashes from a dying city. What could be more appropriate?"

"Oh, my poor girl!" Kalme moved to embrace her daughter but was interrupted by furtive taps on the doorpost.

Dan Roeh straightened, though he looked dazed. "Come in."

Two men entered, both shuffling uncomfortably. Ela had to look twice to recognize them—they seemed so misplaced among the Roeh family. Amar and his father. When recognition took hold, she immediately understood what Amar was trying to work up the courage to say. How could he marry a girl who was supposedly Parne's next prophet? For him, it would be worse than having no wife at all because she could never belong to him. Her life and her heart were no longer her own. Ela's throat tightened as she fought unshed tears. Truly, his decision was for the best.

"Amar," she said, "you and your family are quite admirable. But I must leave Parne tomorrow, so I cannot agree to marry you. Ever."

Amar didn't even have the grace to hide his relief.

Yesterday, Ela knew, she would have thrown something at him.

✦ ✦ ✦

Casting a wary glance around at the borderlands' desolate rock formations and life-stripped soil, Ela knelt in a smooth patch of dirt and allowed Tzana to slide off her back. "Don't wander away," Ela reminded her.

"I won't," Tzana promised. "I just want to find a comfortable place."

"Watch for bugs!" And poisonous lindorm serpents. And stinging plants. And hideous scalns . . . Ela had to stop thinking of the dangers in this wilderness. She'd frightened herself. Seeking composure, she wiped the sweat from her face and drank some water from Father's newest waterskin. He'd insisted she take it. Ela had seen tears in his eyes.

It was an awful, awful thing, seeing Father almost cry, particularly during his farewell with Tzana. He always fretted over Tzana. But they'd been brave at their parting. Even Mother. Would they meet again? Ela frowned, wishing the Infinite would answer that question.

Meanwhile, she and Tzana were here, in this barren waste of rubble, sand, and jagged stone spires and canyons that separated the city-state of Parne from its warring neighbors. Neighbors who were probably much worse than the bugs, the poisonous lindorms, stinging plants, and hideous scalns. Ela tensed, listening for her sister. Not a sound. "Tzana? Tzana!"

"Oh, just wait!" her sister's small voice piped from beyond a huge boulder.

She will be protected here, while you are being trained as My prophet, the Infinite assured Ela.

"How long will I be a prophet?" Ela begged, hoping for a hint of her life expectancy.

Instead of an answer, she received a command. *Place the branch exactly where you are now standing. Tzana will guard it until your return.*

What? Leave her vulnerable young sister in the wilderness with no supplies? "Infinite—"

I told you she will be protected here. Do you think I can forget My promise?

"Just leave her here?"

Yes. Step out of your sandals, and take the waterskin with you.

"Leave Tzana here without water!"

Yes.

"Why are you yelling?" Tzana demanded, tripping her way around the boulder.

"I'm not. I mean, I won't yell again." She begged silent forgiveness from her Creator, then knelt to kiss Tzana's soft, vaguely wrinkled cheek. "Stay here and guard the branch, please."

"Why?" Tzana knelt on the dry sand, her face creased in charming confusion as she watched Ela untie her sandals.

"Because the Infinite asks you to. He promises you'll be safe."

"All right." Tzana lifted a sparse eyebrow. "What about you?"

"I'll be safe too." She hoped. She spiked the branch into the ground, stepped out of her sandals, kissed Tzana once more, and then walked away. In tears.

✦ ✦ ✦

How much longer? She'd been hiking for half the day through too-warm sand, surrounded by these barren rock formations. Her feet were screaming. Well, if they could scream, they would, Ela was sure.

She was also hungry. Tepid water from a skin was not filling. Worse than the hunger, Ela was worried about Tzana, who'd never been alone for so long in her life. Despite the Infinite's promise that Tzana would be protected, Ela's thoughts continually circled back to her little sister. Was she so mistrustful of her Creator? If so, then why had she agreed to become a prophet?

Finally, as Ela hiked into a dusty hollow rimmed by gray stone spires, He spoke. *Stop here.*

Relieved, she halted.

Do you understand what My Presence truly means?

He had perceived Ela's lingering doubts, she knew. "I cannot begin to understand—please tell me."

It will be best for you to understand by experiencing Its loss.

Loss? Was He leaving?

I am leaving you completely alone now. But as I Am, I will return.

28

She felt His presence sucked from her body like air—saw it leave in a whirlwind rising above her. He was gone. No! Ela staggered, fighting to breathe. The mimicry of breath she finally managed was a searing torrent of agony. She tried to raise her hands to her throat, then comprehended that even the dust the Creator had used to sculpt her kind was incapable of holding form without His Presence.

She crumbled into the ground itself. Bereft of a body, her soul collapsed in fiery torment, screaming for death and for Him.

◦ 3 ◦

The world around Ela vanished amid flames, leaving her writhing in agony. Without His sustaining Spirit, she could not endure this measureless cauldron of fire. Where was its end? Where was He? Why couldn't she die? "Infinite! Let me die!"

A touch drew her soul from the fire, and her body from the dust. Alive, she lay helpless, her face resting against ash-tainted desert sand. Clawing the parched ground, which was cold in comparison to what she had just felt, she whimpered, "Please, let me die."

What purpose would your death serve now? He seemed so near that Ela imagined she felt His breath restoring her senses. Her sanity.

She was trembling, unable to even lift her head. How was it possible she still lived? Who could exist without Him?

Not even those who deny Me can live on this world if I withdraw My Spirit, the Creator murmured into her thoughts.

"I've never been without You," she realized aloud, her voice breaking.

Never.

"Never leave me again!" she begged.

Never, He agreed. The word was a promise.

Ela inhaled another cooling breath, sighed, and shut her eyes. Seeing flames, she opened her eyes hurriedly. Wide.

Rest. You are safe. She sensed the Infinite waiting, keeping watch. Guarding her . . .

She woke before sunset, recovered enough to move again. She'd stopped shaking. Her limbs, her whole body, seemed to be wrapped in an invisible blanket. As Ela sat up, her Creator sent her a thought.

Drink your water.

He was right, of course. She guzzled water from the leather bag, which remained full long after the water should have been gone. Particularly after she clumsily splashed herself. Fascinating. At last, feeling restored, she closed the plump waterskin with a firm knot. "Infinite? Was that like death?"

No. That was life without Me. Death without My Presence is immeasurably worse, for it brings eternity in torment, without hope of release.

"What gives us hope? What gives us eternity with You?"

Faith in Me.

If she'd had no faith in her Creator before, Ela was certain she had it now. And she intended to cling to the Infinite and pester Him like a persistent toddler for the rest of her short life. Perhaps He would become wearied by all her questions.

No. He responded to her notion before she formed the words. *This is why I brought you here. To listen and learn. Learning begins with questions. Now, ask.*

"I'm sorry, but what did You do to my water bag?"

✦ ✦ ✦

Death deserved unrelenting black.

Ambassador Kien Lantec eyed himself in the polished metal mirror and knew he was making the correct choice. Tunic, belt, leggings, boots, all black. His people, Tracelanders, the victims of the massacre of Ytar, deserved no less than his country's formal mourning attire.

Sorting and packing gear on the other side of the room, Kien's servant Wal grumbled aloud. "I still say we ought to leave immediately. Without a word. We should have left last night! Who knows what the Istgardians might do. They have almost no sense of honor and even less self-control." Wal approached now, sounding almost desperate. "Sir, please reconsider the black. If you appear in the king's formal audience chamber and insult him while wearing *that*, you will incite war on the spot. The king's guards will surely kill you."

Kien turned and thumped his nervous attendant on the shoulder. Though Kien was younger, Wal was the one behaving like a frightened child. "Control yourself. I will not insult the king. I give you my word. I'm going to walk into the audience chamber, protest the massacre, return my insignia, and leave. We will reach the border by nightfall. Are the horses and carts ready?"

"Yes, sir." Wal's voice was hushed.

"Will you follow me into the audience chamber?" Kien knew what Wal would say, but he couldn't resist asking. Just to see the expression on Wal's face.

The thin man's gray eyes bugged, and his mouth gaped. His pale skin went ashen. "Ah. No, sir. I'll stay with the horses. You won't actually say the word *massacre* to the king, will you?"

"Yes, I will. The 'skirmish' at Ytar *was* a massacre, no matter what the Istgardian commanders claim." If Kien thought of the massacre too deeply, he would be in a killing mood when he walked into the royal audience chamber, and he needed to be calm. His father would counsel coolness. But how could any loyal Tracelander remain cool, thinking of the slaughter, the enslavement, and the burning of a peaceful city?

The instant Kien reached the border, the Tracelands would declare war on Istgard. He would be sure of it. Those enslaved citizens had to be freed. Ytar must be avenged. "Where is my sword?"

"Sir!" Wal squawked. "Do not wear your sword!"

"Istgardian protocol demands a ceremonial sword," Kien reminded his servant. "Where is it?"

Wal sat on Kien's clothing chest. Blinking.

Kien grabbed the smaller man by the shoulder and wrist and dumped him to the floor. "You can ignore protocol if you think it will guarantee your own safety, Wal, but—excuse me—I will not."

Wal jumped to his feet. Agile. Kien had to allow him that much of a compliment. The man was also determined—admirably so, when he wasn't being annoying. As he was now. "Sir! I promised your father I would advise you. . . ." Wal hesitated, like one who has said too much.

"Advise me? Concerning what? My youthful foolishness? My failures in etiquette?"

Wal turned away, not denying Kien's words.

Kien glared. So Wal finally admitted he'd been hired to be a nursemaid. Or an etiquette master. Both options were insulting. Kien knew his conduct had been almost irreproachable throughout his service in Istgard, despite multiple opportunities that tempted him to indulge in less-than-exemplary behavior. Seething, he flung open his clothing chest and rummaged through it for his ceremonial sword. Wal—the maggot!—had hidden it in the bottom of the chest. Well, scheme as he might, Wal couldn't part Kien from his weapons. Not his sword. Not his boot knives, nor his buckle knife. Wal would screech like a seared fowl if he ever learned of Kien's hidden cache.

Kien slung the leather baldric over his shoulder and buckled the sword at his side. Wal, not quite remorseful, offered Kien his black cloak. "I pinned your insignia to the shoulder."

"Because I can't be trusted to pin it on correctly?"

Wal huffed in obvious disgust.

"If anyone has the right to be offended here, Wal, it's me." Kien stepped past his servant and rechecked his image in the mirror. Excellent. The triangular gold insignia gleamed impressively at his left shoulder. A pity he had to return it today. He should keep the gold and have it hammered into coins for the widows and orphans of Ytar. No, the Istgardians would deem such charity to be theft, and Kien's left arm would be shortened one hand-length.

He stalked to the door, calling orders on the way out. "You'll have enough time to send a cipher to my father and the Assembly. They'll want to know what's happening. Be ready to depart the instant I return."

"Yes, sir. Right away."

Kien strode outside and marched along the smooth block-paved street toward the palace. Ruddy dawnlight sculpted countless graceful temple spires and the stodgier walls and massive towers of Istgard's capital, Riyan. How could he ever have admired this view? Built by savages to honor their kings and their nonexistent gods.

All things Istgardian turned Kien's stomach now. He'd been too trusting. Too eager to be the perfect ambassador. If someone had told him yesterday that King Tek An sanctioned the destruction of a peaceful Traceland border town, Kien would have scoffed like the Tracelander dupe they'd deemed him to be. "Stupid!" he told himself.

He should have seen the truth the instant he arrived in Riyan. Wasn't his ambassadorial residence—arranged by Tek An—the most cramped and unimpressive in the capital? Even the fact that it was within walking distance of the palace was an insult. No doubt Tek An had been spying on Kien from that first day. He'd been a fool.

Looking around, Kien realized he was still a fool. Palace guards were loitering along the broad street, in doorways and various arched stone gateways. Not ordinary red-cloaked military guards, but palace guards. Watching him. A chill slid over Kien. Should he advance or retreat?

Ahead, he heard horsehooves and a sharp whistle. A light single-horse chariot emerged from the palace gates and turned toward Kien. An elderly charioteer, in a plain brown servant's tunic, managed the reins. Beside him stood a young noblewoman, her golden ribbons and veils fluttering over her dark hair and blue mantle in frivolous contrast to her somber face.

Tek Lara, a cousin to the king.

As Kien moved aside, Lara's gaze met his, and he saw her serious eyes widen, alarmed. While her charioteer guided the vehicle past, Lara leaned toward Kien and cried, "Leave! Hurry!"

Evidently perceiving this as a command, Lara's servant snapped the reins and chirruped to the horse. As the chariot sped away, Tek Lara looked back at Kien, her distress still visible.

Was he walking into danger? Unlike most Istgardian noblewomen, Lara was neither silly nor a flirt. Best to heed her warning. Kien turned, intending to rejoin his servants and leave Riyan immediately. But five massive green-cloaked royal guards converged in the street before him, blocking his way. Gloating.

Extensively trained, the king's guards were armed with short swords, helmets, plate-armor vests, greaves, and spears. In tribute to his rank, their burly leader sported a vertical crest of black hair on his helm, sculpted to trail down his back. Hair, no doubt, sheared off the lead guard's hapless victims.

There would be no hair-shearing today if Kien could help it. He fought down nervousness and faced the guards proudly, a hand on his sword. "I am returning to my residence. Why are you stopping me?"

The leader's smirk darkened. Hardened. "Kien Lantec of the Tracelands, I arrest you by order of the people of Istgard, according to their high laws, on suspicion of conspiracy to murder their beloved king, Tek An. You are now stripped of your rank and privileges as ambassador. You will lay down your sword and come with us."

Conspiracy to murder Tek An? Ludicrous! "Why are you arresting me on false charges?"

Without warning, the lead guard drove his fist into Kien's stomach.

Doubled over, fighting to breathe, Kien felt another blow to the back of his head. He crashed to the pavings. Stunned, Kien tried to focus. How could this be happening?

As Kien gasped, the lead guard bellowed, "You call the people of Istgard liars?"

Yes.

His movement hidden by his cloak, Kien slid his hand to the knife concealed within his buckle. The lead guard gut-kicked him.

"Ah!" Kien curled, clutching his stomach, sick with pain. If he'd eaten breakfast, he would have lost it with the force of that kick. Was the man wearing metal boots?

The lead guard carved Kien's gold ambassadorial insignia from his cloak with a dagger. "Take his sword. Search for any other weapons. Be sure he cannot so much as lift a hand against you."

The other guards seized Kien's sword, then took turns kicking his back, belly, and ribs until Kien could do nothing but welcome the darkness that followed.

Pain brought him to consciousness again. Curled up on his side, Kien checked his wounds. Right eye swollen shut. Left temple pulsing with an open wound. Ribs stabbing miserably. At least his hands and legs moved. Kien summoned the strength to look around. He was lying in blood. And musty straw. On a stone floor. Prison? Was he actually in a prison?

Behind him, a door squeaked open on its pivot. A man laughed none too kindly. "I see you're awake. Good! Get up. I am your warden. Some friends are patiently waiting for you."

Who? His servants? Or perhaps interrogators . . .

"Hurry, Tracelander." The man kicked at Kien's shins.

More wounds might incapacitate him altogether. He had to stand before this beast kicked him again. Fighting agony, Kien forced himself to his feet. Balance would be easier if the walls would remain still. Hit by dizziness, Kien wavered.

His warden laughed. "For a pile of bloody bones, you've done well. Here, now. Look out the window."

He shoved Kien toward a narrow stone window, gripped Kien's hair, and pushed his face into the opening, which was only one hand width wide. "See 'em? I'm told you have to see 'em."

See what? Who? Kien turned his face until he could see through the slit stone window with his left eye. He finally managed to focus on several long bundles. Bodies, neatly placed side by side in the dirt below his window. One was . . . Wal. The others, his groomsmen.

All dead. So many wounds. Even Wal. The battle must have been horrific. His fault.

"No," Kien rasped, barely recognizing his own voice. Sword. Where was his sword?

We should have left last night! Wal accused Kien in his thoughts. *I promised your father I would advise you. . . .*

Blinded by grief, Kien slid down the wall to his knees. He hadn't listened. He'd failed Wal. His servants. Father. Himself. Everyone. He deserved to die. "Sword . . ."

Dazed, Kien patted his sides, his leggings, his boots, seeking his missing belt, his weapons. Becoming desperate as the warden laughed.

Sword. He needed to fall on his sword.

✦ ✦ ✦

Ela watched the dawn, the last stars fading from the roseate sky. Had she ever felt such calm in her soul? Never. She could stay here forever, questioning, listening, learning. Parne—indeed, the whole world—had faded from her thoughts. Nothing compared to His Presence. "Infinite? I don't want to go."

Return to your sister.

Naturally, He had the perfect reply. Now she wanted to go. Tzana needed her, and she missed Tzana. How many days had she been here? Seven? Ten? She prayed Tzana wasn't frightened, believing Ela had forgotten her. Was she in desperate straits by now? No, the Infinite promised Tzana would be protected while Ela was gone. But what had Tzana been eating all this time? Perhaps nothing. Only an endless source of water, somehow provided by their Creator's will.

Ela's water bag was finally a bit slack this morning, no longer replenishing itself. Another signal that she must leave. As she tied the bag, Ela's stomach growled loudly. Painfully. She'd been fasting for days. "What will we eat?"

Why are you worried about food? Return to your sister.

Ela scrambled to her feet and slung the water bag over her shoulder. She climbed the side of the dusty hollow, seeking the path she'd taken before. There. Her bare feet slipped a bit over the dirt, causing her to flail her arms as she made her way along the sloping path. Ugh, she was graceless! How could the Infinite wish to be represented by someone so clumsy?

She hesitated at the unspoken question, expecting a reply. Silence.

Her stomach growled again, urging Ela onward. Already the sunlight was heating the air. Soon the ground would be searing hot. She had to hike quickly.

Half the morning passed, though swiftly, hastened by Ela's eagerness to return to Tzana. In the center of a small canyon, she paused to take another drink. Such peculiar rock formations in this canyon—red rocks streaked with yellow-green minerals and blue shadows, their lines and colors interrupted here and there by snags of dead trees, some fallen, some hollowed, all leafless. Lifeless.

Ela retied the water bag and slung it over her shoulder again while she studied the snags. What had happened to the trees here? A blight, perhaps. Or a particularly severe storm. At one time, these had been large trees, probably beautiful. And shady. Ela peered through the canyon, hoping to find another shade tree.

A low gurgling broke the canyon's hush. Was that her stomach? If so, she hadn't felt the rumble. The gurgle sounded again, echoing off the canyon's red walls. Definitely not her stomach. Baffled, Ela looked around. Was there a waterfall nearby, playing tricks on her thoughts and sending sounds ricocheting off the rocks?

Again the gurgle resounded, ending with a hiss this time. A distinctly snakelike hiss. But snakes didn't gurgle, did they? And water wouldn't hiss like snakes. Or would it?

Now an odor reached Ela, thick and heavy, wrapping around her like a cloak of rotting meat. A shudder traced its way down Ela's back. She was being watched. She felt it. Not just watched, but stalked.

Prey. She was being stalked by a . . . The gurgle echoed more deeply now, its reverberations thrumming through her entire body. Warm, putrid air seemed to slither about her ankles. The gurgle, the hiss, the rotten stench . . . it could not be.

Ela forced herself to swallow. To look over her shoulder. The hideous creature approached her, soft-footed. The size of a ram. But this was no ram. Bloodshot yellow eyes, flat as stones, watched her from a broad skeletal face, plastered with a thick red skin that coated its powerful body like coagulated blood. "Scaln!"

She went lightheaded. Think. Breathe. To faint, to trip, to fall, would be fatal.

Never run from a scaln, Dan Roeh's voice whispered through her memories. *Scalns can outrun you in a charge. Your only hope is to stay, fight, and avoid being wounded.*

Fight with what?

The creature padded toward her, slobber glistening and dripping from its mouth, as if anticipating the taste of her flesh. No, not slobber. Venom. *Scalns paralyze their prey with venom,* Father whispered.

She was going to be paralyzed by venom, then devoured bite by flesh-shredding bite.

The scaln hissed again, its malodorous breath reaching her in a warm, air-thickening current. Another thread of venom dripped from its broad mouth, from those jagged, blade-sharp teeth.

"Never run from a scaln," Ela warned herself.

The creature eased nearer. Too near. Against all her self-warnings, Ela ran for the nearest snag beside a canyon wall.

She flung herself at the snag's weathered gray trunk, panting as she swiped toward the sanctuary of its limbs. Please. Please! She gripped a limb.

The scaln's gurgle became a growl, then an ear-piercing hiss. Rocks spattered behind her and another current of warm, fetid air lifted toward her, skimming her bare feet and legs.

Something stabbed her right calf, then her left, searing as it tore downward to her feet. Ela screamed, clutched the barren limb even tighter, and hauled herself up, sobbing at the pain.

Perched on the limb, Ela looked down at her foe. The scaln lurked at the snag's trunk, flat yellow eyes ravenous, its desire to feast evidenced by its outpour of venom. Clearly, it was frustrated. She was safe.

"Today, you starve!"

The scaln hissed, gouged its vicious red claws into the gray snag, and began to climb.

✦ 4 ✦

Ela shrieked and threw her water bag, pelting the scaln's red nostrils. The creature dropped to the ground, hissed fiercely, then stabbed its claws into the snag to climb again.

She was going to die. "Infinite!"

Listen!

Ela gulped down a sob, listening hard. Watching the scaln bunch its rear legs onto the snag. Climbing nearer.

Who am I?

"My Creator!" The scaln approached striking distance, nauseating her with its stench.

And the scaln's Creator. Tell the scaln, by My Holy Name, I command it to depart.

Gurgling thickly, the scaln swiped her shins with a blood-red claw and dragged her downward. Ela screamed in pain, clinging to the snag with all her might. "By His Holy Name, the Infinite commands you to depart!"

The scaln recoiled, flattening against the snag's trunk. Ela saw confusion in those yellow eyes. To her stupefaction, the creature dropped to the ground once more and lunged away, not looking back.

"It's gone? So easily?"

Creation must acknowledge its Creator.

Hands shaking, Ela swiped the tears from her face. Part of

her longed to indulge in hysterics. A heel-drumming fit. Most improper when questioning the Infinite. "But why create a scaln? Or any such monster?"

Even monsters have a place here. Each has its purpose—and a lesson to teach.

Ela hoped she'd learned this lesson well enough never to repeat it. She muffled another sob and rubbed at fresh tears.

Tell Me what you did wrong.

Wrong? What had she done wrong? "I ran?"

Pitiful answer. She'd failed the test, obviously. What else could she do but entreat compassion from her teacher? "Please, tell me what I did wrong."

If you had called My Name immediately, the scaln would not have wounded you.

Humiliated, Ela accepted the rebuke. It made sense. Why would the Infinite allow her to die, prey to a scaln, before she'd truly begun her work as a prophet? She should have realized this. However, she was expecting death at any time, from every direction. And she hadn't had much experience in such situations. Wasn't it natural for her to panic just a little?

An impulse of humor—not her own—slid into her thoughts. "Aw! Infinite!" Was He laughing at her pain?

No, the Infinite responded, allowing her to sense His love and indulgence. *I do not enjoy your pain. Rather, I treasure your spirit.*

She was treasured. The thought made her almost smile despite her wretchedness. If she was treasured . . . "Will You always save me so quickly if I command things in Your Holy Name?"

Will those commands reveal My power, spirit, and glory?

Oh. This was what He wanted her to remember. His will must be revealed in all her words and actions. "Help me to remember, Infinite. I'm begging You." Would it be silly of her to beg for no more confrontations with scalns? And how could His glory possibly be revealed by her inglorious defeat?

Her thought-questions remained unanswered. Instead, the Creator reminded Ela of His previous command. *Return to your sister.*

"Yes." She'd almost forgotten. Ela slid down the snag's weathered gray trunk, flinching and sweating. Blood dripped from her wounds. The scaln's claws had cut more deeply than she'd realized. Her legs were burning. Less as she moved. Sighing, she regathered her thoughts.

Tzana. It would be wonderful to see Tzana again.

Ela limped forward, moving more quickly than she would have believed possible. By the time she neared the place where she'd left Tzana, however, Ela's legs were heavy—pain biting with each unwieldy step. She was dizzy. And the inside of her mouth felt powdered despite multiple sips of water. Her wounds were puffed now, deep red furrows cut into both legs. Worse, the blood hadn't stopped dripping. Wasn't this where she'd left Tzana? Ela's vision blurred, the landscape rippling before her as if suffused by rising waves of sultry heat.

She faltered, realizing she was ill, poisoned by the scaln's wicked claws. Venom? Whatever it was, her symptoms were becoming unpleasant. Faintness threatened, and she would have allowed it, except that she knew she was in serious trouble. "Help me, Infinite."

Staggering now, Ela imagined cool water lapping at her toes, then washing her ankles. Hallucination, of course. Grass. Precious grass flanked each side of the stream. In this desert? Definitely a hallucination.

"Ela." A young woman splashed into the stream and grabbed her arm, half dragging her along, into a pool of water. Ela wobbled, then fell, submerged beneath the pool's crystalline chill.

✦ ✦ ✦

Kien stared at the bowl of congealed gruel. Would he die more quickly by starving himself or by eating that rotten stuff?

A delicate skittering in the straw alerted him to the approach of a mouse. The tiny creature emerged from the straw, paused for an instant, then sped across the stone floor to the bowl of gruel.

"You are welcome to it," Kien told his companion. "I hope you survive."

The ringing thump of the warden's key and the rasp of the bolt sliding aside made Kien turn. The heavy door pivoted open and the warden tramped inside, followed by a palace guard—the ugly smirking lout who'd arrested Kien in the street last week.

"I'm honored," Kien told him, sarcasm ladled on as thick as the prison gruel. Not bothering to stand, he eyed the guard's sword. Could he wrest it away long enough to use it on himself? Perhaps the guard would kill him first.

Definitely an option worth considering.

The guard intercepted Kien's glance and slapped a protective hand on his sword. To the warden he snarled, "Get him to his feet and bind him."

Approaching Kien, the warden threatened, "You fight me and I'll strike you hard enough to send you to the next realm."

"Do it!" Kien lunged for the man's ankles and took him down.

The warden's head thumped against the floor—cushioned by the straw—and he yelled, "I'll kill you!"

The man tried to remove a wooden cudgel from his belt. Instinctively, Kien snatched the weapon away and hammered it against the warden's kneecap. The man's agonized screech pierced Kien's ears. A small victory, but nowhere near enough to avenge the Tracelands for Ytar.

"Stop!" The palace guard grabbed Kien's shoulder. Kien retaliated, cracking the cudgel against the guard's hand with all his might. The man swore. "Demon! You broke my finger!"

He pressed one greave-clad shin into Kien's side and yanked the cudgel from Kien's grip. "I'm commanded to bring you alive to the palace, but you don't have to be in one piece!"

The greave's metal plating pressed into Kien's already-cracked ribs, provoking breath-stopping pain. Kien yelped. He was ready to die, but couldn't the palace thug just knife him quickly and plead self-defense over Kien's corpse?

It would be a magnificent death. Almost.

Until then, he would be wise not to fight. Kien willed himself to rest as the guard clumsily bound his hands behind his back and growled about the pain from his broken finger. Finished, the guard shoved Kien and hauled his bound arms upward. "Get up!"

Nearby, the warden said, "I can't stand."

"I'll send someone for you," the guard muttered. He wrenched Kien's arms again, and Kien managed to push one knee forward for balance enough to rise. The guard yanked him impatiently, prompting ferocious stabs from Kien's ribs. "Move, Tracelander!"

Clenching his teeth against the need to yell with pain, Kien stood. At least his legs worked. But the warden's didn't. Kien nearly grinned at the thought. Life was almost worth living.

He hoped they hadn't crushed the mouse.

Outside, a small contingent of guards met Kien's surly captor, apparently to escort them to the palace. Kien blinked against the sunlight. He hadn't realized it was so warm outside—his cell was miserably cold. For an instant he turned his face skyward to bask in the sun's rays. Until someone in the prison courtyard spat on his cloak.

A blunt-faced citizen clad in an ordinary workman's tunic and worn sandals glowered at him. "Assassin!"

"I haven't killed anyone!" Kien protested. Unlike the Istgardians. Other subjects of Istgard, evidently forewarned of Kien's progress, gathered just beyond the prison's gate. They taunted him, spat on him, and laughed. Someone threw a clump of moldy bread, which bounced from Kien's shoulder to the guard's.

"None of that!" the guard bellowed. He ordered his companions to walk ahead in the street and warn onlookers against throwing refuse or spitting on the prisoner.

"I've been condemned without a trial," Kien said to no one. Not that it mattered. Condemnation meant execution, didn't it? Perhaps he was walking to his death now. Good.

The barrage of rotten food and spittle ceased, but not the taunts and curses. Why had he ever thought the Istgardians were sociable people? Had he actually considered them to be people? They sounded like animals.

Men, women, and children howled at him from the doorways,

then merged behind him in an unruly herd, screaming abuse, wishing him a painful death. Kien glared, despising them all. As the guard hauled him through the immense arched palace gates, Kien said, "Unhand me. You have weapons and my arms are bound. I won't run."

To Kien's surprise, the guard—though obviously displeased—didn't argue. Perhaps his one little broken finger hurt too much. The man should experience a few broken ribs.

Not bothering to disguise his contempt, Kien eyed the Istgardian courtiers as he passed them. Lingering near the king's ornate fountain, several elaborately cloaked noblemen regarded Kien with undisguised sneers. Their jewel-adorned wives and daughters, however, gasped when they saw him, clearly upset. He'd flirted with most of them at receptions and balls during his ambassadorial service. "Never again," Kien muttered.

His boots echoed loudly against the polished marble floor as they entered Tek An's vast audience chamber. Soaring white columns flanked either side of the hall. Golden lampstands glistened before each column, and a broad path of sparkling golden marble guided all eyes toward the king's throne, a deeply cushioned marble-pedestaled bench, positioned before an elaborate gold screen.

On the royal bench, watching Kien's approach, Tek An sat like a gilded statue, his crown and robes threaded with shimmering metals and garnished with deep green gemstones. Impassive, he watched his noble subjects. They were remarkably quiet, Kien realized. Listening. Probably eager to see him condemned, then watch him die.

Did the bloodthirsty creatures expect him to fight? Perhaps he would. If only to take a few of these deceivers with him when he died.

As he approached the steps before Tek An's throne, Kien saw Tek Lara. She looked ill. Had she been crying? She glanced at Kien, her somber red-rimmed eyes widening, her expression crumpling a bit as if fighting tears. Was she so worried about him?

Kien allowed his contemptuous glare to soften as he returned her glance. Lara's dark eyes brimmed, reflecting undeniable compassion, and her lips parted slightly as if she longed to speak to him. Instead, she looked away. Tek An was speaking—his words saturated with royal plurals.

"Kien Lantec, you are accused of conspiracy against us. Just before they died, your servants were caught sending ciphers by messenger pigeon. The Tracelanders plot against our life and the well-being of our realm. Can you dispute this?"

Kien scowled. Clearly Tek An and his minions hadn't interpreted and read the ciphers, because none of them hinted at plots against Tek An. There were no such plots! Moreover, how could Kien—or anyone—dispute a charge conjured out of thin air?

"I deny it completely. I've never sought to harm you in any way, O King."

Tek An scoffed, his broad brown face with its thinly sculpted black beard showing nothing but disdain. "You declare yourself and your country as being on friendly terms with us?"

"We have been." Pausing for cold effect, Kien added, "Until the massacre at Ytar."

He watched the king go livid. Losing a measure of royal dignity, Tek An blustered, "Ytar was a preemptory blow against a threat already brought about by your people! You are nothing but a pack of rebels, plotting against Istgard!"

Rebels. Kien snarled at the word. Now Tek An's courtly mask was gone. As was Kien's mask. Good. Let the truth be told. After seven generations—seven!—Istgardian kings still regarded all Tracelanders as mutinous subjects. Kien managed to speak politely through his teeth, though Tek An deserved no courtesy. "How, O King, has my own generation, or my father's generation, threatened you?"

"How? Do not pretend!" Tek An jerked his chin toward a stout, pompous official in green and gold robes who stepped toward Kien, unsheathing an ornate sword.

Kien braced himself. Now he would die.

Exuding contempt like a bad odor, the official stood just beyond arm's length and displayed his sword with both hands, as if holding an exceptional gem. Kien eyed the blade and froze, recognizing the metal's rippling dark blue and gray seascape pattern. Azurnite. The official was correct. That blade was as precious as a large gem of rare quality. Kien's father owned a similar sword. Apart from its beauty, Azurnite was derived from newly discovered Tracelandic ores, which produced much lighter, stronger blades—so sharp and amazingly flexible that they were already revered by the few officials wealthy enough to afford them.

Had this Istgardian looted this sword from an assemblyman or a swordsmith in Ytar? No doubt it was at least part of the reason Tek An threatened Kien with conspiracy. The king and his officials wanted information. The conspiracy charge was a mere bargaining ploy.

Kien shrugged. "That's not my sword. Why are you showing it to me?"

"You know of similar weapons," Tek An prompted. "Your countrymen will produce more, then attack Riyan."

"I know nothing of an attack."

The king abandoned his rigid, majestic posture completely and leaned forward. "Do not scorn us as a fool, Lan Tek!"

Noting the king's emphasis on both syllables of his surname, Kien paused. What sort of game was Tek An playing by emphasizing the ancient form of the Lantec name? Kien's descent from a rebel Lan Tek prince of Istgard was hardly his own fault. However, Tek An pronounced the name as if Kien, not his ancestor, was the noble rebel. Kien glared. "It is the truth. I know nothing of an attack—it's all in your royal imagination. As for the sword, what if I *have* seen other such blades in my homeland? What does it matter? We are all entitled to carry weapons for our own protection. And if those weapons happen to be works of art—all the better." He wasn't about to discuss the Azurnite, much less reveal the locations of the metal's precious ores, if that was what Tek An wanted.

"These are not ordinary weapons." Tek An motioned Kien's guard forward. "Demonstrate. Refresh his memory."

Kien almost told them he didn't need a demonstration. But the thought of what was about to happen proved too irresistible. Particularly when it involved his lout of a guard.

The guard trudged forward, drawing his sword with his good hand, while bringing the injured one protectively close to his side. The pompous official holding the blue Tracelandic sword grimaced in snobbish distaste, but nodded to the guard, who bowed. They circled, parrying each other's attacks tentatively. Both men began to perspire. Tek An quickly lost patience. "Attack!"

The guard yelled and lunged as if to kill. The official—eyes bugged—parried viciously. Their swords rang on impact. A metal shard flew at Tek An's feet, clanging against the throne's marble base, making him gasp and jump.

Kien suppressed a laugh, though it would have been worth the pain from his ribs. What had the king expected?

The guard uttered a low curse, glaring at his broken sword, then at the official, who sneered. Kien smiled.

"Tell us you did not know about these new swords!" Tek An snapped.

"I knew." Kien hardened his voice and eyes. "I've seen them forged. But I'm no swordsmith. I don't know the proportions of the ores they smelted for the metals. Or the exact mixtures of the metals. So why are you asking me anything?"

"You know enough, Lan Tek. These are the ores, are they not?" The king snapped his fingers.

Amid much jostling, one of the official's green-clad subordinates emerged from the crowd, lugging a wide trough. Within the trough were large, glittering blue crystals—similar to ones Kien had seen near a Traceland swordsmith's forge.

Tek An jerked his bearded chin toward the trough. "Where did they acquire these ores?"

Kien noticed the Istgardians were missing subtle but important details. Like small children, they focused on dazzling crystals when they should pay equal attention to what surrounded those crystals. Dark blue stone striations. Sand, leaves, and vinewood. "Ask the swordsmith in Ytar!"

When the king pursed his lips hard as if tasting something sour, Kien guessed, "Your marauders killed him. Didn't they? And your guards killed my faithful servants—one of whom might have had the information you seek!" Wal. Wal had served several of the Traceland's most prominent Assemblymen. Wal might have known about the ores' locations. Kien clenched his bound fists as he pushed away the image of his servant's pale, worried face. Yet the memory, brief as it was, calmed him. "I have nothing more to say. Why don't you just kill me now?"

"Is death what you seek?" the king asked, eyes narrowed.

Lara gasped, causing Kien to look at her. Golden robes flaring, she rushed to the steps and knelt before the king. "Sire, please, remember—"

Tek An waved her back impatiently. "Do not fear, Cousin Lara. We have forgotten nothing, including our ancestors' writings." Fixing a baleful look on Kien, he said, "Kien Lan Tek, of the rebel son of King Lan Tek, our blood is the same." Murmurs and exclamations rippled within the crowd of courtiers like a small, disquieting current. Tek An lifted a hand, silencing them. "Yet, Lan Tek, you ask us to kill you. By this, you prove you have indeed conspired against us. You are trying to bring the curses of all gods upon us."

"No, I am not. My family renounced their titles when they signed the Charter forming the Tracelands," Kien argued, hiding his frustration. His remote Istgardian heritage was nothing to him. An irritating obstacle to be overcome. "We were disinherited by the rebellion."

"You do not use your titles, but you carry our blood. And we will not be cursed by killing you."

"Likewise, curse or no curse, I never plotted against you," Kien said. "Nor will I. Your accusations against my good name are unjust, and I ask you to dismiss them. I'm no assassin."

"You've proven nothing, yet admit you hid knowledge of these new weapons from us!" Tek An sat back, studying him coldly. "You are indeed guilty and must be punished."

He'd be punished for his country's advancements in metalwork? Preposterous! "How could you punish me for such a . . . a non-crime? It's insane! Nevertheless, you refuse to kill me. So now what? Do you intend to let me rot in prison for the remainder of my life?" The very thought twisted Kien's stomach. He pulled in a deep breath and was rewarded by stabs from his ribs. Kien bit his lip hard to distract himself from the hurt. Even so, he winced.

Tek An smiled, evidently pleased by Kien's pain. "Perhaps rotting to death is your fate. Rebel son of Lan Tek, pray to your gods for strength."

Controlling himself, Kien straightened proudly. "Tracelanders need no gods."

He'd managed to offend everyone in the royal audience chamber. Even Tek Lara looked hurt, her gentle face paled. Kien hated seeing her misery. Of all the Istgardians he'd met, Lara and her father, Tek Juay, were the most principled and admirable. Even now Kien didn't want to destroy Lara's good opinion of him. He bowed his head, honoring her, before turning to scowl at his guard. "Remove me from this place!"

The guard's complexion resembled clay. He glanced at the king, who waved a furious dismissal, then he faced Kien. "Sir . . . my lord," he began, flustered.

Kien lost patience with the man's fear of his renounced royal blood. " 'Tracelander' is fine! Please, just call your men and return me to my cell—my arms are killing me." He wished the words were true. Death would end his misery.

"Yes, sir."

Kien shook his head as they left the audience chamber. Would Tek An really keep him imprisoned for the rest of his life?

No.

He must escape. And if he died trying . . . "Good."

"What, my lord?" the guard asked, his anxiety evident as he peered at Kien.

My lord? Ugh. Such absolute servility was enough to make a good Tracelander puke. Unless that Tracelander suffered broken ribs.

"Nothing," Kien told his agitated guard.

His thoughts sped onward, pondering his escape.

Or at least, his death.

✦ 5 ✦

The young woman tugged Ela above the pool's sparkling surface and cried, "Ela! I'm so glad to see you! Though I almost forgot you were gone."

Ela found her footing, rubbed the water from her eyes, and studied the girl's sweet face. Her vivid brown eyes. "Tzana?"

"What?" the young woman asked in Tzana's voice, with her usual happy impatience.

Ela stared at her sister, unable to comprehend this transformation. "Infinite?"

She is safe in My presence.

And perfected, Ela realized, still staring at her sister, who smiled, radiant. Almost normal height, with delicate, beautiful features, thick dark curls, and slender, straight fingers. This was Tzana, set beyond the world's destructive forces of disease and pain. Amazing.

Clearly oblivious to Ela's shock, Tzana hugged her. "I'm sorry I forgot you! But I've been busy."

Busy? Just guarding the prophet's branch? Ela looked around, incredulous. The barren rock-edged desert was now lush—a grass-carpeted garden hedged with countless varieties of plants and watered by a stream, which fed the pool where Ela stood. The stream's source emerged from the base of a sparkling tree—the most glorious tree Ela had ever seen.

Numerous varieties of fruits, flowers, and leaves flourished amid the tree's branches, all shimmering as if subtly lit from within. And its broad, wonderfully sculpted trunk twisted upward in a sturdy spiral that tempted Ela to climb it and reach for those appealing fruits and flowers. The trunk resembled . . . vinewood.

"That's the branch!" Ela waded from the pool, enthralled by the sight. How could one slender staff become such an enormous tree? And so quickly? "Infinite, You're wonderful! How beautiful!"

She approached the tree. Movement shivered the sparkling leaves above. Small animals and jewel-bright birds flitted within the branches—each creature perfect and lively, seeming to invite her to play.

"They love having me feed them," Tzana explained, clasping Ela's arm as they both looked upward. "Really, they can feed themselves, but they prefer the food from my hands. The messengers said it was also my job to tend the tree and the land around—"

"Messengers?"

"Yes. Every morning they bring me instructions from the Infinite. Have some fruit, Ela. It's delicious!"

Obviously Tzana had been utterly pampered while Ela was falling to pieces and being mauled by scalns in the desert. "How is this fair?" she cried to the Infinite as Tzana stared.

Did I keep My promise?

She couldn't mistake the amusement in His question. "Yes, but . . ."

Rest here. Enjoy the tree and its fruits. When you leave, everything will be as it has been.

Would Tzana's restored body remain? Ela asked inwardly, not wanting to distress Tzana.

No. His tone requested patience. *When this place is removed, the world's effects will take hold of her again.*

Ela's pang of grief was halted by another hug from her sister. How could she be miserable, seeing Tzana so healthy? Even Ela's fever and wounds were healed in this place—though the scars remained. It was impossible to cling to sorrow here. She returned her little sister's hug and added a hearty kiss to Tzana's thick, gleaming curls. "It's good to know you've been happy!"

"Yes, and I'm happier now that you're here—even if you're yelling and talking to yourself. Come up the tree, Ela, it's amazing!"

Watching her little sister, limber and graceful as she clambered up the tree, Ela rejoiced. Instead of climbing, however, she knelt and covered her face with her hands.

Worshiping the Infinite.

❖ ❖ ❖

Ela sighed, clasped Tzana's hand, then touched the magnificent tree's trunk. Like a gently inverted whirlwind, the branch drew in its fruit, flowers, and limbs in a spiral, while the birds flew away and the smaller animals scampered into holes and shelters, hidden in the sand and nearby cliffs. The branch conformed to Ela's hand now, slender, the wood's grain gleaming delicately. Itself again. Only a small hoard of precious fruit remained, tucked within Ela's folded mantle, secured by her tunic's belt. No other evidence lingered as testimony to the branch's previous glory.

Tzana too was as she'd been. Fragile, tiny, wispy-haired, and slightly wrinkled, her fingers once again gnarled like an old woman's. But her eyes still glowed as she grinned up at Ela. "We'll see it again, won't we?"

"Yes," Ela sighed. "I'm sure we will. Or one like it." She smiled, cherishing Tzana's inward radiance. No wonder the Infinite pampered and indulged her. Tzana's spirit was so lovely. Not perfect, but trusting and accepting. As Ela ought to be. "Come on. We have a long walk ahead of us."

"Where are we going?"

"Across the border to Istgard." To proclaim the Infinite's will.

Mindful of Tzana, Ela allowed her to rest occasionally. At midday they shared some of the nourishing fruits and drank from Father's now-scuffed waterskin. Toward evening, Ela noticed more vegetation and lower rock formations. Surely this was Istgard.

Ela was carrying Tzana on her back when they noticed something dark curved against the base of a boulder.

"What's that?" Tzana demanded.

A body, Ela realized, sickened. "Tzana, cover your eyes."

When Tzana obeyed, Ela approached the corpse. A soldier. Obviously wealthy. His weapons and armor were superbly sculpted and embellished with gold. But the armor hadn't protected him. Lacerations marred his desiccated face, and a gash was cruelly visible across his throat. Oddly, his belongings—rich as they were—hadn't been stolen. "Infinite? Who was this?"

The one righteous leader of Istgard. My servant, betrayed and murdered for refusing to countenance evil.

A vision seeped through Ela's thoughts and expanded. Overwhelmed, she knelt shakily, lowered Tzana to the ground, then clutched the branch, trying to endure the vision's pain. When she returned to herself, Ela wept into the parched soil, heartbroken. Beside her, Tzana cried, seeing the soldier's wounds. Ela covered her sister's eyes, then closed her own. She shuddered, seeing this Istgardian's death again. His murderer attacking—

Take his sword.

Ela couldn't bear the thought of disturbing the valiant man's body. And she most definitely didn't want to carry his sword—or any sword. Even so . . . She nodded.

Mourning the ravages of death, she unbuckled the dead soldier's sword.

✦ ✦ ✦

"I need to find a comfortable place," Tzana announced, shifting on Ela's back.

Ela paused. "So soon?"

"Yes, and it's not so soon."

"It is. Look. The sun's not overhead—it can't be midday."

"Then it's too early to eat?" Tzana sounded disappointed. "I want more fruit."

"I don't blame you. I love it too. But after our meals last night and this morning, we have only three pieces left. We need to save them for our midday rest."

"Only three?" Tzana sagged against Ela's shoulders. "I thought there were more." After a brief silence, she tweaked Ela's long braid and asked, "What will we eat when the fruit is gone?"

"The Infinite will provide food." Through the Istgardians. Ela shied away from thoughts of Istgard. However, each step took her closer to a confrontation with one of its most violent citizens.

She didn't relish demanding justice from a vicious wrongdoer who'd convinced himself he was blameless despite his evildoings. A man utterly oblivious to the sorrow he'd caused his victims and the Infinite.

A man unwilling to understand how vital the Infinite was to his existence.

Really, she didn't want to meet, much less say anything, to this reprobate.

And yet . . . Ela's throat tightened, parched by the memory of searing torment, of existence without the Infinite. Did she wish such agony—eternal agony—on anyone?

"Let's continue." She tried to sound enthusiastic, encouraging herself as much as her sister. "Watch the shadows and tell me when they're almost too small to see. That'll mean it's midday, and we can stop to eat."

"All right," Tzana agreed. In about twenty breaths, she fell asleep.

Ela felt her sister's small body go limp. Her head lolled against Ela's shoulder. Good. If Tzana slept, then she wouldn't recognize Ela's fear. Balancing her precious load and miserably aware of the sword slung at her side—a perpetual reminder of death—Ela trekked on, watching the landscape.

At last, with the sun nearly overhead, she halted. A wall of boulders and shrubs loomed to her left. The ravine she saw in her vision was now to her right, full of trees, briars, and vinewood. And that narrow dirt path between both formations was exactly as the Infinite depicted. How eerie to see familiar landmarks in a place she'd never been. Worse to know that these landmarks fit a most unnerving scene in her vision. She studied the now-minuscule shadows beneath the rocks and shrubs. Yes. This was the place, and almost the time. She knelt, set down the branch, and gently nudged Tzana awake.

"Climb down, silly! You were supposed to tell me when the shadows became almost too small to be seen."

"Like me?" Tzana mumbled drowsily. "Amar said I was almost too short to be seen."

"Well, Amar was wrong!" How dare he! If she hadn't already called off their future wedding, she would have called it off now.

Tzana tugged at Ela's sleeve. "I need a drink."

"Of course you do." Relieved to push aside thoughts of the traitorous Amar, Ela offered her sister the waterskin. But the waterskin's knot proved too much for Tzana's painfully bent fingers. If only poor Tzana could have retained even part of her temporary healing in that miraculous oasis! Ela untied the skin, then unpacked the last of the fruit as Tzana drank.

The fruit glistened in the sunlight, almost too beautiful to eat. Ela chose a plump, iridescent violet globe crowned with a bright green-stemmed cap. Pressing it between the heels of her hands, she split the fruit's vivid skin. Five perfectly white segments nestled within deep violet-red pulp. Ela tied up the waterskin, offered three segments to Tzana, then ate the remaining two.

She wished she could enjoy the sweet fruit, but thinking of the encroaching clash drained her appetite. However, her next meal would be long in coming, and not much to look forward to. Best to eat more now. She peeled the faceted green skin from the second fruit, ate half of its creamy center, then gave the rest to Tzana. Distant laughter from within the ravine stopped her as they were eating the third piece of fruit.

Men laughing and shouting raucously. Soldiers. If Ela closed her eyes, she would see them again, from her vision.

"Who's that?" Tzana asked, through a mouthful of the creamy fruit.

Sweat started over Ela's skin. Her raw, puckered scars, tokens from the scaln's attack, began to itch. "They're soldiers. You mustn't say a word to them, Tzana. Promise me."

"I promise." Tzana shoved the last bite of fruit into her mouth and nodded, asking with her mouth full, "Are you going to talk to them?"

"Yes. But they won't want to hear what I'm about to say. Whatever happens, just be quiet and stay close to me." Infinite? Ela pleaded, shaking inside, sickened. As she stood and gripped the branch, a consoling hand seemed to rest on her shoulder.

I am with you.

His voice strengthened Ela's wavering resolve. She wished it would banish the itching of her wounds. Was the itching a reminder of her previous failure?

Sounds neared. Metal clinked. Horses whickered, their hooves thudding against hard-packed dirt. The first horse—a formidable, massive black beast—emerged from the ravine and charged upward onto the path.

If this horse could breathe fire, it would now. Thankfully, Ela didn't recall the creature breathing fire in her vision. Even so, this monstrous beast, with hooves the size of platters and a foul disposition, snorted and glared as if it wanted to stomp Ela flat. Its rider, Ela knew, was equally horrendous.

Sunlight glinted fiercely off the soldier's crested metal helmet, his chest and leg armor, his weapons, and his shield, which was adorned with Istgard's symbol, a scaln's snarling face. No surprise, but still repulsive. Ela shuddered.

Spying Ela, the lead rider coerced his awful warhorse toward her. Tzana gasped and huddled into the folds of Ela's mantle, her small body shaking. Her obvious fear inspired no hint of compassion in the soldier's dark eyes. He called out, "Who are you, and where are you from?" His authoritative demeanor required an answer. "Are you refugees?"

"No!" Ela lifted her chin. "I am Ela Roeh of Parne, and this is my sister, Tzana."

"Huh! Parne's a dustbin, full of nothing but future slaves for Istgard."

His contempt infuriated Ela, but she fought to control her temper. The Infinite must not be represented by a prophet indulging in a tantrum. She exhaled a prayer. Let this man and his compatriots hear the truth. "You've taken enough slaves, Taun—pillager of Ytar."

The soldier stared, then scowled, his already-severe tone turning hostile. "Beggar! How do you know my name?"

"Your Creator told me your name, Taun." She shifted the branch cautiously, feeling its hidden light working toward the vinewood's surface. "I've been sent to warn you that He has seen your wickedness. He knows everything you've done. You must repent before you are condemned."

"My Creator?" the man sneered. "Who is this Creator? He's nothing to me!"

Four other soldiers were now urging their massive horses along the path from the ravine. As if to prove its dominance over the other creatures, Taun's frightful horse curveted, kicking out its back hooves and snorting unmistakable threats. Taun managed to keep the beast under control. Barely. It huffed toward Ela now, tossing its head, then flattening its dark ears. Its huge black body collar, equipped with handholds, footholds, and weaponry, added to the beast's menacing form. Ela didn't recall the horse charging her, for the vision had concluded with her warning to Taun. And Taun wasn't listening. Not with that beast throwing such a fit.

Beneath her breath, Ela implored the Infinite, "Tell me Your will!"

His voice commanded, *Tell that destroyer-horse, in My Holy Name, to be still.*

Gladly. Conveying her Creator's sternness, Ela looked the beast in the eye and called out, "In the Infinite's Holy Name, be still!"

The horse stilled, dark eyes watching her. Not even its tail flicked.

Taun sucked in an audible breath and checked his steed. The beast didn't move except to breathe and blink as it watched Ela.

"Witch!" The soldier looked offended, as if she'd insulted him beyond endurance. "What did you do to my destroyer?" He kicked, prodded, smacked, and chirruped, but the warhorse didn't budge. "Lift your spell!" he cried to Ela.

"This is no spell. Your destroyer obeys its Creator. As you should."

His lips pressed tight in his weathered face, Taun jumped from the horse onto the hard-packed trail. Using the blunt end of a spear, he beat the destroyer fiercely. The animal didn't stir. At last, the soldier threw down his spear, drew his sword, and advanced on Ela. "Lift your spell!"

Tzana ducked beneath Ela's mantle, shivering. The branch was glowing now, its brilliance unmistakable, even beneath the midday sun. Taun paused and his fellow soldiers dismounted, hushed, squinting against the branch's radiance. Ela summoned her courage. "Taun, I am no witch. Please, I've been sent to speak to you! Listen to your Creator's warning. He—"

"Shut your mouth!" He brandished his sword at her. "I do not obey witches! And whatever spell you're casting—break it!" Shading his eyes against the branch, Taun approached. "Give me that toy!" He stopped abruptly, his gaze fixed on the baldric slung over Ela's shoulder, then on the sword at her side. Moistening his lips, he asked, "How did you acquire that sword?"

A younger soldier, flushed with eagerness, edged near, shielding his eyes against the branch while studying the sword. "General Tek Juay's sword! Did you steal it from him, witch?"

"I am no witch," Ela repeated, squelching the impulse to scream. "The Infinite told me to remove this sword from your general's body, and to demand justice for his murder. You—"

"Liar!" Taun's bellow overpowered Ela's explanation. "If he's dead, then you killed him! For that, you deserve to die!" He tried to yank the branch from Ela's hands, but his fingers passed through it like insubstantial shadows. Snarling, Taun struck Ela. A blow that should have knocked her flat.

Ela's face stung at the impact, but she remained standing, supported by the branch. It seemed alive in her grasp now, an astonishing white-blue column. Ela shut her eyes and listened to the Infinite, sickened. She forced the words past her lips. "Taun, if you try to strike me again, the Infinite will remove your life's breath."

Her experience in the desert, within the agony of a bottomless cauldron of fire, seared her yet again. She could see the flames against her eyelids. Desperate to prevent anyone else from suffering its eternal fire, she looked up at her accuser and begged, "Please! Please, accept the Infinite's warning. He offers you this chance to atone for your crimes and to be reconciled to Him. It's not His will that you suffer!"

Taun hesitated. For the merest breath, Ela thought he might be convinced to listen. Instead, the soldier shook his head and raged. "You fraud! Who paid you?"

"No one! Please listen. You know I'm telling the truth. In a vision, your Creator showed me your general's death. The face of his murderer, approaching him from behind . . ." Ela weakened, seeing the image again. "Because Tek Juay renounced you for your cruelties, your greed, and your failure to follow orders, you took your dagger and—"

Taun lifted his sword, roaring a battle cry.

Certain she was about to die, Ela wrapped an arm around Tzana, hoping to protect her. "Infinite!"

Midswing, Taun choked. His eyes mirroring absolute torment, he lost control of his sword. Its blade struck the branch and shattered against the now unbearable glow. The soldier collapsed before Ela, his mouth wide open as if sucking air, his eyes staring horrified into his eternity.

"No!" She could almost see the flames reflected in his eyes. His agony of complete separation from the Infinite. "Why couldn't you listen?" Ela dropped to her knees and sobbed.

"Commander?" The young soldier crept over to the body, hands shaking as he checked Taun's throat, clearly seeking evidence of life. At last, he sat back and stared at Ela, his narrow face losing its ruddiness. "You've killed him!"

She shook her head, struggling to speak coherently through her tears. "He r-refused to listen. If only . . . if only he'd accepted the Infinite's warning."

Tzana extricated herself from Ela's mantle. She looked from the dead soldier to Ela and whimpered. Ela pulled her close, shielding them both with the branch, which faded, returning to its usual form.

The other soldiers dismounted, gaping. At last one of them spoke to Ela, his voice frayed with obvious fear and rage. "Whoever you are, I must charge you with Commander Taun's murder. Come with us."

Go *with them*, the Infinite commanded Ela.

Numb, she stood, prepared to obey.

✦ 6 ✦

Infinite, I'm not old enough to be a prophet! I'm failing at everything!" Ela whispered, unable to scream the words aloud. Actually, if she weren't carrying the dozing Tzana on her back, Ela would do more than scream. She would throw herself to the ground and surrender to despair. For Tzana's sake, however, she trudged onward, following the lead soldier who'd assumed command after Taun's burial.

Ela looked up at the man, riding straight and lordly on his black destroyer. She longed to beg him for a brief rest. Her arms burned with the ache of balancing both Tzana and the branch, light as they were. Irritating rivulets of sweat slid down her back and her face. And grit worked through her sandals, grinding at her now-blistered soles. But these discomforts were mild, compared to the burden that dragged at her soul and crushed her resolve. Was this her life as a prophet? Always stumbling? Never successful? She sniffled and gave in to tears.

"Infinite? What use am I to You if I continually fail?"

Peace infused His response and covered Ela's misery like a balm. *You believe you have failed. But you—created from dust— cannot see as I see.*

As Ela gulped down a sob, He continued. *You are My prophet. No more, no less. I reveal My will to you, and you must speak it to reveal My glory.*

67

"Yes," she agreed softly, not craving details so much as an answer to enduring her seemingly pointless struggle. "I want to . . . but why do I feel like a failure?"

You must speak My will, whether evildoers listen or fail to listen. The failure is their own.

"It still hurts." Tears fell and mingled with the sweat on Ela's cheeks as she thought of the soldier Taun. His look of horror when he died . . . The memory cut like a blade. If only he'd listened! Why couldn't—

"Aaaah!" Tzana croaked awake and wriggled against Ela's back. "It's licking me! Don't let it eat me!"

Ela whipped her thoughts away from her own wretchedness and spun on her heel to confront Tzana's assailant. Taun's massive black destroyer. It halted.

Forcing down her fear, Ela eyed the creature sternly. "What *are* you doing?"

The beast blinked at Ela, mild as a newborn. Waiting.

As she returned the destroyer's look, Ela sent up a wary question: Why is this monster following me?

Are you certain it's a monster? Tell Tzana to stretch out her hand.

Ela faltered, then said, "Tzana, stretch out your hand."

"Whyyyy?" Tzana rasped, still sleepy-voiced, but obviously suspicious.

"Because the Infinite commands you."

Tzana shifted on Ela's back, then cautiously stretched out one tiny gnarled hand. The destroyer nuzzled her swollen fingers gently, as if understanding that a more vigorous nudge would cause Tzana pain. Tzana's little-girl laughter trilled in Ela's ear. "That tickles!"

Ela grinned and some of the ache faded from her soul. Her sister's joy was as irresistible as breathing. "Thank You, Infinite. You always have the perfect answer."

Almost climbing over Ela's shoulder toward the destroyer now, Tzana cried, "He's our pet! Can I ride him?"

Ela glanced around and saw their four captors had halted. They looked disgruntled by the delay. Well, she could certainly move faster if Tzana rode. If they both rode. Moreover, the Infinite had prompted her to befriend this horse. Wasn't it logical to believe she and Tzana would be allowed to ride it? And the monster—destroyer—seemed agreeable. Her decision made, she boosted Tzana toward the horse's war collar. "Climb up, move forward, and grab a handle on his collar. I'm riding too."

"We shouldn't allow this!" one of the soldiers protested. "Not only did she kill Commander Taun, but that's his destroyer—and women don't ride destroyers!"

"Are you going to stop her?" the lead soldier asked the protester.

Ela hesitated. Surprisingly, the irate man didn't try to stop her. But he brooded, grim-faced, as if, having lost a battle, he were plotting revenge. She ignored him.

Seating Tzana was easy. Seating herself would be more difficult. This creature was entirely too tall for Ela to simply bound up onto its back—the collar's lowest footholds were too high. She studied the landscape and saw her solution.

Trying to convey a request, she stroked the beast's neck, then walked toward a boulder. "Will you come with me?" she asked. The destroyer followed at an amiable saunter, prompting delighted giggles from Tzana.

Branch in hand, Ela climbed the boulder and reached out to stroke the big horse's wide neck again as it paused before her, incredibly meek. Encouraged, she adjusted the branch to avoid hitting Tzana, pushed General Tek Juay's sword aside, then climbed onto the thick rider's quilt and settled herself sideways, mimicking the few female riding traders she'd seen in Parne. Tzana sat astride in front of Ela, tiny and heedlessly young, her long tunic bunched just above her thin, knobby knees. A child with a new toy. She turned to Ela. "Can we keep him?"

"He's not ours," Ela answered. "We're only borrowing him."

Branch clasped in one hand, the destroyer's reins gathered in the other, Ela urged the animal to follow the lead soldier, who had ridden onward.

The soldier who had protested Ela's decision to ride goaded his destroyer alongside her. With a smile that wasn't a smile, he said, "That addled beast is the last creature you'll ever bewitch. Mark my words, you'll be executed in Riyan."

"Mark my words: I won't," Ela replied, suddenly realizing it was the truth. She gritted her teeth as glimmers of a vision pierced her thoughts. A king. A battle. Soldiers falling. Dying. And she, Ela Roeh of Parne, would be at least partially responsible for their deaths.

No!

Inexplicably, the destroyer halted. Ela prodded him to move onward, then she implored her Creator to reconsider. "Please, Infinite! I'm not clever or expert enough for any of this. I don't want to tear down a bird's nest, much less a kingdom or nation. Particularly if it causes others to die!"

Silence answered.

Argh! Just like Father when he considered a discussion ended.

Ela fumed awhile, glaring past Tzana at the destroyer's shining black mane. Finally, her attention shifted to his large, listening black ears, which perked back and forth. Amusing ears. She enjoyed watching them, actually. And she liked riding.

Think of it . . . scrawny Ela Roeh and her afflicted little sister, riding a gigantic destroyer that sought their attention. Who in Parne would ever believe her?

Already Ela's feet, back, and arms felt better. Wasn't this a gift? Hadn't the Infinite offered her this respite? And here she sat—Ela could just see herself—sulky and ungrateful as a spoiled child.

Not to mention thoroughly wrong.

"Infinite?" Ela knew He saw and felt her remorse. "Thank You!"

Even if she and Tzana were riding into the chaos.

✦ ✦ ✦

70

Had she ever imagined such a dazzling city? Ela gawked at Riyan. Early evening sunlight gilded the city's exquisite towers and spires, their bases misted by curling wisps of smoke. Above the slender spires, dules of doves fluttered and soared high into the golden sky, their ethereal white forms offset by the looming deep blue mountains beyond Riyan. "How beautiful!"

"We're too late for the sacrifices," the always-irritable soldier grumbled loudly to his companions as they rode behind Ela.

"At least we'll be fed," the new commander replied. He looked back at Ela now, his tanned, powerful face dispassionate. "Tonight you will sleep in a cell. Unless your trial convenes immediately."

"It will," Irritable announced, sounding smug. "I intend to speak to my uncle at once."

Was this boorish soldier's uncle a magistrate? Ela would have never guessed.

The commander fixed Ela's foe with a severe look. "Ket, you will allow us time to stable our horses and eat."

"If the witnesses are hungry, the trial won't be delayed," Ket pointed out, smugness intact.

"If the witnesses are hungry, they won't testify!" someone else cried. His rage made Ela turn. It was the youngest soldier, who had first recognized General Tek Juay's sword. He jutted out his black-whiskered chin, truculent, as if baiting Ket. Riding behind him, the fourth soldier merely belched, then glared and nodded agreement to the youngest soldier's antagonistic retort.

Ket leaned forward on his destroyer and growled, "Is that a threat, Tal? I can have you imprisoned for refusing to cooperate!"

"You mean your uncle, the judge, can have me imprisoned, don't you? But I'm willing to bet my evening meal he's not as fond of you as you believe."

Ket drew his sword, the thin, dangerous ring of metal sliding across metal accentuating his reply. "Dung heap! Do you think I'll take insults from you?"

"Stop!" their leader snarled. "Ket, I gave you an order. You will not speak to your uncle until we've eaten. Put away your

71

sword or I'll have you cleaning cesspits for the next year! Tal, drop that smile off your face. I order all of you to be quiet! The citizens are listening, and you sound shamefully like squabbling brats instead of trained soldiers."

The three miscreants straightened and responded in trained unison. "Yes, sir."

Tzana plucked Ela's sleeve and leaned back. "*We're* not squabbling," she announced, sounding pleased with herself and Ela.

"No, we're not," Ela agreed. "And I think we've more reason to squabble than they do."

Behind them, Ket snorted and uttered a vicious oath. Somehow, the noise provoked Taun's destroyer, and it kicked back toward Ket's destroyer, huffing apparent threats, jolting both girls in the process. Tzana squeaked, and Ela hastily smoothed the animal's glossy black coat. "Shh. It's useless to lose your temper—though we appreciate your instinct to defend us."

"Just when I thought that beast had become a mouse," Tal said. "It has some spirit left after all."

"Quiet!" the commander ordered. "Tal, when we reach the barracks, you will scrub the floors and practice keeping your mouth shut."

"Yes, sir."

The destroyers' hooves thumped against stone pavings as their small party entered the first street in Riyan. A chill descended on Ela as they passed one of the exquisite spires she'd admired earlier. This spire—indeed all the spires—evidently marked the city's temples. "So many," she whispered. She longed to cry. She prayed instead.

A vision opened within Ela's thoughts. She braced herself, pressed the branch hard against her forehead, and shut her eyes as she tried to make sense of what she saw and heard.

Burly craftsmen carving wood, chiseling flawless stones, painting the carvings and adorning them with gold and gems. Kissing the floor on which the ornate objects stood.

Proclaiming the objects gods.

See how these carvers work! They use half of their wood for their fire to keep warm, and they sculpt the remaining half to form their little gods, who do nothing for them. Can these gods send blessings? Lightning? Or rain to nurture their crops?

Ela felt the Infinite's contempt. *Where are these gods? I do not see them here beside Me! These people cannot understand how foolish they are, trusting clumps of wood, metal, and stone they've sculpted with their own hands. Look!*

At His urging, Ela opened her eyes and looked skyward. At the fluttering doves. *My creatures are compelled to signal the useless sacrifices these fools have just made to their false gods. Sacrifices to nothing!*

Smoke filled the street as Ela passed one particularly large temple. Burning spices added pungency to the smoke's scent, not quite masking an underlying stench of scorched flesh. Ela covered her eyes and saw the sacrifices in her vision now. Doves. Lambs. Horses. Children.

She suppressed the need to vomit. But she couldn't hold back her tears.

"What's wrong? Why are you delaying us?" The commander rode toward Ela. She blinked, realizing the destroyer had stopped.

"Forgive me." Ela wiped her tears.

Tzana leaned back against her, concern fretting the wrinkles in her small face. "Ela, are you sick?"

"Very." Unable to bear her sorrow, Ela looked the leader in the eyes. "Istgardians sacrifice children!"

His expression quieted. "Some do. They give what is most precious to their gods."

"But what if their sacrifice is useless? Their gods aren't even—"

"Don't talk foolishness. Sacrifice to the gods is never useless, and I will not listen to you spouting blasphemy." He turned his destroyer about sharply. The dark creature reared in protest.

Ela protested, "The desire to protect innocent lives is never blasphemy!" When the leader said nothing, she seethed. Why didn't he care?

You will not be the first of My prophets to speak against this evil in Istgard. But this time, you will not only speak the truth; you will warn these foolish people of disaster beyond their imaginings. I am about to judge Istgard's leaders for encouraging such evil.

The delicate hairs on the back of Ela's neck prickled and she shivered. "What sort of judgment?"

Oh no. Why had she asked?

✦ ✦ ✦

A cool breeze touched Ela's face, calming her, easing her headache. What a mercy she hadn't fallen off the destroyer. She opened her eyes and sucked in a deep breath. At least this vision was more tolerable in force, if not in substance. Fear shook her limbs.

"Are you *quite* ready to proceed?" The lead soldier looked fit to roar with impatience. "If you don't move that idiot destroyer, I'll have it butchered and drag you to the prison myself!"

Had the destroyer halted again? Ela straightened, perplexed. How did the creature know when she was overcome by visions? Were all horses so perceptive? She rubbed the destroyer's neck and urged it forward. "Go. You mustn't allow my visions to stop you."

Tzana chirped her own encouragements. "Ela's awake now, Pet! You can walk."

"Pet" walked.

Behind them, Ket groaned in obvious disgust, and Tal cried, "*Pet?* She's named him *Pet!*"

The fourth soldier, a gloomy-faced laggard who spoke rarely and belched often, was evidently offended beyond endurance. "To name a destroyer *Pet* is—it's wrong! Lacks dignity! It's bad enough that you've stolen Commander Taun's horse, but now you lower that once-magnificent creature to nothing! The commander will rise from his grave and hunt you down for this, witch."

"Pet is still magnificent, and I'm not a witch," Ela said.

"Huh! You're casting spells and having visions!"

"Silence!" the commander bellowed. "Ket and Osko, you will join Tal at the barracks tomorrow and scrub the floors.

Three times. And if I hear a word of complaint, you'll muck out the cesspits."

"Yes, sir!" the soldiers called in unison.

Their leader redoubled the pace. Jolted, Ela leaned forward, clutching Tzana and the branch tight. Men, women, and children backed off but watched as Ela rode by, some of the women looking compassionate. Ela welcomed their compassion and prayed for the women. How many of them had been forced to offer their children to the flames beneath those exquisite spires?

Elegant buildings eventually gave way to a long, stout wall, crowned by ungainly watchtowers, which were covered with drab shingled roofs. Grim spear-wielding guards stalked back and forth on the wall walk above.

The leader called up to the guards, "Open the gates immediately! We have two prisoners."

As they rode inside, Ela felt bleakness drop over her like a sodden blanket. What a dismal place. But what else could she expect? Perhaps she could be of use here. "This is our home for a while," she told Tzana. "We need to make the best of it."

"It's big," Tzana said, looking around, remarkably bright-eyed.

The commander dismounted, marched over to Pet, and looked up at Ela. "Give me the child, then climb down. No scenes, please."

Please? Ela looked into the man's stern brown eyes, seeing him instead of a soldier-leader. His soul contained more than she'd suspected. Honor. Even a hint of kindness.

Why hadn't she noticed this before?

Child of dust, can you withstand too much knowledge at one time? the Infinite asked. *No.*

Now, imagery, like a memory sent to her from the future, made Ela smile. "Tsir Aun, the Infinite sees your heart and will bless you for your kindness to us. He asks you to seek His will and be worthy of your future."

For an instant the commander looked stunned, as if he'd been thrown by his destroyer. "How do you know my full name?" But then he waved off her reply, seeming to dismiss a foolish notion. "Never mind. My future is of no concern. Let me fulfill my duties. Give me the child."

She scooted Tzana toward him and watched as he set the fragile little girl down carefully in the courtyard's trampled dirt. Then Ela managed her own awkward descent from the huge destroyer's back, nearly falling off the war collar's last foothold. "Ugh!" She stumbled and dug the branch into the dust, seeking balance enough to stand.

Ket jeered.

"Eat, then go find your uncle," Ela commanded him as she dusted off her tunic. "I'll speak to him tonight. Then the king and his family will send for me."

"The king and his family?" Ket huffed. "How you talk! As if they'll greet you with a feast and joy."

"There will be no joy for the king, or for you. Remember my words, Ket. It's not too late—your Creator offers you the contentment you've never known."

The haughty soldier's face went blank, then took on the bewilderment of a child. "I don't know what you're talking about, witch."

"Again, I'm no witch. Only Infinite's servant. Eat, then go to your uncle."

She turned her back on him and found the commander, Tsir Aun, staring at her. "How old are you?" he asked, as if trying to figure out a puzzle.

"Almost eighteen." She felt much younger. Her knees were shaking. Knowing what was going to happen tonight didn't make matters any easier.

Pet whickered plaintively as Ela and Tzana walked away. A twinge of remorse surprised Ela, and she stopped long enough to reassure the huge destroyer. "Be patient. Let the soldiers feed you and don't worry. We won't be far."

The big horse calmed a bit, though with an air of grumpiness that made Ela smile.

Tsir Aun shook his head in apparent disbelief, then led the girls inside the prison's main tower.

✦ ✦ ✦

Starvation, Kien decided, was not his preferred method of dying.

But now, staring at his meager ration of parched bread and a bowl of hot water with a single wilted leaf foundering beneath its surface, Kien realized starvation was his intended fate. The warden's wife would see to it.

Stringy-haired and haggard, with her wrinkled white head-dress flapping above her gray sweat-stained tunic, the warden's wife stood beside a large kettle in the center of the stone-paved prisoners' yard. With the air of a displeased mother, she doled hot seasoned water into bowls, accompanied by hard grain rolls from a basket at her feet. She shoved these rations at the grimy prisoners, who clattered past her in a well-guarded line. To favored prisoners, she served bits of boiled meat and overcooked vegetables, plopping them into the hot water like waste into a privy pot. Kien shuddered, almost glad he wasn't one of her favored prisoners.

He glanced about the yard, planning. By supposed virtue of his once-royal blood, Kien was chained to no one but himself and was always seated beside no one but himself. The situation was ridiculous. Hopeless. How could he possibly connive an escape if, because of undeserved respect, he was continually separated from the other prisoners?

To thwart any dubious honors this evening, Kien pretended forgetfulness and wandered toward some potential conspirators who were chained together in a shaded corner.

"Sir." A guard stepped in front of Kien, waved a hand to gain his reluctant attention, then pointed to an unoccupied wall in the sunlight. "There's your place."

Kien stifled his frustration and headed toward the sunlit wall. At least he would be warm by the time he finished his rations.

Cautious of the bowl—water was water, after all—he sat on the dusty stone pavings and braced himself to eat. He partially dunked the hard roll into his water, waited for it to soften, then gnawed at the mess.

The yard's single doorway squealed open and a prison guard shoved in two more prisoners, then tossed a wooden bowl behind them, which clattered loudly on the stones.

Two girls.

All conversation stopped. Even the warden's wife paused to stare.

What, Kien wondered, had this skinny young female and the tiny Unfortunate with her done to deserve imprisonment with Riyan's most vile miscreants?

The older girl, wielding a slender wooden staff, surveyed the motley assortment of criminals and nodded as if she'd expected to see them. With a tender smile she motioned the child-Unfortunate to sit on the stones near the cauldron. Then she retrieved the wooden bowl, which she silently offered to the warden's wife.

Shaking her white headdress, the older woman scolded, "Don't bother asking for a second bowl! You two will have to share that one—I'll not be chasing up and down the stairs for any wrongdoers."

"Of course." The girl's voice was clear, low, and surprisingly calm, Kien thought. Wouldn't most females in her situation be frightened out of their wits? The girl accepted two hard rolls, slipped them into a fold of her tawny mantle, then smiled as the warden's wife plopped small chunks of meat and vegetables into their bowl of hot water. "Thank you."

Holding her bowl and slender wooden staff, the girl turned away. Kien straightened, intrigued. She wore a wide baldric with an ornate scabbard that could only belong to nobility. Was she noble? And where was the sword? Confiscated, most likely. But without its scabbard? Interesting . . . That scabbard looked familiar. . . .

The girl sat with the child, and they shared the food happily, as if enjoying a picnic. The other prisoners—all men, and understandably distracted—resumed eating. But without the usual lewd banter, curses, and threats normally exchanged during their meal.

"I suppose I'll have to guard you two," the warden's wife complained. "Why they'd send girls here is beyond my knowing! I've enough work to do, tending meals and waiting on a crippled husband!"

Kien didn't bother to hide his grin at the thought of the crippled warden.

"Don't worry," the girl told the warden's wife kindly. "You won't be delayed long. A judge will send his clerk for us as soon as we've finished our meal."

"And I'm the queen of Istgard!" the woman snipped, thunking her ladle into the kettle.

"You wouldn't want to be the queen," the girl answered. Her smile faded. "Pray for her."

"Pray for her! Why? She has everything I can only dream of!"

"Soon, unless matters change, she will only be able to dream of everything you have."

Kien wondered at the sorrow suddenly shadowing the girl's thin face. The tiny Unfortunate patted her hand as if to console her, and they resumed eating. Soon after the new prisoners finished their food and set aside their bowl, the solitary door opened. A stout man, handsomely cloaked in gray and pinned with a silver law clerk's insignia, stepped into the yard, his movements finicky, as if he feared treading in manure. And he might.

"Ela of Parne!" He noticed the two females and said to the girl, "I suppose that means you. Come with me. You're called to the court of Judge Ket Behl."

"I was expecting you." Her walking stick in hand, the mysterious girl stood politely, forcing a smile as if she'd been invited to a party she'd rather not attend. She and the odd child followed the clerk from the yard.

Questions buzzed in their wake, whispered by Kien's fellow prisoners.

Just before a guard slammed the door, blocking the girl from Kien's sight, she said, "You must return the general's sword to me."

The general's sword? Kien devoutly hoped he'd see the girl again.

✦ 7 ✦

You must give me General Tek Juay's sword!" Ela charged after the self-important clerk in the stone passageway. "I need to return it to his family."

"If you are so concerned about the general's family, then why did you kill him?" The clerk pivoted on his booted heel to face Ela so swiftly that she jumped back a step and nearly trampled Tzana.

"I did not kill the general. I found his body."

"A common defense. And a useless one, Ela of Parne."

"It's the truth," Ela insisted.

Tzana leaned around Ela and piped up. "We found a dead man—his face looked like bark."

The clerk recoiled a bit at this description, but then he recovered and smiled at Tzana. "So you are a witness, eh?" Looking at Ela again, he said, "Too bad. She's too young. And"—he squinted at Tzana's earnest, wizened face—"perhaps not altogether . . . shall we say, 'all together'?"

What a snide man! Ela itched to slap him. "I should think that my sister's obvious innocence would make her testimony more trustworthy than an adult's."

"More easily led, I should think," the man replied. "Now, having settled this matter, let's hurry along."

He strode ahead, leading Ela and Tzana through several

guarded doorways before they stepped outside to the prison's main yard, where evening shadows purpled the stones.

Determined to make the clerk listen, Ela halted beside the prison tower's steps. She tucked Tzana behind her and planted the branch upright in the dirt at her sandaled feet, like a guard with a spear. "We've settled nothing. I will not go until you bring me General Tek Juay's sword."

The clerk's face went deep red, and he blustered, "Do not order me about like a menial!"

"I apologize if I've offended you. But I won't leave until I receive the general's sword."

"You have been summoned by the Honorable Ket Behl, and you must answer the summons immediately. If you do not, you will be severely punished, I promise you!"

"Why are you making promises you cannot keep?" Ela asked.

Puffing out a breath, the impatient clerk tried to grab Ela's arm. She swung the branch toward him, and his fingers sizzled as they hit the vinewood. "Ow! You *are* a witch!"

Witch. Again. Ela closed her eyes and begged her Creator for patience. For His guidance. She looked up at the angry man and spoke loudly, so everyone in the prison yard could hear. "Sir, I am the Infinite's servant—not a witch. Furthermore, I give you my word I intend to follow you without delay, as soon as General Tek Juay's sword is returned to me. Oh . . . and I'm sorry about the three large blisters on your fingers."

The clerk looked at his fingers, then at her, a line creased between his dark, wiry eyebrows.

Ela smiled. Certain that all the guards and grubby hangers-on in the yard could hear, she said, "Your blisters won't swell and rot your fingers off *if* you bring me the sword. In fact, by the Infinite's mercy, your blisters will heal the instant the sword is in my hands. Your choice, sir."

Clearly exasperated, and perhaps a bit unnerved, the clerk whirled about and yelled at the guards, who lurked near the tower's metal-studded doorway. "Where is General Tek Juay's sword? One of you rogues bring it to me at once, or the Honorable Ket Behl will know why!"

Even as the clerk was shouting, Tsir Aun emerged from the doorway, wearing a clean tunic, polished plate armor, his bright red cloak, and a gleaming black-plumed helmet. General Tek Juay's sword rested flat in his outstretched hands. Distinctly formal, he bowed his head to the clerk and offered him the sword. "Sir, this was in the warden's quarters. I regret you had to wait so long." More quietly, he added, "My men and I are witnesses in this matter. If you will allow us to accompany you, we'll be sure the prisoners cause you no further delay."

"Yes, yes. Of course." The clerk accepted the sword and offered it to Ela, tentative now. Did he expect her to attack him?

"Thank you." She secured the branch in the crook of one arm, accepted the ornate sword, and slid it carefully into the glittering scabbard. As she straightened the baldric and took Tzana's hand, Ela glimpsed the clerk furtively checking his fingers. He blinked hard, then opened his eyes wide, as if he didn't trust what he saw.

Or what he didn't see.

Ela smiled. "Your blisters are healed because you've obeyed the Infinite. As He said."

The clerk opened his mouth, then shut it again. Marching toward the gate, he motioned the guards to let them pass through. Outside, Tai and Osko waited, helmets casually beneath their arms. Both appeared damp, as if they'd recently doused their heads in a pool and allowed the water to drip onto their cloaks and tunics.

Tsir Aun's face hardened, and he glowered at his subordinates, unblinking.

In response, the men donned their helmets, adjusted their swords, and smoothed their cloaks, then stood at attention. Tsir Aun looked away, his displeasure eased.

With a scornful snap of his now-healed fingers, the clerk motioned a humbly clad assistant to bring a smallish glossy brown horse. Almost groveling, the assistant led the horse forward, struggled to boost the clerk onto the beast, then gasped, "Thank you, Master Piln!"

Tal, the guard to Ela's left, snickered as if trying to restrain himself. Ela understood why. The brown horse was a mouse compared to any destroyer. Beneath his breath, Tal chortled, "Ha! Look at that pretty brown . . . mite!"

"Cesspit duty, after you scrub the barracks floors tomorrow, Tal," Tsir Aun commanded.

"Yes, sir!" Tal wheezed and managed to stifle his mirth.

Beside him, Osko smirked.

"I miss Pet," Tzana told Ela, her small voice mournful. In sympathy, Ela bent and picked up her little sister. The walk couldn't be too far. Nothing compared to their forced march through Istgard's countryside. Ready, she looked ahead. Hopefully, the clerk, Master Piln, was riding his pretty horse as a point of status, not necessity—the leader of their motley procession.

A wormlike assistant, two tattered girl prisoners, and three soldiers—two of them bumptious oafs. Yes, a striking procession. Ela sighed. "Onward," she murmured to Tzana.

They had just turned onto a side street when deep thuds echoed off the walls. More horsehooves, Ela guessed. The ground thrummed with vibrations. A big horse's hooves. As shrieks and pandemonium filled the street behind them, Ela sucked in her breath, appalled. Could it be—

Tzana looked over Ela's shoulder and squealed. "Pet!"

"Wrath of all the gods!" Osko snarled a spate of oaths that made Ela flinch. "Who released that befuddled thing? I chained him in the stables with the others!"

"Osko," Tsir Aun said, with the merest hint of satisfaction in his voice, "You've failed. Cesspit duty with Tal, after the barracks floors tomorrow. Argue and the penalties will double."

"Yes, sir," Osko muttered.

By this time, Pet was breathing down the nape of Ela's neck, wilting her braid. She glanced back and exhaled in retaliation, though her breath was nowhere near as fulsome. "You would have enjoyed the stables more, Pet, I'm sure."

Osko snorted. Pet snapped toward him, then sighed into Ela's braid again. Tzana burst into giggles. She chattered and crooned to Pet, offered him her hands to sniff, and tried to scratch his neck. If Judge Ket Behl's clerk had imagined himself at the fore of a dignified procession, well, that delusion was surely sinking with the evening sun.

As Master Piln looked over his shoulder at the commotion, his little brown horse lapsed into a skittish fit and tossed him off. The clerk rolled helplessly in the street, finally coming to rest nose and toes up, blinking at the sky. His silence made Ela nervous.

"Master Piln!" The clerk's assistant rushed to his side and squawked, "Are you dead?"

"Of course not!" Piln swatted away his flustered, fluttering servant. "Fool! Go catch my horse! Can't you think?"

As his servant scrambled after the now-distant mount, the outraged clerk hefted himself to his feet and pointed a finger at Pet. "Remove that destroyer—it frightened my horse!"

"Pardon, sir, but a destroyer cannot be removed against its will." Tsir Aun looked both polite and uncompromising. "This is, or was, Commander Taun's destroyer, and it is now besotted with these girls. My men insist this is the effect of a spell—which, perhaps, will interest the Honorable Ket Behl."

Ela grimaced at his words. But why should she feel betrayed? Tsir Aun spoke the truth.

Master Piln evidently realized the truth as well. He stuttered, "Then—then—keep that—that *reprehensible* beast out of my way! And you'd best hope my servant finds my horse again, or that animal will be forfeited!"

"He doesn't like Pet?" Tzana sounded stricken.

"You were afraid of Pet when you first met him, weren't you?" Ela squirmed as she spoke. Pet was snuffling at her shoulder. She hoped he wasn't blowing his nose.

"The prisoner will maintain her distance from you," Tsir Aun told the clerk, with a sidelong frown that demanded Ela's obedience. "The destroyer will remain with her."

"You be sure she does!" The clerk shook his cloak into order, regathered his tattered dignity, and—with admirable fortitude—limped ahead, up the street.

Tsir Aun allowed the man a lead of twenty paces, then motioned Ela to follow, with Tal and Osko on guard to the left and right of the street. The formidable commander walked beside Ela now, measuring his steps to hers. "My fear is confirmed," he said. "This destroyer has pledged itself to you and your sister. When either of you sets foot outside a building, unless you command this destroyer to wait, or unless he is chained—as he should have been—he will follow you."

"He's going to be breathing down my neck for the remainder of my life?"

"Or for the remainder of his life. If you are in danger, he will die trying to defend you."

Wonderful. No, horrible. But, why . . . "Why didn't he defend Commander Taun?"

"He did," Tsir Aun said. "Remember? He threatened you. And he was about to charge. However, you told him to be still and he halted. Which is why my men believe you are a witch. Destroyers never pledge defense to anyone without a direct order from their current master. And usually, the master must earn the destroyer's complete devotion over the course of months."

"The Infinite told Pet to be still," Ela argued, aware that Tal and Osko could hear. "I simply said the words aloud."

"Well, now you have a pledged destroyer, Ela of Parne," Tsir Aun said dryly, as if trying to decide how to deal with the problem.

"You mean we can keep him?" Tzana whooped in Ela's arms.

"What would you do with a destroyer, little one?" Tsir Aun asked, his dark eyebrows lifted.

"Play with him!"

"Of course." The commander looked vaguely sickened.

As Tal and Osko grunted and frowned, Ela smiled at her sister.

"What *are* we supposed to do with a destroyer?" she wondered aloud.

"First, you must survive this night." His voice neutral, Tsir Aun asked, "Are you afraid, Parnian?"

"Always." Aware of their listening attendants marching alongside, she said, "Though the judge will ignore the charges set against me."

"How?" Tsir Aun demanded, as his comrades stared in disbelief. "Each charge against you requires a death sentence, and you cannot possibly prove your innocence."

"I am innocent. And if the Infinite defends me—as He will—I cannot be condemned." Remembering the end of her vision, she shivered and kissed Tzana's face. "We'll face more worrisome troubles tonight, Commander. When all seems well to you and your men—be ready."

✦ ✦ ✦

Ela marched through the high-arched stone gateway, eager to be finished with this trial, yet dreading what waited beyond. A beautiful tree-and-shrub-edged courtyard tempted Ela's attention. But she followed her guards, climbing the steps to Judge Ket Behl's courtroom.

Pet halted just inside the gate and rumbled noises of complaint, stomping his understandable disapproval.

"Wait!" Ela called to the uneasy animal. "We won't be long."

Tzana toyed with Ela's damp braid. "What are we doing?"

"I must tell a judge what happened—why those two men died. But you must not speak unless the judge questions you. Agreed?"

"All right. But I can't like this," Tzana whispered. "I want to leave."

"So do I." As she walked into the handsomely tiled chamber, Ela prayed and hugged Tzana again. Must her vision end in the terrifying darkness she'd seen? "Infinite, please."

You are safe enough for now. Do not consider the darkness until you must—and know that I will use evil for good.

"Evil for good?" Ela repeated. "What . . . Oh, never mind." She sighed. Did she really want to know *what* evil?

Tsir Aun was frowning, as if he questioned her sanity. Not a defense tactic she wished to use. Ela set Tzana down and stretched slightly, easing her shoulder, adjusting the branch.

Master Piln, dignified again in his clerkly role, mounted a stone dais at the far end of the chamber, limped across it, and rapped grandly on a door. "Your Honor, they are here."

A muted voice called out an unintelligible reply, which the clerk seemed to understand. He hobbled to the single item of furniture on the dais—a finely carved, cushioned chair—and adjusted its thick green pillows. A tight smile lifted the corners of his mouth. Evidently satisfied, he crept off the dais and arranged himself on a chair before a scroll-strewn table.

The far door opened and Ela's antagonistic guard Ket emerged, haughty as usual, his polished helmet in the crook of his arm. Tal and Osko both shuffled. Tsir Aun frowned. Ket ignored them.

A man, resplendent in a decorously pinned and draped gray cloak, sauntered after Ket. Ela immediately saw the family resemblance. The smugness. The irritability.

Ela wondered if Ket had told his uncle-judge the truth.

Mouth pursed in his puffy, jowly brown face, the judge eyed Ela. "You are the accused?"

"I am Ela of Parne. Servant of the Infinite."

"Pish," the judge said. "Parne is nothing."

Almost exactly the same reaction as that pillager Commander Taun. Obviously, a fair trial was not forthcoming. She prayed for peace and waited as the judge settled into his chair.

At his little table, Clerk Piln clinked vials of ink and scratched quills across scrolls. An important man. During the delay, Ela's scars—souvenirs left by the scaln—began to itch up and down her legs. She bit her lip against the urge to scratch. Most undignified.

Ket Behl stared at her, scornful, as if Ela was already condemned. "You deny murdering our general Tek Juay?"

"Yes. The general was dead days before I found his body."

Sickened by the memory, Ela added, "The air, sand, and sun had dried his skin. Baked it." She shifted a foot slightly, trying to ease the maddening itch of the scars. "Moreover, about the time General Tek Juay must have died, I was recovering from a scaln's attack."

"Impossible!" The judge scowled. "One does not recover from a scaln attack!"

"I have the scars," Ela said. "The Infinite healed my wounds. Otherwise, I would have died of the venom."

Everyone stared now. Even Tsir Aun. Ket Behl sneered. "Show us these scars."

Heated embarrassment flooded Ela's face. But she stepped forward, pressed the branch against her side with her elbow, and cautiously lifted her tunic until the hem was almost to her knees. The scars showed violet-red, and deeply furrowed, on the fronts and backs of both legs.

The judge cleared his throat. "Record that the said scars do exist, being deeply incised into the legs of the accused and are, ahem, recent. Colors are . . . purple and red. The flesh severely creased and marked in the, ah, patterns one would expect to be inflicted by a scaln."

Master Piln's quill scraped and scratched furiously across his scroll. No one said a word. When he looked up, Ket Behl was more respectful. "These scars are impressive. You should be crippled. But they cannot be scaln's scars. No one has ever survived such a mauling."

"The scaln stalked me in a canyon," Ela said. She lowered her hem and gripped the branch with both hands, sweating as she saw the scaln's face once more. "I heard the gurgle first. Then the hiss. Its breath was rotten. Its face—"

She relived the attack, her terror. The pain. The blood that would not stop dripping from her wounds. Her hallucinations and the fever. "The Infinite healed me, according to His mercy. And for His glory. My scars are reminders of my failure to call on His Name immediately."

"Your Infinite need not be mentioned here."

"Yes, He must. He healed my wounds, though I should have died."

"She didn't know me," Tzana said, her thin, clear voice unexpected.

"Child, you will hush!" the judge ordered, making Tzana gasp and hide in Ela's mantle. "And you, Ela of Parne, will not argue. What other evidence can you offer in your defense?"

"Only my knowledge, given by the Infinite. Commander Taun attacked General Tek Juay from behind and slashed his throat because the general condemned his cruelty and failure to follow orders halting the massacre at Ytar." Ela nodded toward Ket, Tal, and Osko. "They witnessed their commander arguing with the general shortly before the murder."

Tal nodded, as if he remembered the argument. Ket glared at him. Osko shuffled from one foot to the other and looked away. The judge saw their discomfort, and his face reddened. He stared at his nephew, who lowered his gaze. Quietly, each syllable clipped, Ket Behl said, "You are neither condemned nor excused in the general's death, Ela of Parne. The accusation is discarded. Tell me, what weapon did you use when you killed Commander Taun?"

How smoothly he dismissed the charges for the sake of his nephew's good name—and his own. As if no one would notice. Even so, Ela blessed the Infinite and disputed the next charge. "I did not kill Commander Taun. I begged him to listen to me—to live. And to confess to his crimes. Instead, he struck me. I warned him . . ." Ela swallowed. The memory was too raw. Despite the sting of tears, she continued, "I told him that if he struck me again, the Infinite would remove his life's breath."

"Again, you defend yourself by naming the Infinite," Ket Behl pointed out. "He does not exist. Your testimony is invalid."

Ela dashed a hand at her tears. "I am the Infinite's servant. Does a servant speak of work without mentioning his or her master?"

Unmoved, the judge said, "Rephrase your answer."

"You have dismissed the Infinite."

"Yes. Rephrase your answer."

Infinite, how? After a brief pause, the answer came. Nauseated, Ela said, "Very well. I told Commander Taun not to do something that would cause his death. I *begged* him to listen to me! He did not. He fell while raising his sword to strike me—though I wielded no sword. And when he died, I mourned his passing. I still mourn. Am I responsible for his death, Your Honor?"

"Is this true?" the judge asked Tal and Osko.

"Close enough, Your Honor," Osko muttered as Tal agreed.

"Then I have no choice but to ignore these charges."

"Uncle," Ket argued, "you cannot excuse her! If she had not been there, Commander Taun would still be alive. She caused his death by some form of witchery!"

"Silence." The judge narrowed his gaze at Ket. "Witchery is a nonexistent charge. Five self-proclaimed witches and soothsayers ply their trade on this street alone! I can count twenty nearby. Half of Riyan pays fortune-tellers, and the other half wishes they could afford to pay them. This case is ill-considered, and I am deeply disappointed with those who have wasted my evening here."

Ket growled, making Ela wish Pet could snap at him. This afternoon's vision buoyed to the surface of her thoughts. She must conclude matters here. "May I speak?"

Bored, the judge waved agreement.

"Thank you, Your Honor. I am no witch. My words are from the Infinite and can be tested, because they will be fulfilled. Always. Now, Judge Ket Behl, your king has sent for me. His messengers approach your gate. But before I leave, I am required to warn you. Because you have dismissed the Infinite, He has dismissed you."

"What does that mean?" Ket Behl stood, his gray cloak swaying with his indignation. "Are you threatening me?"

"No, I am not. But tonight the Infinite has judged and

condemned your family. His sentence will depend upon your own heart. Your choices."

"You are demanding a bribe!" Ket accused, his eyes now bright and hard, like a man about to eradicate his prey. "How much money do you require to lift this curse?"

Ela trembled as the Infinite's wrath overcame her own petty exasperation. This man exemplified the superstitions and evils that were destroying Istgard. "You work of dirt! The Infinite has no need of silver or gold—He created all the wealth that's ever existed. The only thing you can possibly give Him is genuine remorse, and plenty of it! Your time is short, Ket. Unless you change!" Her accuser cowered and stared, silent. Ela shook out her mantle, then bent and picked up Tzana. "It's time for me to leave. Your king's men have found me."

Sharp whistles resounded from outside. The courtroom door banged open. A tall, green-cloaked official barged in, followed by four guards, also clothed in green, their weapons clattering. The official could not have looked more disdainful as he addressed Judge Ket Behl. "We are looking for an Ela of Parne. She is summoned in the name of the king."

"Here," Ela told the man. He blinked at her. "I'm ready to go."

Tzana tapped at Ela's shoulder, and whispered, "I liked your hair. It looked like the branch!"

"What?" She noticed the branch fading. It was ablaze? "Oh."

No wonder everyone stared. She managed a smile, then turned to the door.

✦ ✦ ✦

"What's happened?" Disbelief made Ela almost stumble. She set Tzana on the steps before Judge Ket Behl's courtroom, then rushed down to the courtyard. The Infinite hadn't warned her of *this*.

The miniature trees and flowering shrubs she'd admired in the court's garden were now twigs and nubs. And all along the borders of the now-obliterated plants, she noticed formerly decorative stones overturned, dirt-sides up, wildly out of order. Seeing a familiar form, Ela gasped. "Pet! You've destroyed the judge's garden! He will probably fine us!"

Pet crunched down his mouthful of shrubbery, unperturbed. Ela was almost certain she saw a you-shouldn't-have-left-me-alone glint in his dark eyes. How could one admittedly large horse do so much damage so quickly? No wonder they were called destroyers.

Tzana cried out from the steps, "Oh, Pet! You're in trouble!"

"You must not leave!" the king's official called to Ela. He descended the steps, his comrades following, all five of them clearly ready to chase Ela down. Immediately, Pet flattened his ears, snorting out dire threats toward the king's men. They backed away.

Tsir Aun took charge. "Ela, order him to follow Tal and Osko. They will take this creature to the stables, *feed* him, then secure him for tonight. Ket, you will accompany me and resume guard. Osko, you will rejoin us later. Wait in the palace entry until we meet you—after the audience with the king."

"Yes, sir." The commander's men agreed in unison. But Pet balked.

Ela went to her pledged destroyer and smoothed his glossy black coat, murmuring, "Go with them, you rascal. I'll survive, I promise. You'll see me . . . later." She almost believed Pet nodded. Tal and Osko coaxed him away, though he looked back at Ela and huffed.

The instant Pet was out of sight, the king's men surrounded Ela. The stout bureaucrat said, "The king wishes to hear the circumstances of General Tek Juay's death. Tsir Aun"—he turned to Ela's guard—"we were told you and your men witnessed the general's death."

"No," Tsir Aun corrected the man politely. "But I can explain the circumstances to the king, if he wishes."

"He might." The official was so overbearing that Ela felt Tsir Aun deserved an apology.

Seeming unoffended, the commander-guard spoke to Ela. "I will follow you." He lowered his voice. "Did you realize that the general was the king's nearest cousin?"

Ela recalled her vision of Tek Juay, and nodded. "Yes. I knew." Now she must face his grieving family.

And the darkness beyond.

✦ 8 ✦

Hemmed in by their guards, Ela urged Tzana forward in the long, echoing marble corridor. Without warning, Tzana stopped and cautiously bent to touch the golden veins sparkling here and there in the floor. Ela couldn't blame her. The marble, indeed the whole palace, was so glorious that Ela half believed they'd entered a colossal treasure chest. Every aspect of this passageway dazzled and distracted her. She could only imagine how stunning it must seem to Tzana. However, the guards were almost tripping over the little girl. And tripping was *not* in any portion of Ela's vision. "Shall I carry you?" she asked.

"No." Tzana sat, suddenly stubborn. "I want to look at the floor."

Ela would have preferred to look at the floor too. Nap on it, actually. This had been such a long day, and she wasn't looking forward to its apparent end. But duty was duty. She knelt and whispered, "Tzana, I need you to walk with me now. Please."

"Why?" She sounded as tired and testy as Ela felt, without the fear.

"Because others are waiting for us, and we cannot be rude." She teasingly offered Tzana her hand. "So help me up."

"All right." Tzana stood and smiled as Ela made a show of being helped to her feet—enjoying their make-believe. Pretenses aside, Ela wished she could scoop up Tzana and run away. What

95

would happen to them tonight? The Infinite was present to her, of course, but markedly silent concerning her vision's inexplicable end, which made Ela suspect she'd rather not know the meaning of that fearful darkness.

"Thank you," she told her sister. "You're my favorite helper."

"Better than Pet?"

"Better than Pet. But don't tell him. We mustn't hurt his feelings."

Standing behind them, Ket made a low, angry noise in his throat. Tsir Aun coughed. Ahead of them, the king's snooty green-robed representative waited before a tall, gilded door. His eyebrows were lifted higher than Ela could have imagined possible. Even Matron Prill of Parne was outdone by this official's air of condemnation. Sounding so nasal that Ela wondered if he had a cold, the man intoned, "One does not keep the king waiting."

"The king is not waiting," Ela informed him, remembering her vision. "One of your subordinates saw us and told him we are here. He and his family are coming down from their rooms this instant."

The man looked askance, as if wondering how Ela dared to be so forward. Without another word, he led her, Tzana, and their guards into the room, and motioned them to wait. He departed, his robes aswirl.

"Do I have to be quiet here too?" Tzana demanded.

"Probably," Ela murmured. She fluffed her sister's thin, wispy curls. While they waited, she looked around. This was not a large room, but it was as opulent as Parne's temple, with golden screens and lamps glistening throughout. The temple, however, didn't have metal mirrors set into the walls. Ela frowned at the nearest ceiling-to-floor mirror.

A brown-skinned apparition with tattered robes, huge dark eyes, and a long black hair braid stared back at her. Was she really so gaunt? And ragged? Ela hadn't seen her reflection in any fragment of her vision, but why should she? Her appearance was of no consequence compared to the souls of Istgard—and its king. Still, she looked wretched.

Footsteps sounded in the corridor. As her guards stood at attention like statues, Ela turned toward the doorway.

✦ ✦ ✦

The king, Tek An, entered first, exactly as Ela had seen him. Crownless, unhurried, and stately in green robes and slippers sumptuously edged with gold embroidery. His broad brown face appeared calm, but small wrinkled pouches sagged below his eyes, betraying his weariness. His grief.

An elegant woman trailed behind him, her pale garments whispering, her dark hair pinned high on her head and crowned with jeweled gold flowers and a sheer veil flowing down behind her shoulders like a misted waterfall. The queen. Her son, Tek An's heir, followed. He was taller than his father, but with the same squared face, rich attire, and lordly bearing.

He eyed Ela, so speculative and intense that if she hadn't seen this in her vision, she would have been extremely uncomfortable. Instead, she returned his gaze, serene as possible, then looked past him to the person who interested her the most.

Graceful and somber in a soft blue tunic and a gold-hemmed veil, a young noblewoman entered the room. Her dark eyes were reddened and slightly swollen. She'd been crying, of course. Despite being forewarned, Ela's breath caught with pity at the sight of her.

King Tek An spoke first. "You are Ela of Parne?"

"Yes—a servant of the Infinite." She exhaled a silent prayer and stepped forward. "If I may, there is something I must return to a member of your family."

Inscrutable, the king motioned his consent, though he flicked a look at her guards, as if warning them to monitor her every move.

Intentionally slow to avoid alarming anyone, Ela maneuvered the branch between her fingers, then lifted the wide leather baldric from her shoulder, careful to untangle it from Father's water bag. She folded the baldric against the sword and approached the sad-eyed young noblewoman.

"Tek Lara." Just saying the girl's name wrung Ela's heart. She composed herself and continued. "I am so sorry. I was instructed by the Infinite to remove this sword from your father's body and bring it to you. I know you recognize it as his."

Tek Lara nodded faintly. Unshed tears glistened in her dark eyes, but she faced Ela with dignity. Ela wished she had half the young noblewoman's poise. And courage.

Respectful, Ela said, "Your father, General Tek Juay, was the most honorable man in Istgard. The Infinite regards him as righteous—and now he rests in his Creator's eternal peace."

Lara cradled her father's sword. Tears slid down her cheeks, but she smiled, tremulous. "Thank you, Ela of Parne."

Ela nodded and backed away. The royal family watched her, evidently astonished that she—a stranger in their land—was able to identify Tek Lara, much less speak of her father's soul. The king's tired eyes were now wide, amazed. "You claim to be a servant of Parne's Infinite?"

"I am His servant." Ela set the base of the branch on the floor, with a quiet thump that emphasized her point.

"Can it be true?" Tek An surveyed Ela from head to toe. "Has Parne finally cast out another prophet—a *girl*?"

"So it seems," Ela agreed, pleased by Tek An's grasp of history, even if he disparaged the Infinite's decision to choose a young woman as His prophet. She wasn't afraid of the king. How could she be? Her first task was to counsel this most unrealistic man. To keep him from destroying himself. To save his dynasty. And his kingdom.

Tek An hesitated, smoothed one hand over his thin beard, then asked, "You are not descended from Eshtmoh, the last prophet?" He sounded a bit worried—a fear Ela understood. Seventy years past, one of his own ancestors had died at the sight of Eshtmoh.

Ela fought down a grim smile. Was her ancestry so important? Half of Parne could claim some blood tie to one of the prophets of old. "My father's family name—Roeh—bears the designation of an ancient prophet. My mother was invited to become a prophet. But she refused. As far as I know, I am not descended from Eshtmoh."

Tek An relaxed. Imperious, he waved his family to the only seats in the room, a series of cushioned benches, while he appropriated the single green-tufted chair for himself. He arranged his gleaming robes, then frowned at Ela. "You are not descended from Eshtmoh, but it seems you are doubly descended of other prophets. Perhaps we should be afraid."

Perhaps? He was indeed afraid. Ela hoped Tek An's fear would inspire him to listen to the Infinite's warnings. To encourage him, she asked, "Are there reasons for your fear?"

"Certainly we have reasons for fear!" Tek An huffed. "To begin, seventy years is an ominous number, is it not? A most telling and fateful number in Istgard."

On the bench to his right, Tek An's heir shifted, visibly exasperated by this conversation. His father stilled him with a glance, then faced Ela again. "If you are indeed a prophet, then the death of our most favored cousin cannot be the only reason you were sent to us. Nonetheless we will also discuss what you know of his murder. Tell us plainly, why else are you here?"

Apprehension prickled the hairs on Ela's scalp. In her hands, the branch exuded heat. "The Infinite has judged your kingdom and your people. Disaster will overtake you and your family—and your kingdom. Unless you change."

Tek An lowered his chin and glared at her from beneath his thick black eyebrows. "In what way must we change? Istgard is ruled by a just and mighty king!"

"You are wrong," Ela argued. "Istgard is no longer ruled by a king."

Tek An's heir gasped and bounded to his feet, his right hand moving to his left side, clearly seeking a sword. Fortunately he wasn't wearing one.

Tek An lunged and smacked his son's arm. "Sit! Do not interrupt us!"

The young man sat, but he glared at Ela. The queen too was offended, her exquisite dark eyes kindled with anger. Tek Lara didn't move. Seated on her own bench, she stared at her father's sword.

"Explain this outrage," Tek An ordered Ela as he settled into his chair again. "How do we no longer rule Istgard?"

Did all kings refer to themselves in plural? Or was Tek An's opinion of himself so high that he needed plurals to express his views? "Fear and superstition rule Istgard," Ela said. "Soothsayers and so-called witches play on your terrors of the unknown, for no reason. You lift your souls to little non-gods of wood and stone that preside over useless, cruel sacrifices—all detested by the Infinite, your Creator! He is the only One who can help you—or save your kingdom. But you shun Him."

"He does not exist!"

"He does. He was once beloved to Istgard," Ela told the flushed king. "You are a student of history. Seek the Infinite's name in Istgard's most ancient writings, and you will find Him. He blessed Istgard's beginning. Now He decrees its end. Unless you and your people abandon the love of evil."

The branch glittered now, more radiant than any gold or gems in the room. The mirrors and polished marble surfaces all reflected its light—directly into the faces of the royal family.

Tek An covered his eyes. "Yes! We will consider your warning!"

His sincerity was unmistakable, as was his fear. Ela exhaled. She'd heard him say this in her vision. Why, then, should relief and hope overtake her? Nothing was certain. "Do more than consider," Ela urged. "Follow the example of Istgard's first citizens. Love and fear Him."

The branch's glow softened, to the royal family's apparent relief. They squinted toward her now. Lara studied Ela with perfect calm, but the queen uttered an unintelligible exclamation while her son jumped up and fled for the door.

"You have frightened our family." Tek An straightened and looked around, wary.

Ela refused to be sorry. "The Infinite desires you to see that your kingdom's survival depends upon your actions."

The king's natural feistiness took hold, as he seemed to realize he would not drop dead at her feet. "What actions might you suggest? You are a prophet! Advise us."

Tek Lara shifted on her bench and she looked away, but not before Ela caught a glimpse of her interest—evident despite her grief.

"Advise you?" Ela asked. "I've already advised you, according to the Infinite's will. Search your heart, O King. Search your country's most ancient writings. You will find the Infinite and His words. Trust His wisdom, not your own."

"You will not answer further questions?"

"Of course I will."

"Then answer us now. What does the Infinite require of us?"

"A contrite heart. And that you love Him with all your might, and all your soul."

Tek An chuckled at this. "With no love remaining for our family?"

Wonderful that he could be amused in the midst of a dire warning, Ela sighed. "Your heart, if you allow it, O King, has an endless capacity for love of your family, your friends, and strangers. But your love for the Infinite must come first."

"This is true with you?"

"Yes." Remembering her soul's torment when separated from the Infinite, Ela said, "He is my entire reason for existence. Once I heard His voice, I could not endure the thought of living without it."

The king leaned forward. "Now you truly interest us. How do you know it is the Infinite who speaks?"

Did Tek An believe she was deluded? Most likely. "I know the Infinite's voice because He tells me everything I don't want to hear, sends me where I don't want to go, and asks me to fulfill tasks I consider impossible. Above all, He is forever right."

"And you always obey Him?"

"With all my heart. Why wouldn't I?"

"Huh." The king's royal fingers tapped restlessly on his royal knees. He sat back, frowned, and abruptly changed the subject. "Tell us what you know of our dear cousin's death."

Aware of Tek Lara's listening silence, Ela said, "He was murdered by one of his commanders. Taun, leader of the raid on Ytar, was reprimanded by the general for his cruelties. He attacked Tek Juay from behind. The general didn't suffer."

"How do you know so much?" Tek An peered at Ela intently. "Were you there?"

"In a vision. Yes."

The king scoffed. "You ask us to believe only a vision?"

"Yes. It is the truth. And because of this truth, Commander Taun tried to kill me."

"But you killed him instead?"

"I did not kill Commander Taun." Prepared for this dispute, Ela kept her gaze sternly fixed upon the king's equally severe stare. "I warned Taun that if he attacked me, the Infinite would remove his life's breath—which is exactly what happened."

"You claim all these things because of visions." Tek An stroked his thin black beard again. "How are we to believe you are not simply a witch?"

"Because everything the Infinite tells me is fulfilled." A slender thread of a vision unfolded within Ela's thoughts. Understanding, she said, "And because the Infinite is merciful, you will be allowed an example. This evening, as I was walking into your palace, you sent soldiers to find your cousin's body." The king gaped. Ela continued, "General Tek Juay's body will be exactly where I found it, at the base of a boulder, just beyond Istgard's limits. Within three days, your men will place his body here, where I stand. You will be notified and when you arrive here, your men will tell you that they were shown their general's body—its location—in a dream. You will see your cousin's fatal wound and know I have told you the truth."

"You cannot possibly say this! Our soldiers will certainly have to scour the borderlands for weeks!"

"Three days. The Infinite declares that you will find your men waiting for you here. All Riyan will grieve for their good general. But they will not grieve for you, their king. Unless you call upon the Infinite and trust Him."

As he had in her vision, Tek An spluttered his indignation. "You—you predict our death? This is treason! Should we let you walk free from this place?"

"No. You are about to tell me I will be locked up for life in your prison."

His face went ashen, then brilliant crimson. Exactly the same shade in her vision.

"You were about to say so," Ela challenged the royal.

The queen shook with such rage that the delicate gold flowers quivered atop her head. "Witch! How dare you . . . charlatan!" Her husband waved her off.

"Yes, Parnian!" Tek An stomped his slippered feet. "What you say is true! You will be locked up for life in our prison!"

"You will become too frightened to keep me here. Even in your prison," Ela informed him. "Within three months—unless you follow the Infinite—you will devise a way to have me killed."

"If we do, will we succeed?" Tek An growled.

She replied with silence.

The king fumed. "You have nothing else to say?"

This question she must answer. Rejoiced to answer, in fact. "Indeed I do have more to say. All the slaves sent to you from Ytar must be freed. The Infinite commands it."

She watched the king rant, roar, and storm from the glittering room.

Precisely as she'd seen in her vision.

✦ ✦ ✦

Evidently unimpressed by all the turmoil, Tzana had fallen asleep on the marble floor while Ela confronted the king. She scooped up her sister's limp form, nuzzled her small, softly wrinkled face, and waited as the guards surrounded her. They all radiated disapproval like heat from a furnace.

"You could have walked free!" Tsir Aun scolded Ela as they retraced their path through the palace. "Why did you provoke our king?"

"He provoked himself. I told him the truth." Ela felt beads of sweat raise over her skin. More trickled down her back and made her shiver. The end of her vision was near.

Infinite?

I am here.

Courage. Ela exhaled, reminding herself she wasn't going to die. Not yet. Why then had such fear flooded her vision? Holding Tzana and the branch closer, Ela looked up at Tsir Aun. Ashamed of the terror breaking her voice, she said, "Sir, I . . . I warned you, remember? That when things seem well—to you and your men—be ready."

"I remember," Tsir Aun answered, sounding coldly displeased. "What of it?"

"It's near."

He didn't reply. Osko was waiting in the grand main entry to the palace, just as Tsir Aun had commanded. As Tsir Aun received Osko's respectful salutation, the antagonistic soldier, Ket, sidled up to Ela. Gloating, he murmured, "Do you know how *glad* I will be to see you locked up for the rest of your miserable life?"

She saw his probable fate and trembled, ready to burst into tears. Her throat tight with fear, she said, "Guard yourself, Ket. And please—I beg you!—call to the Infinite now, or you won't live to see me locked away."

He didn't reply, for Tsir Aun approached and resumed his place at her side. However, before they could leave the palace courtyard, the commander of the king's guards forestalled Tsir Aun, saluted, and said, "We give you custody of the convicted. You will take her to the prison and be sure the warden is informed of the new charges."

"Of course," Tsir Aun agreed.

The palace guards disbanded, heading off in various directions, no doubt glad to be relieved of their duties. Tsir Aun motioned to Ela. "Come." As they walked to the gate, Tsir Aun sighed. "We will finish our final obligation for the night by returning you to the prison. At least you'll be safe there."

"And all will be well?" She couldn't help asking the question.

"Yes," Tsir Aun replied. But he hesitated in the deepening night. As if disquieted. To Ela's profound gratitude, he readied a hand on his sword's hilt—clearly alarmed.

At least someone had listened to her.

They turned onto the street outside the palace and headed for the prison, their combined footsteps sounding too loud over the street's stone pavings. Ela's mouth went dry. The palace wall to their left. That death-black street corner to their right. Her last few steps.

"Tsir Aun," she begged, "I'm about to face darkness. Pray for me, please."

Before he could reply, they turned the shadowed corner toward the prison and were besieged by a rush of scuffling footsteps. Masked faces. Muted cloaks.

Ela clutched Tzana and the branch to her chest and sucked in a terrified breath to scream.

Her cry was stifled.

Vanquished by the darkness.

✦ 9 ✦

Ela fought her way up from the black nothingness, into miserable consciousness.

Her parched tongue seemed glued to the roof of her mouth. Piercing drumbeats pounded inside her aching head. And her shoulders hurt so intensely, it was as if her arms had almost been torn from her body. Worse, her arms were empty. No branch. No Tzana. What had happened?

Infinite?

Her silent plea—her desperation to hear His voice—was answered with a waiting calm. She sensed His presence, and it was enough for now. But . . .

Unable to open her eyes, Ela worked up enough moisture to swallow. She forced her tongue to move. "Tzana?"

"Hush," a soft voice urged. "Rest."

"No," Ela mumbled, scared because the voice wasn't Tzana's. "Where's my sister?"

"She is resting."

Had Tzana been injured? Ela coerced her unwilling eyelids to lift. To see the owner of that soothing voice. Big, serious brown eyes, an oval face framed by a gilded veil. "Tek Lara."

"Yes. I'm so glad you remember me!" To Ela's confused amazement, the young noblewoman began to cry.

Ela found that her hands and arms worked, though they felt heavy, as if made of stone. She patted Lara's arm clumsily, consoling

107

her even as she scanned the stark stone room, looking for Tzana. "Why . . . are you crying? Where's my sister? Was Tzana injured?"

"Yes, but believe me, your sister will recover. She was injured when you were knocked to the street. She has one arm in a sling and a few impressive bruises, but nothing else. I must say, your sister is remarkably good-natured."

Ela's panic eased. Swiping at her tears, Lara continued. "The warden's wife is caring for her. However, the warden's a bit annoyed at the situation. I suspect they've never had children of their own, the way his wife dotes on Tzana."

"Dotes on her?" Ela tried to gather her wits. "How long have I been unconscious?"

"Almost a full day. See?" Lara gestured toward a single narrow window, which framed the blaze of a crimson sunset. "Perhaps part of your trouble in recovering is that you were simply exhausted. Do you remember what happened?"

Moistening her lips, Ela said, "I warned Tsir Aun to be ready. I'd foreseen this darkness. Men—several at least—attacked us not far from the palace. Their faces were masked. I know nothing more." She understood less. Why hadn't the Infinite allowed her to escape this attack?

Was this another lesson she'd failed?

Tek Lara began to whisper, evidently fearful she'd be overheard. "Listen. I was told this morning that you were nearly dead. And that one of your guards died—though the two who survived fought off your assailants. You're bruised everywhere and have, most likely, a concussion. My dear royal cousin hopes your prophetic abilities have been knocked out of you."

They have not, the Infinite declared within her thoughts.

Such a swift answer to a question she hadn't even formed coherently. Ela wanted to shake her head, but it hurt. "Your royal cousin will be disappointed. When can I see my sister?"

The thought that her sister might be in pain made Ela struggle to rise.

Her noble caretaker lifted a restraining hand. "No. Stay here until my physician has seen you. I'll have Tzana brought here, but not until you and I have talked."

Ela didn't resist. Her head was spinning, and she couldn't imagine walking anywhere without toppling over. "What do you need to discuss?"

"So many things—I should have written a list. Wait. Drink this first." She offered Ela a delicately carved white stone cup.

Still lightheaded, Ela held herself up long enough to drain the cup of broth—and to notice she was wearing a clean robe. Tek Lara's orders, no doubt. Finished, Ela sank back against the pillow, fighting the impulse to close her eyes. "Thank you for everything you've done. The broth, the robe, Tzana—"

Tek Lara placed the cup on a nearby tray. "My thanks will be to see you recover."

"I will," Ela assured her. "You said one of my guards died? It was Ket, wasn't it?" She knew it couldn't be Tsir Aun, yet the thought twisted her stomach.

"You do remember some of the attack," Lara murmured. "Yes, my servants said the soldier's family name was Ket."

"Actually, I don't remember much. The Infinite warned me Ket's death was near." And she'd failed to reach Ket. Ela pushed away the thought, unable to endure it. "The men who tried to kill me—were they captured?"

"No!" In an offended whisper, Lara continued, "Worse, there's been no effort made to find them. I cannot believe my royal cousins would condone such an attack, but what other explanation is there? Promise me you'll say nothing of my suspicions. It won't help either of us."

"I'll say nothing."

"I'm such a coward." The young woman sighed. "I'm sorry you were attacked. At least my fears for your safety gave me enough courage to demand the king's permission to visit you. I told him that I owe you an irreparable debt of gratitude, and that I could not rest until I'd thanked you, so he agreed."

She gripped Ela's hand. "You see, I knew my father was dead.

I knew! Whenever Father was gone, no matter how far, I received a daily letter or gift from him. And I always replied. But then his letters ceased. When his personal attendants returned to Riyan two weeks ago and said that he'd failed to return after a supposedly short jaunt through the borderlands . . . I was going insane with the uncertainty." Lara swiped at fresh tears, adding, "Thank you for bringing me his sword. You cannot know how much it means to me!"

"The Infinite knew." Ela shut her eyes, fearing Lara's inevitable disbelief—so prevalent in Istgard.

"Yes," Tek Lara agreed. "I'm amazed to think of His consideration in sending you with Father's sword." She dug through a small leather pouch slung at her side, retrieved a pristine cloth, and blew her nose. "How foolish of me to be surprised. I should have expected He would provide comfort."

Ela stared at her, bemused. "How foolish of *me* to be surprised. You serve the Infinite."

Lara tucked away her cloth, looking older, calmer. "Ela, prophet of Parne, you should know this. Where do you think the wise Eshtmoh resided while he lived in Riyan?"

"With your father's family?"

"For three years." Wistful, Tek Lara said, "When I first realized you were a prophet, I hoped to continue my family's tradition and offer you shelter for as long as you stayed in Istgard. But you've seriously offended the king. Now I must either gain a pardon for you—which could be impossible—or break the law and steal you and your sister from this place."

"Don't break the law," Ela pleaded. "Anyway, perhaps the Infinite intends for me to serve Him here."

"I'll visit you often," her benefactress promised. "But first I'll send my physician to confirm you and your sister are recovering. I also intend to see that you're fattened up a bit. You are as thin as that twig you carry."

"The branch!" Ela sat up and wished she hadn't. She clutched her aching head. "Where is it?"

"It's on the floor with your water bag. There." Lara nodded toward the opposite side of Ela's makeshift bed. "My grandfather once said that the prophet's branch simply couldn't be lost. Which was useful because Eshtmoh was such a daydreamer—hopelessly forgetful."

The branch couldn't be lost? Why hadn't she been told? What other useful little being-a-prophet facts didn't she know?

Ela clutched the light, fragile-looking staff and immediately felt better. Soul-wise, at least. Her body seemed to be one large bruise. And her head ached mercilessly, while dizziness and nausea threatened like twin scoundrels battling for control of her senses.

"You haven't been a prophet for very long, have you?" Lara asked.

Ela sank back into the bed and shut her eyes. "Not very long. Weeks. I think. Or perhaps more than a month." She'd lost track of time. Eshtmoh must have felt the same way. No wonder the Infinite had created the branch to be permanently unlost—if Tek Lara's story pertained to this same branch.

"I wish I had your courage," Lara said.

Ela opened one eyelid and almost smiled. "Yesterday, I wished I had only half of yours."

"I'll need all of our courage in two days. Pray for me, Ela, when I see my father's body." Before Ela could reply, Tek Lara made a wry face and changed the subject. "You look awful. Are you sure you don't want me to sneak you and your sister out of this place?"

"You, of all people, cannot break the law," Ela scolded with all the force she could muster. "Besides, I'm certain our Creator has some duty for me here, as His servant."

"If you change your mind, send me word." She gave Ela a brief hug and left the cell.

✦ ✦ ✦

Her head aching, Ela used one hand to balance herself against a wall in the prison's narrow access corridor while she wielded a large wooden ladle with the other. It would have been helpful to lean upon the branch as she walked, but she needed both hands free to accomplish her current task.

Really, when she'd told Tek Lara of serving the Infinite in prison, Ela had no idea it actually meant *serving* the prisoners. Well, at least she was out of her cell this morning. Most important, she believed the Infinite's will was somehow accomplished by her work.

Slung over one aching shoulder like a canvas bag of rocks, Ela carried the hard rolls that were served at the noon meal. A none-too-pleased guard trudged behind her, pushing a half-filled kettle of lukewarm broth on a creaking trolley.

Stopping at each narrow door, she unbolted its horizontal food slot, lowered its small shelf door, and called to the prisoner inside, "Bring your bowl!"

Every prisoner unfailingly scurried to the door and handed his bowl through the slot—usually licking dry lips and urging her to be generous with the broth. The prisoners seemed to know better than to say more than a few words to her. None of them thanked her. Not that she needed thanks. She returned each filled bowl with an apologetic smile, a tooth-breakingly hard roll, and a kindly parting, then bolted the food slot again.

"Hurry," the guard grumbled. "No need to be all tidy with the broth and bread. And don't worry about the manners. Not for these dregs."

"They are men with souls, not dregs," Ela corrected. "Besides spilled food is a waste, and it attracts vermin."

"Just hurry!"

"As best I can." She supposed that years of working in this prison would make anyone short-tempered—if they didn't have a sense of humor. "Smile," she urged the guard.

He bared his moldy teeth at her. Ela cringed. He was right to keep his mouth closed.

At the end of the last corridor—and after numerous refills of the kettle and rolls—she sighed. "Finished."

"No, we've one more above in the tower." His voice turned exaggeratedly sweet. "The coddled one."

How could anyone be coddled here? Although Ela had to admit that the warden's wife was certainly spoiling Tzana while Ela worked. "So we have to climb the stairs?"

"You're a bright one, aren't you?" The guard snorted. "Of course we have to climb the stairs. You keep hold of the bread bag, an' I'll haul what's left in the kettle."

The very thought of climbing those circular stairs in the corner tower dizzied Ela. When *would* she heal? Of course it had only been three days since the attack. Three. Tonight the king's men would return with General Tek Juay's body. Ela's heart skittered in agitation. She knew what King Tek An's reaction would be. But what about Lara?

Ela distracted herself from the dizzying stairs by praying for Lara. And the king. At the top of the stairs, she steadied herself, then approached the only cell that was closed and occupied. The one difference in this prisoner's treatment, as far as Ela could see, was that these few tower cells were larger and airier. And perhaps quieter, being separated from the occasional shrieks and groans of the prisoners below. Otherwise, they were just as stark and uncomfortable.

The guard gestured with his head to the last cell. Ela rapped on the door, unbolted the slot, and lowered its narrow shelf door. "Bring your bowl!"

A young man studied her through the slot. His eyes were remarkably bright gray—not brown like Parnian or Istgardian eyes. "It's you!" He sounded surprised, and pleased, as if greeting a much-missed friend.

She couldn't help but smile. "Who else would I be? Where is your bowl?"

"Oh. Yes." He grinned, his teeth very white amid dark whiskers. Charming enough to make her blink. Worrisome, that charm. He handed Ela his bowl, still talking as if they were enjoying a sociable visit. "If I may be so bold, but I fear I've forgotten . . . What is your name?"

"I am Ela. Of Parne." She ladled the broth into the bowl, ignoring the guard's glare.

The genial young prisoner accepted the bowl, but paused. "Parne? So we're both strangers to Istgard. Did you also offend the king?"

She almost laughed. "Sir—"

"I am Kien Lantec, former ambassador of the Tracelands. Please call me Kien—it's not as if we're obligated to stand on ceremony here, is it?"

"I suppose not," Ela agreed. Ceremony or no ceremony, she shied away from using his name. "But please don't think I'm going to criticize the king to you."

"Of course not. And I wasn't about to disparage him either. Forgive me." He grinned again, peeking through the slot. Much too fascinating for his own good, or for hers.

To hide her face, Ela rummaged through the slack folds of her canvas bag and snatched the last roll, while she prayed for strength of will from the Infinite.

Still bent on conversation, Kien Lantec said, "You intrigued me when I saw you in the courtyard several days ago. Have you and the little Unfortunate been well?"

"Unfortunate?" Ela froze, the hard roll clasped in her fingers.

"Yes, the child with you. I've—"

Unfortunate. He'd called Tzana *Unfortunate* as if she were regrettable! Ela slammed the roll through the slot and felt its impact against his face.

"Ow!" He staggered backward several steps, a hand to his left eye, in obvious pain.

"How dare you!" She banged the slot's door shut and bolted it with a resounding thump—ferociously glad to lock him inside. Why did everyone seem to regard Tzana as lamentable? *They* were the unfortunates! Fools!

Beside her, the guard cackled, delighted. "That's a sight to pay for! Wait'll the others hear!"

Maddeningly dizzied, Ela sat at the top of the spiral stairs. "Infinite, forgive me."

This was not how His prophet should have reacted. Where was her kindness? Her spirit of forgiveness?

Unfortunate.

"Augh!" If she'd had another roll, she would have hammered him with that one too!

She clutched her head, in serious need of rest. And self-reproach, remorse, and prayer. But not just yet.

She was much too pleased she'd hit him.

✦ ✦ ✦

Kien dipped an edge of his cloak into the last cold drops of water-broth, leaned back against his cell's stone wall, and rested the makeshift compress against his eye.

"Ugh!" His cloak stank.

But what did it matter? Let it rot as he was rotting. He probably reeked worse than his cloak. As for his beard, what he wouldn't give for a razor. To cut his whiskers, his hair, his veins . . .

Offensive as he looked and smelled, this Ela of Parne *should* have thrown the food at him and run away shrieking before he'd even said a word. Instead, she'd bashed his eye with a prison roll simply because he called an Unfortunate an Unfortunate. The last time he'd seen a girl so furious at him—or anyone—was when he'd used his sister's dolls for target practice. Beka's screech echoed in Kien's ears to this day. He chuckled at the fond memory, but his mirth faded as he considered Ela of Parne's wrath.

Were customs different in Parne? Or was the girl overly sensitive regarding her little sister? He, an ambassador, should have suspected that the casual Traceland idiom might offend this Parnian. Foolish of him.

A few weeks in prison had wreaked havoc on years of courtly training. Yet the damage was done, and an uncomfortable fact nagged at Kien.

He had to apologize to Ela of Parne.

Thus far, she was his one hope to maneuver an escape from this place. Or to acquire some sort of weapon—though she'd just proven he could arm himself with the prison's rolls. Well, at the very least, she might be able to smuggle him extra food. Kien's stomach growled, as if on cue. "Disgusting."

Now he was talking to himself. At least talking to the mouse in his previous cell was partially excusable. However, conducting a solitary dialogue must surely be a symptom of failing sanity. Soon he would be banging his head against the wall, Kien was sure.

Why had he been so stupid?

Tired of his own thoughts, Kien shut his eyes for a nap. At least his dreams were often interesting. He might even see home. Father, Mother . . . Beka.

The sound of jangling keys woke Kien. Bleary-eyed, he noticed the deepening shadows in his cell. Was it time for the evening meal? Bad as the meals were, Kien wished he could have several servings at once. How could he organize a coherent escape plot while suffering from malnutrition?

"Tracelander! Step to!" A big, genial guard opened his cell door and grinned. "Well, look at that eye—beaten by a girl! And a scrawny one at that."

"I'm glad you're amused." Kien stood, yawned, and shook out his cloak. "Lead on. I'm ready to eat."

The guard exuded a rude noise. "We're not going to feed you—it's too early for that. You've been called for by the king."

❖ ❖ ❖

The guard hurried Kien through the dim passageway by jabbing him in the ribs. The pain was tolerable, which was good. In a few more weeks he'd be fully recovered from the beating inflicted upon him by the palace guards. He feared, however, that by that time, he would be too weakened by starvation to escape.

If only . . . Kien stopped mid-thought and mid-step as he entered the main entry's yard.

Ela of Parne waited there, clothed in a clean linen tunic and neatly draped mantle, all simple but very well made. With the exception of a water bag, her staff, and that now-missing sword, she hadn't been carrying any extra gear when Kien first saw her in the small inner courtyard. Who had supplied her with new clothes? And where was the Un—the child?

She saw Kien and shut her eyes, as if disgusted.

Considering his previous offense, and his ruffian appearance, he couldn't blame her. Regardless, he intended to apologize in his most courtly and winning manner.

It helped that the guard was goading Kien to stand beside the offended girl.

Matters would also be helped if—for pity's sake—this Ela of Parne would open her eyes and acknowledge his existence.

He stared at her, and waited.

✦ 10 ✦

Ignoring the Tracelander, Ela kept her eyes shut and leaned heavily on the branch. She'd overexerted herself today. Myriad pains raked through all her muscles, and the dizzying headache persisted, consuming much of her ability to think. And the sunlight, despite its blessed warmth, was making her headache worse. If only she could curl up in a dark room and beg the Infinite for relief.

However, her ailments were short-lived physical miseries. Nothing compared to the spiritual needs of others. Unnerved, Ela began to pray.

The king had summoned her to dispel his fears. Ela saw him in her thoughts now, weeping over his cousin's body and contemplating his own death with such terror that his hands shook. Regrettably, only Tek An could end his fears . . . if he would simply forget his pride and listen to the Infinite.

Within this muted fragment of a vision, Ela watched Tek Lara kneel beside General Tek Juay's body. Like the king, Lara was crying, but without Tek An's terror. Lara needed Ela's presence this evening—

Ela's vision ceased, somehow disrupted by Kien Lantec's continued stare.

Audacious man! Why was he there?

She allowed Kien a sidelong glance. Immediately, her headache worsened. He was staring at her, and his eyelid was deeply reddened and puffy. This was the first time she'd ever truly hit someone, and she was appalled at his appearance. Really, the prison's hard rolls should be offered to the Istgardian army as sling stones.

Of course, she was being ridiculous. Her temper, not the rolls, had caused Kien Lantec's injury. "I'm trying to be remorseful for injuring you," Ela told the Tracelander.

"I wish you success." He smiled, not the least bit sarcastic. "I'm pleased to report that I *am* remorseful for offending you. I apologize with all sincerity and vow to never repeat the offense against anyone. Do you wish me to kneel before you and openly proclaim my wrongdoing and my regret?"

Despite his smile, he was serious. And entirely too glib. Ela muttered, "Don't you dare!"

"Are you sure?"

"Quite sure. Thank you."

"You're welcome." Kien grinned, all his previous charm intact despite the incongruous eye. "Has the king also summoned you?"

"He's summoned *you*?"

"Yes. No doubt to charge me with more crimes because he's affronted by some misdeed he imagines my country might commit."

"Infinite," Ela complained in a whisper, gripping the branch tight, "couldn't You have warned me?"

The young man leaned near. "I'm sorry? I didn't hear what you said."

"Nothing." Ela sighed. It seemed that the Infinite had plans for this talkative young man. Well, whatever those plans were, she didn't care to know. The guards opened the far gate, drawing her attention away from the troublesome Kien.

A contingent of red-cloaked guards marched into the entry yard in two columns, bearing huge red shields and wearing plate armor and swords.

Tsir Aun commanded them. His uniform was different today, Ela noticed. Instead of the ordinary soldier's squared plate armor, he wore gleaming fitted armor. The crest on his new helmet was longer, and a thick gold stripe bordered his red cloak. His sword too was more elaborately decorated. Ela doubted Commander Taun had been so impressive.

His voice deep and ringing, Tsir Aun ordered his men to halt. After surveying their ranks, he instructed them to turn and face the entry gate. Then he approached Ela, eyeing her sharply.

She almost hopped to attention. Despite her headache, the realization made Ela smile. "Commander. I'm glad to see you are well."

"Thank you." With a formality that clearly required her to offer more than a courtesy response, he asked, "How are you?"

"I've a severe headache, dizziness, and exceptional bruising."

"No surprise. Will our walk to the palace be too much?"

"I think not—if I don't walk too quickly."

"Good." His stern eyes allowed a hint of a smile.

Quietly, she asked, "Have you been promoted?"

"Yes. I'm a high commander." He grimaced as if displeased. "How is your sister?"

"She is recovering, thank you. She's staying with the warden's wife this evening."

"Perhaps it's for the best, considering the situation at hand." He studied Kien disdainfully, as if deeming him unfit for duty. "Who is this?"

The Tracelander offered an elegant half bow. "I am Kien Lantec, former ambassador of the Tracelands, now the king's prisoner. I have been summoned, it seems, to be charged with further crimes."

Looking only a little appeased, Tsir Aun spoke to Kien, with a nod toward Ela. "She was injured during a street skirmish several evenings past. You will assist her. Alert me if she seems unable to continue."

"Yes, sir," Kien agreed, sounding so respectful and soldierlike that Ela stared. Did the ambassador have military training?

Pivoting on his heel, the new high commander raised his voice. "Let's proceed." He led them to the center of his deputation of guards and motioned them to halt.

While they waited for their guards to receive and respond to Tsir Aun's marching orders, Kien gave Ela a serious, quizzical glance. "You were injured?"

"Knocked unconscious," Ela admitted.

"I never would have guessed it earlier today." The Tracelander's observation sounded like a compliment. Though Ela suspected that everything he said would sound like a compliment. How could anyone trust such a man?

He offered her his arm. Ela frowned. "Thank you, sir, but there's no need."

Kien returned her frown. "Accept my assistance and don't be stubborn. I won't have your soldier-friend crushing a few more of my ribs just because you've tried to be brave."

"Hmm." Not a bit of a compliment in that order. Perhaps her previous opinion of his character was wrong. Perhaps. She accepted his arm, but depended equally on the branch.

Pleasantly, as if they were enjoying a tranquil stroll while accompanied by soldiers, Kien said, "Quite a few guards they've sent for us. I wonder why?"

"You don't want to know." She wished he would hush.

"You're wrong. I do want to know."

Ela braced herself, saying the words while fighting off the memory. "A few days past, I found General Tek Juay's body in the borderlands. He'd been murdered. This evening, the king's soldiers brought his remains into the palace—as I said they would. The king is near mad and wishes to assure I'm not killed before he can confront me."

The Tracelander missed a step and hushed.

✦ ✦ ✦

"You brought this disaster upon us!" Tek An stormed toward Ela, his voice ricocheting off the marble and gleaming mirrors. "You are the cause of our pain! So now you will gloat, seeing your scheme come to pass. Do not think we will forgive you!"

He was perspiring, trembling. A wave of compassion swept

over Ela. More so as she looked down at the general's mummified body—at Lara huddled, weeping beside her father's corpse. Tears burned Ela's eyes, and she allowed them to fall freely as she faced the angry king once more. "I do not expect your forgiveness, and I am *not* gloating. Do you think I haven't mourned, O King? I do! Istgard will suffer because an evil man took your cousin's life!"

Before Tek An could say another word, Ela kneeled beside Tek Lara, hugged her, and cried, the Infinite's sorrow pouring through her soul.

❖ ❖ ❖

All the hairs on Kien's scalp tingled as he knelt on the marble floor near the general's body. Wails lifted around him as if unleashed by a signal he hadn't heard, but fully understood.

General Tek Juay—always so vital, amiable, and quick to laugh or argue politics with Kien—was truly dead. Kien couldn't bear to look at the preserved body, half curled beneath his military cloak in sleeplike peace. Instead, Kien stared at the girl who claimed she'd found the general dead in the borderlands.

Ela of Parne. Three days ago, no one in Istgard had even heard her name.

Now he'd seen this Ela defy the king and exchange hugs with Tek Lara as if they were sisters.

Incredible. A citizen of lowly Parne had entered the royal courts and now mixed with the royal family as if she'd lived among them for years. How could anyone possibly explain something so astonishing?

A flurry of motion caught Kien's attention. The king hurried from the chamber with his guards, as if he could no longer bear to remain near his cousin's body. Beneath the doorway's arch, however, he turned and pointed at Ela of Parne. "We will speak to you! And your miserable conspirator! Lan Tek, you will follow us."

The king's heir strode from amid the mourners. "My lord-father, may I attend you?"

"Yes, but you will be silent."

Lips pressed tight, his expression mutinous, the heir stalked out after the king.

A swift-whispered squabble erupted among the king's men. Two green-cloaked guards stepped forward, motioned to Kien and to Ela, and led them into the corridor.

Kien noticed the girl lagging. Her face went ghastly, as if she were ill. He wrapped an arm around her shoulders and helped her along. The instant they stepped into the king's smallest antechamber, however, the little wretch elbowed Kien's ribs. Painfully. He released her.

He might have been at home, quarreling with Beka.

"We are correct!" The king seemed infuriated, yet oddly triumphant. "You two have planned a conspiracy against us."

Kien nearly growled. More royal conspiracy madness. "Forgive me, O King, but I've never spoken to this young lady until today. One of the guards at the prison can describe our conversation— we suffered a misunderstanding."

The heir snickered. "She bashed your eye?"

"I deserved it, young lord." Kien hoped he could keep his temper. He'd always disliked the youth, who was far more arrogant than the king.

Tek An flicked his son's arm. "If you cannot control yourself, you will leave us."

The heir turned away in a sulk.

Determined to speed up this foolish interrogation, Kien prompted, "What conspiracy are we charged with, O King?"

"Do not pretend ignorance!" Tek An reached inside his robe, extracted a scroll garnished with numerous wax seals, and flung it at Kien's chest.

Kien caught the scroll and recognized the seals. Father's tower-etched signet imprinted the largest wafer of wax. Twenty smaller seals were affixed alongside Father's—one from each Tracelander in his nation's Grand Assembly. The sight made Kien grin. Without asking permission, he opened the scroll and skimmed it. An ultimatum.

. . . Innocent lives have been destroyed. Peaceful citizens have been abducted from their homes and enslaved in Istgard. In response to this outrage, it is the will of the Traceland's people that we not submit to such unwarranted and deplorable violations of our most elemental rights. The Tracelands must defend itself.

Our motive is not one of conquest, but concerns the protection and well-being of our people. . . . Free those you have enslaved . . . return, unharmed, those you have imprisoned. . . .

Kien stopped skimming the document and eyed the king. "If you restore my office and release me from prison, we can begin negotiations to prevent war."

"Why?" Tek An blustered—a defensive tactic, Kien knew. "Your country has long planned this invasion! You seize any excuse, even turning our own self-preservation against us."

The Parnian girl finally spoke, low and stern. "Istgard's justification concerning Ytar is a sham. A lie to excuse your greed. I saw Ytar burn. It was not a battle but a savage butchery!"

Kien stared, stunned. She'd seen Ytar burn? No doubt she had—he saw tears in her eyes. Kien listened hard as she continued. "Do you think your actions will be excused and forgotten?"

"This was another vision," the king accused her.

"It reveals the truth!" She pressed a hand to her forehead, looking ill again. "Three nights ago, I told you that the slaves from Ytar must be freed. Nothing has changed."

Tek An protested in an obvious attempt to sidestep the issue. "You disturb us extremely!"

"I am meant to disturb you!" Ela frowned at the king, her courage stealing Kien's breath. "Do you think I want to see you die—watch your kingdom fall? Your safety and your eternal soul concern the Infinite. Extremely!"

The Infinite? Kien's admiration fell into a swamp of confusion. Wasn't this Infinite the God of Parne?

Tek An, however, was listening to Ela. Until his heir interposed. "My lord-father, forgive me, but why should we take note of this foreigner? This *Parnian*. She's nothing to us!"

"We told you to be quiet!"

The heir began to wheedle, his face a younger, craftier image of his father's. "Sire, forgive me. I will be quiet—I simply could not bear their insults and lies any longer! How can they have your best interests at heart, as I do?"

Tek An thawed a bit toward his son. "We know you are concerned for us. Nevertheless, obey our wishes—listen and learn in silence. Have you not perceived their conspiracy? This former ambassador demands we free our slaves. The Tracelanders threaten us with war unless we free our slaves. This girl-prophet declares her Infinite will curse us if we do not free our slaves. It is clear they have plotted together to rob us of our victory!"

Prophet. Kien exhaled. So Ela of Parne had proclaimed herself a mystic and the king probably believed her. Interesting.

Straightening, Ela said, "We have not conspired together, O King. Freeing Ytar's captives is the Infinite's will. Of course, you can choose to believe or disbelieve us. However, if you reject the Infinite and refuse to follow Him, you and your son will die with General Tek Juay's murderers. The Infinite will bring new and honorable leaders to power in Istgard."

The heir seethed. "Your Infinite discounts *me*, and that is a mistake! Forgive me, my lord-father. I cannot obey you if I remain. Please, excuse me."

To Kien's relief, Tek An waved his son out of the room. "Yes, take your distractions and leave. What will you ever learn of being a king?"

"You have said more than you realize, O King." Ela of Parne leaned upon her staff, obviously listening to the heir storming along the corridor outside. His echoing footsteps silenced as the guards closed the antechamber door.

Glad to be rid of the heir's unstable presence, Kien waited for Tek An's rage to ease. Perhaps he could begin peace negotiations now and free himself from prison in the process.

The king, pacing and fuming, eventually perceived the Parnian girl's words. "What? Explain what you meant—that we have said more than we realized."

"You are in despair over your son's failure to learn his royal duties. Rightfully so. As we speak, he is making choices that might destroy his future."

"How can his foolishness be prevented?" Tek An's demand made Kien gawk. The king was asking this girl for advice? Tek An's cronies would go into fits if they heard.

"Talk to your son," Ela urged the king. "Remove his so-called friends and advisors from the palace, then give him official duties and encourage him to follow General Tek Juay's example in leadership."

Tek An snorted in offense. "What of our example? Are we nothing to our son?"

"You need to be available to him. Be a true father to your heir."

The king waved her off, his lips pursed in disgust. He faced Kien instead. "This was your answer then, Lan Tek? Negotiate to avoid war?"

Taken aback, though he should be used to the king's impetuous turns by now, Kien recollected himself and smiled. "Yes. That is my advice. Reinstate me as ambassador. Send me to more appropriate quarters and let us begin formal negotiations with the Tracelands."

Tek An scoffed. "You have no need to leave your current residence for us to accomplish these tasks. Tomorrow, we will send you writing materials and instructions."

"Dictation is not negotiation." Kien wanted to shake the man, king or not. "If you think I will lend myself to your lies and delaying tactics, while you build your army and let me rot in prison, you are mistaken!"

Ela rested a hand on Kien's arm, almost startling him, though her voice was calm. "We can say nothing more tonight that will convince him we are working in his own best interests. Sir . . ." She gave the king a warning look. "It's too late to stop your son's wild scheme this evening. Soon, you will hear of his recklessness, and you will see his injuries. I beg you to use his recovery time wisely. Advise him. Befriend him. If he listens to you, and if you listen to the Infinite and abandon your pride, your kingdom will be saved."

"What? What!" His green robes flaring, the king sped out of the room, bellowing for servants to find his son.

Leaving Kien holding the Tracelands' declaration of war on Istgard.

Kien smiled, scrolled the document carefully, and slipped it beneath his cloak.

The girl tugged at Kien's cloak until he looked down into her eyes. Lovely eyes, actually, though as tired as her voice. "I hope you're ready for a small adventure, sir. I'm not."

❖ II ❖

Aware of palace spies, Kien leaned toward the Parnian girl and questioned her softly as they walked along the corridor with their guards. "What did you mean, 'a small adventure'?"

"We're going to be attacked as we return to the prison. Again."

Her obvious distress made Kien wish for his sword. "What sort of attack?"

"The heir is waiting with his reprobate guards to ambush us."

"Oh." Kien shook his head as his confusion cleared. "This is part of your mystical vision concerning the heir's downfall, which might not happen."

"Yes—I pray he mends his ways and turns to the Infinite."

"You are admirably persistent," Kien said in as polite a tone as he could muster. The palace guards led them outside, down the marble steps into the public courtyard. Ela stumbled on the last step. Kien steadied the girl, determined to set both her thoughts and feet aright. If she was his only available coconspirator in a potential escape plot then he couldn't allow her to destroy everything with wild Parnian flights of imagination.

He bent, whispering, "Listen, Ela. It's clear the king considers you a prophet, and that's a good, useful thing. He's quite superstitious. But you cannot spout streams of commands based on your 'visions' and expect the rest of us to simply obey you."

Ela's chin lowered, and she gave him such a look through her lashes that he nearly checked to see if she'd equipped herself with another prison roll. She lifted her hand from his arm. "You don't have to obey *me*. The Infinite doesn't coerce anyone—we all have choices."

"Good. We're agreed on that." As much as possible anyway. Perhaps he could plot around her delusions of Parne's Infinite. Kien forced a smile and proceeded to his next complaint. "Now, forgive me, but I feel obligated to warn you that you cannot behave as if the king is your student. He's not. He's—"

"Though Tek An is a king, he has a soul," Ela said, clearly unmoved. "And other souls depend upon his decisions, so he must receive good counsel."

Kien felt his patience ebbing. Maybe he was the delusional one, believing he might depend upon this girl to help him escape. "You're hardly old enough to be any sort of counselor, much less a king's."

She glared at him. "Age has nothing to do with good sense, or with the Infinite's will. I do not provide counsel. *He* does. But these aren't your concerns, so why are you upset?"

"I'm not. Actually—" He decided to be rudely honest. "I am. You're going about this advisor role all wrong. Your actions defy every expected protocol!"

"Hmm. Well, following courtly protocols hasn't worked for you, has it? Abandon them."

Stung, he grimaced. "I suppose your Infinite told you this."

"Yes. And it's true. Forget etiquette for now. Follow honor." Her tone turned to gentle mockery. "What else might the king do, Lan Tek? *Kill* you?"

Kien stared. She was talking as if she'd witnessed the previous confrontations he'd had with the king and his men. How did she know?

The green-cloaked palace guards handed Kien and Ela over to the red-cloaked military guards. As the red-cloaks formed lines to their left and right, Kien finally mustered words. "How did you know?"

"That the king is afraid to order your death? The Infinite showed me, of course. But you don't want to hear about Him." She rested her forehead against her slender walking staff and didn't look up until her superior soldier-friend approached. "Tsir Aun."

"Any warnings?" The high commander was perfectly solemn, Kien realized. Worse, the girl answered him just as seriously.

"You were planning a longer alternate route to return us to prison, but you might as well save steps and take the more direct streets. Ambushes are planned for us in either direction. Tell your men to be ready with their shields."

"Do you know everything?" Kien asked her as the commander strode away, issuing orders.

"No. If I did, your insult this morning wouldn't have taken me by surprise. I'm wondering if that was another test."

"Ah. Let me know when you learn the results of your test."

She shrugged, and her brown eyes went wistful. "I usually fail."

"Really?" Somehow, her confession restored his hopes. Perhaps this little wayfarer from Parne wasn't as irrational as he'd believed. He couldn't resist teasing her a bit. "Then I'm not alone. In failing, I mean."

Ela's answering smile was disappointingly weak. In truth, she appeared exhausted, which reminded Kien of his duty. He straightened his musty cloak and offered the girl his arm. She accepted, and they followed Tsir Aun's lead. "Are we ready to brave our little adventure?"

"I'd rather not, sir. But we don't have much choice."

They walked together quietly for a while, crossing various streets and turning corners, which seemed to make her increasingly on edge. At last, grasping for a bit of conversation to divert her, Kien said, "I wish I had my sword."

"It won't do you a bit of good. This time anyway."

"What do you mean?"

"You'll know later."

Kien almost halted. "You're saying that you know my 'later' now?"

"I've received a few hints." She was looking up at the highest surrounding buildings.

Kien followed her apparent line of vision and squinted at an ancient tower to their left, which was gilded by the evening sunlight. A glint in one of the tower's highest windows caught his attention. Was that a—?

Kien snatched Ela's hand, freed his arm, and pitched himself and the girl onto the stone-paved street, just as an arrow slammed into his cloak.

✦ ✦ ✦

"Augh!" Ela gasped at the pain as her knees smacked the stones. Knowing her fall was going to happen didn't lessen the hurt a bit.

Tsir Aun bellowed, "Shields—cover!" Instantly his men converged, almost trampling her and Kien as they maneuvered their shields skyward to form a makeshift roof. A series of thuds rained onto the metal-plated shields. "First rank!" Tsir Aun called out, "to the tower!"

Half the soldiers departed. The remaining guards repositioned themselves, creating a smaller, but still effective, roof of shields. "Stay put!" one of the soldiers ordered Ela and Kien as more arrows pelted the shields. "Don't move until we tell you."

"How can we?" Kien said to Ela, none too quietly. "They're standing on us."

She didn't reply. He was holding her too close for her own comfort. Not that she wasn't grateful for his protective instincts, but . . . To distract herself from thoughts of being held by a charming young man, she breathed a prayer, then focused on the moldy, vile, *awful* smell wafting from his cloak. Better. She looked up as shouts echoed from the tower.

Some of the guards were actually grinning. Were all Istgardians so in love with the idea of war? At least Kien seemed somber as he looked about, studying their situation. The arrows ceased to fall.

From a distance, Tsir Aun ordered, "Second rank—march!"

"Stand!" a soldier ordered Ela and Kien. "Move!"

Kien's breath rasped as he helped her to stand. "Ow—the arrow!"

"You can't be wounded," she told him. "I didn't see you wounded."

"What . . . about . . . a long scratch?"

"Well, yes, there's *that*. But it's not really bleeding. Soon you won't notice it."

"You're not the one with the scratch."

The guards lowered their shields and urged their prisoners forward. While they walked, Kien fished through his cloak for the arrow and wrenched it free. "This attack could have been a well-gauged guess on your part, you know."

"Believe what you want to believe." Her head thudded miserably, worse than before. She hoped this Tracelander didn't intend to prattle all the way back to prison. If she must accept Kien's presence, couldn't the Infinite offer her a solid glimpse of his future to explain matters?

Seeming oblivious to her misery, Kien wielded the arrow like a sword. "I have a souvenir. Do you suppose they'll let me keep it in prison? They've let you keep that stick."

"No. And it's not a stick. The branch is my insignia." Was he trying to provoke a quarrel? She truly didn't have the strength to endure more commotion.

The guards quickened their pace. Despite herself, Ela clutched Kien's arm, almost sick with the pain of her headache. She couldn't continue at this rate. Infinite . . .

Thuds echoed in her ears. The headache. No, cruel as it was, her headache wouldn't cause the buildings to reverberate in horse-hoof patterns. Ela said, "Oh, Infinite, thank You!"

"Listen." Kien's voice lowered in alarm. "That must be a destroyer coming toward us."

"It is. He's coming for me."

"We have to get out of the way—" Kien halted and stared. "What do you mean he's coming for you? Ela, now is not the time to indulge in another vision. We must leave the street!"

"I'm not having another vision." Ela patted her companion's arm. "Just stand quietly and trust me. You won't die. Not even if you still want to."

"I wish you would stop telling me what I want to do."

"I can't help it. Anyway, I'm right, you know."

The soldiers were all backing away, focused on the next street corner. Ela waited in the middle of the street. Kien exhaled and stood his ground beside her. Ela smiled at his courage. Even armed, none of their guards was willing to face an irate destroyer.

Pet bolted around the street corner, formidably huge, black, and undoubtedly prepared to trample anyone in his path. He snorted a threat, his eyes almost rolling in fury. Until he saw Ela.

Her heart skipped at the sight of him, but she lifted the branch and spoke sternly. "Walk!"

Huffing with obvious impatience, the destroyer walked. The instant they were within nudging distance, he stopped and greeted Ela with a mild bump to her shoulder and a sigh that infused her braided hair with moisture. She rubbed him and crooned, "Dear rascal. You're too late to save me from the arrows, but I'm so glad to see you. And Tzana will be thrilled. Kien—" She offered her slack-mouthed companion an imploring glance. "Help me up, please?"

"Onto . . . the destroyer?"

"Of course."

✦ ✦ ✦

Kien backed away as Ela settled herself on the monster-horse and urged it into a jaunty walk.

Unbelievable.

Not just the fact that this baffling girl was riding a living natural disaster, but also those discolored, unforgettable scars he'd glimpsed striating her lower calves and ankles. Kien had seen curving lacerations identical to those.

On a dead man.

Ela of Parne had survived a recent scaln attack. How?

Immediately, Kien shoved the question from his thoughts. He knew what she would say. Her "Infinite" had probably saved her. Kien considered the destroyer instead. A helpful—

"Move, Tracelander!" One of the guards shoved Kien from his dazed musings into the present reality of being a prisoner. "The girl's behaving for now, but if she tries to escape on that animal, we have to be ready."

To mask his interest in escaping with one of Istgard's prized warhorses, Kien shrugged. "She won't try to escape, I know. But if she did, how could you possibly catch her when she's riding a destroyer?"

"We'd chase her down using other destroyers." The soldier sounded as if he begrudged every syllable. "But you'd have to be in your cell first, so move along."

Kien hoped they weren't too late for the evening meal.

✦ ✦ ✦

"I wish Pet could have stayed with us yesterday," Tzana said, fiddling with her arm sling as she sat beside Ela in the prison kitchen.

"I wish so too." Ela reached for another knotted brown root vegetable, doused it in the tub of dingy water before her and scrubbed it with her rag. An improvement, but still not much to look at. She tossed it into a large wooden bowl and reached for another.

Tzana plucked at Ela's rolled-up sleeve. "Stop scrubbing and play with me."

"I can't. You want to eat tonight, don't you?"

"Well . . . yes. But I'm very sad."

The warden's wife entered the kitchen that instant, laden with a huge canvas bag of rolls. "What is my girl so sad about, eh?"

My girl. Ela bit down her welling anxiety. Infinite, please, let her suspicions be wrong. The warden's wife, Syb, had all but taken over Tzana. Would she create a fuss and demand to keep her when Ela was finally forced from the prison? Ela prayed

135

the Infinite would work out a solution, because Tzana was also becoming fond of Syb. And, surprisingly, fond of the warden.

"I want to see Pet again." Tzana clutched the folds of her new red tunic and tripped over to Syb, as if knowing she had an ally who would do more than sympathize with her.

"Of course you want to see your Pet again." Syb set down the rolls, which clattered like unappetizing chunks of wood. Picking up Tzana, she fluffed the little girl's thin curls. "I've a notion that your Pet wants to see you more often too. One of the guards told me Pet's been fussy in his stable without you, so we'll ask to have the poor thing brought around to visit."

"Today?" Tzana rested her knobby uninjured hand on Syb's ruddy face.

"Tell you what." Syb kissed Tzana's cheek. "You be my good girl today, and I'll speak to the next red-cloaked guard I see. We might have Pet here tomorrow, all right?"

"Aw. All right."

"Meanwhile we should leave Ela alone so she can finish her work and get the soup heating in the courtyard."

Just as the warden's wife was about to leave with Tzana, someone pounded at the kitchen's courtyard door.

"Delivery!" A stocky man stepped inside, his grizzled face and watery little eyes as appealing as the vegetables Ela had scrubbed. "Salt-meat an' flour for you, ma'am."

"We didn't order salt-meat." Syb's brown forehead furrowed beneath her veils. "Nor flour. I don't do baking here. You have your orders wrong."

"Here I was told an' here it stays." The deliveryman folded his big tunic-draped arms. "You just ask the warden."

"I just will." Holding Tzana, Syb swept from the kitchen, her headdress fluttering.

Ela's arms prickled as an image slid through her mind.

The grizzled man stepped closer and grinned, clearly emboldened by the fact that they were alone. "You're the cook, girl?"

"For now." She wiped her hands and used the branch for

support as she stood. Not bothering to hide the iciness she felt, Ela looked this miscreant in the eyes. "Why do you ask?"

"Now, don't be all priggish, girl. I've a small task for you. Nothin' to it at all—an' you'll earn a bit of money. For your dowry, I'd say. Pretty as you are, you're sure to marry soon."

His smarmy manner made Ela long to give him the same sort of black eye she'd given Kien. A silly desire because the Infinite's plan was already perfect. Naturally. She willed her expression to ease. "What sort of task?"

Evidently certain of his victory, the man's small eyes crinkled and watered even more as he grinned. "Why, it's nothin'. An easy chore that won't take but a breath of your time. The female prisoner—I'm told there's but one—ought to have a bit extra tonight with her meal. Slip this into her food and be sure she eats. My master will pay you well."

He dangled a small leather pouch before Ela's eyes.

Her heart thudded, but she smiled and reached for her intended death.

❖ 12 ❖

Ela shifted the branch into the crook of her arm, picked at the bag's tie, then peered at the white powder inside. How odd to encourage this man to discuss her own murder. "Will it make the prisoner sick?"

The deliveryman beamed. "Why, it'll cure all her ills. My master's been fretful about her."

"He must be indeed." Inspired, Ela asked, "How much will you pay me this instant?"

The rogue rubbed his whiskers, clearly taken aback. Ela knew, despite his assurance, he'd had no intention of paying a poor, duped cook to commit murder. "Ah. One dram now an' three when it's clear she's cured." He fumbled with a leather bag strapped to the side of his tunic. "Here y'are."

Ela accepted the coin. That's all she was worth? Lovely. "Thank you. I'll put it to good use. One more question?"

He had turned away, but faced her again, offering a being-patient smile.

Ela asked, "Would you, please, pull up your sleeves? I'm terribly concerned about your arms."

"Not a thing's wrong with my arms, girl. See?" He pushed up his tunic sleeves. Sores gaped, oozed, and teemed white-crusted over his skin. Worse than a powdered mold covering decomposing fruit. The deliveryman shrieked. "By all gods an' furies! What's this?"

Squeamish at the sores, Ela said, "Your nonexistent gods and furies have nothing to do with your arms. The Infinite, your Creator, has decided to allow your body to reflect the state of your soul."

"What d'you mean? My arms—they're goin' numb!"

"Do you want to be cured?"

Eyes wide as they could open, he said, "Mercy! I was just followin' orders!"

"Forget your orders. The Infinite is disgusted by your behavior and has made you a living sign of corruption to your master, the heir."

"You're *her*." The man whimpered low in his throat.

"Yes. Now, if you want to be cured, listen carefully." Certain he was paying strict attention, Ela said, "You will go to the heir and tell him what's happened. Do not lie or exaggerate to make your behavior seem better to your master. Tell the truth! Show him your sores, then tell him that the Infinite hears all his thoughts and sees all his actions. Warn your heir-prince that his life is at stake if he doesn't repent and call upon his Creator."

"Then I'll be cured?" Real tears coursed down the fraud's whisker-stubbled face.

"Once you've told the heir exactly what I've said, go outside to the main fountain in the palace courtyard. Submerge yourself seven times and pray aloud to the Infinite for forgiveness before you step out of the fountain. He will have mercy and cure you."

"In the king's fountain? But—"

"Do you want to be cured?"

"I'm beggin'! I can't feel my arms."

"Then hurry and obey your Creator. Before the sores spread."

Arms outstretched, the would-be conspirator fled. Leaving his small hand cart with its load of salt-meat and flour outside the kitchen door.

A blessing for the prisoners, if the food wasn't spoiled.

Her movements slowed by her stiffened, bruised muscles, Ela dropped the bag of powdered poison into the coals of the kitchen's giant raised hearth. The bag burst into unnaturally green flames. Ela shuddered and knotted the thin coin inside a fold of her mantle, beneath her belt. "That's all I'm worth?" she asked the Infinite.

Should you be worth more than I am in their eyes?

An image of the salt-meat and flour popped into her thoughts, and she laughed. "Very well! One measly coin, and some meat and flour—yes, I'm happy!"

Her bruises and aches seemed insignificant now. She nudged the blackened bag of poison to disperse it in the coals. Then she went back to work.

Syb sailed into the kitchen again, looking smug, with Tzana still perched in her arms. "Didn't I say we ordered no salt-meat and flour? Now—" She became miffed. "Where's that idiot deliveryman?"

"He had to leave. The salt-meat and flour are outside the door, but he didn't demand payment. Can I ask one of the guards to bring the bags inside?"

"I suppose." Syb's face lit with joy. "He didn't demand payment? Ha! Foolish of him."

"He was foolish indeed, poor man." And clearly the warden's wife was perfectly willing to take advantage of the situation. Ela smiled at her little sister. "I'll be taking the broth and rolls out to the other prisoners soon. Would you like to walk with me?"

Tzana wrinkled her tiny nose. "Nuh-uh. Warden promised to play kings and pawns with me before I take a nap."

"It's a good game," Syb explained. "Bores them both right to sleep."

"I'm sure it does." Ela's dejection renewed itself, but she smiled at her sister. "May I have a kiss before you leave?"

"All right."

Ela received her little sister's distracted kiss, then Syb scooted toward the door, issuing parting orders. "If you call a guard to haul in those bags, Ela, also ask him to place the largest kettle on the hearth in the central yard, then fill it with water for your vegetables this evening."

"Yes, thank you."

The instant Syb departed with Tzana, Ela poured out her complaints and fears to the Infinite. "She's stealing Tzana! What if Syb and the warden want to keep her? What if Tzana wants to stay in Riyan? How could I ever explain that to Father and Mother?"

Silence answered.

✦ ✦ ✦

Kien glared at the writing board, scrolls, reeds, ink set, and written "suggestions," which had been left for him by the king's scribe.

Did Tek An truly believe that Kien would slavishly copy Istgard's warped justification of the massacre at Ytar? If so, the royal man was deluded. As a representative of the Tracelands, Kien must write the truth—and what ought to be the results of that truth.

"What else can the king do?" Kien asked himself. "Kill you?"

Ela had said much the same last night. A useful reminder.

He sat cross-legged on his straw pallet and wrote a description of the massacre, followed by—sarcastically—Istgard's formal apology and pledge to immediately free Ytar's captives, with restitution for their sufferings. Grinning, he added Istgard's offer to rebuild Ytar.

Ludicrous to imagine such a marvel would happen, but why not?

Now, to sign his name. Kien rubbed the writing reed's tip against the stone wall behind him to sharpen it. As he finished signing, the food slot rattled and squeaked open.

Ela's dispirited voice said, "Bring your bowl."

Kien set down the reed and stood. "Is something wrong?"

"Nothing you can help. Please, bring your bowl."

"Only because you said *please*." He handed his bowl through and she returned it soon after, filled with broth that was actually broth, not water. Shocked, Kien nearly dropped the bowl. The roll, however, was the same as always, fit for nothing but blacking a man's eye. On impulse, Kien yelled before Ela shut the food slot. "Wait, wait! Do you have any more rolls?"

"No. You're allowed only one. Anyway, the warden's wife counts them all."

"Do you really think I'd want a second one of those rocks? Actually, I wanted to be sure you're unarmed. Because if I offend you, I don't want you blacking my other eye." While she sniffed her resentment, he asked, "Do you read?"

"Of course. Is that your offensive question?" She peeked through the slot, her voice brightened, her eyes interested. "What do you have for me to read?"

"Only this. What do you think?" He resisted the impulse to swat Ela with his scrolled masterpiece. Instead, he offered it to her with such grace, his mother would have been thrilled.

"Here, now!" the guard protested, unseen to Ela's right. "I'll not stand here while you waste time *reading*."

"Go on and rest," Ela told him kindly. "I give you my word that I'll hurry downstairs the instant I'm finished."

"Be sure you do! If I have to chase you down, you'll regret it!"

Kien watched as best he could while Ela skimmed the document. By the end, she was actually smiling, showing tiny dimples around her mouth. She rerolled the document and returned it through the slot. "The king will have a fit! You know he will."

"Yes, but he won't kill me. I have to amuse myself somehow, don't I?"

"You won't be amused if you're bruised," she quipped.

"When Tek An is ready for honest negotiations, I'll be serious. Until then—" he brandished the scroll— "I'll write the most favorable conclusion for my people."

"Then I'll pray for you to escape with as few bruises as possible."

"Thank you." What could her prayers hurt? Kien smiled. "By the way, you have beautiful eyes."

She looked skeptical. And, equally surprising, wary. Before she could take offense, Kien said, "I don't know about Parne, but in the Tracelands, if an honorable man pays a lady a sincere compliment, then it's correct, even commendable, for a lady to accept."

For an instant, Ela seemed to be listening to someone else. Her frown faded, and she allowed him a shy smile. "Well . . . thank you. I'd best go before my guard decides he must return. He's supposed to help me with the food tonight, so I don't want him to become upset."

Before Kien could say another word, Ela closed the food slot and departed, her footsteps echoing along the narrow passage outside.

He was just about to sit down again when he realized he'd forgotten to ask her about the destroyer. Did she own the creature? "Dimwit!" He thwacked himself on the head with the scroll and flung it across the room.

Consoling himself with the savory broth, Kien realized Ela hadn't mentioned the Infinite once. Odd. Was she ill? At the very least, she'd needed cheering up.

All the better, then, that he'd amused her with his scribblings. She had a lovely smile.

✦ ✦ ✦

Ela wandered down the stairs, bemused. Kien's compliment made her nervous. And the Infinite's prompting—*Behave. Be polite*—hadn't helped matters. What was she to think?

"Hmm." Flatterer. Also, Kien's defiant imaginary "negotiation" between Istgard and the Tracelands made her long for more to read. Particularly the sacred writings of Parne. Reading them would certainly hearten her and make her forget a certain flattering ambassador. Ela pondered the sacred words and whispered, "Who is like the Infinite . . ."

She turned a corner from the stairwell and nearly collided with a green-clad royal official in the prison's main passageway.

The man shoved her aside without a glance or apology and stomped up the stairs toward Kien's cell. Ela exhaled a prayer. "Infinite, please protect Kien!"

Calm slid into her morose thoughts like a ray of sunlight through darkness. Encouraged, Ela returned to the kitchen. While she finished chopping a mountain of salt-meat and vegetables, she questioned the Infinite. "If You're willing to acknowledge Kien's situation, then won't You please answer me concerning Tzana?"

Do you believe I know what is best for Tzana?

"Yes. But—"

Finish your work. You have visitors.

Ela obeyed. While she tossed the massive heap of food by handfuls into a large empty kettle, she glimpsed fragments of the remainder of her afternoon, akin to portions of a vivid fabric woven within her thoughts. She wished the Infinite would stitch the whole pattern together so she could understand everything immediately.

Doubtless, He knew she'd be overwhelmed and drop like a rock beneath such a massive vision.

Just as she finished, a guard thumped at the kitchen's doorpost. "You've visitors on the way, prophet-girl. Might as well talk with 'em here. Better than your cell."

"I suppose." Ela started to retrieve the branch from its corner, but remembered her vision. No need of the branch for this visitor, much as Ela wished she might use it.

The guard dragged a small stool to the cleanest part of the kitchen. He looked nervous, as if he wanted to flee, and—considering who was about to enter the kitchen—Ela couldn't blame him. She offered him a smile with the chance to escape. "The warden's wife asked that these vegetables and the meat be added to the largest kettle in the central yard, with water. I'm not feeling strong enough to lift it yet. Could you—"

He accepted eagerly. "You want a lid on the mess?"

"Yes, thank you."

With a grunt, the guard lifted the full kettle. "Heavier 'n usual."

Footsteps sounded in the passage. The guard shifted the loaded kettle and scuttled through the delivery door like a panicked rabbit. No sooner had he vanished when a haughty female in a graceful rose tunic and sheer mantle glided through the kitchen's passageway door.

"Tek Sia," she said, as if Ela ought to be impressed.

The imperious woman stepped aside, making way for an even more self-important and elegant lady, swathed in a pale green tunic and shimmering gossamer draperies. A thin, plain-robed girl— almost eleven years old, Ela knew—slipped into the kitchen after them and hid behind Tek Sia and the superior serving woman.

The exquisite Tek Sia surveyed the kitchen, her full lips pursed in distaste. She noticed the stool and motioned to the young girl. The child hurriedly carried the stool nearer Tek Sia, thunked it down, and brushed its surface with her small hand as if to be sure it was clean. Tek Sia gazed upward and sighed in exaggerated impatience. "Be done, clumsy little dolt! Move!"

The serving girl stepped away, so downcast that Ela ached at her misery.

Tek Sia sat on the stool, shedding various draperies like an exotic bird in molt. At last, she deigned to look up at Ela. "You know why I am here."

"The Infinite has a purpose for your visit, yes." Ela watched the noblewoman and her servants. And waited.

Tek Sia fidgeted. "Well?"

Maturity-wise, the woman was a child. Completely spoiled. Ela studied her, sickened. "You could have accomplished so much with everything the Infinite has given you, Tek Sia. You are sister to a powerful king, and you have unlimited wealth. Yet you sit here, bored and idle, wanting your Creator to perform for your amusement and to resolve your petty troubles—which are all your own fault. He refuses."

"Oh!" The noblewoman stiffened, offended. "I didn't come here for a scolding!"

"You deserve a scolding."

Tek Sia stood and arranged the longest of her sheer scarves about her throat, clearly ready to take her offended self out of the kitchen. "That's all you have to say to me?"

"Yes. Unless you want to hear the truth."

The noblewoman paused, eager. "The truth? About my future? Will my life improve?"

"You mean will you be happier than you are today?" Ela shook her head. "Only if you change. Follow Tek Lara's example and—"

Tek Sia sniffed. "That mealy-mouthed little do-gooder? She's dull as dirt!"

If Ela had the branch at that instant, she would use it on this woman. "Tek Lara is happier than you will ever be, even now, while she's in mourning for her father. Everything you ought to be—she *is*."

"You cannot possibly compare me to her!"

Tek Sia was great only in her own mind, but no one could tell her so. Ela temporarily surrendered. "Here is the truth: With the exception of your life, you are about to lose everything that you've never appreciated. If you want to be happy, think of others instead of yourself. Go home. Be kind to your slaves, befriend your husband, stop quarreling with the queen, and pray for the king and Istgard."

"You are insolent! If I quarrel with anyone, they deserve it."

Ela bit down an unworthy response. "Be that as it may, I've told you the truth."

Her tunic and scarf rustling and gleaming, Tek Sia swept from the kitchen, followed by her elegant, now-scared attendant. The youngest servant lingered, her thin face anxious as she shook straw from Tek Sia's discarded scarves. Ela went to help the child, who jumped with fear.

"My lady will be so a-angry," the girl stammered as she dropped one of the soft veils. "She wanted to hear good news from you, because everyone plots against her."

"I can only tell her the truth." Ela retrieved a length of fragile material and folded it. "You and your mother were captured in Ytar, then purchased to serve the king's sister."

"Yes." The girl stared at Ela, her soft brown eyes wide. "How did you know?"

"I saw you in a vision." Realizing the girl had to hurry, Ela gave her the folded scarf, then reached for the coin paid to her by the would-be assassin that morning. "Here. Give this to your mother when you see her. It'll pay a doctor. And when you meet others from Ytar who are also enslaved, tell them to pray to their Creator, the Infinite. He is working toward their freedom, and yours. Work hard for your owners, but encourage each other and stay strong!"

Teary, the girl sniffled. "How did you know my mother needs money for a doctor?"

"The Infinite told me." Ela bent and gave the child a swift hug. "Hurry now. Remember what I've said. Pray to the Infinite!"

The little servant ran.

"Thank You!" Ela breathed, grateful to help at least one of the captives cope with a burden.

She prayed for their freedom.

✦ ✦ ✦

Tsir Aun strode into the kitchen and halted, his expression so severe that Ela winced. She tossed aside her scrubbing rag and reached for the branch. Glimpsing Tsir Aun's stern look in her vision didn't lessen the impact of his disapproval.

The aggravated soldier took Ela's arm. "Ela Roeh, I thought locking you in prison would keep you safe and out of trouble. It seems I was wrong."

❖ 13 ❖

Ela doubted sarcasm was proper for a servant of the Infinite. Yet she imitated surprise as she faced Tsir Aun. "I'm in trouble because the heir arranged to have me poisoned? Delightful!"

The soldier's voice lowered, grim as he escorted her from the kitchen to the prison's dim, musty passages. "That is not your offense, and you know it. Regardless, you cannot accuse the heir publicly—it would be useless. His previous actions have already been excused."

"Not by the Infinite."

In an obvious attempt to courteously change the subject, Tsir Aun said, "I pray your Infinite will continue to protect you and your sister."

"Thank you. But He is also *your* Creator, so you mustn't refer to Him as if He's mine alone." Ela halted in the gloomy passageway. Tsir Aun stopped willingly. Ela suspected he wanted to talk. She eyed a new gold emblem on his cloak, brilliant even in this murky light. "You've received another promotion, haven't you?"

Tsir Aun sighed, betraying his troubled soul. "Yes. And I mistrust it. I suspect it's a bribe, meant to cover the heir's crime. He fell down the tower steps while trying to avoid capture after he and his men attempted to pick off you and the former ambassador, Lantec. When we realized the prince was crippled, I carried him to the king."

Almost grumbling, the soldier continued. "The next thing I knew, King Tek An was praising my abilities and ordering my promotion to a crown commander. I now report to the king personally. Daily. No doubt to monitor my behavior."

"You'll be perfectly safe if you prove yourself worthy—as the Infinite intends."

"What do you mean?" Tsir Aun studied Ela in the dim light.

"Have you ever heard of another soldier being raised through the ranks so quickly?"

"No. This is why I mistrust my situation, and myself."

"Tsir Aun, don't you remember the day you brought me here? I told you that the Infinite asks you to seek His will and be worthy of your future. This promotion is what I spoke of. And it's only the beginning. If you remain honorable. And humble."

"Why me? I'm an ordinary citizen. The most I'd ever hoped for was to become a high commander following years of service. But suddenly I'm *this*." He flicked at the gold emblem, clearly baffled. "I haven't done anything to merit such a tribute."

"A perfect example of your humility." Ela waited for the proper words, then said, "The Infinite blesses whomever He pleases. It pleases Him to bless you with this honor. But why listen to me? Seek His will yourself. Pray to Him."

The crown commander hesitated. When he finally answered, his voice conveyed unease. "That would be a rebellion against everything I've been taught. My kinsmen would be appalled." Abruptly, he motioned Ela along the gloomy passage. "Come. The king waits."

Guards also waited, surrounding Kien in the public yard.

Despite his awful black eye—so dark that Ela turned sick with guilt—Kien looked cheerful. Particularly when he saw her. "I know what *I* did to deserve being summoned for a reprimand, but what did you do, Ela?"

"Oh, everything despicable. I thwarted a murderer this morning and insulted the king's sister this afternoon. The king's had an earful of complaints. Worse, I'll be severely scolded tonight for adding extra meat and vegetables to the stew. Imagine having enough to eat."

"Tonight's stew?" He seemed genuinely dismayed. "Will we miss the evening meal?"

"You'll receive your share," Ela told him. "Aren't you interested in the murderer? Or that I've insulted the king's sister?"

Obviously remembering Tek Sia, Kien grimaced. "She deserves to be insulted. As for the murderer—I'm sure you dealt with him." He touched his black eye. "You were warned beforehand, *weren't* you?"

"Yes." Ela decided to ignore his affable taunt. "You're enjoying this mightily."

"What else can I do? What's wrong with you? I'm disappointed by your lack of awareness. Didn't you know I'd be happy today? Or that I wouldn't be concerned about the murderer, whom you've obviously escaped?"

Her headache was returning. "I don't know everything."

"At least tell me why we're waiting here. You do know *that*, don't you?"

"Pet is coming. And stop teasing or I'll command him to sit on you."

"Forgive me. The thought of eating real food tonight has made me giddy."

Pet rounded the gate with two handlers guiding him—or attempting to guide him.

Ela recognized her former guards, Tal and Osko. With a pang, she remembered their dead comrade, Ket, slaughtered in the heir's first attempt on her life. Memories of the antagonistic Ket led to thoughts of his uncle, Judge Ket Behl. Ela hastily pushed aside her worries over the judge.

She concentrated on this evening's fears.

Ignoring Tal and Osko's attempts to restrain him, Pet stalked across the yard and snapped at Kien. Ela pushed the branch at her destroyer. "No! He's not an enemy unless I say he is."

Pet grumbled. Ela caught him giving Kien a sidelong ear-flattened glare that implied future bruises.

Kien returned the destroyer's glare, without the ear-flattening, and without retreating. "What did I do to offend him?"

"I don't know," Ela said innocently. "You *never* mock me."

"Where's your sense of humor?" Kien asked Pet.

Pet stomped. One of the guards, Osko, finally lost patience. "We've orders to leave at once. Step up!"

Obedient, Ela stepped into the guard's linked hands. He pitched her onto the destroyer's back so roughly that all her bruises were jarred. She gasped, hurt. And her headache intensified with the jolt.

Pet retaliated, nipping Osko's shoulder, making him curse.

Ela gripped her destroyer's war harness and scolded, "No! I understand you're upset, but you can't bite everyone. You must behave."

Timeless irony prodded Ela's conscience and made her cringe. Like prophet, like destroyer. "You're right," Ela told the Infinite, dizzied by the effort of trying to sit up straight. "Please, forgive me."

She sensed pardon instantly. Encouraged, Ela wondered to her Creator if sarcasm was allowed in certain situations.

It evidently pleased Him to allow her to wait. Giving up, Ela prayed.

❖ ❖ ❖

She was talking to herself. Or to her Infinite, but the effect was the same. Even so, Kien admired Ela's fortitude. Besides, hadn't he been talking to himself recently—though with fewer delusions?

At least Ela held sincere delusions. However, all delusions were sincere to the deluded.

"Tracelander." One of the destroyer's handlers stood beside Kien now. Not the oaf the destroyer had just bitten, but a younger, obviously tired soldier. "You will walk beside me. Not behind the destroyer."

"Of course. I had no intention of allowing that natural disaster the chance to kick me."

"Wise," the soldier muttered.

The destroyer swung its huge head around and stared at Kien as if perceiving his "natural disaster" comment. Kien returned the massive beast's gaze with outward calm, but his heart thumped. Hard. Were all destroyers so intuitive? This creature looked as if he'd just read Kien's mind and was plotting retribution.

He could not allow this mountain of horsemeat to intimidate him. Determined to prove himself a worthy opponent, Kien lifted his chin at the destroyer. "I'll behave if you do."

The destroyer snorted and turned its head, as if deciding to ignore a gnat.

"Good bluff," the soldier said, eyes forward, attention seemingly fixed on Tsir Aun.

"Thank you." Kien mimicked the man's stance, prepared to march to the palace.

As they passed through the prison's gate, Kien glanced up at Ela. She leaned forward, gripping a handle on the beast's huge collar, while she clutched her staff tight against her cheek. Her face went clay-like, her lips paled, and she shut her eyes.

The destroyer altered his pace, moving cautiously, as if balancing something fragile.

Was she about to faint? Kien measured his steps to the destroyer's and kept watch, hoping to break Ela's potential fall.

✦ ✦ ✦

She wouldn't scream, though she longed to. This new vision was as horrible as the massacre at Ytar. At least she hadn't fainted.

"Infinite," Ela begged, eyes wide open now, "is there no hope?"

Until the last instant.

Between her vision's impact and the effects from her earlier injuries, Ela knew that if she shut her eyes to pray again, she would topple off Pet's back and create a scene. Instead, she told herself to be calm. Breathe.

Looking ahead at the street, the towers, temples, and dignified homes of Riyan, Ela prayed. A breeze glided past her face, drying tears she hadn't realized she'd cried. The vision resurfaced, provoking more tears. And sobs, which she fought to muffle. Not behavior suited to the Infinite's prophet. Why couldn't she be dignified?

Walking alongside Pet, Kien motioned to her, clearly concerned. "Are you ill? Should we ask to return to the prison?"

Ela sniffled and looked away. "No. Thank you. I'm better."

Evidently unaware of Ela's distress, Tsir Aun led their procession through the city's streets. The palace gates opened before him swiftly, and he halted his men and prisoners in the courtyard. A green-cloaked wall of palace guards waited inside the courtyard, glittering spears readied.

An official garbed in stark white robes and a gold insignia stepped forward, his mouth tensed like a man being forced to eat filth. He glared up at Ela. "*You* will wait here."

Tsir Aun motioned his men back, leaving Ela, Kien, and the destroyer under the watchful scowls of the green-cloaks.

Courtiers were filing from the palace now, all of them wearing white robes without their usual finery except the gold emblems marking their ranks. Ela wondered at their robes until she saw Tek Lara descend the palace steps. Lara was swathed in stark white garments, her hair covered by a hooded white cloak instead of her veil.

Mourning, Ela realized. They were mourning Lara's father. New tears threatened. Ela rubbed her face and waited. Pet shifted beneath her. Partially concealed by the edge of her hood, Lara gave Ela a sad but subtly encouraging smile.

Ela wished for Lara's composure.

The king finally appeared, majestic in white and gold, accompanied by the queen and his sister. The queen was impassive. Tek Sia, however, gave Ela such a killing look that Ela feared Pet might charge the noblewoman.

When Ela met the king's gaze, the Infinite allowed her to hear Tek An's thoughts as if he'd spoken aloud. The tyrant's contempt was so evident that Ela almost forgot her vision. Good. Anger would allow her to confront the king without crying. "Thank you, Infinite."

Tek An motioned Ela to dismount.

Ela guided Pet toward the fountain. A central geyser spilled water from an elegant raised bowl into a huge, round main pool. The fountain's classic design was offset by a tarnished statue of King Tek An, majestically posed atop an ornate, oddly stair-stepped wall enclosing the back of the fountain. No doubt the king had ordered the elaborate, awkward wall and grandiose statue to be added to the fountain's original plan to please his own vanity.

Ela dismounted on one of the ornate stone ledges. Balancing herself with the branch—and praying she wouldn't fall ingloriously into the pool—she descended to the lowest stone seat that curved around most of the fountain. Then she hugged Pet in a temporary farewell. "No biting or kicking anyone."

Pet grunted and clattered in a restless circle near the pool while Kien lingered beside the pool's low wall, both of them unmistakably guarding Ela. Perfect. She stepped down to the courtyard's stone pavings and waited.

Tek An approached, his white and gold robes gleaming in the sunlight, at odds with his rage-flushed face. He looked nothing like his statue. "You told a leprous beggar to wash himself in our fountain!"

"He was no beggar!" Ela retorted. "This morning, he was sent to arrange my death, on orders from his master, and *you* know his master's identity!"

The king's crimson face purpled. "Insolent girl! You will clean our fountain! That *beggar* left his disease in our water!"

Ela raised her voice, making certain all the hovering courtiers heard. "As I live, O King—and I do!—the Infinite cured my would-be assassin in this fountain and removed every trace of the disease. This water is pure."

As if to support Ela's claim, Pet bent toward the pool, nosed the water's surface into a sparkling tempest, then began to drink. Loudly.

Tek An glowered at the destroyer, then at Ela. "We say our water is tainted! Clean this pool. *Now.*"

Ela surveyed the fountain's shining water, its rust-tinged stones, the time-darkened stonework, and hints of underwater mosses flecking the pool's basin. "Who will judge when the fountain is clean?"

"We are the judge." The king squared his shoulders.

"As I am," a proud feminine voice added. Tek Sia stepped forward to join her brother. He didn't argue. Indeed, he smiled furtively, as if he'd guessed his sister's intentions.

"You will judge honorably, of course," Ela said. "Though I must warn you that your Creator is judging you both."

"You talk only to delay work." Tek An signaled to a handful of servants, who were armed with pails, scouring stones, and cleansing powders. Obviously the royal siblings expected Ela to spend days toiling here.

How little they knew.

Remembering that morning's vision, Ela gripped the branch to balance herself, then prayed at the top of her lungs. "Infinite, Creator of kings, You formed these stones at the beginning of time. All water is Yours, as are all the lives dependent upon Your presence. You alone are able to truly cleanse this fountain. Show these foolish, stubborn people Your will!"

She dipped the branch in the fountain's moss-tinged basin. Light radiated from the slender vinewood staff and flashed through the pool—so intense that Ela had to look away.

The king and his sister retreated, covering their eyes. Pet skittered backward.

Within a breath, the light subsided, leaving the fountain undeniably perfect inside and out. Gold veins and delicate crystals glimmered through the white stones. Every crevice was pristine, free of moss, leaves, debris. Not a hint of grime remained anywhere.

Except on Tek An's tarnished statue.

Even when the fountain was first carved by Riyan's royal

stoneworkers, Ela knew it had not been so spotless and gem-like. The king stared, openmouthed.

"You are the chief judge." Ela lifted the branch from the water. "Is the fountain clean?"

He nodded, mute. Beside him, Tek Sia puffed out a breath and shook her head. "I say it is not. *You* were supposed to clean this fountain!"

"Do you argue with the Infinite's will, lady?"

Tek Sia bridled. "It's an illusion. The fountain's filthy, and you've escaped your work."

Proud, headstrong, idiotic noblewoman! Ela clicked the branch against the pavings directly in front of Tek Sia. "Be careful, and be truthful. Your Creator is judging your reply. He has cleansed this fountain. Do you say the muck remains?"

"Of course it does! You're nothing but a witch."

"The Infinite disagrees. And to prove the filth has been removed from this fountain, your Creator gives it to you."

Moss and decaying leaves coated Tek Sia's robes. Rust tinged and stiffened her meticulously coiffed hair. And pungent grime encrusted her skin like baked mud. Tek Sia sucked in a horrified breath. Before she uttered a sound, Ela warned, "If you say one more word against me, or the Infinite, He will also give you the rotting leprosy cleansed from my intended murderer this morning. Go home, scrub yourself, and pray to the Infinite for your soul."

Tek Sia burst into tears and fled. The crowds of courtiers in her path parted, shrieking, obviously afraid the king's sister might taint them with her touch.

Ela faced the swaying, sweat-beaded Tek An. "As I rode here, I saw your death, O King." Tears brimmed in her eyes as she recalled the image. "Why couldn't you listen to me?"

Tek An fell, unconscious.

✦ 14 ✦

Palace guards rushed toward Ela to strike her down, she knew. Before they were within arm's length, Pet charged the guards, scattering them like craven green-winged birds. Huffing threats, the destroyer shielded Ela from her potential attackers.

Curses and quarreling arose from the frustrated, now unseen guards. Ela prayed for Pet's safety, reminding herself that destroyers were revered in Istgard. And in her visions, she hadn't seen Pet being slaughtered by fanatical soldiers.

Walled from Ela's view, the queen sobbed while courtiers buzzed, sounding like bees from a distressed hive.

Someone touched Ela's shoulder. Kien. "We could escape. The gate's open."

"It's not the Infinite's will, and I won't leave without my sister. Besides, think of the scandal."

"True." Kien's mouth twitched as if he'd suppressed a grin, and he took a deliberate step away. Just as Ela considered pushing him into the fountain, he sobered. "Is the king dead?"

"No. He's about to open his eyes, protest that his statue remained tarnished, and he will demand my presence. He believes the tarnish is an omen of his death, which is partly true."

"So you'll wait?"

"Yes." Ela soothed Pet now, rubbing his neck and shoulders. Like Kien, the destroyer seemed to think escape was Ela's best option. Pet signified his wishes by repeatedly nodding toward the gate. Ela continued to smooth his glossy coat. "Patience. Everything will be fine. For now."

An unseen chorus of *oh*s and sighs of relief lifted throughout the courtyard at what she assumed to be the king's awakening. Soon Tek An's voice complained, "Our statue is blighted! Should we accept this insult? Where is the Parnian?"

"I'm summoned," Ela murmured to Kien. She eased Pet's nervousness by scratching his gleaming, twitching neck muscles as she stepped around him to face the king.

Tek An now resembled his statue. Blighted. His complexion mottled where it wasn't fear-blanched. He snarled. "Why was our likeness insulted?"

"You know the answer. But why should I say anything if you won't heed my words?"

"Correct your work!"

"The Infinite declares that statue reflects its subject. The day is coming when this same likeness will shatter into a thousand pieces—unless you change your ways, O King."

"Your Infinite is wrong!" Tek An gestured furiously to his servants, who scrambled to help him stand. Fortifying his lost dignity with wrath, the king yelled to his guards, "Bring her and that Lan Tek inside!"

"My lord," the queen protested, chasing after the king, her white veils fluttering. "You're unwell. I beg you to rest before speaking with these frightful people."

"You will not argue! Go tend our son."

The queen stopped. Ela saw her shoulders lift then droop, as if the woman surrendered the battle. But she turned and gave Ela such a malicious glare that Ela nearly stepped back. Any courtier would have fled in terror, targeted by that look.

A soldier approached Ela now, obviously intimidated by Pet looming behind her. Beneath his breath, the soldier begged, "Have pity. I don't want to lose a hand to your destroyer."

"I'll go with you quietly," she promised. Ela gave Pet a brief hug. "Wait here and don't fret. Oh, and don't eat anything or anyone, *please!*"

As Ela walked away, the destroyer whickered so low in his throat that the noise sounded like a growl.

Several guards urged Kien to move away from the destroyer's vicinity. Kien obeyed, but slowly. Was he still plotting to flee? The instant he stepped up beside her, Ela warned in a whisper, "It's not time for you to escape."

Kien offered her his arm and a glint of exasperation. "I suppose you'll eventually tell me the proper time."

"Yes." She rested her hand on his arm. "I thought you were in a good mood."

"I was."

"The time for escape will arrive when you've the best chance to survive it."

Kien's dark eyebrows lifted high. "And when might—"

A guard cut off his question. "Shut your mouths!"

Flanked by the palace guards, Ela and Kien proceeded up the steps and through the magnificent golden corridors. Tek An was pacing through the small, gilded antechamber, a gem-studded cup in his hand. "Leave us!" he ordered the guards.

"Sire—" one of the guards squawked, obviously horrified.

"Stand outside the door. If they kill us here, you must hack them to death at once, and butcher the destroyer. Now depart!"

The guard quietly shut the huge gilded door. Tek An stopped before Ela, so close she could feel his breath. "Why do you continue to torment us? Even from prison you control our subjects until they talk of nothing but you! You afflict our son's chief guardsman and command him to taint our fountain, then you shame us before our most eminent subjects! When will you die?"

"When my death serves the Infinite's purpose." Ela despaired, studying the king's blunt, hard-eyed face. He refused to see the truth. Nevertheless, she had to persevere. To persuade him to be accountable for his actions. "Why have you pardoned your son?"

Tek An scoffed. "What shall we do? Execute our heir?"

"No! Restrain him. He plans murders, and you excuse him. King, he no longer has a conscience. *Your* conscience is severely weakened, but even you realize he is unfit to rule."

"He is a Tek, and that is enough."

"You're going to see him die in battle!"

"We ordered him to remain in Istgard," the king retorted, clearly proud of his cleverness.

As if the heir would obey. Ela thunked her head against the branch, wanting to scream. To cry. Failure taunted her until the Infinite whispered, *Why are you grieving? The heir has made his choice, as has Tek An. Therefore, I have chosen others to replace them.*

A rebuke, but an almost consoling one. She listened, and looked up at Tek An. "As you prefer, O King. The Infinite gives you and your son over to your own wishes. I won't speak of this again." She must not think of their eternities.

"Good." The king smiled as if he'd gained a victory. He drained his cup, then cast a sneering, sidelong look at Kien. "Now that we are agreed upon this, tell us why you tolerate a man whose nation conspires against us, returning our ambassador in disgrace."

"Excuse me." Kien's voice was ice-edged, his gray eyes equally cold. "At least Istgard's ambassador returned safely home. And there was never a conspiracy. Your attack on Ytar, the enslavement of innocent Tracelanders, the slaughter of my servants, and my imprisonment are all due to your . . . misperception."

"We were not speaking to you," Tek An scolded. "You, who appear before us continually wearing the stinking Traceland color of aggression and rebellion!"

"If my black attire offends you, cousin, then perhaps you should return everything you've confiscated from me. I have nothing else to wear."

The king turned away, as if he hadn't heard. Instead, he spoke to Ela. "Answer. Why do you assist this man, our enemy-kindred, in his plots against us?"

Why was she wasting her breath? "I do not assist the former ambassador, and he is not plotting against you. I speak the Infinite's will. *He* is angered by your dealings."

"Why should your Infinite care what we say and do?"

"For honor, righteousness, and—as I've told you—for the sake of your soul. He is your Creator. Don't you think He should be concerned about you?"

Tek An slammed his empty cup on a polished stone table. "We will not betray our gods for your Infinite, who insulted us by leaving our statue tarnished."

Ela marveled at the king's sudden resemblance to his spoiled sister. "You are willing to forsake your kingdom because you perceive your Creator's warnings as insults?"

"They are insults! And we will discuss nothing until your Infinite removes this evidence of His slur against us."

"Your pride will be your death." Fear chilled Ela as a premonition took hold. "From tonight onward, nightmares will shatter your sleep. The palace will wake to your screams. I can do nothing for you."

Tek An's dark eyes widened, flickered with uncertainty. But then he puffed out his chest in a show of bravado. "You can do nothing? Then why should we believe anything you say if you are so easily defeated? Indeed, every question we have asked tonight, you have evaded."

She wouldn't bother to respond. As Ela looked away, Kien said, "Forgive me, but how can you believe the Parnian is easily defeated? She survived a scaln's attack."

"A lie! The gods made scalns invincible. Our strongest soldiers cannot survive an attack despite all our physicians' remedies. Prove your claim. Show us your scars."

"Nothing will convince him," Ela muttered to Kien. "Not even my scars." Nevertheless, she lifted the hem of her tunic just enough to reveal the peculiar, curving violet-red disfigurements incised along her shins and calves.

Tek An circled Ela, staring in silence. At last, he stood before her again, but refused to meet her gaze. "We congratulate you on such meticulous fakery." He swept from the antechamber, his robes flaring.

Kien laughed. "I knew it! He's so upset that you've obviously survived a conflict with Istgard's symbol that he's forgotten to punish me for authoring my imaginary peace treaty."

"You used my wounds to distract him from your offense?" Ela pretended to wallop the Tracelander's shoulder with the branch. He laughed and grabbed at the shimmering vinewood, but his fingers passed through the wood as if through air. Kien's grin faded.

The guards waved them from the antechamber. Looking perplexed, Kien offered Ela his arm. "There's an explanation for everything."

"Yes, there is," she told him sweetly. "But you don't want to hear it."

In the courtyard, Pet greeted Ela with a wet muzzle and an air of pride. The water level in the king's fountain was reduced considerably. And the pavings were marked with calculated yellow puddles.

Ela shut her eyes and prayed for rain.

✦ ✦ ✦

Ela patted soft thin rounds of dough onto griddles above the kitchen's hearth, glad to comfort herself with work. She'd already made dried-fruit pudding and toast. Tzana's favorite breakfast— as ordered by Syb. Yet she hadn't seen her little sister even once that morning. Was Tzana forgetting her completely?

A girlish giggle echoed from the prison's passageway, lifting Ela's hopes. Tzana—

Instead of Tzana, however, a young white-and-gold-clad noblewoman flitted into the kitchen, followed by her servants. Seeing Ela, she squealed and rushed to hug her. "Ooo . . . I cannot tell you how thrilled we were when Tek Sia ran out of the courtyard yesterday, covered with slime! It was marvelous retribution. Thank you!" The young noblewoman hugged Ela again, as if they were dear friends.

Confounded, Ela blinked at the girl, a delicate teen with wide brown eyes, rosy brown skin, and dimples. Who was this? Infinite?

He didn't reply. And He hadn't offered even a hint of warning or advice on how to cope with this pretty, fluttering little aristocrat. She perched on Ela's closed bag of flour, chattering. "Royal or not, Tek Sia's earned every bit of humiliation you can serve her! She's snubbed my family for years. What's next? Can you tell me? Everyone's dying to know."

Was this a test? Ela smiled, but continued to pat out her rounds of dough. She had meals to prepare and no time to waste with a gloating, silly noblewoman. "What is your name?"

"Oh! How rude of me. Everyone knows who I am. Except you, of course." She swiped back her long dark curls with a dainty, well-tended hand. "I'm Lan Isa. And you're Ela of Parne."

Hmm. Ela supposed it was good to be reminded of her own name. Despite her frustration, she chuckled. "Lan Isa, I'm pleased to meet you."

"I know." Isa wriggled on the huge bag, as if trying to settle its lumps. The remaining flour would have to be sifted twice before Ela could use it. Oblivious, Isa beamed at her. "So, tell me! What else will happen to Tek Sia?"

"Pray for her." Ela slapped another soft, grain-flecked round onto a griddle. "And pray for yourself. Tek Sia, the royal family, and everyone in Istgard is about to suffer immeasurable losses. Today you wear white, mourning for one nobleman. Within three months, there will be so many noblemen to mourn for that white fabric will be impossible to obtain."

"What?" Lan Isa hesitated. But then her eyes brightened, and to Ela's dismay, she tittered. "Oh! You're teasing! Never mind, then. I can see you don't want to discuss Tek Sia, and I can't blame you. She's *vicious*. Tell me, instead—because I know you've talked to him—what do you think of Ambassador Lantec?"

Startled by the question, Ela almost seared her fingers on the griddle as she turned a flat circle of bread. Thankfully, Lan Isa didn't require an answer. She babbled on as if she were related to Kien. And, distantly, she probably was.

"Have you ever seen anyone so handsome?" The girl fanned herself with the edge of her cloak as her hovering maidservants exchanged knowing glances. "He's had all the ladies swooning over him for the past year, though he ignored us for his duties—it's insulting! However, my friends and I forgave him. We couldn't help ourselves. Can you think of anything more romantic, seeing him dragged from prison wearing black . . ."

Romantic? Ela recalled the smell of Kien's black attire now. That cloak. Ugh.

". . . we were certain he'd be killed. Oh, but he was so brave!"

This poor young woman was seriously infatuated. Ela listened and tried to be patient as her visitor chattered. But after a while, even Kien Lantec's admittedly excellent traits seemed tedious, being detailed in an endless rush of girlish adoration.

Ela continued to pat out fresh rounds, while silently begging the Infinite to be merciful and send her a vision—a massacre-of-Ytar-sized vision that would hammer her senseless.

✦ ✦ ✦

Jubilant, Kien rummaged through his clothing chest. With the exception of his razors and his weapons—and, naturally, his money—everything was here. Boots, baldrics, leggings, tunics, mantles, light cloaks, formal cloaks, hoods, belts . . .

He stared at a particularly long sword belt, his euphoria fading.

Only a few weeks ago, he'd longed to have this exact belt to create a noose for himself.

He could use it now, if he wished.

A tap sounded on the door and the food slot dropped open. Ela's voice called, "*Ambassador*, hand out your bowl."

Was she taunting him? Grinning, Kien snatched his bowl and went to the door. "The king ordered my gear returned. You must have scared him witless last night."

"I'm so glad, Ambassador." Her voice was dust-dry, edged

with mirth. He heard the clang of the ladle against the emptying kettle. The slosh of liquid as she filled his bowl. "I've just spent half the morning with your most ardent admirer."

She was indeed taunting him. Kien laughed. "Really . . . Who?"

"Lan Isa."

Who? Kien picked through his memories and finally recalled a blushing little girl without a voice. "She spoke to you? She's never said a word to me."

"How heartbreaking." Ela passed the bowl through the slot. "She must have been too overcome by your amazing eyes to speak. Or was it your marvelous eyelashes? She talks of almost nothing but you."

"I'm 'nothing'?" He looked into the bowl and forgot to complain about Ela's choice of words. Meat nearly overwhelmed the rich sauce. And vegetables, perfectly cooked. With barley. Kien set down the savory stew. If a mouse headed for this, he'd stomp the creature.

Ela handed him two thick folds of flatbread. "Actually, I don't want to discuss you any further. I'm sick of you."

Kien stared at the soft flatbread, reverent. "Ela, I love you."

"No you don't. It's just the food. Eat, then practice with your sword."

Practice. Why hadn't he thought of this before? Amazing idea, except—"They didn't return my swords."

"Pretend, please. You need to practice."

"Why? Did you see me dueling in a vision?"

"Don't flatter yourself." Her voice went serious. "Just practice. Every day." She closed the food slot and locked it.

Kien settled in the straw to eat. He kicked away the sword belt, glad to be alive.

✦ ✦ ✦

Ela emerged from the stairwell, planning her afternoon's work, hoping she would see Tzana. A guard stalked toward her. Without a word, he gripped Ela's braid at the nape of her neck, swung her around, and rushed her along the passageway.

"Let go—you're pulling my hair!" Ela wished she had the branch. She'd strike him with it. "At least tell me what I've done! Where are you taking me?" Infinite? What's happening?

Silent, the guard opened a door and shoved her inside a cell ominously fitted with chains, spikes, ropes, and a gargantuan wheel. Were they going to interrogate her?

Ela stared at the cell's occupant and prayed.

✦ 15 ✦

Shrouded in white, Judge Ket Behl advanced on Ela, his dark eyes intent, though they glistened with sudden tears. "You should suffer the misery you've caused my family!"

Keeping her voice gentle, Ela said, "I did not cause your misery." She sent up a silent prayer and a plea. How could she best counsel this proud man, so plainly broken with grief for his nephew? "Yet I grieve whenever I think of your loss, sir. I warned Ket. I begged him to change his ways—to *live*."

All dignity gone, the judge sagged against the massive wooden wheel and cried, shielding his face with one smooth hand. Between gasps, he apologized. "That was not what I meant to say. Forgive me. My nephew wasn't perfect . . . by any means! However, he was my heir. . . ."

"Your future isn't lost," Ela murmured. "The Infinite wishes you to prepare an inheritance for new heirs. Not only wealth and status, but a worthy reputation and a righteous soul."

She waited as the judge calmed himself and wiped his eyes. At last, he exhaled. "The night Ket demanded I bring you to my court . . . after you were taken away, I went outside and saw my garden . . . ruined."

Pet. Ela winced, remembering the gnawed, uprooted, mulched shrubs and miniature trees. Before she could express regret, Ket Behl said, "I knew, then, that I'd been wrong. Not for pardoning you, but for my motives in doing so. I should not have dismissed the Infinite."

He'd considered her words. Questioned himself. Someone had finally listened! Ela gripped a nearby iron stand for support.

The judge continued. "You warned me that my choices would condemn my family. I am a man of the law. The last thing I desire is to see my loved ones destroyed by my failure to act as I know I ought. What must I do?"

Why couldn't she hear the king say these words? Ela swallowed. "Excuse me, but I have to ask. As a judge, you realize that the law merely points to your own wrongdoings. Knowing this, can you say you've been perfect throughout your life?"

The judge shook his head. "I feel the weight of everything I've ever done—every bribe I've accepted, every threat I've bowed to, every miscreant I've pardoned . . . every innocent . . . wrongly sentenced . . ."

"Make whatever restitutions you can," Ela urged. "It won't absolve your wrongs, but the Infinite will bless you."

Ket Behl's mouth twisted. "Yet He judges me. How I regret my failures!"

"The Infinite judges us all," Ela agreed. "He compares us to Himself, and we all fail."

"Then what can I possibly do to redeem myself?"

"Nothing." As the judge sagged again, Ela continued. "Only your Creator can redeem you. And He will. He longs to. He's simply waiting for you to trust Him. Call to Him."

"I'm not fit to speak to Him."

"Neither am I. Yet He loves us. May I pray for you?"

Her offer seemed to hearten the miserable man. "You would pray for me?"

"Yes." She hesitated, a bit nauseated by her question, but needing the truth. "Tell me: Have you worshiped Istgard's gods, and sacrificed to them?"

Ket Behl reddened. "No. I fear I have been my own god."

Ela held out a hand. "Will your self-worship end now?"

Placing his hand on hers as if making a legal pledge, the judge nodded.

Ela bowed her head.

✦ ✦ ✦

Ela drifted back to her work, blissfully thankful that at least one soul in Riyan had listened to the Infinite. This afternoon's chores would be a delight, eased by the knowledge of Ket Behl's newfound peace.

She wandered into the kitchen and looked around, stupefied. Leather bags of grains and flour rested in corners. Dried meats, vegetables, and fruits dangled in mesh bags from hooks in the rafters, alongside garlands of dried herbs. Jars of vinegar and oil stood in rows against the wall opposite the huge fireplace, flanked by bins bearing the promise of additional foodstuffs. And fragrant slivers of wood filled the big arching hollow beneath the open, raised hearth, ready to use.

While Ela tried to absorb the sight of such treasures, a gentle voice called from the outer doorway. "May I help you?"

Tek Lara stepped into the kitchen, smiling, pushing back her softly draped white hood. "I'm not supposed to be away from my family until the official mourning ends, but they're all squabbling, and I couldn't endure it any longer. I needed some peace. Father would agree."

"You sent all this?"

"Yes, though I should have sent it sooner."

"Thank you!" Ela exclaimed—to Lara and to the Infinite. "Some of the prisoners are near to dying of starvation. I've been adding a little more to their meals each day, but . . ."

"Now they'll be fed," Lara promised. "Including you. So what must we accomplish first?"

"We?" Ela stared at the young noblewoman. Lara hung her hooded cloak on a wall peg and stood waiting in a plain brown tunic, her dark hair braided back like any servant's.

"Yes. You'll have to endure me." Lara approached the hearth

and tested a griddle with her fingertips. "I need to talk to you, and I need to keep busy. What are you cooking first?"

"Oh." Ela looked around. "I was going to scrub and chop vegetables with the last of the dried meat for tonight's stew. The water's already simmering in the courtyard—I'm behind in my work."

"All the better that I'm here. No doubt the Infinite sent me."

"No doubt!" Blessing the Infinite for this amazing surprise, Ela rushed outside to the water barrel, filled some buckets, then sat beside Lara in the open doorway to scrub and chop the heaps of vegetables. After a brief silence, Lara asked, "Have you received word from the Infinite? I mean, what's going to happen? I've been so uneasy lately."

A brief series of images and explanations whisked through Ela's thoughts, leaving her breathless. "You're uneasy because you know the truth and don't want to admit it. The kingdom is about to fall."

Lara's color faded, but she continued to chop at her vegetables. "My royal cousin—"

"Is about to die. Unless he listens to you. It's not too late." While she scrubbed vegetables, Ela leaned toward the young noblewoman. "Listen. Please warn the king to stay in Istgard and to bring the Istgardians back to the Infinite, whom they once trusted. Declaring war will be disastrous, particularly if Tek An goes into battle. Warn him openly."

Knife stilled, Lara eyed Ela. "Why openly?"

"Because you must speak the Infinite's will in Istgard. Soon, if Tek An fails to listen, I'll be gone. Your duties—your public duties—must begin now."

Lara went back to chopping, her knife clacking hard against the board. "Istgardian women do not have public duties."

"And Parnian women don't become prophets." That made Lara stop. Ela continued, "Is anything impossible for the Infinite?"

"I'm sure you're right, but—"

"You're a royal general's daughter, Lara. The Infinite's child.

And as the king would say, you are a Tek and that is enough. Truly, you'll be the only living Tek the people trust, and you won't fail them. *If* the king goes into battle."

"I don't want to consider it!" Lara chopped a carrot ferociously, betraying her distress.

"Even so, listen." Ela set the baskets of scrubbed vegetables between them, positioned her knife and board, and began to mince an onion. "If the worst happens, believe me: You will gather allies and rebuild Istgard within days."

"Days? Rebuild a kingdom within days? Ela—"

"Not a kingdom," Ela corrected. "A nation. First you must send word to Judge Ket Behl and request his counsel. He now worships the Infinite and will support you."

"What?" The young noblewoman put down her knife and grabbed Ela's arm, her pained expression giving way to joy. "I thought my servants and I were the only believers in Istgard. Oh, how wonderful!" She picked up the knife again. "I'll call on the judge this evening, after I leave here."

"Not this evening." Ela reached for another onion. "Give him a week to adjust. He's full of plans right now, and his family is in turmoil. In addition, you're both in mourning."

Lara's elated glow dimmed. "For one lovely instant, I'd almost forgotten." She focused on the vegetables for a time, then sighed. "How can I convince my cousin to give up his resolution to go to war?"

"Only speak to him. He must listen while there's still time. I'll be praying for you all."

"This morning, he woke us by wailing through the corridors in a nightmare."

Ela shivered, watching a silent image of Tek An shambling along the palace's golden corridors, disheveled and howling. "What was he screaming?"

"He was crying for his son."

Ela forced the mournful imagery from her thoughts. "He has two months to change."

✦ ✦ ✦

Kien sensed his enemy's oblique approach, sword lifted to kill—

A brisk tapping jarred him to reality. Disgusted, he swung toward his imaginary foe, then straightened, facing the cell door. "Enter!"

It was ridiculous to give permission to enter his cell. Anyone with a key could admit themselves. Already, the lock was freed and Kien heard the bolt sliding away.

This was unexpected. It wasn't time for him to be led outside, and he'd had no formal visitors for many weeks. Almost two months, actually. He'd begun to think the king had kindly forgotten him and that Ela's visions were nothing but Parnian whimsicalities.

Ela's soldier-friend, Tsir Aun, strode into the cell. "You are summoned."

"Alone?"

"Yes. And I won't bind you if you don't fight." The crown commander gave Kien's dark garments a cold, sweeping glance. "The king will be displeased that you still wear black attire. At least it's clean. Have you burned that old cloak?"

"With what? The fire in my nonexistent hearth?"

Kien laughed as the crown commander made a face, acceding silent defeat. Tsir Aun prompted Kien from the cell. "When we return, Tracelander, you will hand over that foul cloak. I want to watch it burn in the courtyard."

"I'll consider it. Who knows? Perhaps the prison will catch fire." Kien had actually stuffed the old cloak down an outside privy several weeks past, unable to endure its mustiness any longer. However, this Istgardian soldier didn't need to know such details. "Why have I been summoned?"

"I am not at liberty to speak."

To provoke the crown commander—and to amuse himself—Kien began to guess. "The king has finally accepted my terms for Istgard's surrender to the Tracelands?"

"No." Tsir Aun goaded Kien toward the stairwell. "Watch your step."

"The king has decided to set me free?"

"Decidedly not."

They clattered down the stairs. In the prison's main passage, Kien snapped his fingers. "You're actually part of a sympathetic conspiracy, and you're planning to free me yourself?"

"One more question and I'll knock you senseless." The soldier followed his threat with an impressive glare. No wonder his men obeyed him. Kien hoped Tsir Aun wasn't in charge of the whole army yet. The Istgardian military would be entirely too disciplined and organized.

"Are you now the crown general?"

Tsir Aun shoved Kien into a wall. Once he'd gathered his senses and checked his face for dents—and found none—Kien said, "Sorry. That question escaped me."

The crown commander marched Kien outside, where four soldiers waited. Without shields. "A rather small contingent today."

Narrowing his eyes, Tsir Aun said, "It's doubtful anyone will try to assassinate you after all these weeks. Nor is it likely that we'll have to fend off rampaging destroyers."

Meaning that *he*, Kien Lantec, was a dull prisoner?

Kien had to admit the ensuing walk was boring. Couldn't Ela have caused enough mischief to accompany him for this rebuke—or whatever his meeting entailed?

Inside the palace, Kien was shown to a chamber filled with noblemen and their peculiar odors. Their mincing manners. And their sneers. He could only surmise that he'd been brought out of the prison for some royal idea of entertainment.

However, his first glimpse of Tek An was hardly amusing. The man looked twenty years older, though it had been only two months since Kien had last seen him. The king had lost weight. His skin sagged in loose jowls, and the pouches beneath his eyes were now so pronounced they seemed to rest on his cheekbones.

"Lan Tek." The king scowled toward Kien's black attire. "Have you no other colors?"

"Brighter garments seem inappropriate for prison. Or for someone mourning massacres."

Tek An's advisors muttered among themselves. The king waved them to silence. "Have we not decided to end his rebellion? Be still and let us speak!"

He faced Kien again, ill-tempered. "Your presumptuous country has declared war against us. For defending ourselves! Because you are our kinsman, we believe it proper to tell you our plans. You will be joining our army."

"Not likely!" Kien snapped.

"Unarmed." A malicious gleam brightened Tek An's tired eyes. "Clothed as a footsoldier. Unrecognizable to our enemies."

Kien controlled himself. "You hope my own countrymen will slaughter me in battle?"

"They will."

The heir limped forward to stand near his father. "Unless I kill you first. You and that little witch."

Ela. The whelp continued to threaten Ela? Not that she couldn't defend herself, but the heir's malevolence toward the young woman was despicable. Kien smiled, making his voice too polite to be mistaken for concern. "I heard you fell down some stairs during a sad misadventure. Are you healed from your injuries?"

"Enough to cut you to pieces," the young fool promised.

Tek An shook his head at his son. "You will not accompany us—have we not commanded your obedience in this?"

"My lord-father, I cannot stay here like a coward while everyone else claims the glory of conquering the Tracelands!"

"You will remain here! If you wish to argue, you must leave this council now."

The heir sulked. His father smiled at Kien. Not benevolently. "Thus, the gods repay you for all your wrongdoings. Unless you perish along the way, you will certainly die in battle."

"I will certainly not." If these fools supposed Kien would falter, whine, and beg for mercy, they were going to be disappointed. "Your gods don't exist. However, if they did, they would be nothing beside Parne's Infinite."

No doubt Ela would be delighted to hear him. Kien continued, straight-faced. "I also remember a certain prediction. Something about you living just long enough, O King, to see your son die? I'll be interested to see who prevails. Istgard's gods, or Parne's Infinite."

"Remove him from our presence!" Tek An snappped. "Prison has driven him mad."

Kien indulged himself with kind-sounding partings. "My compliments, by the way, on the continued cleanliness of your fountain, O King. Marvelous, isn't it?"

Tsir Aun was already hauling Kien out. Over his shoulder, Kien taunted, "I wish you a peaceful sleep, *cousin!*"

The crown commander gave Kien a sobering shake. "Consider yourself fortunate that I wasn't ordered to have you beaten!" But as they descended the palace steps, he asked quietly, "Are you now pledged to Parne's Infinite?"

The man was Istgardian. Why tell him anything?

Kien stomped through the courtyard. He couldn't help but admire the fountain—its gemlike brilliance flawed only by Tek An's tarnished statue.

No doubt the king shuddered every time he saw the fountain and his statue.

Kien grinned.

✦ ✦ ✦

Shivering, Ela tried to burrow more deeply into her pallet. Sleep finally settled upon her, easing the chill and her heartache. She'd lost Tzana. . . .

High, piercing screams shattered the darkness. Jolted awake, Ela opened her eyes and sat up, listening.

A child's terrified screams.

"Tzana!"

✦ 16 ✦

Tzana!" Ela pounded on her cell's door with both fists. "Let me out! I have to reach my sister!"

Tzana's screams neared, so shrill and desperate that Ela thought her own knees would buckle beneath her fear. "Tzana!"

A guard's roughened, surly voice snarled, "Move away!"

Ela retreated. The door squeaked open. The guard stepped inside and brandished a torch at Ela, a silent command for her to stay put.

Tzana's cries ceased. Ela heard her little sister sniffling and gulping outside in the passageway. Syb's voice scolded gently, "I cannot believe you'd create such a scene! Do you hate me so much?"

"N-no," Tzana stuttered. "I l-love you. But I n-need to see E-Ela!"

Syb swept into Ela's cell, her hair in two disheveled plaits, her tunic trailing, a long mantle pinned haphazardly at her shoulders. In her arms, she held the distraught Tzana. Syb scowled at Ela. "She wouldn't be calmed until she saw you."

Coughs and complaints echoed up and down the passage as the other prisoners stirred, no doubt wakened by Tzana's screams. Ela took her sister from the warden's indignant wife.

Tzana hugged Ela's neck. Ela patted her small back and murmured to Syb, "Thank you. I'll keep her quiet."

179

"Be sure you do. She needs her rest." Syb rubbed Tzana's arm. "I hope you're happy now—screaming to wake the dead. Such a fright! I'll visit you in the morning, Tzana."

"Yes, m-ma'am." Tzana sounded remorseful.

The warden's wife rustled out, and the guard followed with his torch. He slammed the cell door shut and thudded the bolt into place.

Ela stood in the now-hushed and dark cell and held her sister. Tzana sucked in a quivery breath, then sighed and rested her head on Ela's shoulder. She was heavier, Ela realized. And she smelled sweet, as if she'd been rubbed with flower oils. Poor, pampered little girl. Ela smiled. "What was all that dreadful screaming about?"

"You left me!"

"I've been right here."

"No, you left me for real! And you took Pet."

"Ah. That's it. You thought I took Pet."

"And you left." Tzana gulped. "I saw you leave, and someone said, 'You will not see her again in this life' and you took Pet. . . ." Her words became whimpers.

"Tzana," Ela rocked the little girl in her arms, soothing her. "Was this a bad dream?"

"M-maybe. But it was the worst dream. You can't leave without me!"

"I won't. I promise. But we will leave this place very soon. Are you sure you want to come with me? You'd be warmer and better fed with Syb."

"It's not the same," Tzana protested. "She's not you!"

Ela gave her sister a kiss and knelt to settle her onto the pallet. "Hush now and move over. There's room for us both. Do you feel better?"

Tzana sniffled moistly. "Mmm-hmm. You won't leave without me?"

"I won't leave without you." Ela tucked the coverlet around them both and snuggled Tzana close.

A chance dream? Ela smiled, recognizing her Creator's care. "Thank You!"

"You're welcome," Tzana mumbled, already sounding half asleep.

Ela relaxed. Raindrops pattered against the stones outside, filling the air with the scent of moisture. *Infinite? You planned this separation from Tzana. Why?*

You had duties to fulfill, and she needed to rest and recover from her injuries. Moreover, Syb and her husband needed your sister's company.

Were the warden and Syb so burdened that they needed reasons to laugh? She hadn't noticed. But the Infinite did. Had He allowed Tzana to draw the couple nearer to Him?

Silent affirmation passed through Ela's thoughts.

Comforted, Ela drifted toward sleep, briefly aware of the rain intensifying. Spring rain. In her dreams the lands encompassing Parne bloomed with plants that hadn't been seen for years. And Father and Mother walked through the dazzling fields, gathering flowers.

✦ ✦ ✦

"I'm in disgrace," Tek Lara whispered to Ela as they stood beside the hearth, patting flat rounds of bread onto the griddles. To Ela's dismay, the young noblewoman began to cry, tears streaking her gentle face. "I spoke to the king openly, as you suggested. He's banished me from his presence for daring to praise the Infinite aloud. And . . . he took my father's sword, saying I'm unworthy of such a treasure!"

Ela blinked at a silent vision, seeing the sword removed from Tek An's death-stilled grasp, then reverently placed in Lara's hands. An image she couldn't mention to Lara—the noblewoman would be too shocked by the vision's final implications. "You'll receive the sword again, from someone you can trust with your life."

"What do you mean?"

"Exactly what I've said. So don't grieve that you've lost the sword. Instead, rejoice that it will be returned to you, with the Infinite's blessing."

"Then I must content myself with trusting the Infinite." Obviously shifting her thoughts away from her banishment and the confiscated sword, Tek Lara smiled. "Speaking of blessings, I called on Judge Ket Behl yesterday. I've become friends with him and his family."

"And?"

"Ela of Parne." Lara's wet-lashed eyes shone. "Why are you asking what you probably already know? He and his entire family now trust the Infinite. They begged me to visit them again tomorrow."

"I knew it." Ela laughed. "I'm thankful you'll have others to talk with after I leave."

It would be difficult to leave Lara, knowing everything the young woman must soon face. Hating to trouble her with yet another duty, though an important one, Ela asked, "Will you remember the prisoners after I leave?"

Some of Lara's joy faded. "I give you my word I will, though I wish you wouldn't go."

"Don't cry. You won't be rid of me that easily. If the nation of Istgard misbehaves, and if I live, the Infinite will send me to scold you all."

"I'm so glad!"

Ela smiled. Was it cowardly of her to not tell Lara that Parne's prophet would die during the battle?

✦ ✦ ✦

Ela watched as Syb fretted and hugged Tzana in the prison's public yard. "You be safe, my girl, and stay well. Eat all your food—promise me!"

"I promise." Tzana peeked over Syb's veiled shoulder at the prison's main doorway and giggled. Ela turned to see the cause of her delight. The warden limped outside, supporting himself with a cane and squinting in the sunlight. Tzana reached for him. "Warden Tired! I need to tell you good-bye."

Ela thought the man would start blubbering as he struggled to speak. "It's Warden Ter, not *tired*—you've forgotten again."

Tzana kissed his grizzle-bearded cheek. "I'll remember you always."

The warden and his wife burst into tears. Ela hastily turned away, just in time to see Kien stalk from the main entry clad in a basic soldier's rough tunic, boiled-leather vest, worn sandals, and faded red mantle. He met Ela's gaze and stormed over, avoiding the guards. "Did you know they'd plan my death with this disguise?"

"Yes. You needn't worry. You'll survive the battle."

"I might not survive these sandals—they could have at least allowed me my boots."

"Yes, but the sandal leather is so battered and soft that you won't become blistered."

"Stop being optimistic. I want to complain. I'm wearing *used* sandals!" But he grinned. Captivated by the warmth of his gaze, the appeal of his sparkling gray eyes, Ela had to look away for an instant. The rough attire certainly hadn't lessened Kien's charm. If she weren't going to die, Ela quite believed she'd fall madly in love with him. Would Kien remember her when she was gone?

"That's all you're carrying?" Kien drew Ela's attention to her plump water bag and the branch in her hands.

"For now. I've packed Tzana's gear on Pet." She'd had to gently refuse numerous gifts from the warden and Syb. Fortunately, Tzana hadn't complained, reasoning that she needed room to ride Pet. Ela, however, was sentenced to walk to her death, as was Kien—a punishment from the vengeful Tek An.

Kien cast a sidelong glance at the warden, then muttered to Ela, "I see someone has finally recovered."

"No thanks to you."

He smirked. "This from a girl who greets strangers by blackening their eyes."

"You have no intention of forgetting that, do you?"

Kien leaned closer, his voice softening. "If you don't know, then why should I tell you? It would ruin my fun."

He was flirting with her. She retreated to take charge of Tzana.

The warden wiped his eyes, then grumbled at Ela. "Because of you, the prisoners are so fat an' lively that I'll spend the next year quashin' rebellions an' escape attempts."

"You're welcome." Ela smiled, watching Pet frisk through the gate, accompanied by a detachment of guards commanded by Ela's former captor, Tal.

Tzana saw the destroyer and dived for Ela's arms. "I want to ride Pet! Please, oh please!"

While Syb burst into fresh tears, the new commander, Tal, dropped a backpack of supplies at Ela's feet, including dried foods, a clanging cooking pan, and an empty waterskin. Another soldier dumped an even heavier hoard in front of Kien.

The Tracelander lifted one dark quizzical eyebrow at Ela.

"No," she answered before he could form his question. "The Infinite hasn't shown me these rather large details, but I'm sure it'll do us no good to complain. Anyway, dealing with unexpected burdens is character building."

"You sound like my mother."

"I do not. I sound like mine."

✦ ✦ ✦

Sweat slithered down Ela's neck beneath her pack's wooden frame as she trudged along, amid an endless line of soldiers, horses, and carts of supplies. She felt like a pack horse. As a prophet, Ela supposed she ought to pray and not allow herself to become irritated. But irritation was more difficult to fend off as this journey stretched into several days. "Infinite . . ."

Young charioteers drove past her on the dirt road, laughing as the clattering chariot wheels raised clouds of dust that choked Ela's plea. Could she pray for those impudent young men to be blighted?

Could she forgive herself if she prayed and those young men indeed rotted with blight?

No.

Infinite? She hated to whine, but . . . Grit rasped between Ela's teeth. Trying to be neat, she stooped and spat into the stubbly grass alongside the road.

"Are you ill?"

"Thank you, but it's nothing—just a mouthful of dust." Ela glanced up at Kien, who had stopped beside her at this less-than-graceful moment. Dirty rivulets of sweat streaked his face, running down into his scruffy beard. She felt as grimy as he looked, though without the beard, she hoped. "I suspect the charioteers are deliberately raising dust as they pass us. Notice they're slowing when they're among the other soldiers."

"The king probably ordered them to torment us."

They resumed walking. Kien chuckled and nodded at Tzana, who rode Pet just ahead of them and chattered at anyone willing to listen to her. "At least one of us is having fun."

"Pet seems happy too," Ela agreed. Indeed, the destroyer's walk was sprightly. "I'd almost suspect he knows we're going into battle soon."

Another charioteer drove past, roaring a battle cry and leaving a whirlwind of dust in his wake. Ela covered her face against the grit, biting back blighting wishes.

✦ ✦ ✦

"How do I know you won't run away?" the guard demanded, scowling down at Ela.

His hostile tone provoked Pet, who rumbled a threatening noise low in his throat. Mindful of Tzana still perched on the destroyer's back, Ela reached over and stroked the huge horse to let him know she was safe. But she returned the guard's scowl. "I give you my word I won't run away. I simply want to go down to the river and rinse off before the sun sets. Everyone else has permission to do so—why shouldn't I?"

The soldier snarled, "Leave your gear and your walking stick with me! And don't dawdle. I've plans for tonight."

Drinking and gambling, Ela knew.

She lowered her pack to the ground and rested the branch beside it. Planning, she removed her small bronze cooking pot from the pack, a comb, a change of clothes for Tzana, and a long mantle for herself. Then she stood and beckoned Tzana and Pet. "Let's walk upriver."

"To scrub?" Tzana clapped her hands. "We need to wash Pet too—his hair is all dirty."

"Pet first, then us." Ela calmed herself during the walk down to the river. Listening to birds chittering in the trees, the rustle of grasses—which lured Pet to graze along the way—and the sighing rush of the current was the perfect remedy for her bad temper.

As they approached the river, Pet's hooves splatted against the soggy ground. Ela relished the chill of water against her toes. She didn't need to coax Pet into the river. He entered the current eagerly, but he blocked Ela from moving into water any deeper than her waist. "Don't fret," she murmured. "I know how to swim." Not well, but Pet didn't need to know that.

The destroyer didn't budge.

Ela resigned herself to pitching water at the destroyer's glistening sides, then handing up the filled cooking pot to Tzana repeatedly, until the water ran off the giant horse's back, sparkling and clear. Pet's beautiful mane and tail were rather knotted. Wasn't she supposed to comb him? She must speak to Tsir Aun or Tal later about caring for her destroyer.

Satisfied for now, she coaxed Tzana off Pet and gave the little girl a careful head-to-toe scrubbing with fine-grained clay from the riverbank, then doused her thoroughly.

Fearing soldiers might see her, accidently or otherwise, Ela wore her tunic in the river, scoured herself cautiously, then ducked beneath the water. Until Pet nosed her above the surface.

"Silly!" she scolded him. "I'm fine. See?" The destroyer

grumbled his impatience. Ela sighed. "You're right. We'd best return to our gear."

She waded to the riverbank, worked Tzana into a clean tunic, then wrapped herself in the mantle. No doubt she would dry quickly near a fire. Scanning the river one last time, she noticed a series of dead trees to her left. Grayed snags, their bare branches clawing at the sky as if imploring for mercy from whatever had destroyed them. Why did those snags look so familiar?

A memory surfaced, unbidden and unwelcomed, of the rough borderlands between Parne and Istgard. A canyon of red rocks with yellow-green striations, all shadowed and garnished by snags of dead trees. Trees poisoned by a— "Scaln!"

Now, imagery presented itself. Not just one scaln, but an ambush of five scalns. Downriver. Stealth-footed. Approaching . . .

Ela's feet seemed stuck in the sodden riverbank. Her thoughts froze. Until the Infinite sent her a stern mental shake. *Must men die because you are afraid?*

"Pet!" Ela shrieked over her shoulder, "Stay with Tzana!" *Run!*

17

To die of a scaln attack just when his will to live had been restored . . . Maddening!

Trapped between the river's edge and five slavering scalns, Kien wielded a dead tree branch, fending off the largest, most aggressive creature.

Flat yellow eyes narrowing in its broad, blood-red face, the scaln gurgled thickly. Venom oozed from the corners of the creature's nonexistent lips. A muggy rotting-meat stench swept over Kien in a noxious, stifling wave.

Kien held the dead limb aimed at the predator, waiting for it to lunge. He would attempt to fork its mouth and keep those poisonous red claws at a distance. Above all, Kien hoped one of his two guards would somehow assist him. Or at least kill him before the entire ambush descended upon him. "Throw me a weapon, you cowards!"

"Swim!" his most distant guard urged. "Scalns don't swim."

"That's a lie!" Kien bellowed. "When they finish me, they'll stalk you!"

Though he dared not look away from the lead scaln, Kien became aware of another soldier warily approaching the ambush from behind, his sword raised, shield readied.

Someone else was running toward him from the left—Kien heard footsteps spattering along the riverbank. But his would-be defender slipped and tumbled directly in front of the lead scaln. Horror washed over Kien as he recognized his fallen rescuer. "Ela!"

Her charge startled all five scalns enough that they skittered backward. Briefly. In unison, the animals regrouped and advanced on her, their gurgling expelling fresh venom. Frantic, Kien urged, "Ela, hold still! I'll try to ward them off."

Ela didn't respond. Just as the lead scaln stepped within striking distance, she sucked in a raspy breath and cried, "By the Infinite's Holy Name, He commands you . . . depart!"

The five scalns flattened themselves as if they'd been smacked down on the riverbank. Almost immediately they recovered and dashed into the river as one, seeming desperate to escape Ela. Confounded, Kien watched as the whole ambush hit the rapids mid-river and was swept gurgling and hissing downstream. Who would believe such a thing? By all accounts, scalns did not retreat from prey. Ever.

Kien lowered the dead tree limb and knelt beside Ela. "Were you scratched?"

She shook her head, silent except for wheezing attempts to catch her breath. And she was trembling as if she'd been caught in a winter's chill. His fingers none too steady, Kien unpinned his coarse red cloak and draped it over Ela's shoulders. Her hair and clothes were drenched. Had she fallen into the river?

Kien's other would-be rescuer joined them. Tsir Aun. Sword still in hand, the soldier swung his shield onto his shoulder, hunkered down, and looked Ela directly in the face. His voice deep and solemn, he said, "Thank you. I'm sure you've saved more than just two lives this evening."

Ela nodded and looked away from the crown commander. Leaning closer, Kien saw Ela blink at tears. And her chin quivered, making her seem as young and vulnerable as her little sister. Clearly the girl had been terrified, yet she'd faced the scalns anyway. Had he ever witnessed such courage?

Kien stifled an impulse to fold Ela into his arms and kiss her.

It would be safer, and less scandalous, to tease her from that state of near shock. "Ela, thank you—though you took a terrible chance. Scaln stench alone is enough to rot a person alive. No wonder your eyes are watering. Can you stand?"

"Not yet." She wiped her lashes.

Kien's two guards approached now, both shamefaced. Tsir Aun addressed them dryly. "If our entire army shows your level of courage, we've lost already. Return to camp!"

"Yes, sir." They hurried up the riverbank with several backward glances. Kien heard them whispering harshly to each other while they departed.

"As for you . . ." Tsir Aun smiled at Ela. "I wish every soldier in this army had your valor."

Kien chuckled. "I'm glad they don't."

"Careful, Tracelander, or I'll send you downriver after the scalns."

Fresh commotion erupted to Kien's left. A child's voice piped a stream of complaints amid much splashing. Pet trotted up, dangling the offended Tzana by the back of her tunic as she kicked her scrawny legs and flapped her arms like an aggravated bird.

"Pet, stop splashing! And you're drooling on me—Ela's going to be mad if I'm dirty!"

The destroyer halted beside Ela, plopped the untidy little girl in her lap, then bared his teeth in an obvious grimace before swinging his big head away with a loud huff.

Was the monster sulking? Kien bit back a laugh.

"Why did you run away?" Tzana demanded. She yanked a long, dark wet lock of Ela's hair. "You should have let us come with you!"

"Be glad you weren't here," Ela said, her voice low. "Pet would have died of scaln scratches."

"You won't let him die," Tzana argued. "You love him."

Interesting perspective. Kien longed to quiz Ela or Tzana for more details, but judged it safer to leave his curiosity unspoken. And unanswered.

Tsir Aun sheathed his sword and broke the sudden silence. "Let's return to camp and dry out. Child"—he held out his hands to Tzana—"will you allow me to carry you?"

"All right."

Was this a strategic retreat on the crown commander's part? Kien hoped so. He bent closer to Ela and murmured, "If you cannot stand, I'll have to carry you."

Ela stood, though she wobbled visibly. Kien gripped her elbow. "That's better," he encouraged. "Where's your walking stick?"

"It's not a stick!" She sounded almost affronted.

Definitely better.

The destroyer, however, seemed to disagree. As they reached the crest of the riverbank, the monster nosed his way between Kien's shoulder and Ela's, coercing Kien to release his hold on Ela's arm.

Kien complied, but glared. At least the black fiend wasn't biting.

"Tracelander!" A foot soldier motioned toward him. "Get over here and start setting up tents!"

Smiling as if deferential, Kien pondered ways to sabotage the tents.

✦ ✦ ✦

Ela left Tzana dozing near a fire, with Pet standing guard—freed of his war collar and eating his massive ration of feed. She had to retrieve her gear. If only her knees would stop shaking. Imagine! A prophet too distressed to walk straight. Ridiculous.

She had every reason to celebrate. The Infinite, in His mercy, had protected Kien and Tsir Aun. And most likely the scalns were dead, swept away in the river, unable to kill anyone ever again. But what if she'd hesitated an instant longer? Ela shuddered.

Ahead, a cluster of guards hovered around Ela's backpack and the branch, laughing and jostling one another. What were they doing?

Ela ducked between the men and saw a soldier kick at the

192

branch. When his heavy-sandaled foot swept through the vine-wood as if through air, the soldier's companions and Ela's guard guffawcd at his failure. They were making a game of trying to destroy Eshtmoh's branch!

Anger strengthened her wobbly legs. "If you truly understood what you're doing, you'd be scared spitless—all of you! Instead of behaving like a pack of little boys, why don't you pray to your Creator for mercy in the coming battle? You'll need it."

"We haven't gone to war to listen to a woman's carpin'," one of the soldiers sneered. The others cackled or nodded agreement.

"Fine. You're on your own. Forget your Creator." Ela hefted the pack of gear onto her shoulders and snatched up the branch. She elbowed past the grinning soldiers and returned to her cook fire. Tzana hadn't stirred. Good. Ela filled her small kettle with water from this evening's allotment, then added the grim assort-ment of grains, dried vegetables, and meat.

Ela's guard sauntered up and sat before the fire, clearly amused. Did he think she would cook for him after he'd allowed his comrades to try to destroy the branch? Not likely.

Evidently sharing her sentiments, Pet abandoned his feed and loomed over the guard, nipping at his hair and shoulders until the man stood, aggravated. He was clever enough though to keep his voice pleasant. "You need to control your destroyer, prophet-girl."

"What if I approve of his behavior?"

"I hope you don't." The guard sneered. "I hear you chased off seven scalns."

"Seven? It seems your countrymen are well informed, as al-ways."

"You, there!" Tsir Aun's deep, authoritative voice beckoned Ela's guard. "Call your companions to prepare tonight's waste area, and be sure they use it properly."

"Yes, sir. With permission to ask, sir, what about my prisoner?"

Tsir Aun neared. "I'll keep watch over her for now. March!"

"Thank you," Ela murmured as her guard hurried away.

"He will be reassigned. I saw what was happening." Tsir Aun scowled, still watching the guard and his companions as they grabbed several picks and shovels. "It's understandable if they regard you as an enemy—"

"Oh, perfectly understandable!"

"However," Tsir Aun continued as if Ela had said nothing, "they need to treat you with more respect."

Shamed, Ela sighed. "If all Istgardians were as honorable as you, sir, we wouldn't be marching toward this futile battle now."

"Will it be futile?" The crown commander neared, his words hushed. "Can you tell me?"

"You'll survive. Few Istgardians will."

"What about you?"

His kindness almost made her cry. Ela shook her head. "Everything I've seen can only be explained by my death." Before he could ask another question, she said, "I'd like to groom Pet properly before the battle. While the soup simmers, would you mind showing me?"

"I suppose I could offer months worth of training in a few words. First, you ought to start by giving him a more dignified, battle-worthy name."

Ela chuckled. "You'll have to argue with Tzana over his name— I had nothing to do with it. What did Commander Taun call him?"

"Scythe. In battle, your destroyer cuts down everything in his path."

"I can imagine." More than imagine, unfortunately. Ela almost cringed, catching a new glimpse of Pet—Scythe—tearing through a bloodied battlefield, enraged as his rider. Ela gasped. Infinite? When would this battle take place? Obviously it hadn't happened yet, but . . .

Tsir Aun disrupted her thoughts, and the unsettling vision. "Listen. I might not have time to repeat myself." Removing combs, picks, nubby rags, tufts of bristles, and wooden flasks from Ela's supply pack, the crown commander talked rapidly.

"When grooming a destroyer—or any horse—work down and around. Head to hooves. Also, check his teeth several times a year. Pledged masters are the only ones allowed that privilege."

Ela cringed. "No one's been tending his teeth?"

"No. But he's young and isn't dropping his food or losing weight, so I'm sure he's well. If he stops eating, that means he needs a brave physician or someone to tend his mouth. And the pledged master holds him still during any surgeries." Tsir Aun handed Ela a wooden vial. "This oil untangles his mane and tail. Use it sparingly."

Ela armed herself with a comb and eyed Pet's mane and impossibly high back. Tsir Aun grinned. "It would help if you were taller."

"It would help if he would help." Ela leaned against her destroyer. "Pet, can you sit, or kneel, or lie down, or something?"

The destroyer sniffed, as if offended by her question. Almost haughty, he knelt, then settled onto the grass. Ela laughed. "You rogue! Why didn't you show me this trick before?"

Under Tsir Aun's direction, she oiled, rubbed, brushed, and combed the big horse until his neck and back shone in the deepening dusk. His tail was wildly knotted—particularly underneath. A lesson in patience, Ela decided as she worked out the tangles. She ordered him to stand, then brushed his sides and smoothed his legs with a liniment. Ela finished by rubbing him with a damp, nubby cloth.

"Check his teeth,". Tsir Aun prompted. "Slide your thumb into a corner of his mouth in the gap between his teeth and push up. When he opens his mouth, grab his tongue and pull it to one side."

"Grab his tongue? Are you sure?"

The crown commander lifted an eyebrow. Undoubtedly sure.

Ela stifled her fears and faced Pet. "Don't you dare bite me. And no burping."

Pet plainly disliked the procedure as much as Ela, but endured it, his raspy-wet tongue lolling. Amused, Tsir Aun asked, "Are any animals, trees, or human limbs stuck between his teeth?"

Unamused, Ela studied her destroyer's gleaming teeth, then let him draw in his tongue and close his mouth. "No. There aren't." Remembering Pet . . . Scythe . . . in his future battle, and the glimpse of her own lifeless body, she asked, "Will he obey someone else? If I tell him to?"

"Yes, but he won't be happy. His purpose is to tend you for as long as you live."

"What if I've died?"

"Then, if he survives your death, he will pledge to another master. Particularly one you've previously commanded him to obey."

"Or perhaps the Infinite will command him to obey—" She stopped herself.

Tsir Aun frowned at her. "Do you truly expect to die soon?"

"Yes. Now . . . how can I command him to obey someone else?"

"You grab his muzzle, turn him to see the prospective pledge, and command him to obey that person."

"That's all? Simply 'Obey'?"

"Obey. And be stern." The crown commander stepped nearer. "Is there anything I can do to help you?"

"Pray to the Infinite for your own safety—and for Istgard."

He allowed her a trace of a smile. "I have. And I will."

There wasn't a hint of ridicule in his expression. He'd spoken the truth. Infinite, thank You! She almost dropped to the ground in relief.

As if he'd said too much, Tsir Aun cleared his throat. "The king will be expecting my report. By now he's heard about the scalns."

"The king will be irritated to know we've survived," Ela said. "But that reminds me . . ." A glimpse of the upcoming conflict between Istgard and the Tracelands resurfaced, stopping her midsentence. Tsir Aun must think she was addled.

The crown commander frowned. "Yes?"

"When the battle begins, you must stay with your countrymen.

Fight for the king and the heir until the very last. Do not cross over to join the Tracelanders."

He stared. "Why would I do such a thing? I'm no traitor!"

"Trust me, sir. You'll be tempted. But the Infinite wills that you fight for Istgard."

Silent, the commander bowed his head and departed, clearly upset.

He would understand later. And forgive her. Even so, she ached as if she'd lost a friend.

By now, Pet was nuzzling Tzana, waking her. Their food was ready.

✦ ✦ ✦

Insulted or not, Tsir Aun kept his word and reassigned her abusive guard to other duties, replacing the man with the recently promoted Commander Tal. Obviously pleased with his new status, and respectful of Ela, Tal greeted her with a smile. "Give me and my men your word that you won't try to escape, and we'll leave you unbound for tonight."

"I give you my word. Anyway, why should I run? My work here isn't finished."

While his men prepared for watch duty, Tal dropped his gear and unrolled his sleeping quilt, seeming satisfied to sleep beneath the stars, near the fire. He yawned, stretched out, and shut his eyes. "Tell me about the scalns."

She'd rather not. But at least he would hear the truth and, perhaps, discern the Infinite's will. Before she'd finished, though, Tal was snoring. Ela nestled on her bedroll beside Tzana, and they looked for images in the fire until they both dozed off.

The flames had dwindled to glowing coals when Ela awoke. Myriad insects chirped and rasped in the darkness, a vibrant, unstructured chorus. Had she actually slept through all this noise? Moving gently, she placed several pieces of wood on the coals and checked Tzana and Pet. Both sound asleep, and both on their sides. Satisfied that she hadn't awakened them—or the exhausted guards—Ela slung her water bag over one shoulder and crept toward their camp's designated latrine area. Mercifully, the narrow privy trench was shadowed.

Finished with her duty, she splashed water over her hands and dried them. Instead of returning to the fire, she lingered near the trees and gazed up at the nighttime sky. If she weren't a prisoner on her way to a bloody battle—and her own death—she might enjoy being here. Apart from the scalns, this river valley was a lovely place. Greener than Istgard or Parne, with tall, lush trees. Beautiful. Yet the sky was the same. Ela stared up at the stars, blessing their Creator.

Muffled footsteps sounded behind her. Before Ela could turn, two large hands clamped over her nose, mouth, and throat in a murderous grip. After trying to scream, she simply fought to breathe.

❖ 18 ❖

Infinite! Please . . .

Ela struggled to pry her assailant's huge hands from her nose, mouth, and neck. But his grip tightened, particularly along the sides of her throat, making the blood pound in her temples. Her senses darkened. Faded. Just as she felt herself sliding into unconsciousness, her attacker gasped and let her fall. Ela tumbled into the grass, too overcome to prevent herself from rolling.

As she sucked in air, thuds pulsed through Ela's head. And through the soil. Massive dark hooves charged past Ela's dim line of vision. Bleary, she tried to concentrate. Pet?

No. Not Pet. Scythe charged her would-be murderer. Stomping him. Ela shook off her disorientation and tried to lift her head. She heard snaps, like twigs. Her attacker screamed. Then hushed. Still in a fury, the destroyer grasped the man's limp form between his teeth, flung him aside, and trampled him again.

Ela propped herself on one elbow and managed a whispered plea. "Pet! Scythe . . . Stop!"

Though her voice sounded pitifully weak, the destroyer heard. He left his target and nudged Ela, as if urging her to her feet. She couldn't stand. But she stroked his face. "Thank you."

Vertigo washed over Ela, and she retched into the grass. Pet snuffled at her, then whickered. By now, the guards were running toward them, calling, "Who is there? Identify yourself!"

Pet whickered again, mournful. Apparently encouraged by his gentle tone, the guards approached Ela, their swords drawn. One of the guards cursed. "It *is* the girl. We're gonna be punished—lettin' her escape."

Disgusted, Ela spat to clear her mouth. Her voice emerged as a feeble, painful squeak. "I didn't escape. I used the latrine."

"Step back!" Commander Tal ordered the foul-mouthed guard. Tal kneeled beside Ela. "What's happened?"

Ela tried to push her voice above the raw whisper. "I was half strangled."

"By whom?"

Giving up, Ela gestured toward her assailant's shadowed, trampled form. The man hadn't moved. Hadn't survived. Pet killed him. For her. A horrifying, ghastly thought. Sobs worked up through Ela's bruised throat. Her weakness apparently worried Pet enough that he nuzzled Tal.

The soldier sighed. "Can't you two make it through one week without causing disaster?"

"I'm n-not the one who tried to strangle me," Ela protested, fighting tears. The top of her head felt as if it might explode.

Without asking permission, Tal scooped up Ela and stood. She hoped she wouldn't be sick again—the helpful commander would bear the brunt of her illness. Tal's subordinates were inspecting her assailant's body. "Stone-dead," one of them announced.

"Bring his body to the fire, and expect an interrogation," their commander ordered.

"No," Ela pleaded in a thready whisper. "Tzana will see his body."

Unmoved, Tal said, "She can cover her eyes."

Heartless man! To be fair, Tal was handling her cautiously. Most Istgardians would have regretted Ela's survival. But perhaps Tal's caution was due to his fear of Pet, who lurked behind them. Ela could feel her destroyer's breath against her arm, saturating her tunic's sleeve.

Tal hunched his shoulders. "When you're able to stir yourself, find a grain cake and give it to your destroyer with a bit of praise. He saved your life."

Yes. Her life was saved. At the cost of her assailant's eternally suffering soul.

✦ ✦ ✦

"Can't I look?" Tzana demanded, hidden beneath her make-shift tent, which sheltered her from the dawn light spilling over the dead man.

"No." Ela frowned, trying to sound severe despite her hoarse voice. "You don't need to see this, I promise you." As far as Ela was concerned, Tzana had already seen too much death on this journey.

"But what if I want to?"

"You don't." Ela shivered, contemplating the crushed, blood-ied corpse. She whispered, "Infinite? Couldn't You have warned me?"

You didn't want to know.

True. But . . . "I would have avoided the privy."

You could not have avoided him. He and his master have loved evil too much.

Ela saw her attacker's face. And his master's face. She sighed. Of course it was *him.* She should have realized this would happen. Infinite, Ela implored in her thoughts, I know I'll die soon—and I accept that—but to *almost* die repeatedly beforehand is exhaust-ing! Must my enemies always try to kill me?

They are My enemies, attacking Me, through you—yes.

He allowed Ela a tiny hint of His anger toward the evils she'd suffered for His sake. A glimpse of His judgment. She cringed and nearly crawled into Tzana's tent. Not that it would have helped.

A shadow passed between Ela and the ruddy light of dawn. Tsir Aun's shadow. She straightened as he half knelt beside her. He studied her throat, then the sides of her face. His observations finished, the crown commander looked Ela in the eyes. "What can you tell me?"

"The heir is here," Ela rasped. "Against his father's orders, as the Infinite said."

"Where, exactly?"

"He's among the foot soldiers. But there are too many. You won't find him until just before the battle—in two days."

"Will he attack you again?"

"His men are too frightened by their comrade's death. And he doesn't want to betray his own presence." Ela worked up courage to form her next question. "Are you still angry with me?"

The crown commander leaned forward, whispering, "I wasn't angry with you. I'm worried. It's a fact that all your predictions have come true. And I've seen the Infinite's power with my own eyes—which is why I trust Him. But now you've warned me that I'll consider betraying my country. . . ." He shook his head, unable to continue.

"For the best reasons, Tsir Aun, yes, you'll be tempted. But I'm praying you'll summon the strength to resist."

"What reasons?" He actually looked desperate.

"Just before the battle, because you now trust Him, the Infinite will show you everything that I've seen concerning the slaughter. But you must stay with the king. For Istgard's sake. And the Infinite's."

"As you say." Despite his obvious apprehensions, Tsir Aun shrugged and changed the subject. "The king continues to suffer his nightmares. Every night he wakes, screaming and wailing in terror. It's affecting all the noblemen and my fellow commanders. As it is, the king's advisors are foolish and making costly mistakes, but now they are sleepless and befuddled. Their drinking alone will cost them this war."

"I know. But the Infinite has already given the victory to the Tracelands. Unless you persuade the king to turn to the Infinite, his nightmares will continue, and he will lead most of the army into death."

"Unless I can persuade him to change?"

"Yes. The Infinite is merciful. He will restore the kingdom, up to Tck An's last breath—if only the king will listen to Him."

Tsir Aun pondered for an instant, then said, "If I speak to the king and urge him to consider turning to the Infinite, will he dismiss me as he dismissed Lady Tek Lara?"

Ela hesitated, knowing he'd be unhappy. "Yes. You'll be banished from the king's presence. However, the king won't remove you from your command. He depends upon you more than you realize. And he won't survive your dismissal for long."

The crown commander grazed his knuckles along his dark-whiskered jaw, the motion of a man struggling to make a decision. "I'll go speak to the king now. After he's dismissed me, I'll search for the heir. If nothing else, a father and son ought to be together when facing a battle." He threw Ela a sad smile. "If I'm dismissed, at least I'll be able to sleep tonight."

✦ ✦ ✦

"I heard the commotion last night." Kien aligned his steps with Ela's as they trudged along the dusty road. "I was sure it had to do with you, but my guards had me bound hand and foot so I couldn't come to your rescue."

Raw-voiced, Ela muttered, "Thank you for your concern. It was another of the heir's assassination attempts. Scythe rescued me."

"Scythe?"

"Pet," she amended. "His battle name is Scythe."

Kien laughed. "Perfect! I'll call him Scythe from now on. No doubt he was impressive."

"I'd rather not think of it."

His amusement faded. Like Tsir Aun, Kien surveyed her face and throat. His expression turned grim. "Sorry. It's clear the attack nearly succeeded. I hope you're feeling well enough to walk through the day. If not, I'll carry your gear."

Why did his sympathy make her feel as if she were coming apart like a bit of raveled fabric? Unable to speak, Ela nodded.

Kien exhaled. When he finally spoke again, he seemed aggravated. "What sort of loving Creator would compel a young woman to endure everything you've suffered?"

Despite her misery, Ela's soul gave a small, elated skip. Kien Lantec, actually questioning her about the Infinite! She forced herself to be calm and answer him. "I wasn't compelled. My Creator *asked* me to become His prophet. And I agreed."

"Why? I mean, if your Infinite is the Creator—the one true God—then why can't He simply say, 'Listen, mortals, everyone behave!' and have them be perfect? Why drag you into this mess?"

Ela prayed to the Infinite for words, then spoke carefully. "Because He loves us. And love does not demand enslavement, but . . . love desires a partnership. Our Creator seeks true communication between us and Him. He won't force anyone to love Him. We decide for ourselves."

"Therefore, your role is . . ." He sought the right word. Ela had to laugh.

The laugh hurt. She put her free hand to her throat. "You, of all people, should know the word. I'm an ambassador. His ambassador. I inform, negotiate, and hopefully win spiritual peace treaties. I speak for my Lord in foreign courts."

The Tracelander's gray eyes sparkled irresistibly. "I deserved that."

"Yes, you did."

"Fair enough." He frowned. "It's rude of me to ask you questions when you're so hoarse, so I'll keep quiet today."

"Can you?" Ela pretended disbelief, then smiled.

Kien's attempt to look offended was bested by a grin. "Ha, ha."

As the day progressed, the landscape changed, becoming more luxuriant. Ela couldn't help but admire the beautiful, widening river valley. She'd never been there, but those colossal trees and magnificent cliffs in the distance were familiar. Her breath faltered. "We're approaching Ytar."

"You're right." Kien glanced around, his dark eyebrows lifted.

His profile, strong and cleanly cut despite his whiskers, was so appealing. . . .

Ela looked away, deliberately recalling her vision of Ytar.

✦ ✦ ✦

Kien stared at Ytar's charred ruins. At the broken, blackened stone and timber buildings. Worse, at the scattered fragments of bones. Tracelanders' bones. The sight caught at Kien's heart. His people had died here. This place should be sacred. Instead, celebratory shouts echoed off Ytar's burnt walls.

Around him, Istgardian soldiers were laughing, jeering. A charioteer clattered past Kien on the weed-strewn main road and taunted, "More of the same to you, and all Tracelanders!"

"Enjoy yourself!" Ela hissed toward the charioteer's back. "This is the last celebration you'll have!"

Kien blinked, stunned by Ela's ferocity. She met his look with such hurt and rage that anyone would have believed her a Tracelander. Swiping her tears, Ela said, "Just wait! Within a year, Ytar will be reborn."

He wanted to kiss her. Really kiss her.

A rush of seriously inappropriate thoughts followed Kien's impulse, and he averted his gaze. Clenching the straps of his backpack, Kien willed himself to think coldly. She attracted him because of proximity. He'd been near her and no other marriageable female for months. She was unsuitable. She was a Parnian. And truly not appropriate . . . or admirable . . . or lovely . . . or . . .

He berated himself. Liar!

✦ ✦ ✦

"Here's another rag," Tzana chirped, offering Ela a thick, nubby square.

"Thank you." Ela swiped the rough cloth over Pet's shimmering sides and legs. She hoped she'd finished crying. But encamped as the Istgardians were in and around the devastated city, she was easily overwhelmed. Every angle of Ytar brought back her vision. Much better to concentrate on Pet's gleaming darkness and nothing else.

Besides, Pet deserved pampering. Tomorrow morning he would face a true battle. "You be safe," she scolded him tenderly, glad her voice was recovering. Perhaps the destroyer could hear her fondness. "I don't see you fatally wounded, but—"

Tears stung the edges of her already raw eyes. She hugged the warhorse and dragged her ragged emotions together. A sharp whistle beckoned. Kien trudged toward her, his arms and back laden with firewood.

The soldiers had loaded him down as if he were a pack mule. This was her chance, Ela realized. She grabbed Pet's muzzle between her hands and turned him to see Kien. Becoming fierce, she muttered, "Obey! Do you hear me? Pet *and* Scythe obey him!"

The destroyer groaned.

Tzana clambered to her feet, her brown eyes bugged with worry. "What's wrong with Pet? That was a big grumble."

"He thinks he has a stomachache," Ela guessed. "But he'd best get over it soon." It was, after all, the Infinite's will.

Kien dropped some wood near Ela. Pet shut his eyes and groaned again. The Tracelander stepped away as if fearing the destroyer carried a contagious disease. "What's his trouble?"

"You." Ela smiled and resumed brushing. Until glimmers of light and shadow flicked through her thoughts. New images.

Aware of Kien's approaching guard, she whispered, "Tomorrow morning, just before the battle, we're going to escape."

"What?" Kien seemed ready to dump the load of wood from his back and flee at once. "How?"

"Move, Tracelander!" The guard shoved Kien onward before Ela could speak.

Pet sniffed in unmistakable disdain.

✦ 19 ✦

Finished scouring the cooking utensils and packing her gear, Ela sat before the fire. She ought to curl up beside Tzana for some sleep. But the flames lulled her into a waking dream. A chunk of wood popped, sending sparks upward into the dark sky and dropping ashes to the makeshift hearth beneath.

Ashes from Ytar's broken timbers.

Take up these ashes, the Infinite commanded. *Let them be a sign. . . .*

Reverently, Ela leaned forward and tugged a charred limb from the fire. When the wood was cool enough to handle, she crumbled its coal-dark edges between her fingers and sifted the ashes onto her hair. Ran them over her arms. Smudged them across her face and throat.

"What are you doing?" Tal demanded, staring across the fire as if Ela had gone insane.

"Mourning." But tears must wait. Tonight, she had to be calm. "Tomorrow, you and your men will face battle."

"Huh! You think so? I haven't seen one Tracelander, 'cept Ambassador Lantec. Much less an army."

"They see you, Tal. And they are prepared to avenge Ytar. I pray you survive them." Tal had been courteous to her and kind to Tzana. She implored the Infinite to let him live.

Tal looked around, suspicious. "What do you mean—they see me?"

"They're watching." Ela rubbed ashes into her braid, unraveling it.

"Stop playing with those ashes! You're making me nervous."

"Good. Be nervous," Ela told her guard. "Every man here ought to be nervous, but they haven't listened. Souls will be lost in the morning, to eternal torment without the Infinite's presence." She scooped up more ashes and showered them over her tumbled hair, a dark, warm rain. "Tonight I mourn. And I pray these souls will listen."

"You look like a madwoman!" Tal protested.

Ela retrieved the branch and stood, admiring the vinewood's metallic gleam as it cast light into the darkness. "Grief causes madness. Warn your men, Tal, and yourself. Tomorrow you'll face the fight for your lives and souls. Pray to the Infinite you survive."

She kissed Tzana's tenderly wrinkled cheek and left her sleeping beneath Pet's watchful gaze.

❖ ❖ ❖

Gritting his teeth, Kien broke a chunk off the disc of coarse bread that posed as his evening meal. If he hurled this disc whole at his guard, the man would die of the wound. Clearly the Istgardian army had hired the same baker who supplied the prison, only now the rolls were flattened to stack easily.

Kien doused the chunk of bread in his ration of water and waited. Then waited some more. Resigned to his fate, he finally shoved the mess into his mouth.

Eating this one meal would take him all night.

He worked the rough mouthful between his teeth and convinced himself to swallow just as an apparition appeared, outlined against the fire. A dark wraith wielding a beam of chilling blue-white light. Kien choked, blinked his watering eyes, and gasped.

A woman faced Kien and his captors. Her hair flowed black

over her dark arms and robes, while her eyes—huge, beautiful, and dire—swept them all, including Kien. She seemed the personification of imminent death.

Low-voiced and surprisingly distressed, she said, "Tomorrow each of you will be cast into battle. The fight will not be to save merely your lives, but your souls. Pray to the Infinite, your Creator. Trust Him, please, and escape eternal agony."

Ela. Kien exhaled. She'd genuinely shaken him. The staff in her hands exuded an eerie glow, adding force to her warning.

She vanished before he could say a word—not that he'd had a word to say. He stared at his guards, who sat like carved figures of wood, incapable of speech. At last, their commander, a harsh-voiced thug, said, "Somebody oughta stop 'er."

As one, the soldiers looked at Kien. He shook his head. Stop Ela from terrifying the Istgardians half to death? "No. Not for anything."

The commander growled. "If 'e's not gonna be useful, tie 'im down for the night."

The two guards nearest Kien snared him with cords at his wrists and ankles.

At least he didn't have to finish the bread.

When the guards left him in a knotted heap, Kien twisted around until he could stare up at the stars. Ela wasn't bound each night, was she? Were the guards so frightened by the Parnian that they didn't dare touch her? Unfair.

Actually, considering the way she'd startled him, Kien understood their fear. As he remembered Ela's words, realization crystallized. Ela had included him in her warning. Why? Kien frowned. Wasn't he supposed to escape with her tomorrow morning? Did his escape now depend upon his submission to Parne's Infinite?

Kien stared up into the nighttime sky—a dark, gem-scattered cloak worthy of a king. Or a Creator. Really? His mouth forming words that allowed almost no sound past his lips, Kien whispered, "If You exist, show me!"

His heartbeat quickened, becoming so violent that he coughed in an attempt to slow its pace. A Tracelander calling to the Creator. Unimaginable. And yet, he'd watched Ela's every move and judged her words with more than a little doubt. Even condescension. Now his verdict settled within his thoughts, guaranteed to steal his sleep: Ela was probably right.

"Don't lie," he warned himself beneath his breath. Probably? No. She *was* right. Each of her earlier predictions had either been fulfilled or appeared near fulfillment.

Now, he—an arrogant Tracelander—was questioning the Infinite. And the prospect was more frightening than Ela's darkness this evening. He was wholly unworthy of the Infinite's regard. He was—confess it!—a reprobate. Humbled, he tried again.

"Infinite? Are You there?"

✦ ✦ ✦

Approaching the fire before the green royal pavilion, Ela studied the king's face. Surrounded by his counselors, Tek An jumped in his seat, gasped, then glared up at her. He had become an old man. A hateful old man. Lips parting, nostrils flaring, he snarled, "You, the cause of all our troubles, dare to show yourself here! Do you believe you can frighten us?"

Obviously she'd frightened him and his counselors—they were all slack-jawed. Ela said, "The battle is tomorrow morning. Tonight is your last in this life, and the beginning of your separation from all peace. Unless you call to the Infinite."

Tek An bounded to his feet. "The battle begins when we decree it shall begin! Our scouts have seen no Tracelanders, and you lie only to coerce our obedience to your Infinite!"

"The Infinite warns you, but He will not coerce you or anyone to accept Him."

"Get out of our sight! Our sleep is destroyed by your curses. Our subjects hate you and your Infinite—we long for you to die!—leave us!"

Aching at his words, Ela sent up a plea. Infinite . . .

Why do you plead for him? He refuses to hear. Look at his counselors. They are unwilling to hear My warnings, therefore I have given their power to others and will turn them to dust.

Ela bowed her head. Finished listening, she gave Tek An a last look. Then a final reminder. "As the Infinite warned, you will see your son just before the battle. At least reconcile with him before your death." She turned, gazing at the counselors and courtiers. "Each of you, pray to the Infinite for your souls. The battle is at hand."

She heard their laughter as she walked away.

❖ ❖ ❖

Kien turned, uneasiness drawing him from sleep. His eyelids twitched, and he rubbed them. With his hands. Wide awake, he stared into the clouded predawn sky and sat up. His hands and ankles had been released. Where were the ropes? Ela stood beside him, her face illuminated by light from the branch. She raised a finger to her lips, then motioned him to stand.

Kien nodded. Escape! Hardly daring to breathe, he stood and straightened his cloak. Ela pointed to the snoring commander nearby. Specifically at the sword resting in its scabbard at the man's side, partially hidden by his cloak. Was Kien supposed to take the sword? Gladly. He slipped the weapon and its belt away from the commander and grinned. At last, a sword. If only he could find his gear and escape with that as well. At least he had his life. And the hope of recovering some of his confiscated belongings after the battle.

He crept silently over the trampled grass, following Ela toward her waiting destroyer and a tiny limp bundle on the ground. Tzana, sound asleep, Kien realized. Ela knelt, gently scooped up her sleeping sister, nuzzled her, then stood. She glanced around and nodded Kien toward the black outlines of the forest edging eastern Ytar.

The group hurried past numerous soldiers' encampments scattered through Ytar's burned-out foundations. As they crossed the eastern fields, Kien held the sword half drawn from the scabbard, readied against any pursuers. Strange . . . the sword's grip felt familiar.

Kien looked over his shoulder just as they entered the forest's darkness. No one followed. Satisfied, he lifted the sword and inspected the hilt in the predawn gloom. Beside him, Ela adjusted Tzana on her hip, then used the branch to illuminate the weapon in Kien's hands. Plain soldier's scabbard, but beneath its wrappings a gold-threaded grip and the pommel incised with a tower.

"My own sword!" His fighting sword. Kien grinned.

"Yes," Ela whispered. "The Infinite says we must hurry. The Istgardians are waking."

They moved on among the dark trees. Seeming eager to rush them along, Pet breathed down their necks. Kien wanted to swat the beast, but feared losing his hand. "Couldn't we ride? Your Pet could carry all three of us."

"We don't want to ride."

"And why not?"

"Because."

"Because . . . ?" Kien drew out the question and waited for Ela to respond. She didn't. Fine. She was suddenly as cryptic as the Infinite.

The branch glimmered as they wove between the big trees, rustling through ferns, avoiding mossy fallen snags. They entered a leaf-carpeted clearing, which was large enough to allow the murky predawn light to reach the forest floor. Kien tried again. "Where are we going?"

Ela stopped and tapped her branch against the ground. "Here."

"Why here?"

"Because."

"Ela . . ."

An archer stepped from behind one of the trees, the outlines of his bow and arrow aiming for Kien. "Put down your sword."

Keeping his movements slow, Kien crouched, gently placed his sword on the carpet of leaves, then stood, hands raised. "Don't kill me. I'm a Tracelander."

"So you say." The archer whistled a birdcall. Two more archers appeared, outlined in the shadows. His voice emboldened by his comrades' support, the first archer asked, "Who are you, sweethearts, and where are you going?"

"I'm Kien Lantec. I intend to fight for the Tracelands, then return to my family."

"And I am Ela Roeh of Parne. Your countrymen are planning to attack the Istgardians this morning, but they need to advance their plans. I must speak with your commanders."

"Why? You a spy? And what's that light you're holding?"

"No, I'm not a spy. I'm the Infinite's prophet, and this 'light' is my insignia. Listen, please! Tell your commanders that they have less time than they believe. They must attack now, not later this morning. As we speak, King Tek An is waking from a nightmare."

"You, a Parnian girl, expect me to snag my commanders from their meeting with your wild ideas? Not likely."

"If the thought makes you nervous, then snag only one! Fetch . . ." Ela paused, as if listening, then said, "Jon Thel."

Jon! Kien gawked at Ela. How could she know his best friend's name? He was sure he'd never mentioned Jon to Ela. "Jon's here?"

"Yes." Ela patted Tzana, who was beginning to stir. "The Infinite told me. Jon Thel is commanding his own troop."

Jon? Already commanding a troop?

"Fetch?" The archer looked as incredulous as Kien felt. "I'm no puppy. And Commander Thel is no one's footboy!"

Losing his patience, Kien snarled, "Can't you see we've got a destroyer breathing down our necks, you dog? Do you want him to stomp you to a pulp because you're arguing? I'm telling you this is important! Fetch Jon Thel *and* any other commanders you can muster!"

To Kien's amazement, the destroyer pressed forward, flattening his ears and snorting at the archer in a credible show of support. Kien almost believed the monster was siding with him.

The archer retreated several steps and spoke to his companions. "Watch these tricksters while I call for Commander Thel." He turned and ran off through the trees.

Tzana squirmed in Ela's arms, yawned, then smiled. "Pet! Where are we?"

Ela set the little girl on her feet. "We're with the Tracelanders now. You slept through our escape."

"Aw! Why didn't you wake me?" Tzana pouted.

"Because you're quieter when you're asleep," Kien teased. Tzana widened her eyes at him, indignant. Resembling Ela in a bad mood. He sighed. Best to say nothing more. He concentrated on fastening his sword belt in the light of the branch.

As Kien expected, Jon wasted little time. Following the archer's lead, he stalked into the small clearing so swiftly that his black cloak flared. He stepped into the branch's glow, garbed in a tunic, leggings, and boots all as black as his hair. In this severe attire, Jon Thel looked older than twenty-three years. And coldly suspicious of Ela and the branch. But the instant he saw Kien, he laughed. "It's really you!"

He grabbed Kien and shook him, grinning.

Until Pet nipped his arm.

Jon leaped backward and half drew his sword. "Is this beast a menace?"

"Only if he believes you're a threat to us," Ela murmured. "Please, sir, don't draw your sword."

"Us?" Kien frowned. "I'm now your destroyer's friend?"

Ela shrugged, avoiding his gaze. "In a way. I think Pet . . . Scythe . . . won't tolerate strangers using their fists on you. And he *won't* be happy if Commander Thel draws his sword."

Jon replaced his sword and stared at Ela. Kien cleared his throat. "Jon, this is Ela Roeh of Parne. I owe her my life several times over. And this is her little sister, Tzana."

Ela nodded to Jon and he bowed his head. "We are in your debt, Ela Roeh. Thank you." He smiled at Tzana's tiny shadowed form. Kien braced himself to stomp Jon's foot if he used the "Unfortunate" idiom, but Jon simply said, "Welcome. Ah. Here's the general. And my fellow commanders."

Other soldiers were gathering around now, their stances revealing less than friendly attitudes. The general, thin, silver-haired, and laden with a gold-garnished cloak, snapped, "Thel!" He made a vicious cutting motion, unmistakable even in the dim light. Jon grimaced and hushed.

Kien stifled a growl of frustration. Wasn't this general one of his own father's friends—a Lantec supporter?

The self-important man glared. "At least one of you is a spy, so you'll have to talk fast if you expect to live. Tell me, Ela of Parne, how did you learn of our battle plans?"

✦ 20 ✦

Ela studied the black-clad Traceland commanders and their general. Not a welcoming bunch, with their hands resting on sword hilts, their eyes narrowed in suspicion. Even Pet, hovering behind her like a menacing tempest, did not lessen their hostility.

Were all Tracelanders so foolhardy—or brave? Ela lifted her chin. "The Infinite, our Creator, has shown me what will happen during this battle."

The thin, silver-haired general's voice was dangerously quiet. "We don't believe in the Infinite."

"You don't have to believe, sir. You don't even have to obey. However, if you do obey, you'll survive. And, though their forces outnumber yours, you'll defeat Istgard."

"How?" one of the younger commanders asked.

His general interrupted, "Ror, we will not discuss tactics with a possible spy!"

"If you believe I'm a spy, then fulfill your duty," Ela dared the Tracelanders. Her words made the general and his men uncomfortable. Not one of them looked at her.

"She is not a spy!" Kien challenged his countrymen. "And the Tracelands does not condemn suspects without an investigation. The law states—"

"This is war," the general interrupted, his voice and gaze becoming remote. "War crimes are separate from civil charges, and we cannot trust her. Under such circumstances, I'm required to have spies executed immediately."

"No!" Kien stepped toward his countrymen and lifted his hands, pleading, "She's saved my life more than once, and the Istgardians have tried to kill her at least three times. You will not do this!"

The general glared at him. "Control yourself, Lantec! Did I say we would kill her now? This is a unique situation. She will be considered a prisoner until after the battle. If we lose, the Istgardians must deal with her. If we triumph, we'll investigate her then. Now, however, we don't have time."

"Thank you," Ela told the general. His silvered eyebrows shot up in evident surprise. Ela persisted. "Let's not waste time arguing about me. You *must* gather your forces and attack now to take the Istgardians by surprise so they'll make mistakes. Most of their charioteers are young. They'll fail to enter the battle *if* you take them by surprise. Please, just place me under guard and proceed with your attack immediately."

The general didn't respond to her plea. Instead, he motioned at the trio who'd initially kept watch over Ela and Kien. "Tie her and guard her."

Kien was shaking his head. "She's not a spy! Why won't you—"

"Kien," Ela pleaded, "arguing will only waste time, and you must take charge of . . ." She flicked what she hoped was an imperceptible nod and eye-roll toward Pet. The destroyer rumbled and stomped, sending a tremor through the soil. Ela growled and stomped in turn. She faced her gigantic protector. "Obey! Go with him now."

Pet huffed and lowered his big head. Ela caught his halter and tugged him toward Kien. She had to send the destroyer away before she was bound, lest the sight send Pet into a murderous fury. "Go! All of you, hurry. Why are you waiting?"

A wind rushed through the forest's canopy, with a roar that made everyone look upward. Ela heard what the Tracelanders did not.

Obey.

She smiled, watching the commanders disband, unknowingly scattered by a Supreme General they'd never heard, much less believed.

While the general barked orders to subordinates who lingered beneath the shadows of the trees, Kien stared at Ela. "You knew this would happen, didn't you?"

"Yes. Don't worry about me—whatever happens, I'll be fine. Now prepare yourself for battle. Your friend is waiting." She nodded toward Jon Thel, who was watching them from a short distance.

Kien scowled. "He wasn't much of a friend just now."

"Why should he defend me when he's not sure he trusts me? You must forgive him," Ela murmured. "As I have."

Kien exhaled, then nodded. He took her hand—still smudged with ashes—and bent to kiss her fingers like a courtier. So reverent—so sweet. She blinked away tears. If there'd been any hope of a future with him . . . Resisting the impulse to touch his whiskered face or to kiss him, Ela smiled. "Thank you. Be safe."

"You be safe," he commanded.

Pet nudged her and huffed into her hair. Ela turned to her gloomy destroyer and smoothed his black muzzle. "Dear rascal, don't worry about me—just go." Whispering, she added, "Protect him always! Even if you must disobey to save his life."

Pet sighed, gusting grain-scented air into her face.

She watched Kien walk away with Commander Jon Thel and her unhappy destroyer. The trio of disgruntled Traceland soldiers remained, watching her as if their lives depended on it. She'd expected their hostility, but her knees were shaking so hard that she had to cling to the branch. A reaction to her confrontation with the commanders? To the horrors of the coming battle and the uncertainty surrounding her death? Or to Kien's protectiveness and his reverent kiss?

Abruptly, she sat on the thick carpet of leaves and scooped Tzana into her lap. But the guards approached to tie Ela's ankles, then her wrists—bound behind her back, the branch in her grasp.

Wide-eyed, Tzana pressed her small, gnarled fingers on either side of Ela's face and begged, "What's happening?"

"The Infinite's will." Clenching the branch, Ela began to pray.

✦ ✦ ✦

Inside his tent, Jon shoved a bundle of garments at Kien. "Here. Use these. I have an extra helmet, but we're scouring the camp for spare armor."

Too angry to speak, Kien folded a thick, protective scarf around his throat, then secured a padded vest over his black tunic. Just as Kien finished the last knot, Jon's attendant returned and offered Kien greaves and a heavy, segmented coat of armor. A bit too small, perhaps, but they would do. Kien accepted the armor with a nod of thanks.

Kien fastened the greaves over his shins. As he knotted the armor down his chest and torso, Jon said, "You've made your point. I don't think you've ever remained silent for so long in your entire life."

"You haven't been in prison with me for the past few months." Kien buckled his sword belt.

While buckling his own sword, Jon said, "You have to forgive me sometime."

"So I've been told. Ela agrees with you."

"But you don't? Kien—"

"What!" Kien glared. "You might have offered a few words in her favor, Jon!"

"I knew it would be useless! None of the others favored releasing her, or didn't you notice? We were outvoted before either of us spoke. At least they've excused you."

"Perhaps your comrades have excused me, but they don't trust me, do they? And although *you* trust me, you don't trust Ela despite the fact that I've vouched for her honorable intentions. She's saved my life as well—not that it means anything."

"I'd never met her until now!" Jon retorted. "And she knows our battle plans. What was I to think, except to wonder if she's a spy?"

"She said those were your feelings. But I'd like to think my best friend has enough courage to speak his mind even if the odds are against him."

Hands fisted, Jon turned away. The tent remained silent except for the clatter of their armor as they fastened daggers to their belts, then laced on their helmets.

At last, Jon said, "You're going to have to deal with your anger, Kien. I'm not only your friend now; I'm your brother. Beka and I were married last month."

Jon and Beka? "What?"

"When I told Beka I'd be leaving with the army, she told me that if I left without marrying her, she would never speak to me again."

A year ago, Kien would have celebrated this news. Not now. He turned, prepared to leave the tent. "I wonder what Beka would think of you this morning." Before Jon could protest, Kien said, "We'll talk later. If we survive. If Ela survives."

"That's unworthy of you!" Jon crossed to the tent's entry. "Let's at least declare a truce in case we die."

Memories of his last squabble with Wal rose to the surface of Kien's thoughts. They'd parted angrily. And Kien hadn't forgiven himself for that anger—which had added to his grief after Wal's death.

Unworthy, Jon had said. A valid assessment. "You're right." Kien offered his hand. "I spoke in haste, and I'm sorry. But we're going to argue over this later. And if Ela is investigated, you *will* speak on her behalf. We'll insist she be defended before the Tracelands' Grand Assembly."

"Agreed."

Quietly, Kien asked, "How is my family?"

Jon grinned. "*We* arc fine—now that we know you've survived—thank you."

"You're persistent with this 'brother' detail."

"Naturally. It's in my best interests right now."

"Stay alive, Jon." Kien went outside and found Pet ripping the last leaves off a tender sapling. Numerous saplings and shrubs nearby were also stripped of leaves. Other soldiers, prepared for battle, were admiring the destroyer from a respectful distance. Kien acknowledged them with a touch to his helmet, then grabbed Pet's halter and muttered, "You don't like me, and I don't like you. But we're going to work together this morning. Do you hear me?"

The black monster huffed and nipped at another hapless sprout of a tree. Watching him chomp down the leaves made Kien's stomach growl. Loudly. Wonderful. He was going into battle half starved. He muttered to the Infinite, "If You're there, protect me, and Ela, please."

As if he had a right to expect any sort of response. Why should he? He was nothing to the Infinite. Anyway, most of the Istgardians would probably fight on empty stomachs this morning.

"Kien!" Jon pitched a small cloth bag at Kien the instant he turned. As Kien caught the bag, Jon said, "Work on this while we wait. That's half my morning's ration, so you'd better appreciate it. Are you ready?"

"Yes." Kien tugged open the bag and stared down at a clutch of smoked dried meat.

Was this a sign? An affirming answer to his unspoken test? "Thank You."

He shoved a chunk of meat into his mouth, chewed, then glared up at the massive destroyer in the grayish dawnlight. He'd seen enough Istgardian soldiers riding these beasts to know how they used the straps and handles built into a destroyer's elaborate body collar.

First, however, he had to climb onto the animal's back. And manage his shield. He swallowed, then said, "Jon! Give me a hand with my gear."

"Of course." Jon grabbed Kien's shield. "But if he bites me, you're on your own."

❧ ❧ ❧

Her bound arms aching, Ela sat beneath the sheltering trees that rimmed the huge field east of Ytar. Black-clad soldiers gathered nearby, their armor muted in the shadows. Ela shut her eyes and watched the silver-haired general motion the Trace-landers to take their positions within the forest. Contingents of archers stealthily scaled the stands of trees overlooking the encampments—as they'd done the evening before, Ela knew. She'd seen them in her thoughts. Felt them watching. Now she prayed for their safety.

Tzana shifted in her lap. Ela opened her eyes and rested her cheek against her sister's curls, then kissed her. "Do you remember the prayers Mother said with us each night?"

Just a bit grumpy, Tzana answered, "'Course I do!"

"Say them now." Ela bumped Tzana off her lap, adding another kiss. "When you run out of prayers, then say all the verses you remember from the ancient scrolls."

"Verses? What if I only remember one?"

"Just pray. And—" Ela softened her voice to a whisper—"I love you! Whatever happens—if I leave, or if I return and . . . fall asleep . . . just stay here. Watch our guards, and wait for Kien. Promise me?"

"I promise," Tzana whispered. "Are you going somewhere?"

"Yes. Wait here. I love you." Ela kissed Tzana again, then felt the branch taking fire, no doubt brilliant as white-hot metal against her palms. In her thoughts, the general raised his sword and signaled. A trumpet sounded. Ela tensed. She didn't understand what was about to happen—or exactly how she would die. Even so, she would obey her Creator. Sweat prickled over her skin. Branchlight glimmered through Ela's body, freeing her of the still-tied ropes around her wrists and ankles. Amazing.

Clutching the radiant branch, Ela stood and walked out from beneath the trees toward Ytar. The clouds roiled above her, their ash-darkness emphasizing the branch's dazzling light. Scattered cries and trumpet blasts echoed from the Istgardian encampments, yet no one paid her heed. How could they not see her?

The first ranks of the Tracelandic army dashed into the open field. The Istgardians' outcries multiplied.

Perfectly aligned with her vision, Ela saw the first green-fletched arrow slicing toward her through the air. "Infinite . . . !"

☩ ☩ ☩

Standing in the sumptuous green royal pavilion, Tsir Aun fought down the impulse to shake the heir and his father. The heir—with Tek An's slap mark livid on his cheek—sneered at the king. "You expected me to stay in Riyan like a coward? When I rule, no man will be able to say I've failed my country!"

Tek An cursed and struck his son again. "You will never rule! How can a disobedient cur be my son? You've walked into that Parnian's prophecy!"

A distant trumpet blast beckoned Tsir Aun. He strode from the tent, the blood quickening in his veins. "It's begun."

Confirming his fear, more trumpets sounded from Ytar's eastern boundaries. With distant cries of panic. "Tracelanders! To arms!"

Tsir Aun motioned to the king's servants, who'd been sent from the pavilion when he dragged the heir in to Tek An. "Get inside, immediately! Arm your king and the heir *now*!"

"Sir," the chief steward protested, "we've been ordered out."

Tsir Aun drew his sword and motioned the man and his quavering minions inside. "I've reversed that order! Arm the king and yourselves before I kill you!"

Tek An's servants hustled into the pavilion.

Istgard's noblemen were peering from their tents, some looking as if they'd just wakened, others dazed with terror. Tsir Aun roared, "Fools! Arm yourselves or die! Move! Hurry!"

His countrymen were full of nothing but talk. Their wobble-legged fear shamed him. The crown commander stomped through the encampments, snapping orders and unleashing destroyers, hoping the beasts would urge their pledged masters onward to save their lives.

Useless. Hadn't Ela warned him of Istgard's defeat?

"Infinite," Tsir Aun pleaded, "be with us." He felt his prayer's futility even as it left his lips. Heartsick, he shut his eyes and regathered his thoughts. "Be with those who trust You!"

A wave of sensing swept him. Opening his eyes, Tsir Aun saw the encampment altered. Huge, unfamiliar soldiers—seemingly made of light as dazzling as Ela's branch—were patrolling the camp, protecting some of the shaken Istgardians, but silently obstructing most.

Beads of sweat slithered down Tsir Aun's face. Before his eyes, Istgard's army was being judged and condemned. He could not stay with such a dishonored nation.

Would not.

He returned to his campsite and unleashed his destroyer. Instantly, the beast shied and fled in an unprecedented panic. "Wrath—!"

He tore after his terrified steed in a futile attempt to catch the beast. A blue-white blaze of light matched Tsir Aun's every move. Unnerved, the crown commander halted and looked up.

Into an immortal warrior's sun-brilliant face.

✦ 21 ✦

The green Istgardian arrow gouged the soil at Ela's feet, directly beside the branch's white-blue blaze. Did the branch draw the arrow to itself? Even in the vision, she'd been mystified. "Infinite?"

He didn't reply. Yet she felt His encompassing Presence.

The Infinite's warriors—messengers, Tzana called them—now controlled the battlefield. Each immortal soldier loomed terrifyingly large and lightning-fierce amid the battle, armed with swords matching the branch's almost unbearable glow. The Istgardians' destroyers were terrorized, clearly sensing their presence. If Ela hadn't known the celestial warriors were fighting for the Infinite, she would have died of fear the instant she saw them.

But the Infinite's warriors weren't going to kill her. Evidently something else would. But what? Ela composed herself with a breath and marched forward until the Infinite halted her.

Stand here, as My servant.

Obedient, Ela spiked the radiant branch into the damp soil, then stood within her insignia's light, weaponless, praying, and wholly dependent upon Him. As His servant.

More Istgardians entered the field, forming haphazard ranks, archers placed before the swordsmen. Another wave of arrows slashed through the air. Despite herself, Ela gasped, watching the arrows' flight—a grass-green downrush like a lethal waterfall.

Aimed at her. Her vision would hold, wouldn't it? When the weapons thudded into the ground directly in front of the branch, she exhaled. No doubt about it. The branch was drawing the arrows. Otherwise she would be dead or dying this instant. Words from the ancient scrolls unfurled in her mind. Give thanks to the Infinite, for He is good. His love is eternal. . . .

She tried to focus wholly on praises. To distract herself from the knowledge that she, the Infinite's servant, was the Adversary's target in this battlefield. An advantage to the jubilant Traceland swordsmen waiting to her left and right.

Unseen by either army, a luminous messenger swung his sword in a dazzling arc, directing the battle's next incident. Black and red Tracelandic arrows rained from the treetops at the field's northern edge onto the unsuspecting Istgardians. Scores of soldiers fell. Astride his destroyer, a nobleman screamed. Ela watched him clutch the black arrow's shaft in his side. He tore the barb from his flesh, screaming again, pouring blood as he fell from his groaning destroyer.

Ela continued to pray and await the initial charge, though she longed to shut her eyes, sickened by violence and carnage.

Again the messenger signaled to the Traceland's archers, slashing his sword downward. Fatal black hail cascaded from the treetops, striking most of the Istgardian soldiers along the battlefield's northern edge. Screams of agony rose from the wounded.

A wail lifted in Ela's throat, and she swallowed it hard. She wanted the battle to stop. Now. Let this instant stay as it was, forever, with no more men dying. "Infinite? Please?"

Child of dust, can you make their decisions for them?

"No, but . . ." Ela froze, watching another fragment of her vision spring to life.

An Istgardian swordsman charged toward her across the open space, his green cloak flaring, his sword lifted as he roared a battle cry. Shadows seethed and twisted around the man, revealing their malicious, ever-shifting spirit faces as they goaded him onward. The Adversary's deceivers. Was she—like the messengers—invisible to everyone else in this battlefield except the deceived ones?

Ela watched the man's approach, horrified. His eyes locked on hers in triumphant certainty of her death. She'd seen the Adversary's immortal deceivers urging him forward. She'd seen— "No!"

The messenger nearest Ela raised his powerful hand and motioned to Ela's would-be assailant. Just as the swordsman dashed within range to cut Ela down, a black and red arrow struck his neck, just below his ear. The one vulnerable gap between his helmet and body armor. Another arrow slammed against his side, knocking him to the damp grass. Eyes huge and shocked, breath rasping, he fumbled at the weapon fatally embedded in his throat. Until his eyelids went heavy, and his focus faded.

Surely now he saw the eternal fire he could never escape. Unable to cry, Ela mourned. If she could have collapsed, she would.

The messenger urged, "Be strong, and pray." Though calm, his powerful face reflected sorrow. The Infinite's sorrow. Ela breathed more prayers, feeling her Creator's love and aching concern for her, and for the men now falling beneath a black cloud of the Traceland's arrows.

Look, the Infinite commanded, as the messenger nodded toward the Istgardians following the royal banner, just visible at the edge of Ytar's ruins. *Even now, I will save them if they repent. As I would save Tek An. Yet, in his pride, he will prefer death.*

Ela watched the gold and green banner ripple in the rising wind. Tek An was entering the field, majestic on his destroyer, the heir riding another destroyer alongside him, their shields upraised against the Traceland's hidden archers.

Not all of the king's soldiers and noblemen were as cautious. The next hail of arrows decimated their ranks. Several destroyers fell. Others scattered, riderless, groaning as Pet did in deep distress.

The ground rumbled, its vibrations horrifyingly familiar. Pet . . . no, Scythe charged past. With Kien. Despite knowing the battle's outcome, Ela couldn't look.

She lowered her head, shut her eyes, and fulfilled her duty. Praying. Waiting to die.

✦ ✦ ✦

Grateful for the command to proceed, Kien pressed his booted feet hard into the leather-clad rungs of the destroyer's elaborate battle collar. "Ha! Forward, you monster!"

Every battle drill he'd memorized with Jon in his training for the army's reserves returned now, blade-sharp.

Jon's expression had been deathly serious as he issued Kien instructions before the battle:

They were to assemble in a crescent formation. The archers would have thinned enemy ranks and weakened them; whatever sunlight there was would be in the Istgardians' faces. And so would Kien. He and the other men must draw them into the field's center. . . .

Kien halted Scythe sharply before the battlefield's open space, making the beast leap.

While Scythe snorted ferocious threats, Kien watched the field. Istgard's destroyers—many now without masters—paced and turned in obvious uncertainty. Had they ever faced an enemy in battle who rode an Istgard destroyer? Evidently not. Scythe's opposition increased the Istgardian destroyers' confusion.

Gleeful, Kien muttered to his mount, "Tell them! We're going to pulverize their forces. They'll be defeated!"

Scythe's equine taunts redoubled as he paced, reared lightly, and tossed his massive black head, shaking out his long mane. Kien grinned. Obviously he was riding the master of destroyer bravado.

Kien kept his own challenge short and fierce. As Scythe continued to huff, Kien whipped out his sword and yelled, "Ytar!"

Alongside Kien, the black-clad Tracelanders roared and echoed his cry. "Ytar!"

Ytar. Wal. Kien's slaughtered servants. Ela . . . Kien clenched his jaw, thinking of all the lives the Istgardians had taken or threatened.

230

As Jon expected, the Tracelandic archers had done their work, thinning the Istgardian ranks enough to even the odds. But they hadn't counted on the riderless destroyers being thrown into chaos as if whipped by an unseen lash. Turmoil rippled through the Istgardian ranks as their unmanned destroyers fled herd-like, trampling nearby foot soldiers.

Odd. Were destroyers so easily routed?

Seeming eager to give chase, Scythe strained forward. "Not yet," Kien warned, holding him back. "Let the enemy come to us."

Around him, Kien's fellow Tracelanders were howling taunts, beckoning the Istgardians. King Tek An's banner neared, fluttering and wavering in the rising wind. No doubt Tek An was reacting like his banner, agitated by his welling fear.

"Come on!" Kien muttered beneath his breath.

How long could he keep this destroyer in check? Scythe's pacing and huffing increased. He reared. Kien dug his feet into the war harness's rungs, amazed he'd kept his seat. Yet the warhorse and his harness were perfectly suited for battle—easier to manage than Kien had suspected at first glance. "Steady," Kien soothed.

Just beyond the king's banner, Kien saw foot soldiers rushing to assemble the short towers used to hold their bolt throwers, tightly wound weapons resembling giant bows. Had Jon or any of the commanders planned for those huge bolt throwers?

As Kien was contemplating the best method for disabling the throwers, the Istgardian heir rode forward. Doubtless without the king's permission. He lifted his sword, bellowed a war cry, and signaled his countrymen to advance. Echoing their heir's battle cry, the Istgardians charged, their attack encouraged by the blaring trumpets.

Pulse quickening, Kien waited and studied the enemy's advance.

The Istgardian ranks frayed. The few noblemen riding destroyers abandoned their formations, while the foot soldiers behaved as individuals instead of a unit. Undisciplined fools!

Tracelanders and Istgardians met in a clattering press of shields and a ringing of swords. The sounds of metal impacting metal were punctuated by shouts of challenge and screams of agony. Several enemy destroyers merged into the clash. Sighting the nearest one, Kien pressed his knees into Scythe, guiding him toward the nobleman and his massive warhorse. "Go!"

The destroyer lunged, eager to obey. Caught in the battle's tide, two Istgardian foot soldiers veered toward them. Scythe bent his massive head, clamped his powerful jaws around one ill-fated man's arm, and flung him into a second soldier, clearing Kien's path.

Obviously alerted by the soldiers' flying bodies, the nobleman turned his destroyer toward Scythe and swung his longsword at Kien.

As Scythe fended off the destroyer, Kien parried the Istgardian's blade with the flat of his sword—so ferociously that the nobleman wavered in his seat. Pressing his advantage, Kien braced himself and swung his sword into the Istgardian's helmet. Stunned, the man reeled.

For Wal.

Kien plunged his sword into the nobleman's segmented plate armor, just as Scythe charged the enemy destroyer. Nobleman and destroyer screamed. Scythe gave Kien no chance to assess the damage. He kicked backward at a foot soldier, then brought Kien about to face another mounted Istgardian. Seeing the golden sash draped at a diagonal across this nobleman's chest, Kien gasped.

The heir.

"Die!" the young man roared. He swung his sword at Kien. Badly aimed. The blade glanced off Kien's armored shoulder.

Infinite! Within the frantic one-word prayer, Kien stabbed his blade at the heir's single visible point of flesh. His throat.

The heir's warhorse retreated. Scythe lunged. Kien's sword pierced its target.

Gaping in disbelief, the young man dropped his sword, then fell after it, silent.

A scream erupted behind him. "No!" Tek An wailed. "My son!"

Scythe dashed away from the king, mowing down more foot

soldiers, who cried out as they fell beneath his hooves. Kien leaned over the destroyer's harness. Surely someone would attack him to avenge the heir's death. Trying to anticipate his next confrontation, he scanned the battlefield. The Tracelanders had folded their army's crescent formation around the Istgardians discordant forces. The entire field was a seething mass of foot soldiers, clashing shields, and ringing swords.

A spear bolt flew past, startling Kien. If he hadn't been leaning forward . . .

He recovered, adjusted his grip on his sword, then urged Scythe onward.

✦ ✦ ✦

Weren't prophets supposed to face their visions?

Ela watched the battle become a massacre. Archers, still positioned in the trees, targeted any soldiers who dared to man Istgard's bolt throwers. The few remaining noblemen were attacked repeatedly until they succumbed and fell, despite their destroyers' valiant attempts to save them.

At last, the Tracelandic army encircled the Istgardian foot soldiers and began to cut them down. Exactly as the citizens of Ytar had been slaughtered. Tek An's banner swayed. Then fell.

"Tek An." Ela recalled his face and grieved. If only he'd forgotten his pride.

If only . . .

A trumpet blared. When the Tracelanders paused, the Istgardian survivors knelt, hands upraised in surrender. An expectant hush stole over the battlefield. The Traceland's general raised Tek An's shredded green and gold banner in his black-gloved fists. "Victory! For Ytar!"

A ragged cheer echoed from the fallen king's position, then grew until the Tracelanders were all whooping and celebrating. Unsettled, Ela looked around. Now? Wouldn't she somehow die now? The Infinite's messengers looked upward, then vanished within the blink of an eye, leaving her.

"Infinite? I don't understand! I saw myself lying dead and . . ."

Ela felt herself whisked from the field, into the trees. To her vision's end—to Tzana, kneeling where Ela had left her, huddled beside a bound, stilled form. The body. Ela stared at her lifeless mortal shell. So waxen, fragile. Had she died without realizing it? "Infinite?"

The instant she breathed His name, calming darkness overtook her, blotting out all sight.

A deep chill and unbearable weight summoned her to consciousness again. Exhausted and unwilling to move, Ela rested and breathed in the scent of dried leaves and damp soil. Her limbs ached. And the bonds chafed at her wrists and ankles. Still alive . . . How? Was she a mere vision within the battle? "Infinite. Who is like You?"

She strained to hear His voice. Instead, she heard only the Tracelanders celebrating, oblivious to the One who had given them this triumph.

Tzana nestled against Ela, then peeked at her, remarkably calm. "Are you awake?"

"Yes. It's good to see you." Ela wished she could hug her little sister. Dear, sweet girl. Obviously she'd obeyed Ela's commands. From the corner of her eye, Ela glimpsed the branch, pallid and sun-bleached, looking as age-worn and frail as she felt. The approaching thuds of hooves made her turn.

Pet. Scythe. Carrying the disheveled Kien toward her. Ela's very soul seemed to leap at the sight. Dear Kien! Safe . . . She longed to fling herself into his arms and hug him. *So* unprophet-like. Thankfully, she was still bound, unable to make a fool of herself. Even so, tears of relief stung her eyes.

Ela struggled, forcing herself to sit upright. Kien dismounted in a clatter of armor and weapons and half knelt beside Ela's feet. Pulling out his dagger, Kien cautiously sawed the cords from her ankles. "The general must be convinced you were correct. I'm granted permission to release you. Are you well?"

"No." Ela swallowed the painful lump in her throat. "But it helps—seeing you two unharmed."

"Just because there's no blood doesn't mean there are no wounds," Kien said, moving to free her wrists.

If only he knew. Why was she still alive?

Pet arched his black neck and leaned down to nuzzle Ela, obviously distressed by the rawness of her wrists and ankles. "It's nothing," she whispered. "I'm so glad to see you!" She rested her cheek against his big face, then hesitated. His muzzle was sticky. She caught a harsh, metallic scent and nearly gagged.

Tzana began to cry. "Pet! You're bleeding. . . ."

✦ 22 ✦

Finished with his tepid water, Pet nudged Ela with his dripping muzzle. Her tunic stained with blood-tinged water, inciting a pang of guilt.

Really, she should be on the battlefield now, tending wounded or digging trenches for the dead. But the Tracelanders had insisted Ela return to their encampment while they questioned the surviving Istgardians.

If she wasn't allowed to help the wounded, then she could at least see to Pet.

"Will he die?" Tzana whimpered. She clutched at Ela's tunic, her small face a fretwork of delicate wrinkles.

"No." Ela ran her hands over Pet's black coat. Her fingertips stagnated over a series of crusted patches. Drying blood from scratches. Beyond the cut mouth, he had no other wounds. His legs weren't swollen or warm. But coagulating blood met her every touch. Istgardian blood. Ela shuddered. "We need to wash him. And his collar."

She tugged at one of the large buckles securing the destroyer's huge black war collar. More blood. The collar's leather bands were saturated. A wave of nausea made Ela lean forward, hands on knees. Perhaps it was for the best she hadn't been allowed to tend the wounded.

"Ela." Kien's voice echoed to her from the trees at the clearing's edge. "Wait. Let me help you."

Her heart lifted at the sound. "Yes, please."

She straightened and eyed the Tracelander as he approached. Kien had removed his armor and doused his face and hair, banishing any blood. If his black garments were bloodstained, she couldn't tell. A mercy.

His gray eyes reflected fatigue. And sudden concern. "Are you about to be sick?"

"Not if I think of something beyond death and battles." Ela warred with queasiness as she reached for a second buckle.

Kien brushed away her hands. "I'll do that." Leaning into Pet's line of vision, Kien narrowed his eyes at the destroyer. "Don't bite me."

Lips curling, Pet bared his big teeth, as if considering Kien too disgusting to eat. Ela didn't dare look closely at those teeth. If she saw more blood, she would definitely vomit.

Oblivious to Ela's discomfort, Tzana giggled. "Pet, what a silly face!"

"We have to wash that silly face." Ela patted her way tentatively around the huge horse and stationed herself opposite Kien. The instant Kien opened the last buckle, she gripped Pet's collar and—on Kien's count—they lifted it off the destroyer.

Well trained, Pet bowed his big head and stepped backward without being urged. Ela and Kien set the collar in the trampled grass. Kien grimaced. "That will take days to clean."

If it could be cleaned. "I need to tend Pet first."

"He's 'Pet' again, is he?"

"For now." She couldn't think of Scythe. Death.

"Are you taking him to the river?"

"Yes." Cautious, she lifted a corner of the thick quilt on Pet's back. No blood. Of course, if there had been blood on this rider's quilt, it would have been Kien's. A horrible thought—her stomach twisted at the very idea. If Kien had died, she would have longed for death herself. She loved him too much to . . . "Oh my."

Kien raised his voice from the warhorse's opposite side. "What?"

"Nothing." Stupid, stupid prophet! She shouldn't allow herself to love him. Too late . . .

Kien helped her unfold the quilt to cover Pet's back, then circled the destroyer to face Ela. "I'll walk with you. The chief commander sent me away. It seems we're the topic of discussion right now. Our fates are being decided."

Avoiding his gaze, she gathered more rags and hoped she wasn't blushing. Silly, unprophetish behavior. Think! Consider the battle instead of Kien. Consider the general and his commanders trying to decide her fate. Ela spiked the branch in the center of the Tracelanders' encampment, picked up Tzana, then turned toward Kien. "Whatever the commanders decide to do with us, their decision won't have much effect. The Infinite's plans overrule theirs."

"Should I be reassured or alarmed?"

"Perhaps both." Yet *she* should be thoroughly alarmed. She was alive. And in love with Kien Lantec. Foolish, irresponsible prophet! Thankfully, Kien seemed preoccupied with leading Pet and lugging his grooming tools. Ela followed him down to the river.

"It's too soon after the battle to douse him in the water," Kien pointed out. "He might become colicky. Of course, I'm presuming he's actually a horse despite his size."

Pet huffed and swung away, slapping Kien in the face with his matted tail. Kien and Tzana laughed. Ela smiled and immediately felt guilty. How could she smile or think of love so soon after such an awful battle?

She set down Tzana, picked up the bucket, and went to the river's edge. Icy water lapped at her sandaled toes, making her gasp. Good. The chill might distract her from Kien.

Shivering, Ela returned to Tzana, Pet, and Kien. The Tracelander was nudging a rock loose with his booted foot. He grabbed the rock and traded Ela for the bucket in her hands. "Look. This is why the Istgardians wanted Ytar. These indicate the ores for our Azurnite swords."

Prophet

Glad to focus on a new subject, Ela studied the tiny blue gems embedded in the dark blue-gray stones. Similar to the yellow-green streaked rocks near Parne. Did Parne's soil contain valuable ores? "I knew the massacre was provoked by greed, but I didn't see these crystals." She quickly handed the blue-speckled stone to the eager Tzana.

As he swabbed Pet's face, Kien said, "Ytar was founded on the main path from Istgard into the Tracelands. If you look along the river, you'll see small holes carved into the sides of the riverbank—and you'll see traces of blue in the rocks."

"Blue traces? This is how the Tracelands was named," Ela realized.

"Yes. Blue traces in the stones also mark most of our main water supplies." Pet swerved away from Kien now, clearly lured by green shrubbery along the riverbank. Kien growled. "You lummox! Fine. Eat. Just stand still so I can wipe you down. First, let's uncover you."

As they removed Pet's quilt and draped it over a sturdy shrub, Ela said, "The ores enticed Istgard to invade Ytar."

"Exactly," Kien agreed. "We've found that these ores surpass all others for strengthening our swords and other metalwork. These new metals will bring great wealth to our country."

Glimmers of imagery slid into Ela's thoughts. Picking up a nubby rag, Ela began to wipe Pet's damp neck. "In addition to wealth, those ores will provoke envy from neighboring countries. You must do everything within your power to prevent your countrymen from becoming as proud and corrupted as the Istgardians have been."

Kien paused and stepped back to survey Pet's massive shoulder. He flicked a glance at Ela, then splashed Pet's shoulder with water. "Is that a hint that I'll eventually have enough power to persuade my countrymen to listen to me?"

"Something like that."

"Does this mean I'll become an assemblyman?" He didn't look altogether pleased.

Absorbed with new images, Ela paused, then smiled. "Your father will discuss your future with you soon. Listen to him."

"We don't always agree."

"This time you will."

Kien shook his head, swabbed Pet's sides, then went to rinse his rag and refill the bucket. He returned and continued scrubbing. "Are you saying I'll see my father soon?"

"Your parents and sister will receive the courier bird's message from the commander this afternoon. They'll be on the road before sunset because they're so eager to see you." Ela paused, reflecting on a portion of what she'd seen. "They've been desperately worried about you, of course. You have a lovely family." Though with a few troublesome qualities.

Kien paused his swabbing. "You've seen all this?"

"In bits and pieces, yes."

"Why in bits and pieces? Why not all at once?"

Ela winced at the question. "Because the Infinite knows I can't endure too many large visions. They're agony. Particularly if the subject matter's unpleasant."

"But you said I have a lovely family."

"Most of my visions aren't lovely—like those of the battle. Tzana!" Ela called to her little sister, who was meandering along the riverbank, evidently searching for more crystals. "Don't wander away. I'm too tired to chase you."

"Pet will find me," Tzana chirped. "Or one of the messengers." She stopped, as if remembering something. "What did the messengers tell you this morning?"

"Only to be strong, and to pray."

Tzana drooped a bit, mournful. "One waited with me while you were sleeping. I wished they'd stopped the fighting. I heard it."

Aware of Kien's raised eyebrows, Ela said, "They weren't there to stop the battle—only to help the Tracelands."

"Help the Tracelands?" Kien interrupted. "Forgive me, but whom are you discussing?"

Ela foresaw without a vision that this would be a recurring

conversation. "The Infinite's messengers. They also serve as His warriors. You couldn't see them, but they were with us this morning."

"They're bigger than Pet!" Tzana fluttered one small hand in an attempt to describe their height. As Pet wheezed, she said, "And they talk to me sometimes. Two of them guarded me in the desert while Ela was gone, and one pushed open a door for me."

"Pushed open a door?" Ela stopped. Tzana and a door . . . "Was that the day you took the branch from Eshtmoh's tomb house?"

"Uh-huh."

"I didn't see a messenger breaking that door." But it made sense. Infinite?

You weren't looking closely enough.

Obviously. Well, her brain had been addled by the vision of Ytar. "Tzana, how long have you been talking to messengers?"

"Um. Well, before, when I didn't know they were messengers, we never talked."

Not helpful. Ela persisted. "How many years have you seen messengers?"

"I don't know." Tzana became irritable. "They're just always waiting."

"She sees messengers from the Infinite?" Kien asked. "You both see messengers—warriors no one else can see?"

"Don't you dare call this Parnian whimsy," Ela warned. She opened her mouth to question Tzana again, but Pet charged into the river, his patience unmistakably spent.

"It'll be easier to clean him there—as long as he doesn't become chilled," Ela said.

"Agreed." Kien waded into the current. "But don't change the subject. Tell me about the messengers."

"Describing messengers can never do them justice." Ela pinned her mantle high around her neck and shoulders. She grabbed the pail and a rag, and waded into the waist-deep water, stationing herself on the side opposite Kien.

While Ela dabbed at her destroyer's scratches, Pet nosed the water as if testing it. Without warning, he raised his head, then lifted one massive hoof and splashed it into the water repeatedly. With such force that Ela was drenched in a storm of frothy waves and rippling currents. From his side of the destroyer, Kien yelled, "You scoundrel! We're trying to work."

Ela surrendered to the drenching. She heaved a bucketful of water over Pet's back.

Kien answered with a splutter and a bellow. "Prophets have terrible aim!"

"Evidently not!" Ela dashed another torrent over Pet's back.

"Hand over the bucket!" Kien started to wade around the destroyer. Pet flanked him, interceding for Ela.

A water fight ensued, with Pet as instigator, changing sides according to his equine whims. Pitting master against master. A clean skirmish with no victor.

"Infinite." Ela praised Him as she caught her breath. "Thank You!" She felt refreshed—outwardly at least. Why couldn't all squabbles be settled this way? And Kien had evidently forgotten about the messengers. A blessing. She was too tired for an interrogation.

"Ela!" Tzana shrilled from the riverbank. Ela turned and saw Tzana clamber to her feet, clutching her hoard of crystals while staring at the bank downriver.

Ela's breath stopped in her throat. A plaintive nicker reached her from a thicket of shadowed trees. Massive forms emerged.

Destroyers. They traversed the riverbank as a herd, their dark heads submissively lowered as they approached. Pet swung his head toward the herd, then sniffed. Languid, he drank from the river as if the herd was beneath his notice.

Ela waded toward the destroyers, intrigued. They all but begged for her attention. She'd never seen the gargantuan creatures adopt such an attitude of meekness.

Except on the morning Pet pledged himself to her service. Pledged . . .

"Infinite, no," Ela whimpered. She halted in the knee-deep water. "Not a whole herd."

Pity them.

A many-plied twist of emotions threaded into her soul. Loss. Pain. Confusion. Finding in Ela a source of undeniable strength. "They see You. Not me," Ela whispered to her Creator.

Yes.

Ela trudged out of the river. The herd clustered around her protectively, breathing down her neck, into her hair. Along her arms.

Sweat chilled on Ela's skin. She was going to suffocate, smothered by a herd of pathetic destroyers.

Be calm.

"Do I have a choice?"

· 23 ·

Despite his envy, Kien grinned as he waded from the river. Ela managed to extricate herself from the herd of destroyers, but she looked like a lost child on the verge of panic.

"Stop!" She lifted her hands at the herd. As one body, the destroyers obeyed, watching her with single-minded intensity. Ela seemed to make a decision. She squared her shoulders and straightened her mantle. "Follow me, all of you. But *no* licking me! And no squabbling."

"Is squabbling in a destroyer's vocabulary?" Kien called out, glad to tease her. Surely amusement would force his memories of the battle to the outermost fringes of his thoughts. He hoped.

Ela glared at him. "Oh, hush! They're not breathing down *your* neck, are they?"

Such feistiness. Her resilience was amazing. Kien was about to snap a suitable retort when Pet—Scythe—nudged his shoulder and snorted into his hair. The destroyer's next move—Kien imagined—would be to slobber on him. He lifted his voice toward Ela. "I see your point!" To Scythe, he muttered, "You're concerned, aren't you. A bit threatened by the herd?"

Kien saw Scythe blink. "Come on. You've no reason to worry—she loves you."

The destroyer sighed. He followed Kien from the river and waited patiently as Kien boosted Tzana onto Scythe's broad, dark back. Once she'd settled herself, the little girl beamed down at Kien, bright-eyed. "Now we have lots of Pets!"

"I wouldn't say that too often, Tzana. Scythe is looking a bit gloomy."

"He isn't happy that his friends came to play?" The child's face puckered with confusion. "I love my friends."

"Yes, you do. But I fear Scythe's nature isn't as generous as yours, young lady."

"His name is Pet," Tzana reminded him.

"He is your Pet, of course." But he was Scythe when Tzana wasn't listening. Kien drained water from his boots and gathered the destroyer's grooming tools. Ela seemed to have forgotten them altogether. She was walking away, leading the herd up the river-bank toward the encampment. Kien anticipated the shock on his countrymen's faces when the waterlogged little Parnian prophet led an entire herd of destroyers into their midst. "Let's hurry."

"Run, Pet!" Tzana clutched Pet's damp mane and whooped as he trotted beside Kien. But as the destroyer began to nip at various members of the herd, she scolded, "No! That's not nice!"

Kien noticed that not a single member of the herd offered Pet—Scythe—resistance. Indeed, they lowered their big heads and shied away from him. Scythe quickly assumed a swaggering gait. The bully. Evidently he'd designated himself as the herd's leader. After Ela.

"What am I going to do with them?" Ela asked when Kien caught up to her.

Ela's imploring dark eyes more than compensated for her bedraggled clothes and wet, tangled hair. Had any other Parnian prophet been adorable? Not likely. He grinned. "I presume you asked the Infinite for a solution."

"Yes, but He seems to be testing my patience. Evidently I must persist until He answers."

"Then persist."

"Can we keep them?" Tzana sounded thrilled by the prospect. Ela's expression became distant. Questioning the Infinite,

Kien guessed. Now and then, different destroyers nudged her, as if pleading for benevolence. She smoothed one's muzzle. Later, a second's black neck. Distracted, like someone trying to pay attention to one conversation while listening to another.

She was so absentminded that Kien feared she would trip over her own feet, causing the destroyers to stampede in a rush to help her. Well, he'd seen enough bloodshed. Kien adjusted the gear and steadied the girl with a hand to her elbow while they walked.

Ela didn't acknowledge him. But the destroyers were discomfited by his gesture. Over Tzana's protests, Scythe bit at several who seemed particularly upset with Kien. They retreated, rumbling low noises, expressing obvious concern.

As Kien hoped, their arrival in the Tracelanders' encampment created chaos—soldiers staring, pointing, retreating in alarm, calling out warnings. "Destroyers!"

Kien dropped his gear and pretended nonchalance, changing his wet boots for dry sandals. As soon as possible, he would return to Ytar and find his confiscated belongings.

Ela finally shook off her absentmindedness. She retrieved her branch and faced Kien's comrades. "When your general returns I'll be resting, but please send for me. I'll be with the destroyers. Tzana . . ." Ela motioned to her sister. "Nap time."

"Aw! I want to play with our pets!"

"Believe me, you'll see them the instant you open your eyes."

Disappointed, Kien watched Ela cross to the clearing. She evidently planned to sleep amid a protective ring of destroyers.

Not a bad idea. He nudged Scythe. "Stay here, you bully, and keep watch while I rest."

Scythe grumbled.

✦ ✦ ✦

"Order them off," the general told Ela. He and his attendants looked past her, clearly unnerved by the herd of destroyers standing guard in a crowded semicircle behind her.

"I can't, sir. I'm sorry." Ela shifted the branch in her hands. Surprising that she felt its inward warmth, because the destroyers were radiating such heat from their nearness that it surrounded her like a sultry cloak. "They're overly eager to protect me. You'll simply have to speak graciously and look pleasant. Otherwise they'll become difficult."

The general smiled. "Is that a threat?"

"It's the truth." Ela didn't return his smile. He was staring at the destroyers again. She cleared her throat. "You were planning to tell me that I'm free to go or stay, as I please."

Silvery eyebrows raised, the Tracelander asked, "Are you sure?"

"Do you deny it?"

He exhaled. "No. We gathered testimony. You're acquitted of being a spy. However, Istgard's surviving commanders have asked to speak with you and Ambassador Lantec. Therefore, if you are planning to leave us—with your herd—I'd prefer you delay your departure."

Istgard's surviving commanders. Ela sighed. The battle's losses weighed upon her spirit like stones. In years to come, would the Istgardians blame her for their dead? For the destruction of their kingdom? She pulled herself back to the present. "Yes, the survivors. . . . The crown commander, four landholders, and three minor commanders."

"Who told you?" The general's edginess provoked a stir among the destroyers.

Ela lifted the branch and called over her shoulder, "Be still!" Obedient, the destroyers all but froze in place, though she could feel their collective breath.

Gently, the Tracelandic leader observed, "They obeyed you perfectly just now. Tell me again why you can't send them away. I'm convinced you've kept them here to intimidate us."

Be patient, she reminded herself. Tracelanders knew almost nothing about destroyers. "Sir, if I send this herd away, they'll believe they have no masters. They were created to serve. If they cannot protect a master, they'll soon turn wild and live up to their name, destroying everything in their path. Knowing this, sir, tell me . . . what should I do?"

His voice softening further, the general said, "Do what you've wisely chosen to do."

"Thank you, sir." Ela shifted, feeling destroyer-induced sweat slither down her back. "As for your request, I'll listen to Istgard's commanders, but I've little to say. And regarding your question— how did I know which Istgardians had requested a meeting?—our Creator informed me of their current plans."

Now the leader's smile was cynical. "The Infinite. Again."

Ela answered his smile with her own. "Yes. The Infinite. Always. And while you're in such a good mood, General, I wanted to ask you . . . How many Tracelanders died in this battle?"

"You claim to be a prophet. Don't you know?"

"I know *you* don't know, sir. But never mind. I'll tell you. None. Not one of your men died—though a few are wounded and will recover."

The Tracelander cast a look at one of his aides. The man nodded. "She's correct, sir."

Ela didn't wait for the general to respond. "How many from Istgard died, sir?"

The general glanced at his nearest attendant. "With permission, general," the aide offered, "we're still counting."

"So you've won an impossible victory. Yet you were outnumbered," Ela reminded the general. "What chance did you actually have, sir, unless the Infinite gave you the battle?"

The general remained silent, his lips pressed tight as if restraining several hundred responses to her question. Ela sighed. "One more thing, sir. These destroyers each need their own master to care for them. Masters they can protect in return. In three days, the Infinite will chose their new owners from among the Tracelanders."

Skepticism etched the general's features. "Your Infinite will select new masters for these destroyers?"

"Yes. He will choose." The branch gleamed in Ela's hands, a bright warning. "I *won't* be bribed or threatened."

"Of course not." He wasn't smiling. "Three days. You are our honored guest until then, Ela of Parne."

He would rather she left this instant, Ela knew.

But, like Kien and every other Tracelander, he must learn of the Infinite. And be tested.

✦ ✦ ✦

Under the general's stern gaze, with the Tracelandic army looking on, Kien faced Istgard's commanders. Why was Ela standing off to the side like a mere spectator? She'd been at the center of this conflict since the day she'd set foot in Riyan.

Of course, being trailed by forty-one destroyers wasn't helpful in conducting orderly meetings. Scythe alone—looming jealously over Ela's shoulder—was a huge distraction.

Moreover, Ela had that half dreaming, pondering expression. A sign that she was, most likely, conversing with the Infinite yet again.

The highest-ranking survivor stepped forward. Tsir Aun. Shadowed by his mournful destroyer, he looked older. Exhausted and clearly conscious of his defeated status. He bowed to Kien. "Ambassador."

"Tsir Aun." Kien offered him a smile. "I am pleased to see you."

"Thank you, sir." The crown commander's tone was dust-dry. "Likewise, I'm pleased you see me."

Subdued chuckles rippled through the nearest onlookers. Even the general smiled. Kien appreciated Tsir Aun's spirit. Bitterness would have been perfectly understandable from the proud Istgardian. Even expected. However, the crown commander obviously chose to face humiliation in a civilized manner.

Wholly dignified, Tsir Aun lifted an ornate baldric and sword in his hands. "Istgard has surrendered. We acknowledge defeat. In addition, we acknowledge that you and your servants suffered at our hands. Please, accept the king's sword with our sincere apologies."

Kien stared at the sword. Its richly embellished goldwork was sadly familiar. "But this was General Tek Juay's weapon."

"Yes, sir. The king appropriated it for his own use before battle.

Therefore, because you represent the victors as much as those our king victimized, we agreed to offer this to you."

"Thank you." Kien accepted the weapon with a bow. "I'm honored. I respected General Tek Juay above all men in Istgard."

"He would have been delighted." Tsir Aun's answer was polite. But he hesitated. Shifted his stance. Took a deep breath.

Kien frowned. Why was the crown commander suddenly so nervous? Hadn't he just successfully faced what must be the most demeaning military experience of his life?

"Sir," the Istgardian began abruptly, "you are a Lan Tek. A direct descendant of the dynasty which produced the Teks."

"Yes," Kien agreed. He squelched the instinct to step back. Every gaze, particularly the general's, suddenly sharpened. Hardened. Fixed on him. "But that was seven generations past. It's unimportant."

"No," Tsir Aun argued, unnervingly deferential. "The Lan Tek clan is vital to us now. Our king is dead. His son is dead. His brother is dead. This morning, we buried Tek An's cousins. Every male directly descended from Istgard's royal line is dead. Except you. And your father."

Kien fought lightheadedness. And won. "What are you saying, sir?"

"You are our logical choice. We ask you to reinstate the Lan Tek dynasty."

No. Kien shut his eyes. Infinite, won't You advise me? His silent plea for divine counsel was met with a waiting silence. An awful sense of heaviness pressed into Kien's being. Obviously, this choice was his alone. And he did not want to make this decision. Infinite!

Kien restrained himself. Opened his eyes. Shook his head. "I cannot and will not be your king. After everything I've suffered in Istgard, I would be unable to rule impartially." As the crown commander started to protest, Kien cut him off with an uplifted hand. "I have neither love nor loyalty for your country, Tsir Aun. Please, accept my decision."

251

"Then, sir," one of Istgard's lesser commanders objected, "What shall we do? We have no king!"

"Therefore you have no kingdom!" Kien snapped. "Start from that perspective, sir, and make the best of it! Because I refuse to become your king. I refuse your offer in my father's name as well—the Lantecs want nothing to do with Istgard."

Ela's clear, low voice cut through the shocked silence following Kien's outburst. "This morning, Riyan woke to find the king's tarnished statue shattered, fallen beneath the waters in his palace's courtyard. They know he is dead. All Riyan seeks white mourning robes."

The surviving Istgardians shuffled and whispered among themselves. Ela raised her voice further. "With respect, Commander, Istgard's leaders will form an assembly similar to the Tracelands' government. Already, judges and councilmen have spoken to General Tek Juay's daughter, offering her their support to avoid anarchy."

Kien seized this opportunity. "Tek Lara is no fool. And she is a Tek—descended from your kings. Trust her." To emphasize his support for Lara, Kien offered Tek Juay's sword to Tsir Aun. "Please, give this to Tek Lara with my sincere regards and blessings."

Blessings? Not a word he'd used before. He counted it toward fatigue. No, to the Infinite.

Tsir Aun's wearied face eased with something close to a smile. "Thank you. After we've buried our dead, I'll convey your message."

Although Tsir Aun was placated, Kien realized the Tracelanders were whispering among themselves. He, Kien Lantec, had refused Istgard's crown. Not only for himself, but for the Tracelands, and for his father—a man known for his love of power.

He'd made a mistake. No, not simply a mistake. A colossal blunder.

Father was going to disown him. Before beating him to death.

✦ 24 ✦

Kien blinked his eyes hard in an attempt to clear his vision and shake off his fatigue. But it was a waste of time. Dejected, he stared up at the tent's expertly stitched leather canopy. The few snatches of sleep he'd caught last night were consistently halted by variations of one nightmare.

Father tossing him from the top of the Lantec lookout tower.

Father holding him beneath the ocean's incoming tide.

Father, quite self-certain, running Kien through with a sword.

Jon strode into the tent, his dark eyebrows raised. "Any sleep?"

"Not enough." Kien forced himself to sit upright on his pallet. "They'll arrive today. I never thought I'd dread being reunited with my family."

Digging through his gear, Jon said, "Well, from what I've been hearing, half the army thinks you're a hero for rejecting Istgard's crown. The other half thinks you're a fool for rejecting it. And everyone is certain your father will try to kill you."

"What do you think, Jon?"

"You're dead. Unless you talk your way out of it—and run faster than your father." Jon shook out a clean tunic, then grinned at Kien. "By the way, thank you."

"For . . . ?"

"Denying your father absolute power over an entire country. By comparison, you've made me the favorite son."

253

"I'm sure you're right."

Jon shrugged into his tunic. "Get up. If you're going to die, you ought to find some clean clothes and make yourself presentable."

"Not until I've helped Ela with the destroyers."

"Huh. Grooming those monsters and keeping them out of mischief is taking most of your time."

"Working keeps me from thinking too hard about the confrontation with my father."

"What argument can you—ah!" Jon stumbled and fell onto his cot as if he'd been shoved. A dark form pressed into the tent, almost lifting the leather and wood structure from its pegs.

Pet. Scythe—whoever he was—suddenly took up half the tent's interior. Kien glared at him. "Out!"

The destroyer sniffed at Jon, as if deaf to Kien's command.

"Haven't you taught this monster obedience?" Jon demanded. Scythe grazed dangerously close to his ear. Jon covered his head. "He's a menace—a thug on hooves!"

"He understands name-calling," Kien warned.

Too late. Scythe bent, clamped his big teeth on the corner of Jon's cot, lifted it straight up in the air, and dumped Jon onto the dirt floor. "Hey!" Jon yelled.

Kien bolted from his pallet toward the destroyer. "Out! Now! Do you hear me? Obey!"

Huffing, Scythe retreated, Jon's cot still clenched between those huge equine teeth. Kien grabbed the cot's frame. "Drop it! Are you arguing with me? You can't eat this—drop it!"

Scythe released the cot, sending Kien to the floor, with the cot landing on his chest. Before Kien caught his breath to yell, the destroyer backed out of the tent. But his huge shadow blocked the morning light from the entry.

Kien wanted to throw something at him.

However, the horse might throw something in return. Like Jon.

The unwitting potential missile stood, dusted off his tunic, and shook his head at Kien. "Are all destroyers like this in the morning? Invading tents, tasting people, and stealing furniture?"

"Not just in the morning." Kien straightened Jon's cot and surveyed Scythe's impressive teeth marks. "Think carefully before taking on one of the beasts."

Scythe's grumble echoed through the tent's entry flaps, which then rippled with the whoosh of an offended destroyer sigh. Jon laughed. "That settles it! I'm bidding for one. Hopefully your prophet-friend has forgiven me."

"If she said she forgave you, then she has." Kien grabbed his boots and began to dress. "But that's no guarantee you'll be chosen." He dug through his reclaimed clothing chest for a cloak and his sword. Scythe's persistent presence bothered him. Why was the brute lurking around him instead of guarding Ela? "I'm going to see if any other destroyers are loose in the camp."

"Alt is cooking rations. Take your share now, or you'll miss them altogether."

"Inspiration to hurry," Kien muttered. Ela's prison cooking was better by far. He flung on his cloak, marched outside, and stared the glum destroyer in the eye. "Why are you here?"

Scythe whisked his tail and grunted as if Kien's question was ridiculous. He shoved Kien toward the field where Ela's herd usually passed the night.

"Worried about her, eh? Though if she's in genuine danger, you'd be defending her, not nagging me." Kien smoothed the monster's black neck. "You have my attention. We'll go—but let me bring her some food."

If rations could be called food. Jon's servant, Alt—scrawnier than a cook should be—was hunkered by a fire, stirring a small kettle of mush. To be served with dry bread and dry meat. Surprise.

Alt grinned at him. "You takin' food to those girls?"

No. Not food. Rations. "Thank you, Alt."

The man whistled a cheerful tune through his teeth as he plopped a generous double ration into a metal bowl. He tossed bread and dried meat into a bag, then handed Kien a metal spoon. "You'll return the spoon, right? Destroyers're eatin' the wooden 'uns."

"Sorry. I'll see that you receive new spoons." Followed by Scythe, Kien crossed the encampment and strode to the destroyers' field. The herd was moving in numerous, roughly elliptical rings arranged like a flower's petals. At the rings' outer edges— along the field's perimeter, the destroyers grazed, tussled quietly with each other, relieved themselves, munched on luckless shrubs, then returned to their unseen focal point at the rings' center. Ela?

"Why am I not seeing her?"

Scythe huffed in clear aggravation. He bullied his way through the herd, leading Kien to Ela.

A zing of fear jolted Kien. Why was she on the ground? Was she ill? Aware of the destroyers eyeing him suspiciously, Kien approached Ela. She was curled up on a pallet beneath a quilt and an oilskin tarp. With Tzana and the branch tucked beneath her limp arm.

Both girls were sound asleep, oblivious to the morning light and the unhappy herd.

Kien smiled at the sight. He longed to wake Ela, but no doubt the destroyers would attack him if he touched her while she was clearly so defenseless. She was certainly the most well-chaperoned girl in the Tracelands. A pity. He could only imagine waking her with a kiss. Several kisses. Or more . . .

Scythe bumped Kien from his enticing reverie. The orphaned destroyers drew nearer, some eyeing Kien, most watching Ela. Did they want him to wake her? That was it. They were fretting because she wasn't alert and tending them. Kien shook his head and whispered, "Let her sleep! You've worn her out—all of you."

One rude young upstart nosed his dark muzzle toward the metal bowl in Kien's hands. Kien shoved the rations beneath his cloak. "Ssst! Back!"

Scythe added silent threats of his own, charging the beasts nearest Kien.

Heaving rumbles of low complaints, the destroyers retreated, allowing Kien space to sit near Ela and Tzana. He envied the girls their sleep. Ela looked so small and sweet beneath the quilt.

Kien admired the delicate lines of her face and throat. Her dark hair frayed in beckoning tendrils across her smooth cheek. Her breath stirred Tzana's dark wispy curls. The child shifted slightly, rested her swollen knuckles on the branch, then stilled again.

Kien fixated on the child's gesture. Was Tzana the only other person allowed to touch the branch? Interesting.

Even now, Kien felt the shock of his bare fingers passing through the branch as he and Ela stood in King Tek An's glittering audience chamber, its light and warmth evading his grasp.

Was that the instant he'd begun to wonder? To silently consider the Infinite?

His mouth only forming the words, he asked, "Will You ever speak to me?"

He listened. And heard only destroyers shuffling about, moving further afield to graze on the tender grasses and shrubs. A breeze sifted through the new-leafed trees. Beyond these few sounds . . . nothing.

Quiet. Calm.

Silence.

✦ ✦ ✦

Ela drew in a long breath, reluctantly allowing wakefulness to intrude upon the first deep sleep she'd had for weeks. Tzana's head, pillowed on Ela's arm, had slowed the blood enough that Ela's arm felt like a dead weight. An axe could fall, and she wouldn't feel it sever her limb.

Alarming idea. Like a glimpse from a vision. What had she been dreaming? Images nagged at the edge of her thoughts but refused to reveal themselves fully. Unsettling situations. Vague recollections of pain and fear. Her own pain and fear. For the hundredth time, surely, she wondered why she'd survived the battle at Ytar. What would happen now? Another duty for the Infinite, no doubt. Perhaps fatal. What would it be? "Infinite?"

Look around.

Ela braced herself and gently tugged her dead arm from

beneath Tzana's sleeping form. She sat up and rubbed her shoulder as she looked around. A body! She recoiled. Wait. Not a body. Kien, sleeping in the grass, more than an arm's length from her pallet. A metal bowl, half concealed, showed beneath the edge of his dark cloak.

Had he brought food for her and Tzana?

Dear man. What a thoughtful gesture. She smiled at his rumpled hair, his whisker-stubbled face, his slight frown. Was he concentrating on a dream? His mouth twitched. Adorable. Until he gasped and flinched in his sleep. His eyes flashed open, wide and gray. Shocked.

He'd caught her staring. Hoping to distract him from her mortified blush, she said, "Thank you for the food."

Kien blinked, then rubbed his face. "You haven't eaten it yet."

Despite his joke, the young man looked dazed. Ela studied him, cherishing his sleep-tousled look. "Did you have a nightmare?"

"Yes. Asleep for one instant and my father pulverizes me with a hammer for denying him Istgard."

"He won't kill you."

"But he's going to be furious."

"You'll survive. And so will he."

"So you say."

Ela chuckled. "The Infinite said so. Not me."

She saw Kien's interest sharpen. "What else did He tell you?"

"That you must be honest with your father about *everything*. Respect him. But don't give in to his demands or the Infinite will make you regret your cowardice."

"That's not terribly soothing." Kien sat up and straightened his cloak.

"I'm not here to soothe you."

"I wish you were." He responded with a sudden gleam in his eyes and that warm grin—positively dangerous.

Prophets must not be enticed. Seduced. Ela gave the Tracelander her most severe look. "Do not be charming."

"Can you be charmed?" He leaned toward her.

258

"Stop!" Ela lifted a warning hand. She'd rather not test his question. She'd fail. But what was she thinking? She'd already failed! Why, oh why, had she fallen for him? They couldn't possibly have a future together. Or could they? Might she be a prophet *and* . . . Kien's wife?

Blushing at the thought, Ela nudged Tzana awake. She needed an ally as she chased off Kien. "*Ambassador*, give me the food, then leave before there's talk that you've been lingering here. Your family will arrive soon."

"Killjoy." His gloom returned, but he smiled and handed her the bowl and a small bag.

Tzana sat up. "What did you bring us?"

"Rations, little one. Forgive me." He stood and bowed, then strode away.

Ela hoped she had the strength to resist him. *If* she was supposed to resist him. She hesitated, afraid to question the Infinite. What if she didn't like His answer?

By now the destroyers were circling her, showing interest in the bowl's contents. Tzana frowned and waved her tiny gnarled hand. "Stay away! This is ours!"

The herd obeyed.

✦ ✦ ✦

It was good to feel rested. Not wrung out like a rag fit for nothing. Ela hummed a lilting Parnian lullaby as she brushed the smallest destroyer—a female, who was elegant, yet still impressively large. Finished with her humming and the grooming, she smoothed the destroyer's glossy dark mane. "You're lovely!"

The destroyer tossed her head, seeming pleased. Good. Ela had been worried about the creature's persistent misery after the battle. Obviously she truly loved and mourned her master. "What was your battle name?" Ela wondered aloud.

Again, the female tossed her head, her mane shimmering and flowing like liquid. It reminded Ela to comb her own hair, still damp from her jaunt to the river.

She'd just finished tying off her braid when Tzana—perched on Pet—called from the edge of the field. "Ela! Visitors!"

Ela flung back her braid, retrieved the branch, and wove her way through the herd to the field's edge. The general. And one of his aides, who carried a tray.

What? A cordial visit from the general? Infinite?

When silence met her question, she prayed for dignity. And for His words, which would undoubtedly be more significant than her own sarcastic inclinations. The general halted within earshot, but still a safe distance from the destroyers. Ela bowed her head. "General."

The general offered Ela a formal bow in return. "Good morning. Forgive my intrusion, but I would like to know your plans concerning these destroyers. Today is the third day."

He'd remembered. Was he taking her more seriously than she'd believed? Ela nodded. "Thank you for asking, General. Yes. At midafternoon, the Tracelanders may assemble here and—one-by-one—request a destroyer. The Infinite will select those He deems deserving of such responsibility. Anyone may ask." A mental image forced her to add, "Including you."

Really? The general too? Infinite . . .

Behave.

Ela sighed unspoken agreement. "Did you have another question, General?"

"My men have been concerned about your well-being," the general said, noticeably ill at ease. "I too have been troubled. Granted, I am . . . strict . . . but not without . . ."

"Honor," Ela finished at a divine prompting. Honor? Seriously? She quashed her impulse of rebellion. Naturally, the Infinite saw what was hidden from her own mortal gaze.

The general blushed. "For one so young, Ela of Parne, you are an inspiring person."

Despite herself, Ela thawed toward the self-conscious Tracelander, giving him a genuine smile. "Thank you, General. However, I'm nothing. Any of my actions that are worthy or inspiring are from the Infinite."

"My men and I disagree." The general motioned to his aide, who stepped forward with a tray. "We hope you . . . and your sister . . . will accept this noon meal—the best we have in camp. We regret we haven't offered you more."

So much for sarcasm. "Thank you, General."

✦ ✦ ✦

Kien caught glimpses of Ela throughout the morning. Leading Tzana and the herd to the river. Grooming some of the destroyers. Braiding her hair. And talking to the general, who stood at the edge of the field, watched by suspicious destroyers. Kien tensed. Was the general causing Ela trouble?

Finished shaving, certain he was outwardly prepared to greet his parents, Kien decided to satisfy his curiosity. If he gathered a bit of destroyer slobber in the process, so be it.

He found Ela and Tzana sitting on their protective tarp, with an ornately carved wooden tray between them. On it were delicacies Kien hadn't seen in months: glazed squab, fresh green herbs and vegetables, soft bread. A fruit tart.

Torture.

Ignoring the picnic, he asked, "Are you well? Was the general polite?"

"Yes, he was most polite. We exchanged compliments, and he offered us this tray as an apology." Ela looked uncomfortable. As if she'd learned a scaln was friendly.

"We have lots of food," Tzana piped up. "Do you want some?"

Manners. "Thank you, little one. I appreciate your offer, but the general's gift was meant for you and your sister." Surely he'd passed some sort of cruel test. Kien focused on other distractions—namely the warhorses. "If I bid for a destroyer, which one will be mine?"

"You've ridden him already." Ela picked at a squab. "There's no reason for you to bid. But we can't discuss him now." She glanced toward Scythe, who was muscling a path through the herd. The big destroyer greeted Kien with a jarring nudge, forcing Kien to step back.

Ela was giving him Scythe? Impossible. Why? He sent her a questioning look.

But she didn't notice. Her expression was distant now, as if listening to the Infinite.

And her eyes, her lovely eyes, became so sorrowful that Kien stared.

25

Mother always complained that Father drove his light chariot too fast. Today was no exception. If anything, Rade Lantec was surpassing his own record, raising a cloud of dust that heralded his approach more surely than any banner.

Dread warring with pride, Kien admired his father's skill as he drew his pair of matched gray horses to a standstill amid the ruins of Ytar.

With all the assurance of a man used to being obeyed, Rade bounded off his chariot without looking back. His horses would wait. Underlings would appear from nowhere to tend the poor beasts and guard his belongings. Woe to anyone who dared to disappoint him.

Like his son.

"Kien!" Rade beamed and held out his arms, his brown eyes crinkled by a warm grin.

Perhaps for the last time, Kien stepped forward and hugged his father, then gasped at Rade's ferocious, unending grip. Finally, Father thumped Kien's back and released him. Kien saw hints of tears in Rade Lantec's eyes. A staggering sight.

"You look well for someone we'd given up as dead," Father joked. He wiped his eyes.

Kien hoped the gesture was sincere, not for show simply

because the Traceland's finest soldiers were watching. "I'm glad to see you, sir."

Father gave him another evidently fond wallop on the shoulders, then turned to greet the general. "Rol. Congratulations—you've won a great victory."

"Don't congratulate me until we succeed in having the captives returned to Ytar," the general cautioned. "We're depending upon your son to assist us in the negotiations."

Kien managed a smile. Kind of the general to mention negotiations to him.

"Kien!" A light, feminine voice called to him from a distance. Beka in a sky-blue tunic and black mantle was waving to him from a large chariot, evidently guiding the horses one-handed. Mother stood beside her, slender and elegant in black. Apparently speechless. Crying genuine tears. Kien hurried to meet them, leaving his father to talk with General Rol.

The instant the big chariot lumbered to a standstill, Kien helped his mother descend. Ara Lantec clung to him and sobbed, trembling. "Oh, my dear boy! You're alive! Oh, you're alive!"

Father hadn't been joking? They'd thought he was dead? Kien kissed his mother's hair. "Yes, Mother, I'm alive. Don't cry. I love you." Wrong thing to say. She cried harder.

"What about me?" Beka demanded, tapping his shoulder. He freed one arm and gave her a hug. She returned the hug, kissed his cheek, and teased, "*I* knew you were alive. Where's Jon?"

"Here," Jon said from behind Kien. Beka turned.

"Oh." She sounded worried. "Why is Father angry?"

✦ ✦ ✦

"You . . . gave up . . . a crown!" Father whirled around in Jon's tent, so livid with rage that Kien feared he would have a seizure. "Without discussing the matter with me!"

"Yes."

Rade Lantec grabbed the front of Kien's tunic and shook him. "Are you insane?!"

Resisting the impulse to defend himself and possibly heighten the confrontation, Kien answered quietly. "No. I knew that if I accepted the crown it would be disastrous."

"Not if I'd been advising you!" Father snarled. "It would have been—"

Civil war.

Kien jumped. "What?" He looked around. No one else was in the tent, but he'd heard a voice. As if someone were standing at his shoulder, offering counsel. Wise counsel. Infinite?

" 'What' nothing!" Rade seethed. He flung Kien back several steps, then turned away, his well-tended hands clenched in fists.

"Father, if I'd accepted the crown, Istgard would have been plunged into civil war."

Crimson-faced, almost purpling, the elder Lantec roared, "You can't possibly know that!"

"I do know. The Infinite said it would happen." Wait. He'd mentioned the Infinite. Kien exhaled. Oh, why not? Bring out everything now. No secrets. If Rade Lantec was about to kill his reprobate son, then make the event worthwhile. "And if the Infinite says something, it's true."

"The Infinite?" Father hesitated and cast a furtive glance around the tent as if scanning for shadows of eavesdroppers. Then he hissed, "Stupid . . . ! I cannot believe I'm hearing this! You're following Parne's Infinite, like some rustic?"

The truth. Ela had warned him that he must tell the truth. Kien lifted his chin. "Yes."

"Fool!" Father shoved Kien and sent him crashing into a storage chest. As Kien twisted around to pick himself up, Rade bellowed, "Not while I live! Forget that idea or you're no longer my son."

"I can't. You may disinherit me if—"

"Kien!" Jon raced into the tent, dragging the shocked Beka with him. As he hauled Beka to the side farthest from the entry, Jon cried, "Your destroyer is coming!"

"No!" Kien scrambled to his feet and rushed to his father.

The huge black beast charged through the entry flaps. Ripping half the tent free of its pegs, Scythe lunged toward Rade, massive teeth bared to attack.

Rade screamed. Beka screeched. Kien yelled, "Stop!" Scythe halted, but stomped and quivered violently, obviously longing to annihilate Kien's assailant. Kien threw his arms around his now-cowering father and kissed his whiskered cheek. "Scythe—steady! Look!" He patted his father's head. "It was nothing." Inspiration took hold. Straight-faced, Kien said, "Don't kill him. He won't taste good. And we're family. See—he loves me." Kien gave his father a shake. "Sir, tell the destroyer you love me before he starts crunching your bones."

Scythe huffed threateningly, moving nearer, fixing a killer look on Father. Rade shuddered and clutched Kien. "I love him! He's my son. I won't hurt him."

"Scythe, look—" Kien kissed his father again, certain of victory over the destroyer and Rade. "We're fine. Smile, Father."

Rade showed his teeth in a terrified grin. Scythe snorted, clearly unconvinced.

Trying to divert the destroyer's attention from Father, Kien asked, "Where's Ela?"

The huge horse shifted. His ears perked over Ela's name. Relieved, Kien continued, "I'm safe. We won't argue again. Go find Ela, and I'll bring you a grain cake. Go!"

Scythe backed out grudgingly, darting a final glare at Rade. The tent collapsed into a peaked heap of slender poles and pale leather billows as the destroyer departed. Jon laughed, though he protested. "Your beast ruined my tent!"

"Father will buy you another tent."

Releasing Kien, the elder Lantec sat on Jon's half-buried cot. "He was going to kill me."

"Yes." Kien sat beside his father. "But we still need you."

Agitated voices lifted outside the collapsed tent. Ara Lantec cried, "Rade? Kien! Are you there? Answer me!"

Kien yelled, "We're fine, Mother! Don't worry."

"Fine?" Father scowled at him beneath the tent's shadowed folds and muttered, "Prison has driven you mad."

"No it hasn't."

"Shut up! I'm deciding what to tell everyone. Prison changed you, Kien. Battle changed you. That's what I'll say." Rade paused, then sighed heavily. "No, it won't work. You'd be considered mentally unstable. Your reputation would be torn to shreds if you tried for the Traceland's Grand Assembly—you'll never survive politics. Defiance. Yes . . . my best tactic . . ."

Good. Kien relaxed and let Father ramble. Behind them, Jon was shoving aside the tent's framework and complaining beneath his breath. Beka laughed. "That was *your* destroyer? He's amazing! Kien—"

"Hush, Beka!" Rade ordered. "I'm thinking. Kien, General Rol praised your battle skills. With your training, you could join the military. As an arbitrator. A martial diplomat and judge-advocate—with some sort of officer's rank. I'll buy you a commission. Perfect. You'll be gone most of the time, we'll avoid scandal, and you'll have a respectable career."

A military judge-advocate? Kien recognized the idea's rightness. Was this what Ela had hinted at? "Father, that is a brilliant idea."

"Of course it is."

Jon waded past them, hands raised to lift the tent out of his way as he rummaged for the entry. "Kien, it's almost time for the bidding, and I'm not going to miss it. Not even for you."

"Bidding?" Beka followed her husband's path, lifting tent folds out of her way. "Jon, what are you bidding on?" She chased Jon outside, demanding answers.

Kien offered his father a hand. "Sir, I regret offending you. Now, if we don't show ourselves at once, Mother will come after you. And I must help Ela with the destroyers."

Rade clasped his son's hand but asked, "Who is Ela?"

✦ ✦ ✦

Branch in hand, Ela waited. The vinewood remained cool, unchanged. Ela shook her head at the burly Tracelander and offered him a regretful smile. His shoulders sagged with disappointment, but he nodded and moved onward. A destroyer would have ruled him, Ela knew.

Accompanied by his wife, Jon Thel stepped forward next. His expression was controlled, his bearing strictly commander-like. As if he expected to be refused. But the branch glistened, exuding light and warmth. Ela almost sighed her relief. She looked over her shoulder just as one of the younger destroyers lowered his head toward her and huffed his breath in her face. Impatient scamp. Before the destroyer could lick her, Ela grabbed the beast's halter and led him forward. When she was sure the young rascal saw Jon, Ela growled, "Obey! Go!"

The destroyer grumbled, but ambled forward. Jon Thel's soldierly composure failed. He grinned like a boy about to embark on a much-anticipated adventure. But the mischievous destroyer stopped, as if daring his new master. Jon frowned. "Come here. *Now.*"

The young monster-horse obeyed. Jon Thel's wife ignored them.

Ela would have recognized Kien's sister anywhere, even if she hadn't seen the young woman in a vision. Her dark eyes dancing, Beka threw Ela a radiant smile, took one step forward, and lifted her chin. Was she bidding for a destroyer?

Ponderous murmurs lifted among the ranks of Tracelanders. Ela hesitated until the branch sent tendrils of heat and dazzling light through her fingers. "Thank You!"

✦ ✦ ✦

"You gave my baby sister a destroyer?" Kien confronted Ela in the camp. Aware of little Tzana watching from her perch on Scythe's back, Kien kept his voice low and his expression agreeable despite his disapproval. He could see Beka bitten. Tossed. Trampled. *"Why?"*

Ela cradled her branch, looking as ecstatic as a caretaker just freed of forty overgrown toddlers. "I don't know. Ask the Infinite—it's His will. Most likely she'll need a destroyer."

Beka needed a destroyer? Kien was about to demand clarification when Ela looked past him. Her bliss faded, replaced by sorrow. Kien turned.

Tsir Aun and the few remaining Istgardians approached them, trailed by a handful of dejected destroyers. The crown commander bowed, evidently on a formal mission. "Ambassador. Is the general nearby?"

"He's coming," Ela said. She tipped the branch at the Istgardians. "Haven't you praised your poor destroyers for saving your lives by fleeing at the Infinite's command?"

"Did they?" one of the survivors asked, sounding shocked.

"Commander Tal!" Ela sounded pleased. Kien stared, displeased. She continued, "Yes. If your destroyers had stayed against the Infinite's will, each of you would have become a target. You would have died in the battle. Stop treating them as if they've failed you."

"Thank you for the advice." Tsir Aun's fondness for Ela was too clear for Kien's comfort.

Ela smiled, a bit mournful. "You and your men leave for Istgard in the morning."

"Yes." The crown commander looked as if a burden had suddenly dropped upon him. "We've identified and buried our dead. Now we must face our people."

"The Infinite will bless you all," Ela said.

Kien wished she wouldn't look at the man so kindly. He'd mistake her meaning. A commotion and a flurry of Tracelanders snapping to attention gave Kien the perfect excuse to interrupt this too-tender conversation. "The general approaches."

With Father, Kien realized. Rade Lantec was walking alongside General Rol, both men engrossed in an expansive conversation, nodding, hands gesturing. Talking about him, Kien feared. Father never wasted time.

Tsir Aun removed a wooden tube from his belt, opened it, and produced a slender role of parchment. As soon as the general halted before him, the crown commander offered him the tube and the parchment. "This morning, a courier arrived. Evidently Ambassador Lantec had been secretly negotiating with King Tek An concerning a possible settlement between our countries. The final document has been found and approved by Istgard's new government."

"What?" Kien tried to cover his surprise. They'd approved his sarcastic peace treaty?

Serious, Tsir Aun added, "The captives from Ytar have been freed and compensated. Istgard will rebuild the city within a year."

"Thank you!" Ela breathed. Tears sparkled in her eyes and slid down her cheeks.

Father glanced at her suspiciously, then straightened and beamed at the general as if he'd negotiated the treaty himself. The general offered Kien a handshake. "On behalf of the Tracelands, we offer you our gratitude."

Kien accepted the congratulations, stunned. As the impromptu meeting dissolved into a celebration—for the Tracelanders at least—Rade Lantec pressed a hand hard on Kien's shoulder. Beneath his breath, he said, "This Parnian prophet. Ela. Get rid of her—and her Unfortunate sister."

◆ 26 ◆

Freed from the destroyers, and grateful for the calm afternoon, Ela knelt in her small army-rationed tent.

What would become of her now? And Tzana?

Istgard was settled. Ytar's captives were free. The Tracelands was assured of peace for a while at least, she hoped. "Infinite," she whispered, amid her prayers, "tell me Your will. Should we return to Parne? Are we finished with our duties?"

No.

"Then where should Tzana and I go? What will happen?"

A headache. She should have known. Blinded by pain, Ela groped for her designated cot and fell into it.

Into a vision.

◆ ◆ ◆

Standing outside her tent, Ela grimaced at her headache and at Kien's words. So she and Tzana would be rejected by Kien's father? No surprise. Indeed, a prophet must become used to being a social outcast. Hadn't all of Parne's prophets suffered rejection? Even so, Kien's words stung.

To his credit, Kien was obviously offended. Now, having delivered news of his father's rejection, he said, "I can't abide by his wishes, of course."

"You must honor him," Ela said. Perhaps this implied parting

271

was for the best. She hadn't seen much of Kien's future. Surely this meant they'd travel separate paths, particularly now that she knew more of what she was facing. "Anyway," she continued her thoughts aloud, "I have work to do, so you mustn't be upset."

Despite his frustration, he looked interested. "What type of work?"

"I'm returning the Tracelands to the Infinite. And soon . . . I'm to rescue His faithful ones . . . elsewhere . . . before they're slaughtered."

Kien tensed, his eyes narrowing. "Slaughter? Where? When?"

"I'm not sure yet. But I saw them. They're waiting."

"Are you well?"

"Yes." For now.

✦ ✦ ✦

Gripping Pet's battered war harness, Ela leaned forward and inhaled the brisk salt-tinged air. They were approaching the Traceland's capital city, East Guard. "We're near the ocean," she told Tzana, doing her best to convey cheer. "We'll let Pet run in the water before he goes home with Kien."

Tetchy from the long journey, Tzana squirmed around to stare up at Ela. "But Pet's ours! Why is he going home with Kien?"

"Because we're going to be busy, and Kien will be able to keep Pet safe and well fed." Swallowing her misery, Ela said, "Don't worry. We'll see Pet again." True. How often, or for how long, Ela didn't know.

Tzana pouted. "All right. But what'll we be busy doing?"

Loud enough for the Tracelanders to hear, Ela announced, "*We* are going on a treasure hunt!"

Riding ahead on her elegant destroyer, Beka Thel heard and called over her shoulder. "What treasure?"

"Come see." Ela turned Pet aside from the main road, up a hill edging the shoreline. Shouts and beckoning whistles lifted in her wake. She'd have witnesses. Perfect. A pity Kien was traveling with his parents and the general at the front of the procession—he wouldn't be happy when he learned he'd missed their expedition.

Pet, however, seemed perfectly willing to bypass this adventure in favor of eating. He munched his way up the hill, grumping a bit at Ela's repeated commands to proceed.

At last, they rode into an overgrown meadow below the hill's crest. Ela's breath caught. The ruins. Haunting stone pillars, weathered to a deep gray, were sheltered by the hill's highest bluff. Some of the pillars had fallen, and bright green moss thickly draped their broken bases. How sobering, to see this once-beautiful place of worship reduced to near rubble. Would Parne's temple eventually suffer the same fate? Ela shuddered.

She guided Pet to a broken pillar base, tested it with the branch, then dismounted. As she reached for Tzana, the little girl asked, "Where's the treasure?"

"It's hidden. But the Infinite sees every secret thing. Hop down."

Jon and Beka Thel joined them with their destroyers, following Ela's example of dismounting on the fallen pillar. Jon frowned. "This old temple has been picked over by every generation for more than a hundred years—there's nothing left of any value here."

"On the contrary. Your people missed the most important treasure of all." Ela paused, shut her eyes, and recalled what she'd seen. Trees. Generations worth of neglected shrubs . . .

Excused soldiers and curious Tracelanders were filing into the clearing, eager to join a promised treasure hunt. Carrying Tzana, Ela led them behind the roofless temple to a grove of ancient, gnarled, lichen-crusted fruit trees planted near the bluff.

Ferns, shrubs, and fragile saplings whispered against her mantle as she entered the grove. Limbs—many leafless and fit only to be pruned and burned—tugged at her hair, forcing her to duck. Oblivious, Pet barged into the orchard to her right, testing every leaf and twig in his way. Behind them, the Tracelanders murmured. Some laughed quietly, doubting her vision.

273

Let them.

There. Behind the small orchard, at the bluff's vinewood screened base. "Pet! Come here. Bring your friends and your appetites."

Tzana tweaked Ela's braid. "What'll they eat?"

"Everything that's in our way." Ela touched her silvery branch to the tangled vinewood screen. The destroyers nosed the vine's leaves, smacked their lips, and crunched through the wood, reducing it to fragrant pulp. Soon they exposed a substantial cairn of moss-covered rocks blocking a door chiseled in the bluff's stone.

"How could we have missed this?" Jon approached the cairn as the destroyers finally retreated. "Beka—go tell Kien!"

"And become snared with him by those long-winded official welcoming committees? Not for anything!" She threw her mantle over a tree limb, grabbed a mossy rock from the cairn, and passed it to the nearest bystander. "Here."

Setting down Tzana and the branch, Ela lugged rocks and prayed, her joy building as the cairn diminished. The branch's light intensified, illuminating the entry into the bluff. When the last stone was removed, Ela grabbed Tzana and the glowing branch and stepped into the passage.

"We can't all fit inside," Jon yelled to the crowd. "Form a line and wait your turn!"

Stagnant, time-aged air beckoned Ela from the darkness ahead to a metal-bound door. Tzana hugged Ela's neck and squealed as the door's aged lock broke, allowing them into a chamber. Gold utensils—reflections of those used in Parne's own temple—shimmered at her from niches carved into the walls. Ela ignored the gleaming metal.

Gently, she set Tzana on the chamber's stone floor, then approached a shadowed niche filled with an orderly series of gemstudded ivory plaques. "Infinite?"

I am here.

Overcome, she reached for the first plaque. Her eyes dazzled by gems winking at her in the branch's light, Ela read aloud the first verses in the ancient traditional temple lettering. "Blessed are you, who hear and obey the Infinite, your Creator. . . ."

✦ ✦ ✦

Kien paced through his mother's chamber. "The historians are quarreling with the lawyers over the artifacts, and the civilians are protesting for access to the hidden writings. And I *still* cannot believe you didn't send for me." He frowned at his sister and mother, who sat in the sunny window seat.

Beka consulted her parchment, then leaned toward Mother. "I suppose we must invite the Siphrans."

"I suppose." Ara pressed a slender stylus against her wax note tablet. "Siphrans are added. Just keep them away from your father."

Kien flung himself onto an empty cushion and scowled. "You're ignoring me."

"Nonsense, dear," Ara reproved tenderly, "we're planning this reception for *you*."

He nudged his boot at Beka. "Have you invited Ela?"

"My reception's a failure without her." Beka showed him the parchment. Ela's name headed her list. "She's now the most revered person in East Guard. In all the Tracelands."

"Father disagrees." Kien issued the words as a challenge.

Mother met his stare, her gray eyes serene. "He'll come around, darling. Trust me. She's gathered too many followers to be ignored. A remarkable girl, really."

"I'm inviting her to stay the night with me after the reception," Beka informed Kien. "But you will have to leave at a respectable hour, sir."

Ela—invited to stay in Jon and Beka's residence? Kien grinned. "You have my word, I'll be an exemplary guest." When was the last time he'd spoken to Ela alone? Not since their arrival in East Guard. His thoughts sped to the reception. He would—

"Kien." Mother's gentle voice became serious. "Your father hopes you will pay attention to some of the eligible young ladies at the reception. We'd like to see you married within the next year or two. Visit with *all* of them, please." Her words were a command.

"Of course." Determined to end this conversation, Kien stood. "I'm going to run Scythe."

"You've just returned from running him," Ara protested.

"Well, we're off again. Boredom makes us cranky."

Beka laughed. "We noticed."

✦ ✦ ✦

Surrounded by lamplight and cantankerous scholars in the no-longer-secret chamber, Ela concentrated on her chart. These scholars perched on stools around her makeshift table were maddening. They had no concern for the Books of the Infinite, only for the historical value of the writings. The sooner she finished the chart, the sooner she'd be rid of the scholars for today. She hoped.

"You are certain?" the eldest interrupted her, his grizzled eyebrows crescents as he clinked a reed pen on a quartz ink vial. "The translations on these tablets are correct?"

"These tablets are not translations," Ela said. "This is the traditional script used in our holy writings. The ancient form of your own script. What *you'll* write, sir, is the translation, which must be correct. The Infinite's Word is sacred. Wouldn't you prefer to learn the ancient characters?"

One of the youngest scholars spoke quietly. "With permission, I will learn." He'd been mute, copying the tablets all morning in the ancient form.

The reed clinker pursed his lips at the youngster. "Do you believe you are better than we?"

"Not at all, sir. Respectfully, I would like to learn the ancient language to—"

"To show off," his elder sniffed, "when you should be concentrating on copying text."

"He's been copying all morning," another disagreed. "You disparage his gifts."

"Gifts?"

The Tracelands' finest minds began to squabble like children in a sand pile. Any louder and they'd upset Tzana, who sat in a lamplit corner, pressing patterns into a wax tablet.

"Infinite," Ela prayed beneath her breath, "grant me patience! And wisdom." She took a wooden tablet, her parchment chart, ink, and reed pen, then joined Tzana at the far wall.

"You're having more fun." Ela sat beneath the lamp. "May I work beside you?"

"All right." Smiling, Tzana scooted over on her cushioned mat and continued her play.

While the scholars continued their quarrel, Ela completed her chart. Each ancient character was noted, with its name, meaning, phonetic pronunciation, and corresponding contemporary letter. Finished, she marched over to the young scholar and dangled the parchment before his nose. "May the Infinite bless you with understanding."

He'd been poised as if ready to parry the eldest scholar's jabs. Seeing the chart, he stuck the reed in a corner of his mouth and chewed, elated. "Might I consult with you as I translate?"

"Not without our permission," the reed-wielding elder said.

Their squabbling resumed. Ela pressed both hands to her head, willing the commotion to fade. Her thoughts whirled with petty scholars, finicky lawyers, and invitations to receptions she'd no wish to attend, even if Beka was the generous hostess. Infinite? Is this really why You brought me to the Tracelands?

Patience.

"Please, bless me with Your patience. Mine is gone."

✦ ✦ ✦

Kien fought down his exasperation. Two weeks of waiting had led to this? A stuffy crowd of pompous bureaucrats, snobbish society women, and no Ela.

Could the guest of honor vanish, now that the reception had begun?

Father gave him a furtive nudge. "There's General Rol's daughter. Go talk to her."

"We haven't been introduced." Kien refused to look at the young lady in question.

Rade Lantec turned crimson. "*You* are the guest of honor. You've been introduced to everyone. Stop making excuses and be sociable!" He led Kien to a thin young woman who looked as if she would rather be anywhere else. "Nia, you look lovely. Are you enjoying your evening?"

"Oh," she murmured, words as vague as her face, "thank you, sir. Really. Rather, I think I'm not agreeing that I'm lovely, but . . ."

Kien bit down a grin and enjoyed every syllable of Nia Rol's drizzling monologue, because it was aimed at Father. By the time the girl finished talking, Rade Lantec's glazed eyes betrayed apathy. General Rol's daughter had the wit and glow of dry porridge in a clay dish.

They excused themselves as soon as possible. Kien said, "Father, you've made your point. I'll speak with Beka's friends at least."

"See that you do."

Dutiful son, honoring parents. He approached one of Beka's childhood friends, Xiana Iscove. He hadn't talked to her in years. She'd become quite pretty . . . glowing skin, lustrous hair.

"There you are," she said, as if Kien should have paid attention to her sooner. Lifting an etched eyebrow, she teased, "I've heard you're quite a hero now. That's wonderful. Just tell me you've given up spitting apple seeds at people."

"Apple seeds?" Kien stared. "What are you talking about?"

"Oh, Kien, for pity's sake!" She sounded impatient despite her flirtatious smile. "How can you have forgotten? The harvest party in Master Cam Wroth's apple orchard."

Master Cam Wroth? Kien hadn't thought of his first tutor in—what?—sixteen years.

Xiana's eyes hardened just a bit. "You were sitting in a tree, spitting apple seeds down into my hair."

"Oh." He remembered spitting in blissful peace, then hearing horrific screams from below. "I was seven. And I didn't know you were there. You remember that day?"

"Of course. I remember everything."

"Amazing." He imagined being married to her. Xiana perpetually reliving all his faults while forgetting her own. *She* had called him a stupid ugly boy. After he'd apologized twice. No wonder he hadn't talked to her in years. "And, I must say, you're as lovely as ever."

Xiana simpered.

Kien visited a bit longer, then smiled and excused himself. He deserved a medal. Or an actor's mask. Another of Beka's friends waved to him. And asked him to introduce her to one of Jon's fellow commanders. Kien hoped the man didn't eventually marry her—he'd blame Kien.

"Kien!" Beka's new friend, Lil, caught his arm in a death grip. He'd never met the girl until tonight. He smiled as Lil paraded him through the gathering as if she'd won a trophy.

Until Beka pried him away, beaming. "Are you enjoying yourself?"

"Beka," Kien hissed beneath his breath, "you *must* find new friends."

"Like Ela?" His sister showed a mischievous smile.

Ela. Finally! "Where is she?"

"That's what I've come to tell you—she's settled Tzana in their room and is preparing herself now. My maidservant will play with Tzana and sit with her for the night. I'm leaving to meet Ela. If anyone asks, I'll return immediately." She swept away.

"Lantec." A sleek-haired, gold-embellished Siphran nobleman bowed to Kien and cleared his throat. "One hears you refused Istgard's throne. And that you will soon accept a position to train as a military judge. Congratulations."

Whoever 'one' was, he or she was well informed. Kien hid his uneasiness. "Thank you. How may I help you?"

"I am Ruestock, Siphra's ambassador. An unsuccessful one thus far."

Unsuccessful. Kien understood his meaning. Siphra's queen, never mind her useless king-husband, was displeased. The ambassador had evidently received threats. "What's expected of you, sir?"

The Siphran sighed. "I appealed to your father and to your Grand Assembly on behalf of my country. Our mutual border through the Snake Mountains is beset by rebels who threaten us all. We ask that you send military aid to help us root out and destroy these evildoers."

"And you're discussing the matter with me because you've received no response from my father or the Grand Assembly?"

"Precisely. You are very perceptive, sir. Istgard has lost a great king."

Kien ignored the non-compliment. "You are asking a nation founded by a pack of rebels to crush another pack of rebels who threaten your king." Better not to mention the despotic queen, who'd provoked rebellion among Siphra's military.

"These are difficulties, indeed. Will you speak to your father on my behalf?"

"You ought to request asylum instead."

The Siphran's answer was a thin smile that barely lifted the corners of his mouth. Fortunately, Beka returned with Ela, who had obviously been tended by Beka's maidservant.

Ela's long dark hair was styled in glossy curls that framed her face and throat. A softly draped gold-embroidered blue mantle and a flowing gold-and-blue tunic, double-tied at the waist, accentuated her graceful form to perfection. The most captivating lady present. But she was pale and clearly nervous. Kien ached to hold her, to tease her and banish her distress. "Ela!" He offered her his hand. Her fingers chilled his.

"Ela," Beka said, playing hostess, "have you met Ambassador Ruestock of Siphra?"

"No." Ela shrank back as if the ambassador were the last person she wanted to see.

Ambassador Ruestock, however, seemed genuinely delighted. "Parne's most beautiful prophet, and the Traceland's talisman! The gods have blessed my prayers."

Ela's grip tightened, almost cutting off circulation in Kien's fingers. She shut her eyes. Hard. Kien steadied her. The last time he'd seen her react this way . . . she'd been enduring a vision.

27

Ela wanted to scream at Ambassador Ruestock. Despicable flatterer. His gods indeed! The Infinite knew what he'd been praying. And so did she. Ela shuddered and pretended the vision didn't exist.

The instant the Siphran ambassador made his elegant excuses and departed, Kien rubbed warmth back into Ela's hands, fretting over her. "Are you well?"

"Yes." Ela ordered herself to be calm.

Kien leaned down and whispered, "You had another vision?"

Ela shrugged, refusing to discuss what she'd seen. Beka was so kind to her—so excited over the first formal reception she and Jon were giving as husband and wife in their lovely new home—that Ela mustn't disappoint her. What was about to happen was probably inevitable. Her Creator's will must be done. Until the vision *happened*, however, she wouldn't think of it.

"Let's enjoy this evening," Ela decided aloud. She smiled at Kien, pleased by his reciprocal grin. With Kien hovering beside her for most of the evening, she devoted herself to Beka's guests. Answering their questions about the treasure cache. The secret room. The Books of the Infinite. And most heartening, about the Infinite Himself.

More than once, she glimpsed Rade Lantec brooding amid the crowd, watching her. At last, when they'd finished the light

283

refreshments offered by the Thels' servants, Kien's father approached and waved Kien off. "Vanish awhile. Go . . . talk to Jon about destroyers. He wants to race that beast of his and you need to advise him—I can't discuss the matter because I've nothing good to say about the monsters."

"Jon wants to race destroyers?" Kien's gray eyes sparkled. He leaned toward Ela. "Don't let my father chase you away. I'll return soon."

Ela nodded, grateful for the chance to talk with Rade Lantec. He was studying Ela as if perplexed. She offered him a cautious smile.

"How should I address you?" he asked.

Traces of Kien reflected in his eyes, showed in his posture, and echoed in the tones of his voice. Ela said, "You may address me as you wish, sir. I understand your misgivings about me."

"Do you?" His quizzical expression too resembled Kien's.

Ela couldn't help giving the man a fond look. "Your son is so like you. I . . ." She stopped, fearing she'd say something foolish. "I pray the Infinite blesses you and your family beyond measure in everything you do." Probably without her. Ela fought to maintain her composure.

Rade Lantec said, "You sound as if you're taking leave of us. Are you?"

She deliberately shifted the subject. "Sir, if I may . . . You've avoided Ambassador Ruestock for weeks. It's wise of you. Please, for your country's sake, maintain your silence and inaction. Siphra's queen is a viper. Soon their military will desert her almost completely. Siphra has been judged and will be—"

Shock widened the elder Lantec's eyes. "Who told you all this?"

"The Infinite."

"The Infinite." Acid edged his courtesy.

Familiar reaction. "Sir, I know your opinion of Parne and the Infinite. And it's your right to hold that opinion. But if I say the Infinite has judged Siphra and will cast down its king and queen . . . it *will* happen. Otherwise I'm a false prophet who ought to be punished."

Rade Lantec grimaced, one corner of his mouth lifting. Like Kien's. "And when will this rebellion, this marvel of Siphran sanity occur?"

"Within the month." She didn't want to think of it now. "Simply continue the game with Siphra as you've played it until now."

His mockery faded. "For one so young, Ela of Parne, you talk and behave as if you've been involved in diplomacy for years."

"I feel as if I have."

Rade Lantec, preeminent representative of the Tracelands, offered Ela his arm. "We don't agree on everything, young lady, but you interest me exceedingly. Now, tell me about Parne. . . ."

❖ ❖ ❖

Soon.

While Jon and Beka closed the doors and directed their servants in the evening's final chores, Ela sneaked outside to their huge garden. Surely fresh air would brace her. She descended the stairs and turned onto one of the rock-edged paths. Gravel pressed into the soft soles of her thin, decorative sandals—loaned by the determined Beka. But the gravel's discomfort was worth enduring for a calming, prayerful walk through the garden.

Jon and Beka's garden was as lovely as their home. The season's first pale lilies were opening, scenting the air. Other flowers Ela didn't recognize also shone silver-white in the moon's glow. All around her, bugs whirred and rasped soothingly in the darkness. She felt better just hearing them.

"Infinite," she whispered toward the stars, "I know You're with me. But about this most recent vision . . . can't I—"

Footsteps crunched on the gravel in the darkness, hushing her. A low voice said, "Ela?"

"Kien." Her heart thudded. He would want to know about the vision, and he mustn't. He might feel obligated to protect her. If Kien interfered, he could be injured, which was completely unacceptable. She loved him too much. "I thought you'd gone with your parents."

"I had to wish you a good night." He stepped so close that she could feel his breath.

Too close. He bent and kissed Ela, enfolding her in his arms, almost lifting her off the path. She'd never dared imagine . . . a kiss. His lips. His scent. The comfort of his arms around her. She allowed herself to cling to him. To return his kiss. Oh, he was so warm—mesmerizing! She wanted to linger with him forever. There'd been no hint of *this* in any vision. Infinite—

"Marry me," Kien urged the instant the kiss ended.

Ela gasped and pulled away. Was this a test? Was she supposed to resist such temptation? Well, she'd failed. She burst into tears. "This is so unfair!"

"Was my kiss so appalling?" Kien teased, but with a suggestion of hurt.

"No!" Ela swiped at her wet face. "It's nothing to do with you. At least, not exactly." Trying to soothe him, she explained, "If I tell you the truth about your kiss, you'll become unbearably smug. Oh, Kien, there's no one else I'd rather marry. I love you, but . . ." Infinite, how could a prophet be so stupid? Babbling and sniffling!

Kien touched her cheek, looked into her eyes. "If you love me, then why are you crying?"

"A silver-haired prophet has failed."

"What?"

"I can't marry you." Pain nearly stole her breath. Ela caught herself and rushed on. "As much as I love you, it would be unfair of me—even cruel." Not to mention hopeless, considering her most recent visions. . . .

"Shh! I don't understand why you're so upset, Ela." He tucked her hand into his elbow, comforting as ever. But his face was very pale in the moonlight. "Let's sit down."

Kien guided her to a bench and waited until she sat. The cold stone made her shiver. As did his sudden formality. He motioned to the space beside her. "May I sit with you?"

Miserable, Ela nodded and dabbed more tears. "Kien, Parne's

elders say 'A silver-haired prophet has failed' because all our prophets die young." And horribly.

He hesitated, then said, "Because of this, you presume—"

"I don't presume. I *know*. I asked the Infinite." Why couldn't she stop shivering? "I'm going to die young. It could happen at any time. Possibly soon."

"But possibly not soon!" Kien sounded angry. Defiant. He wrapped a fold of his mantle around her. "This has you so upset you're trembling. You don't actually know when, do you?"

"No. But it's the reason you need to take Scythe. I've *seen* him pledged to you. So it must mean my death is near."

"Again, you don't know that!"

"But what if it is?" She began to cry again. Foolish tears. "Please give me your word that if I die, you'll return Tzana to my parents."

"Whatever happens, she'll be safe." Kien gathered Ela in an embrace. "She'll be my sister-in-law."

"No, she won't!" Ela straightened in his arms. "Kien, I can't marry you—or anyone. I've considered it, believe me. Prophets ultimately become notorious. *Hated*. I won't inflict such misery on anyone. You know what most Tracelanders think of Parne's prophets and the Infinite. Also . . . what if we did marry and have a child? How could I endure knowing I'll die soon? I couldn't!"

When Kien finally spoke again, his voice was despairing. "*Why* did you become a prophet under such circumstances?"

"Because once I heard the Infinite's voice, I knew I couldn't live without Him."

Kien said nothing. Ela continued, "I cannot reject my role as a prophet. I won't. I love the Infinite."

"More than you love me." Pain and bitterness edged his voice, cutting her.

"Yes." Ela wiped away fresh tears. "But if I hadn't agreed to become His prophet, I wouldn't have met you. I'm grateful I met you." She tried to lift his spirits. And her own. "I do regret the black eye. . . ."

Silent, he hugged Ela fiercely and kissed her hair. She touched his face, wanting to beg him for understanding.

Before she could speak, Kien stood and walked away, his boots grinding on the gravel.

Her hand was wet. He was crying.

✦ ✦ ✦

After checking on the slumbering Tzana, Ela paced through the guest chamber and prayed Kien would forgive her. At least she knew he would live. Hadn't she seen him riding Scythe, unconquerable during a future battle? And he trusted the Infinite. She would console herself with that knowledge. Now, however, she must concentrate on what was about to happen.

"Infinite? This vision must begin to be fulfilled tonight—I realize that. But can't I reason with these miscreants and persuade them to listen?"

You may try.

Ela rubbed her aching head. She would fail at this too. Oh, this was going to be awful.

Pinning her borrowed mantle close, she stepped through the room's outer doors, onto the stone terrace. The entire house was eerily quiet and dark. Looking up at the stars, Ela froze in horror. How had so much time passed? When had the moon shifted?

She sped back inside, kissed Tzana softly, snatched up the branch, returned to the balcony, and shut the doors behind her. At least Tzana would be safe and undisturbed.

Why hadn't she taken time earlier to change into more sensible . . . "Oh no." She'd been so distracted by Kien that she'd forgotten about Beka's sandals. Ela winced, longing for boots instead. If only she could change a bit of her vision. Tweak it just a little. Perhaps its outcome would improve. Hadn't the Infinite said she could try? Ela set aside the branch and leaned over the terrace's wall-like stone balustrade to rummage through the vines below.

Her fingertips grazed over a chilled piece of metal. Yes, there it was. One of the hooks supporting the latticework. Such a sharp tip on that particular hook. Couldn't she—

Two shadows flickered on one of the paths nearby. Ela ducked behind the solid balustrade. No doubt they'd seen her. Heart thudding, she whispered, "Infinite, be with me!"

Waiting stillness met her entreaty. Ela covered her eyes. Foolish of her to hide. But she longed to escape. Couldn't these two miscreants be avoided? Infinite?

Muted footsteps skittered the gravel just below the terrace. Did she hear breathing?

Ela swallowed, listening to the vines rustle on the latticework. Please, let the perpetrators foolishly use the lattice as a foothold. Let them fall right back on their rumps and give up. Let—

A low thump sounded directly in front of Ela on the terrace's decorative stonework pavings. She opened her eyes. The first scoundrel stared at her in the moonlight, loathing twisting his mouth in a grimace.

"Listen," Ela whispered, "I'm Ela of Parne. I know you're looking for me and I'll go without a sound. Just don't bind me. I need to warn you—!"

The soon-to-be abductor knelt, slapped a hand over Ela's mouth, and shoved her head against the balustrade. "Orders is orders, an' we won't have you castin' spells!" He yanked a long strip of fabric from around his neck.

Ela squirmed and fought to speak. "Wait! Listen—"

The man slapped the fabric over her mouth. Wool. Tasting as foul as the vision. He knotted the strip tight, then removed a coil of rope from his belt. After he'd bound her wrists and ankles, he looked around, agitated. "Too easy, this!"

Easily fatal! Ela made a noise of protest.

The wretch shook her, muttering, "Quiet, or I'll bash ya bloody!"

Yes, and that was the problem. . . . In despair, Ela pieced together the fragments of information from her visions. How could she gain her captors' trust enough to warn them?

Her abductor stood and silently motioned to his comrade below. As Ela concentrated on not smelling the awful gag covering her mouth, she noticed the branch lying on the terrace pavings—just beyond her reach. Panicked, she struggled to grasp the precious piece of vinewood. But the scoundrel dragged her upright, away from the branch. Infinite!

The vinewood glimmered, then dissolved. Before Ela could even wonder, a spiral of heat permeated her bound hands, and the branch formed against her palms. Thank You! Ela clenched the insignia and shut her eyes. Next . . .

The first miscreant tipped her off the terrace wall toward his waiting comrade.

Ela's left foot struck the wall. Stabbed by pain, she shrieked into the gag. The metal hook supporting the terrace's decorative lattice had impaled the flesh covering the ball of her foot, exactly as she'd seen. Surely she could affect this one little detail! She struggled, desperate to lift her sandaled foot off the hook. Before the impatient man—

The second reprobate growled and tugged mightily. Ripping Ela's foot from the hook and from the delicate sandal. Pain flared up her leg. Her screech was muffled in the gag. Now might be a good time to faint. But would she? This part of the vision ended here, with blood trickling off her wounded foot, its stickiness agonizingly ticklish. Ela squirmed. The second reprobate cursed beneath his breath and shook her in his arms. "Stop!"

Rustling alerted her that the owner of the loathsome gag was descending from the terrace. He noticed the branch's subdued glow and muttered, "What's this?" When his fingers passed through the wood, he gasped. Both men stared. The first man whispered, "Carry 'er, Claw."

Outrage in his voice, Claw hissed, "Tha's yer job!" His cohort fled as if Ela were lethal.

They scurried through the garden, which gave way to trees. Ela was certain she heard Jon and Beka's destroyers squealing in the distance. She hoped they were well secured. Poor things.

They mustn't interfere. She noticed her captor lagging. He shifted her in his arms. "Hex?"

Hex halted, turned, and stomped back. "I ain't luggin' that Infinite's sorceress."

Now she was a sorceress? If only they knew the truth.

"I'm droppin' 'er," his comrade threatened.

Hissing through his teeth, Hex took Ela. "No tricks, girl, or I'll smash ya!"

Ela shrank inwardly. Smash? Yes, that was the whole problem. With both men. Their violence and their fearful antagonism toward the Infinite and her. How could she change what she'd seen? She must try. But without speaking? Without moving?

Hex pitched Ela over his shoulder like a bag of meal.

Her arms dangled, with the branch bound between her hands. She could whack Hex's backside if she wished. But that would madden him—the last thing she wanted to do.

Trailed by Claw, Hex carried Ela into an isolated meadow. Reaching his destination, he stood her upright. Pain stabbed Ela's injured foot. Sweating, she gripped the branch for balance.

Four grazing horses waited in the meadow, with another man. A nobleman, his gold pins shining on his dark cloak. Ambassador Ruestock.

The nobleman approached and bent to whisper in Ela's ear, "You are indeed the answer to my prayers! My queen has heard of you, Parnian, and demands your presence." The ambassador caressed her face. As Ela tried to twist away from him, Ruestock crooned, "My honor, my reputation, and my life have depended upon obtaining you for the Siphran court. Be sure you do as you're told. That Unfortunate sister of yours will pay the price if you fail us."

Tzana. He was threatening Tzana! Before Ela could hit the nobleman with the branch, he motioned to his men. Hex lifted Ela in his arms. Her feet brushed against Ruestock's cloak, allowing her to kick at him. Pain reminded Ela of her torn foot.

Ruestock chuckled.

Claw mounted one of the horses. Hex pitched Ela over another. Winded by the impact, Ela wheezed beneath the foul gag. Claw soothed her horse while Hex mounted a third animal nearby. Ela squirmed until she could extend her bound arms and hold the branch before her. The branch faded to plain vinewood as the horses moved from the clearing, following Hex's low commands.

Ela watched the shadowed ground jolt away beneath her. She prayed Kien could forgive her the misery she'd caused him—just long enough to protect Tzana.

◆ 28 ◆

Scuffing sounded at Kien's chamber door, waking him. A muffled call beckoned. "Sir?"

Was it morning? Grayish light rimming the tower window shutters affirmed his suspicion. Kien willed himself to think. Why was he fully clothed, sprawled atop his bed instead of beneath the covers? Oh. Yes . . . Ela. Better not to think about her.

The scuffing repeated, irritating him.

"Enter!"

One of the stablehands leaned around the door. "Sir? Your destroyer's gone wild. He's been carryin' on, tryin' to escape the old stable half the night. If the walls weren't solid stone, he'd be long gone, I'd say."

Scythe? Kien sat up. "Why didn't you wake me?"

"Why, sir, wakin' the family fer one crazed beast ain't needful."

Kien bolted from his bed. Scythe turning crazed could only mean his pledged master was in danger. And obviously, Kien wasn't in danger. Frantic, he checked his boots, grabbed his sword, and charged for the door. Ela . . . What had happened?

From a distance, Jon's voice bellowed, "Kien! Where are you?"

"I'm on my way!"

He donned his baldric, then buckled his sword belt and clattered down the spiraling stone steps from his tower room. Jon waited at the bottom of the stairs with Father and Mother, both bleary and morning-rumpled in their robes. As Kien reached the last step, Jon dangled a small torn sandal for inspection. A bloodied sandal.

Before Jon could say a word, Kien asked, "Ela?"

"Yes. We're certain she was stolen. Shrubs and vines were broken, and our stablemen told us our destroyers were in fits long before dawn. This was hanging on a trellis hook."

Kien took the sandal. Blood on the inner sole didn't mean Ela was dead. But what if . . . He clenched the thin sandal in his fist. He would kill whoever had hurt her. Be calm. Think. "Where's Tzana?"

"She's with Beka," Jon said. "Perfectly safe—and a brave little thing."

Kien snapped, "She's a girl, not a thing!"

Mother gave him a reproving look. "Kien."

"I meant no insult," Jon interposed. "And Kien's upset. As are Beka and I. Ela was stolen from our home, and it's a point of honor that we find her. Who were her enemies?"

"Prophets always have enemies." Though Kien couldn't recall a single Tracelander who hated Ela. Vengeful Istgardians, perhaps?

Rade Lantec rubbed his dark-whiskered chin. "Poor girl. Has a ransom been demanded?"

"No. We found no trace of a note. Nothing was touched in her chamber, and Tzana wasn't wakened by any noise during the night."

Kien couldn't bear to stand still. "Excuse me. I need to think. I'm going to check Scythe."

Long before he reached the barred metal door he heard Scythe raging within the stout, ancient stone walls. "Easy, Scythe!" The commotion inside lessened to a barrage of rumbling destroyer complaints. "Be still!"

Except for the destroyer's labored breathing, silence reigned. Kien slid back the metal bars, prepared to leap out of the monster's way if he charged. But Scythe kept still, as commanded. He was lathered in sweat, his big eyes rolling.

Kien glanced around the stable and winced. The destroyer

had demolished every stall in the old stable. Thankfully none of Father's horses were there. Kien wasn't sure they'd have survived. "You've had enough of a tantrum for us both. Don't worry. We'll find her."

The destroyer nudged his big head toward Kien's hand. Specifically to the bloodied sandal. Scenting it, the beast groaned.

"Who would do this?" Kien asked, thinking aloud. "Who hated her? Who did she fear?"

A memory surfaced. Ela at Beka's reception. Pale and reluctant to meet Ambassador Ruestock. Suffering a vision as the man spoke to her.

"Scythe, let's prepare for a visit to the Siphran ambassador."

✦ ✦ ✦

Dark cloak flaring, Ruestock strutted into his ornately paved ambassadorial courtyard. Smug, Kien decided.

The nobleman lifted his chin. "What is so important that you're unable to call upon me in my own residence like a civilized person?"

"The matter is urgent and my destroyer's upset." Kien refused to mince words. "Ela of Parne is missing. Has your network of spies revealed any useful information, sir?"

"I know nothing of the delightful Parnian." Ruestock cast an uneasy glance at Scythe, who nosed toward him.

The destroyer huffed, scenting the ambassador's cloak. An ominous rumble sounded in Scythe's throat, just before he clamped the nobleman's arm and flung him to the ground.

Kien raised a hand. "Scythe, stop!"

The black horse obeyed, but trembled and snorted threats—unmistakably convinced the ambassador had somehow harmed Ela.

Ruestock cried, "You deliberately attacked me! I am an ambassador! Protected by—"

Kien knelt on Ruestock's chest, grabbed the man's cloak, and twisted it hard against his throat, longing to beat the man to death. "You are squealing 'ambassadorial protection' to the wrong man! Talk! Now, or I allow this destroyer to crush you!"

✦ ✦ ✦

"Darling," Mother protested, "Siphra's border is overrun by thieves and marauders who could cut you to pieces!"

"They'll have to deal with Scythe first." Kien bent to kiss his mother.

Standing beside Ara, Rade Lantec fumed. "Ruestock will be expelled from the country. But, Kien, if you create an international incident, there's nothing I can do to help you. We sent our army after Istgard for you and Ytar. Victory or not, I can't convince the Grand Assembly to repeat a similar vote in the same year. Is it worth your career to chase after this girl?"

"Imagine the uproar if we didn't try to find her, sir," Kien countered. "Jon and Beka would be accused of covering up her death or some other conspiracy. Besides"—he aimed a defiant look at his father—"if mother were stolen, you'd go after her."

Father spluttered, "No! I mean, *yes*, but that's entirely different! Your mother's my wife!"

"I'm glad she is, sir," Kien said. He shouldered his knapsack.

"Rade dear," Mother complained, "for a politician, you're not being very tactful."

"Ara, my love, you know I would come to your rescue."

"You'd *negotiate* me out of danger, you know you would!"

"See the trouble you've caused?" Father growled at Kien. "I'll be all day digging myself out of this one. Then I'll have to decide what to tell the authorities about your Parnian's disappearance!"

Ela, his Parnian? Hardly. Kien hugged his father good-bye.

Rade gripped his arm. "You're planning to marry her, aren't you?"

"She won't marry me, or anyone, sir. Don't worry."

A commotion outside caught their attention. Kien reached for the door. "That will be Jon and his beast. And Scythe." He hoped Scythe wasn't eating the front garden.

"Be safe!" Mother pleaded.

His parents followed him outside. Kien halted on the steps. Jon was indeed waiting. With Scythe. And Beka—looking self-satisfied—on her destroyer, Tzana perched before her.

Tzana caught sight of Kien and beamed. "We're going to find Ela!"

Rade bellowed, "No, you are not! Beka, we've just brought Kien home—we *won't* lose you both!"

All three destroyers took offense at his tone. Scythe started up the stairs.

Father dragged Mother inside and slammed the door.

"Thank you," Jon called after them. To Kien, he groused, "I notice he doesn't care if he loses me. So much for being the favorite son-in-law."

"They do love you, dearest," Beka soothed.

Kien gathered Scythe's reins. "Off the stairs. You cannot eat Father."

The destroyer curled his lips.

✦ ✦ ✦

Unbound now, Ela hobbled, using the branch as Hex led her to the campfire.

Her hands and feet were swollen. As was her face—puffy from being slung over that little horse like a bag of grain. She dropped onto the damp, rough grass, set aside the branch, and looked around. Nausea twisted her stomach.

This was *the* clearing. Not quite as she'd seen it yet—the shadows were too short, and the sun not low enough. She had time. But did she dare speak or move?

Both men watched her slightest twitch, mistrust etching their features. Desperate to warn them, she said, "Don't be—"

Before she could say the words *afraid of me*, Hex gripped her hair and slapped a hand over her mouth. "Hush, or I'll loosen yer teeth!"

Ela cringed and hushed. She'd almost instigated the scene she feared. Hex released her with a shove. To quell her nerves—and possibly reassure the men—Ela probed her foot's bloodied inflamed wound. Ugly gash . . .

Claw thunked the evening meal at her feet. Dried meat, steaming water, and a preserved grain cake. She chewed the meat and half the cake while soaking her foot in the salty water. When her foot was clean, Ela worked the remaining cake and water to a rough paste and pressed the stuff into her wound. The disgusting gag had to serve as a bandage. Ela feared it would rot her foot. If she lived.

As she tied the final knot, images repeated within her mind. Queasy with horror, she concentrated on breathing. Shutting her eyes was useless, of course. How couldn't she see visions unfolded within her thoughts?

Infinite, is this unavoidable?

Child of dust, can you change their evil hearts for them?

"Infinite . . ." Instinctively, she reached for the branch.

"No ya don't!" Claw struck Ela's wrist, breaking her hold on the branch. "No spells!"

"I'm not casting a—"

Hex shoved Ela away from the branch as Claw yelled, "Beat 'er senseless!"

"You mustn't strike me!"

Hex flogged Ela, cursing, threatening with each vicious blow, "I'll kill you!"

An immense serpent, a lindorm, slashed into the clearing. Hissing, fanged mouth gaping, scales gleaming in shades of grass and dirt, it whipped at the now-screaming Claw and sank its fangs into his neck. Ela heard a crack. The horses, tethered nearby, squealed their fear.

Hex released Ela and made a frantic dash for his sword, which rested beyond Claw. The huge viper lashed out and struck his shoulder. He howled the anguished cry of a doomed man.

Ela struggled for the branch, though she knew it was useless. By the time she'd grabbed the cold vinewood, Hex was convulsing. Claw lay unmoving, in a death stare. The monstrous reptile seemed exultant, engrossed in savaging its victims. Ela sobbed and looked away, shuddering, remembering the quenchless fire. The agony of separation from the Infinite's care.

Within Ela's line of sight, an unkempt warrior crept into the clearing, shield and axe readied, his gaze fixed on the feasting lindorm. He lifted the axe, warning Ela to silence. A pack of motley fighters followed him stealthily, axes also readied, each intent on the lindorm.

The lead warrior gauged his target and hurled the axe. Its blade sank deep into the base of the lindorm's head. The huge land serpent thrashed wildly, each subsequent axe blow drawing a more feeble response until the venomous creature went limp in death—its gleaming scales fading to dull gray. The men whooped and cuffed each other in congratulations. Their leader's exultation vanished as he checked Claw and Hex.

Useless, Ela knew. She knelt and shut her eyes. If their deaths—the torment of their souls—weren't her fault, then why did she feel such an appalling burden of failure? How could she continue from the end of this vision to the beginning of the next? She didn't have the strength. Resting her head on the branch, she cried beneath her breath, "Infinite, help me!"

"Akabe?" One of the men called.

Ela looked up. The man repeated his call, sounding much too cheerful for Ela's taste. "Hey, Akabe!"

The leader motioned the man to wait. He approached Ela instead, his scruffy-bearded face and light brown eyes the image of regret. In a low, pleasantly lilting voice, he asked, "Were these your relatives?"

"No. I was their captive."

He smiled, a dimple hinting beneath his beard. "Well, now you are free. What is your name? We must return you to your family."

Truly a man of honor. If she weren't soul-sick and thoroughly beaten, Ela might have smiled. "I'm the Infinite's servant—Ela of Parne. And you can't return me to my family. My work's unfinished."

The branch glowed. Spirals of light expanded, encompassing Ela, settling comfort over her like a mantle. For an instant, one breath, she rested in the light. The instant was enough. Strength poured through her. Ela stood and faced the scruffy warrior, who stared openmouthed.

Run!

What did it matter if these woods were full of vicious lindorms and vagabond warriors?

Let them try to stop her!

Sped by her Creator, she turned and ran.

✦ 29 ✦

Ela stood at the edge of the cliff on Siphra's coast, admiring the ocean's shimmering waves and the deep violet-blue of its far horizon. So much water! Siphra's shorelines—like the Tracelands'—were so soothing. The Infinite knew she'd needed this brief respite, His calming gift of beauty. Dry, landlocked Parne boasted nothing this mesmerizing.

Remembering Parne buoyed a sunken ache to the surface of Ela's thoughts. Would she see Parne again? Or her parents and her soon-to-be-born baby brother? Even Matron Prill's sour face would be a joy now. "Infinite, will I survive Siphra? Will I see Parne again?"

Her Creator's voice prompted gently. *They are waiting.*

"Yes." They. Siphra's faithful. But the Infinite hadn't answered concerning Parne. Did He judge—rightly, of course—that she would be unable to endure the answer?

Unnerved, Ela followed the cliff's knife-thin trail. She kept close to the weathered rock wall towering above to her right, while clutching the branch in her left hand—as if it could save her from falling into the cliff's jagged rocks below.

A particularly convoluted twist in the narrow cliff trail made her look up. If she hadn't seen this precipitous stone staircase in her wisp of a vision, she wouldn't have known it existed. She tucked her tunic higher in her belt to prevent it from snagging on the rocks, then pressed her toes into the first foothold. "How many of Your servants have died trying to climb these steps?" Ela demanded.

Mirth infused His response. *If I direct my servants to this place, won't I guard their every step—as I guard yours now?*

She'd deserved that little scolding. "I know You do. Forgive me."

His mercy reassured Ela even as the words left her mouth. She took a deep breath, lifted the branch, set it into the next stone foothold above her, then crushed down her too-mortal imaginings of rockslides. Rogue winds. Fear. Any of these might send her tumbling off this cliff.

Amazing that her foot didn't hurt. Was it healed? She hadn't stopped to check during her journey. Her pace, of course, had been too swift and the wound was nothing compared to this mission. She nudged her bandaged foot into the next barely discernible niche. Then made the mistake of looking down. Rocks . . . the sheer drop . . . she could almost feel the impact of her body striking the stones. Sweating, she shut her eyes. Breathe. Look up. Know that the Infinite guarded each step. "Onward!"

The sun had shifted by the time she reached her goal: a widening in the path. There stood an opening in the cliff, obscured by wind-bent trees. She rested until the branch glowed, lustrous in the midday sun, reminding her of her duty.

Ela smoothed her borrowed gown and approached the opening of the hidden cave. "Priests of Siphra's Infinite, you are summoned! Come out!"

One by one, twelve men stumbled from the cave, squinting in the daylight, their priestly robes ragged and gray, their hair and beards long and matted with knots, their faces hollowed by hunger and fear. The eldest, adorned with the gold chain and diadem of Siphra's deposed high priest, blinked at Ela. "You are the Parnian Prophet? The Infinite told us you would be sent, but He never . . ."

"Never warned you I'm a girl?" By their sidelong glances Ela knew her guess was correct. Failing to hide her amusement, she said, "Hmm. Well, I'm proof that the Infinite looks at the heart, not outward appearances. Do you have the vial of oil?"

The eldest crooked an arthritic finger toward one of his gaunt subordinates. Shakily, the man untied a packet from his belt, unrolled it, and offered a small gold-embossed case to Ela. She breathed a wordless, fearful prayer, set aside the branch, and secured the case to her tunic's decorative belt. Its modest weight made her shiver. Such a sacred, dangerous burden.

The high priest exhaled, relief easing the fretful lines on his old face. He lifted his hands above Ela's head and murmured, "Infinite, bless Your servant. May You be glorified as she fulfills Your commands!" He looked Ela in the eyes. "Our Creator said you would advise us. What is His plan?"

"Leave this place," she told the priests. "The first citizens you greet will provide you with food. When you've rested, travel north until you find the rebels. Ask for their leader, Akabe. He will protect you all."

One of the minor priests groaned and protested, "But before we reach his camp, we'll surely be sighted and killed by the queen's men!"

"The queen and her adherents will be too busy protecting themselves from the Infinite to hunt you. They'll be after me instead. Don't be afraid. Hasn't the Infinite saved you, His faithful priests?"

The high priest nodded. But his hunger-carved face turned wistful. "*She* killed all our true prophets."

A jab of fear made Ela pause. Would the queen add Ela's name to her list of slaughtered prophets? As usual, the Infinite was silent concerning Ela's death. Regarding Siphran prophets, however . . . Ela reassured the unhappy high priest, "Our Creator has appointed new prophets to stir Siphra toward Him. Meanwhile, obey the Infinite and leave this place."

To set the example, she swallowed her dread and began the torturous descent to the rocky beach below the cliffs.

As she set foot on the beach, Ela saw the next bit of her vision unfurl. For an instant, she wished Kien could face this vision with her. Surely he would find a reason to laugh. To offer encouragement. Comprehending the distinct possibility of death, she turned and followed the coastline south.

✦ ✦ ✦

To Kien's irritation, the destroyers rumbled and whinnied at each other through the woods, as if sharing opinions of their meals—leaves and saplings they crunched along the way. Good to know at least three members of their wearied band weren't hungry.

Kien halted Scythe and studied the fern-swathed woods. Did the gaps between those trees ahead look brighter?

Two tree spaces to Kien's left, Beka thumped a mossy trunk with her elegant boot and left a deliberate mark. "We're lost, aren't we? I'm sure I've seen this tree before. Next time we pass it, you'll know I'm right."

Kien frowned at his sister. "Are you finished complaining?"

"I wasn't complaining. I was stating my opinion *and* yours, though you're not about to admit it."

"I don't feel lost," Tzana announced from Beka's steed. Her tiny old-woman face crinkled with concentration as she looked up at the treetops. "Anyway we need to stop soon."

"You're hungry again, Tzana?" Jon called teasingly from Beka's left. "You eat more than I do! She has a point, Kien. It's near evening."

"Be patient, everyone," Kien said. "I'm sure that's a clearing ahead."

"I didn't say I was hungry," Tzana explained, her tone measured as if speaking to someone much younger. "But those men in the trees might want us to stop."

Men in the trees? Wary, Kien looked up.

A dark-bearded man armed with a bow and arrow glared down from the nearest tree. He met Kien's gaze and bellowed a warning toward the trees around him. "They've seen us—and you're right! They've destroyers!"

"Do we kill them?" another voice called.

Kien's heartbeat skipped. "I'd rather you not! Unless you'd prefer to start a war. We're Tracelanders."

Never mind what Father claimed, Kien was certain chaos would result if he and Jon were killed trying to rescue Ela. Not to mention Beka, Tzana, and the three destroyers.

A third man ordered from a distance, "Spare them for now. Actually, I'd prefer not to eat destroyer roasts. Too gamy."

Beka's destroyer squealed. Jon's snorted. Scythe turned abruptly. Kien ducked to avoid a limb scrape. "Scythe!" Had the beasts understood what the man said? Or did they simply hate hearing unseen potential enemies making threats?

Scythe tore through the underbrush, charging straight to the leader's tree. He circled the trunk, snorting in his finest bullying manner. The unseen leader yelled down, "Call off your destroyer, and we'll share this evening's meal—venison and lentils!"

"Not enough! I want your word that you mean us no harm, just as we mean you none."

Scythe reared and hammered the tree trunk with his massive front hooves, forcing Kien to clutch the war harness. The tree trembled and swayed.

Kien expected to see a body fall, but the leader hung on with commendable tenacity. And he spoke to Scythe in a shaken, pleasantly accented voice. "Destroyer, rest assured I do not kill Tracelanders!" As Scythe settled a bit, the wily man pitched a grain cake to the ground. "See, I am telling the truth—I'll feed you."

The destroyer snatched up the grain cake, but didn't leave the tree.

Though unconvinced of the leader's sincerity, Kien decided to end the stalemate before the treed men became desperate enough to use their arrows. "Scythe, back away!"

"Will your destroyer attack me if I descend?" the leader demanded.

"No." As Scythe backed away grudgingly, Kien patted his shoulder and whispered, "Good job! Here . . ." He pitched a grain cake from his stash. Scythe seized it, midair.

The leader, when he finally dropped to the ground, proved as agreeable as his voice—though badly groomed. Kien guessed him to be as old as Jon. The man called up to his comrades, "Look! I'm still alive, and the destroyers are calm! Get down here!" He grinned at Kien. "I gave you my word that we would share this evening's meal, therefore we shall. And we intend to be friends unless you try to deceive us."

His good-natured expression and easy stance settled Kien's nerves. "I won't place my family in danger by trying to deceive you, Sir . . . ?"

"Akabe, of no other name." The leader offered his hand.

Obviously one of the Siphran rebels, loathed by Ambassador Ruestock. Kien chuckled. "Akabe of no other name, thank you for your hospitality, despite the startling reception."

"Forgive us, but we are cautious men. We heard you approaching our camp like an unruly pack and decided to hide ourselves in the trees. Take no offense at the truth, I beg you. Had the little one not noticed us, we would have abandoned this place immediately." Akabe winked at Tzana. "Now, however, we know it will be safe for us to remain here tonight. A man traveling with his family usually desires peace."

By now, the other men had clambered down from the trees, shouldering their weapons. Silent. Less friendly than their leader. Kien decided to reinforce the peaceable image he'd offered the rebels. He introduced himself, Jon, Beka, and Tzana, then explained, "We're seeking Tzana's older sister, who was stolen from Jon and Beka's home several days ago. As soon as we find her we'll return to the Tracelands."

He had their attention, Kien realized. He dismounted, as did Jon and Beka. To a man, the rebels stared at him. Kien cleared his throat. "Her name is Ela of Parne. Have you heard of her?"

Akabe nodded his men toward their camp. They began to

walk. "We saw her. Two days past, we buried her captors. They were slain by a lindorm."

"A lindorm!" Beka gasped and reached for Jon's hand.

"Don't be frightened," Akabe said. "We killed it more than a day's walk from here. Would you enjoy seeing the lindorm's skin? Not pretty—but it proves our victory."

Kien found he'd been holding his breath. "Did Ela survive?"

The rebel leader was silent just long enough to worry Kien. But, with a glance at Tzana still riding Beka's destroyer, he chose his words carefully. "Indeed she survived. Tell me . . . this Ela of Parne, is she somehow exceptional?"

"She is Parne's prophet, serving the Infinite," Kien said. "Why?"

"A prophet!" Akabe halted, raising both fists. "And I doubted my sanity!"

"What happened?" Kien demanded. They waited at the edge of the clearing.

Akabe all but danced in jubilation. "We saw what we saw! My friends," he called to his men, "we imagined nothing—we saw the truth!"

"Who will believe us," the dark-bearded one complained, "if we say she lit and ran off like sunlight in the air, huh?"

"Did Ela's hair turn light?" Tzana asked, interested. "Did the branch become a tree?"

Akabe bowed before Tzana. "Child, sister of a prophet, I beg the honor of carrying you to the seat of tribute. This will be a story to tell my children—if I survive long enough to have children."

To prevent the destroyers from fretting, Kien hastily coaxed Tzana from the destroyer and allowed her to accept Akabe's praise. The rebels rekindled their fire, listening avidly while they finished cooking their meal. In the midst of their stories, Akabe covered his face with his hands. When he looked at them again, he said, "Forgive me. I have not heard the Infinite named since I was a boy. Now we hope that if He, whose name we dared not speak, has sent His prophet to Siphra . . ." He shook his head, undeniably overwhelmed.

Kien laughed. "Believe me. If the Infinite has sent Ela of Parne to Siphra, your king and queen ought to tremble."

Quietly amid the noisy celebration that followed, Beka asked Kien, "Ela has been in East Guard. Should Father and the Tracelands tremble?"

Her question stilled Kien. "I don't know."

✦ ✦ ✦

Ela halted in the pale sand, chilled by recognition. Munra, Siphra's capital, shone before her in the morning light, its pristine white buildings sharply lined against the edge of the ocean's deep blue on one side and lush trees and vegetation on the other. Open terraces supporting elaborate white altars punctuated the highest portions of the city and the palace, as did ornate white towers and arcades of lacy stonework, entwined with luxuriant flowering vines. Fragrant vines used in rituals honoring false gods.

The queen's gods. Or so the queen believed. Ela shuddered, longing for her vision to fade. To never reemerge in her thoughts, or in life.

She wanted to become plain Ela again. In Parne. Fetching water and wood for Mother, while fending off Amar's questing hands.

Amar? Bah! What was she thinking? Ela shut her eyes and willed her thoughts into the barren borderlands between Parne and Istgard. To the agonizing, soul-shredding fragment of existence without her Creator. Surrounded by fire. Unable to breathe, unable to die.

As the memory beaded her skin with sweat, Ela bowed her head. "Infinite, let Your will be done. And if I must die to accomplish Your purpose here . . ." She nodded mute agreement. All she lacked was courage to march toward the vision's beginning.

"Go!" she commanded herself.

Weighted with dread, Ela walked. And watched. From the corner of her eye, she glimpsed a stealthy form emerge from a thicket of shrubs and tall grasses bordering the beach. A wild man now followed Ela, his skin leathery from the sun, his garments badly weathered, his expression as grim as death. One callused hand gripped his sword—prepared to kill.

Ela continued walking.

✦ 30 ✦

Listen!

The voice woke Kien from a sound sleep. He peered through the early morning light at the still-slumbering forms of Jon and Beka. Beyond them, Scythe brooded over Tzana, who lay snug within her blankets. Akabe's men snored opposite the banked fire, while the man himself kept watch, a silhouette against the dawn.

Too distant a silhouette to provide that commanding voice.

Kien frowned. He'd been dreaming. As he turned over to settle himself for a bit more sleep, the voice cut into his thoughts again, stern—beyond doubt not to be ignored.

You will remain here.

Kien froze. Could this be . . . ?

I am your Creator. You will remain here.

Catching his breath, Kien stared up at the stars. "Certainly." What was he saying? He wanted to find Ela. And yet . . . the Infinite was *speaking.* To him. He waited, heart thudding.

I am bringing about what I have planned.

Meaning he, Kien Lantec, a mere mortal, would accomplish nothing by leaving this place? Fine. But if he was hearing the Infinite, would he also have visions? Would he become a prophet like Ela? "I'm listening."

✦ ✦ ✦

311

The disreputable-looking swordsman followed Ela along the beach, then up the stone steps into Munra. Really, he was making her nervous. Why couldn't her vision reveal the man's intent? Beneath her breath, she begged, "Infinite, I know this man is supposed to be here, but why is he following me?"

Child of dust, I commanded him and he obeyed.

"Oh!" The swordsman was also a servant of the Infinite. Did she look as disreputable as this man? Most likely, with her tangled hair, sandy, salt-sprayed garments, and missing sandal. "How did he know where to wait for me?"

I showed him this place in a vision.

Ela's heart skipped. As she wound through Munra's outer streets toward the palace at its crest, she whispered, "He's to be a Siphran prophet?!"

Yes. Say nothing yet. To him or the others.

Others. Of course she'd seen others. Exactly as she was seeing them now.

More men, some rich, some poor, all silent and armed with swords, stepped from doorways and behind pillars. Eyeing each other suspiciously, they fell into step behind her. Ela forced herself to continue walking. Turning to stare would be most unprophet-like. Were all these men to become prophets? "Why does Parne have only me?"

Parne needs only one.

Yet she wasn't in Parne. Ela shivered, setting aside the thought as the next portion of her vision unfolded. The sounds of footsteps behind her increased. A multitude of sandals and boots echoed against Munra's beautiful, smooth white-blocked streets. Each child's wondering face, the buildings, the vendors—all matched her vision.

Following the route she'd seen, Ela turned left onto Munra's broad main thoroughfare. Dazzling white pavings shone beneath her feet. The walkways were adorned with sculptures of haughty, scantily clad gods and sinuous creatures resembling lindorms, scalns, and web-crested leviathans—all with ferocious expressions, many with exposed fangs and claws. Altars stood before these grotesque statues, each heaped with smoking ashes or still-burning offerings from Munra's brightly robed citizens.

Open worship, ensuring open compliance and adoration of the queen's policies and her gods. To offer these hopeless demonstrations of spiritual enslavement, the woman had outlawed all worship of the Infinite and killed all of Siphra's faithful prophets and most of their priests.

Ela seethed. Good. Wrath was better than fear.

The palace stood on a hill at the top of the street, and Ela strode toward it, ignoring the stares. Now, judging by the echoes of their footsteps, a small army of Siphrans followed her. Would they accompany her into the palace? Hadn't she been alone during the confrontation in her vision?

As she proceeded through the vast public square—decorated with fountains, flowers, and sitting areas—Ela heard the soon-to-be prophets' footsteps cease behind her. Obviously halted by their Creator-General.

Precisely as she'd seen and sensed, Ela approached the palace's huge arched stone entry alone. The branch flared brilliant white-silver in her grip. A guard called through the ornately woven metal gate, "Who are you? Why have you come?"

Ela lifted her chin. "I am Ela of Parne. Your queen and the king are eager to speak with me! Haven't your prophets *warned* you?" Was she supposed to sound so sarcastic?

After a squint at the branch's extraordinary metallic glow, the guard lowered the rim of his gilded helmet and retreated. "Wait."

His commander soon appeared at a narrow side gate and slammed a broad L-shaped key into the heavy lock. "Enter. They are at their morning meal, so you'll have to wait. Where are your guards?"

Guards? He was asking about her abductors. "I have no guard but the Infinite."

The commander didn't bother to hide his sneer.

Ela charged past him.

"See here!" the man protested. "You will not enter the royal presences unguarded!"

"Hurry, then. Perhaps you can protect your royal ones from the Truth."

Precious stones—inlaid everywhere within the palace's white marble as trees, vines, and flowers—glistened at Ela. The floor, polished and level, made the difference between Ela's sandal and her rough bandage noticeable. Compared to the palace's jeweled perfection, her lovely gold-embroidered gown seemed quite simple. At least the branch was glorious and inspiring.

Limping, she entered a large banquet room and fixed her gaze upon the two occupants of the dais, King Segere and Queen Raenna.

Both elegant, seated in vine-and-flower patterned marble chairs, their clothes glittering, the royal couple picked at their morning meal as if too good for their food.

Their courtiers, seated below the dais at long tables, were also stylish in elaborately embroidered robes and tunics. Almost as one, they threw bored, delicately disapproving looks at Ela and the guard, then returned to their meals. Amid the courtiers, Ela glimpsed shadows seething and whispering—the hostile spiritual forces dominating the palace. If only the courtiers and their king and queen could see and recognize these rebellious deceivers' shadows. Minions of their Adversary, not—as they believed—aspects of Siphra's gods.

The deceivers hovered most thickly around certain dark-robed courtiers who flaunted gold chains and were attended by servants holding imposing gold and ebony staffs. Raenna's prophets. Every bit as pompous as she'd envisioned them.

The king studied Ela as if bemused, his vague expression betraying a meandering, undisciplined mind. "This is the Parnian?"

He didn't seem terribly interested. Ela hoped to change his condition. "I am the Parnian. But surely you know this. Your prophets told you, didn't they?"

Segere shrugged his narrow shoulders and rested his thin,

well-manicured fingertips at his platter's golden edge. "We are interested only for the sake of our dear queen." His words drifted into a yawn.

The dear queen Raenna frowned, forming creases between her painted, gem-dusted eyebrows. By the look of her skin, gold-dusted and bejeweled like a statue, Ela suspected her of imitating, perhaps aspiring to be, the goddess Atea. In cool, polished tones, the queen said, "Ela of Parne. How agreeable. Where are your guards?"

"My guards, as you call them, are dead. The Infinite sent a lindorm to attack them when they threatened my life."

Raenna's red-edged gilded lips curled. Amused. "Is this a warning?"

"It is the truth."

"The truth! We are most interested in your variations of the truth. Please, continue. Tell us our future."

"The Infinite is the Truth. Any variations are your own. As for your future, O Queen, if your prophets were true prophets, they would have told you what is about to happen."

The queen stood and descended from the dais in graceful whisperings of rich fabrics and flowing movements. She faced Ela. Looked down at her, actually. Ela had never seen anyone so lovely, with such soulless amber eyes. Her voice dropped further, devoid of emotion. "What is about to happen?"

"Ask your unprophets."

One of the queen's prophets swept forward, his face suffused with rage. "You—a child—*dare* to imply we are false prophets?"

Ela braced herself, lifting her chin. "I imply nothing. I'm telling everyone openly that you and your fellow soothsayers have abandoned the truth and worship deceivers—servants of the Adversary. Therefore, the Infinite plans to remove you all from power."

As she expected, the false prophet struck her hard enough to send her reeling. The impact stung her cheek and mouth, but she smiled. "Have you left a mark?"

Before the pretender answered, Raenna lifted a staying hand. She grimaced, fragile lines framing her mouth, weblike creases etching the corners of her eyes. "You claim to know your Infinite's plans. But what are my plans, little prophet of Parne?"

"You consider me to be a living talisman, which is untrue. And you intend to render me useless by persuasion or death, because you are planning to order an invasion of the Tracelands."

Ela's announcement of this hitherto undisclosed information sent hisses and gasps of apprehension throughout the court.

Raenna laughed—for effect, Ela knew. Her gilded lips stiff with a fraud's smile, she raised her voice. "*I* am planning? Oh, Prophet, you are so wrong! My beloved king, my own husband, declares Siphra's plans. And he's said nothing of an invasion." She bowed her head toward the king.

"True . . . true . . ." Segere bestowed a doting look upon his wife—which she returned with marked fondness.

Ela continued. "You also fear the Infinite will remove you from your soul's throne. You hate Him because He requires obedience—though it's for your own sake—like a perfect and loving Father. He cannot be controlled as you control your little gods and your husband."

The queen's eyes widened. She sucked in a breath and laughed again. Heartily. As the courtiers tittered, Raenna muttered to Ela. "You've signed your death warrant."

"You've already sealed it." Ela forced off the fear prickling over her skin. No doubt Raenna's planned execution involved lingering agony and humiliation, personally witnessed by her royal self. Ela met the woman's conceited, paint-veiled gaze. "It may be that you'll kill me. But the Infinite will repay you. By the way, He intends to measure your devotion to your gods."

The Siphran queen's smugness hardened. "My devotion to my gods is immeasurable."

"Not if the Infinite does the measuring. Do you love your gods beyond your life?"

"With all my being." Raenna's voice rang through the chamber, rebellious. And genuinely fervent. "My soul is devoted to my gods—I will never give them up."

Ela winced. Any torment she experienced at the queen's command, Raenna would suffer eternally, a thousandfold, because of her devotion to immortal deceivers. "You've chosen. But even now, the Infinite will have mercy on you, if you repent."

"Patronizing child! I've nothing to repent. You may keep your arrogant, self-righteous, egotistical Infinite!"

Each hate-filled word of insult stabbed Ela's heart. "How has the Infinite deserved such abuse? He has loved you. He's given you everything to be desired in this life, but you ignore those blessings. You grieve Him continually! You create your own troubles, then blame Him. You long to *be* Him!"

The queen's tawny eyes gleamed. "He deserves to be replaced."

"You—and anyone but the Infinite—would destroy all Creation within two breaths of becoming god. But that's unimportant now. The Infinite has judged your corruption and chosen your successors."

"Our successors?" She looked Ela up and down, plainly incredulous. Her gaze fixed at Ela's waist. Upon the golden case holding the sacred vial of anointing oil, traditionally carried only by Siphra's high priest. The queen sucked in a sharp breath. "How did you acquire *that*?"

"Through the Infinite's will." Ela waited, suppressing a shiver. Praying for strength.

Sweat gleamed on the royal face, oozing between the gilding and paint. "Kill her!"

The vision ended.

Ela closed her eyes.

✦ 31 ✦

*L*eave *this place now.*
   The Infinite's words rested, tranquil within Ela's thoughts. She opened her eyes and saw her guard's startled expression—his paralyzing fear.

Numbed, Ela turned away from the outraged queen and left the chamber. The branch glowed softly, lighting her way. Was she supposed to survive? Why? "Infinite, I was ready."

A current seemed to propel her from the palace. No one stopped her as she marched past the exquisite gem-traced white columns. It was as if she couldn't be touched. Or seen. Incredible.

"Why are You saving me? Was that a test?"

Your work is not finished.

Despite His words—or because of them—Ela wobbled. As if recovering from a terrible shock. She reached the palace's small side gate, found it open, and stepped through.

Close the gate.

She obeyed. The lock clicked loudly, seeming to promise her enemies were barred inside until she escaped. Ela stared at the solid-looking lock, dazed. This was like waking up from a dream. Disorienting. Ela gave herself a stern inward shake and hurried from the gate.

Sunlight bathed the huge whitewashed public square, daz-zling her. Amid this splendor, numerous brightly clad citizens of

Munra promenaded or visited each other, laughing and talking, some eyeing her, but most oblivious to her presence. Siphra's newly appointed prophets emerged from the crowds, approaching her from all directions, their expressions eager, anticipating adventure. Obviously, they'd been watching for her, certain she would return.

"Infinite? They knew I would live, and I didn't?" She was going to laugh. Or scream. Ela scolded herself in a fierce whisper. "Be still!" Hysteria was not prophet-like, and no doubt she was still in danger, as were His Siphran prophets. "Infinite? What now?"

A vision unfurled with such force that Ela had to halt and clutch the branch to prevent herself from falling. The vision encompassed Ela. Absorbed her into itself, then released her within a breath, leaving her gasping.

Ela steadied herself, opened her eyes, and addressed Siphra's new prophets. "We've no time to waste."

✦ ✦ ✦

On a broad sea cliff adjacent to the palace, they prayed and prepared for Siphra's sacrifice to the Infinite—the first in almost twenty years.

"This is a death offense," one of the soon-to-be prophets warned Ela, his roughened hand already on his sword as if anticipating an attack. "No one is permitted to acknowledge the Infinite. The king and queen executed our priests for leading worship."

"I, for one, am willing to die," Ela said. "That's why I was sent here. However, your high priest and a handful of other priests remain."

The Siphran's eyes brightened, and his weathered face creased in a grin. "They're alive? Alive! How can this be? We thought they were all dead—we've been mourning for years!"

Ela laughed, though a shiver ran up her arms. Too often, priests and prophets were rivals. Hadn't Eshtmoh been forced out of Parne after his war on faithless believers? She too had been politely encouraged to leave Parne. "Yes, your priests are alive, though frail. The Infinite has protected them through their ordeals."

"But they aren't here to lead the sacrifice. Will you . . . ?"

Was he asking her to officiate over the sacrifice? Ela shook her head.

Several others, who had been listening, now nodded. The wild man, the first Siphran to follow her up into Munra, said, "You must."

You will lead.

"Infinite?" Ela knelt and covered her face with her mantle. How could she, the youngest person on this cliff, lead the sacrifice? "I'm no priest!" Ela pleaded with the Infinite in a frantic whisper. "How can I be worthy to officiate?"

The branch gleamed in her hands and the Infinite's presence seemed to encircle her.

Your Creator has made you worthy because you have been found faithful.

Determined to obey Him, Ela shifted her prayers from fears of her own inadequacies to pleas for these men and their safety, their futures as His prophets. At last, she stood and looked around.

Nearby, on the palace's magnificent terrace, courtiers leaned against the ornate balustrades and watched. Some were entering and leaving the palace repeatedly. Most likely bearing messages to the queen and the doubtless bored king.

Segere would not be so bored if he could stir himself to hear the truth.

In the late afternoon, as the Siphran prophets placed the offerings of a lamb and a calf on the wood, Ela approached the edge of the cliff. Facing the palace, she called to the courtiers and all Siphrans within earshot. "I am Parne's prophet of the Infinite, with Siphra's faithful ones—ready for today's sacrifices. Come worship the one true God, the Infinite!"

More courtiers assembled on the royal terrace. On the open hillsides around the palace and the cliff, citizens of Munra watched, prompted by curiosity.

Queen Raenna and her prophet-pretenders now paraded onto the royal terrace, most seeming indifferent. The queen, however, looked as if she longed to personally kill Ela.

To goad them, Ela shouted, "Listen, you proud, foolish people! How long will you believe the lies of deceivers? The Infinite is your Creator! He is the reason for your existence, yet you've rejected Him to follow your own desires. Now He will drive out your false gods, your false leaders, and your delusions!"

On the hillsides below, Munra's citizens listened, buzzing over the slopes like a hive anticipating conflict. Several from the crowds approached Ela. One older than the rest said, "We've prayed for this day!"

"Your Creator hears," Ela murmured. Her dread increased.

The false prophet who had struck Ela cried out from the royal terrace in ringing tones, "Our ruler of light, Atea, condemns you! May you rot in darkness! May the gods Seibo, Nemane, and Dagar forever torment you in the Nightlands!"

"Who are these little gods?" Ela demanded. "The Infinite has never seen them in His Presence!" To herself, she whispered, "Infinite, open their eyes!"

The queen leaned forward on the balustrade, her hands clenched in fists. "Parnian! If you offer this sacrifice, you will not survive past sunset!"

"Come stop me!" Ela taunted. "Come face the Infinite!"

The queen and her prophets stepped back from the balustrade, visibly squabbling, though they'd lowered their voices.

Ela studied the waning sun. At this hour in Parne, the priests always offered sacrifices to the Infinite. She approached the stone altar and its unlit pyre. Lifting the branch, she prayed loudly, "Infinite, show that You are the One True God, and that I am Your servant—and that we, your faithful ones, have prepared this sacrifice at Your command. Answer us, Infinite, so these people will know that You alone are their God, calling their hearts to Yours!"

Like a massive lightning strike, fire fell from the clear blue sky and shook the cliff. Screams echoed from every direction as the Infinite's sacrifice flared and vanished beneath the heaven-sent flames. The sacrificial wood, the stones of the temporary altar, and the dust around it crumbled, consumed by the roaring fire.

Everyone on the terrace fell to their knees, including the out-raged King Segere and Queen Raenna. The citizens of Munra collapsed along the slopes below. Unlike the king and queen, they screamed, "The Infinite is God! He is God!"

When the flames vanished, Ela turned toward the palace. On the royal terrace, attended by her advisors and the silent king, Raenna pulled herself to her feet. "Ela of Parne, may my gods kill me if I do not kill you!"

Ela stood and lifted the branch. "You will die. The Infinite now gives you to your deceivers—the 'gods' you've chosen over Him."

Before Ela finished speaking, darkness lifted like smoke from all the windows and doors of the palace, fused together in a writhing column, then twisted downward to envelop the queen.

King Segere shrieked and ran to the far side of the balcony. Raenna's advisors scattered as she screeched and lifted her hands in a futile attempt to ward off the "gods" she believed she loved. The dark seething cloud merged with Siphra's queen. She tore at her elaborately coiled, gilded hair—and knocked her crown to the balcony's pavings. Ela heard the metal ring as it settled against the stones. Queen Raenna fled, raving hoarse curses.

Segere rushed to the edge of the balcony and pointed at Ela while calling to his servants, "K-kill her! C-cut her limb from limb!"

Limb from limb? No! "Infinite!" Spurred by terror, Ela skittered downhill, into the valley below.

✦ ✦ ✦

Kien watched Akabe conduct a meeting, issuing orders, boasting of the lindorm's death—and of Ela's amazing transformation and disappearance—before sending his band of rag tag messengers to his deliberately scattered cohorts. While methods of leadership were far less structured than Tsir Aun's had been in Istgard, Akabe was obviously confident of his followers' loyalty. And why shouldn't he be? Kien had never seen any leader so cheerful, so willing to share hardships with his followers. He was also used to giving orders and being obeyed. Was Akabe a rebel nobleman? Kien was convinced of it, listening to Akabe speak.

"Tell the others to cheer up. We are convinced that the Infinite—bless His Most Holy Name—is moving to free Siphra of its tyrants! I am waiting with you, praying you may return to your families." He clapped a hand on a lanky young messenger's shoulder, and added, "Each of you, take a piece of the lindorm's skin and tell the others about our latest kill and our news."

The messengers each accepted a square of pale gray skin and reverently rolled it in protective leather before tucking away the tokens. The youngest messenger grinned, his teeth surprisingly white against his patchy beard. "A lindorm kill means good luck!"

"A blessing," Akabe corrected. "A sign of blessing from the Infinite. Tell the others so."

The messengers dashed into the woods, not one of them questioning Akabe's authority. Satisfaction played across the young man's affable features. He landed a fist on Kien's shoulder. "We need more meat. Will your destroyer cooperate with a hunt?"

"Leading the chase, you mean?" Kien shrugged. "As long as he's fed."

Akabe pulled a whetstone from his gear and began to sharpen his sword with quick ringing swipes. "We've heard of new metalwork from the Tracelands. Your most elite citizens carry invincible swords with blades patterned like the ocean's bluest waves. Tell me about these."

Kien grinned. "No."

"Huh. I'll wear you down, Tracelander. You know I will."

Tzana tottered up, with Scythe grazing his way after her. The little girl leaned against Kien's arm. "We're bored. What are we doing today?"

"The same as yesterday. Gather food for everyone and watch for the enemy." Kien tucked the child playfully beneath his arm, jostling her lightly, making her giggle and squeal. Distressing Scythe. From the corner of his eye, Kien watched the huge beast pace in agitation, obviously longing to protect Tzana, but reluctant to injure Kien.

Jon and Beka rode up, their destroyers huffing. As he helped Beka to dismount, Jon called over his shoulder, "We've company approaching. It seems they're carrying a body."

A body? Kien's throat constricted with a sudden strangling fear. "Ela . . ."

+ 32 +

Stones gouged Ela's feet, bruising her wound as she scrambled downward into the valley. Her breath stabbed with every gasp. This morning she'd been prepared to die if she must to fulfill the Infinite's will. But being hacked apart limb by limb? Well, certain circumstances demanded resistance.

Half the population of Munra seemed to be milling through this small, open valley, laughing and calling to each other as if celebrating a victory. The other half of Munra clogged all the pathways from the city. Men. Women. Beautiful wide-eyed children. All in simple tunics of crimson, blue, green . . . Ela halted amid the throng. What was she doing?

If she stayed here, the king's guards might butcher innocent Siphrans.

A man to Ela's right called, "Here's the prophet! She's rescued us from the tyrants."

Someone—a white-robed old woman—clasped Ela in an embrace and wept. Ela tried to extricate herself. "Please, let me go! The king's guards might kill you trying to get to me."

"So be it!" the old woman yelled. "I'm sick to death of those fiends and their lies. They killed my husband and son for refusing to sacrifice to the goddess Atea. I want revenge!"

"It won't be revenge if you don't live to see it," Ela warned. She stared the woman in the face. "I don't want you to die with me."

The aged woman's eyes brightened with mischievous inspiration. "Why should either of us die?" She screamed louder, hurting Ela's ears, "Save the prophet! Citizens of Munra, use your weapons. Protect our prophet and His servants!"

Her cry was repeated by others until it became an uproar. A short distance away, Ela saw one of the Infinite's new Siphran prophets leap onto a rock and raise his sword in triumph. As Ela shuddered at the sight, he bellowed, "Now is the time to resist! Show your weapons! Defeat the tyrants who've held us in fear. For the Infinite!"

The king's guards were descending from the palace, swords and shields readied. Until they saw the countless numbers of swords and daggers lifted overhead by the mob. Several retreated and ran for the palace again.

The remaining soldiers turned, joined the mob, and added a battle cry of their own. As if they'd been planning for this day. "Take the palace!"

Ela clutched the branch, stunned, watching a revolution unfold. "Oh, Infinite . . ."

The old woman laughed and hugged her again—frolicsome as a child. "We've waited for you!"

✦ ✦ ✦

Kien joined Akabe and lifted a barrel of flour from a tradesman's cart. Jubilant, Akabe said, "Yesterday olive oil and dried fruit. Today flour. What gift will tomorrow bring?"

"Let's hope such generosity continues," Kien agreed.

Their guests, Siphra's long-lost priests, had certainly caused a stir with their appearance. Gifts streamed from nearby villages. Kien welcomed their generosity. Hospitable as Akabe and his men were, their meals had left much to be desired before the priests' arrival.

As Kien and Akabe lowered the barrel of flour near the cooking fire, the ailing high priest, Johanan, sat up on his bed of furs. His color was better today, Kien noticed. A great improvement

since his subordinate priests had carried him into Akabe's encampment. The old man looked like a wax figure that first day.
Indeed, his followers had given him up for dead.

Johanan beamed at Kien and Akabe. "Amazing how the Infinite provides for us! Had I known we'd be met with such generosity, we would have left our hiding place long ago."

"It was not safe," Akabe protested. "Have you forgotten how
the kingdom was searched? How anyone suspected of loyalty to
the Infinite was tormented or killed?"

Kien suspected Akabe had suffered torment, but the young
man rarely voiced personal details. The high priest shrugged.
"Surely our sufferings are finished."

Akabe laughed and teased, "Your sufferings continue, I fear.
Not one of my men can bake."

"Ah, but mine can," Johanan said, to Kien's relief. "Who do
you suppose baked bread in the Infinite's temple? When the
temple existed . . ."

They fell silent, no doubt remembering a glorious place,
long gone. Akabe sighed. "The Infinite's temple will be rebuilt.
Someday."

For the remainder of the afternoon, the camp was devoted to
talk of the Infinite's temple, and baking bread. Soft, puffy rounds
of flat bread, so similar to Ela's style of baking that Kien paused
to stare at it during their evening meal. Where was she? "Please,
keep her safe," he muttered. If he could be sure Ela was safe,
nothing else mattered.

"Did you say something?" Beka asked, seated between him
and Jon, with Tzana nestled in her lap.

"I was thinking of Ela."

"Oh." Beka's face expressed silent sympathy.

"She'll come back soon." Tzana sounded more hopeful than
certain. Kien saw the little girl blink, as if trying to combat tears.

He was setting aside his bread to console her when the watch-
man cried from a treetop, "More visitors—a herd!"

Visitors, the man had warned. Not enemies. Even so, Kien

grabbed his sword and joined Akabe. Standing orders were for all armed men to station themselves along the approach to the encampment and give warning to the others if the visitors were deemed unfriendly.

Unbidden, Scythe trotted up to Kien and nudged him, while crunching down the remains of a shrub. Kien patted the destroyer's shining neck. "You took long enough to respond, you glutton. Let's go have a look at our visitors."

The destroyer sniffed, twitched, then charged down the slope. Without Kien.

✦ ✦ ✦

Ela dismounted the petulant donkey, kindly loaned by her feisty elderly protector—the unsung leader of the valley uprising, Tamri Het.

From her family's crowded, cushioned cart in the procession behind her, Tamri called out, "Is my beast misbehaving again, Ela-girl?"

"Not too much," Ela called back. "I simply need to stretch. We're almost there."

Tamri cackled and threatened genially, "Don't you dare have adventures until I'm there, little prophet."

"I won't. But hurry along!" Ela hoped her adventures were finished for a while. After this comparatively mild one, of course. She climbed the hill, using the branch for support. Her wounded foot was only a bit tender—a mercy.

Trees shaded portions of the path here. Familiar trees. Ela smiled. A deep-throated rumbling whinny echoed to her from the distance—the most welcomed sound she'd heard in weeks. "Pet!"

The destroyer bolted out from the trees at the crest of the hill, impressive, and so perfectly glossy black that Ela almost sighed in admiration. Pet hesitated, then charged for her. Ela gasped. "Slow down!"

Pet stopped just short of knocking her over, but gave her such a bump with his nose that she stumbled backward. Ela caught her balance and laughed, then hugged the monster's neck. "You dear rascal! Oh, I didn't dare pray you'd be here." And if Pet was here . . .

Ela stepped back and looked up the path. A black-cloaked figure marched out of the trees. "Kien."

Why did she want to cry? Even from that distance she saw his grin. He dashed down the path to greet her and gave the destroyer an ineffective shove in passing. "Scoundrel! Couldn't even wait for me, could you? Out of my way!"

Pet grunted and stepped aside. But he flicked his tail, whisking Kien's hair. Ela laughed at them both. Kien slapped the destroyer, then grabbed Ela's hand and kissed it warmly, gazing at her so fervently that her knees wobbled and her thoughts fell to pieces. Truly, she'd been more confident facing monsters and assassins. Before she could compose herself, Kien pressed his advantage, pulling her close and kissing her cheek. "You're safe! We were just talking about you. Though you probably know that."

If he'd intended to fluster her, he was succeeding. Ela had to speak slowly. "So . . . you've forgiven me . . . a little?"

"Completely. When I thought you were dead—" He hesitated, clearly so overcome that he was fighting to speak. "Nothing else mattered. I needed to know you were safe."

Ela blinked away tears, then gently stepped out of his embrace—though she didn't want to. But he wouldn't relinquish her hand. She worked up a smile. "Thank you. However one day I won't be safe. And you cannot protect me. Nor can Pet."

"Scythe."

"Fine. Scythe. Just promise me that when I'm gone you'll go on with your life."

"I promise you nothing, except that I still love you."

"Kien, you cannot continue to—"

"Yes I can." He smiled, but his gray eyes were serious. "I can and will pursue you for the rest of our lives. And if you argue, I'll be pleased to debate you. I'll win. You know I will."

"You hope you will!"

"I sense false bravado."

She tipped the branch at him, half threatening. "You're calling me false?"

"Not you. Only the bravado." He looked over her head at the cumbersome procession winding its way up the hill. "What's this? Who are all these people?"

"A Siphran welcoming committee. You must be serious now and stop flirting with me."

"Who is flirting? I'm quite serious. I intend to marry you."

"You're hopeless!"

"I'd say quite the opposite."

"May I change the subject?"

"Of course. As long as the new subject concerns us."

"It does. We have business to attend to, Ambassador." She tugged her hand from Kien's and led the way to the encampment. Akabe met them and started to speak, but Ela warned him to silence with the upraised branch. "When everyone has gathered, I'll speak to you."

"What are you doing?" Softly, Kien chided, "Ela, why did you silence Akabe? He's—"

Ela murmured, "He will soon understand. This is not an ordinary visit." And she must behave with prophet-like dignity.

"Ela!" Tzana scampered toward her, a grin crinkling her little face—breaking Ela's composure.

"Oh!" She knelt, caught her baby sister, and hugged her, kissing her wispy curls. And crying. Not proper prophet behavior. Or was it? She didn't care.

Still holding Tzana, Ela stood. Beka waited nearby. With a sweeping glance and a lifted eyebrow that perfectly mimicked Kien, Beka said, "Look at all those wrinkles and spots on your clothes." She sighed, as if disheartened. "At least you started out well dressed. Never mind; I'll dust you off and spruce you up when we return home."

Had Beka already decided that the Tracelands was Ela's home? Kien! Beka was in league with Kien.

As they hugged, Beka whispered, "I'm so glad you're safe! Who cares about anything else? How is your wound?"

"Healing. Thank you." She waited until Tamri Het and all the Siphran prophets and officials from Munra were gathered and respectfully silent. With a kiss and a pat, Ela set down Tzana. Then she beckoned the high priest. He hobbled toward her as swiftly as his arthritic limbs allowed. Raising her voice so everyone could hear, Ela said, "You are the chief witness."

She rested the branch in the crook of her arm, unlaced the sacred vial from her belt, opened its case, then broke the golden seal.

Akabe retreated a step as she approached. She couldn't blame him—the branch glowed in her hand, probably making Akabe fear she'd transform him somehow. And she would. On tiptoe, she poured the delicate stream of golden oil over his head. "Akabe Garric, this is what the Infinite says . . . 'I anoint you king over Siphra.' " She stepped back. "Call to your Creator in every matter, King Akabe. He will advise you."

Siphra's new king looked confounded. But the high priest shuffled toward him, dignified, a hand upraised. "May the Infinite bless you and grant you wisdom as you obey His will."

The prophets and Munra's officials gathered around Akabe, clamoring. He must go with them at once to take control of the capital and the palace. He must hunt down Segere and Raenna's cohorts and their false prophets, and bind them over to face their victims' relatives. He must . . .

Akabe's followers and Tamri Het hurried to concoct the largest feast they could muster. But Kien faced Ela, much too serious. "You knew this would happen the night you were stolen from East Guard."

"Somewhat." Ela bent to pick up Tzana, who was tugging her mantle. "I didn't expect to survive. And I didn't know the Infinite would anoint Akabe until a few days ago. The situation in Munra was . . . difficult." For Tzana's sake, she changed the subject, teasing Kien. "I hope you made good use of your time while visiting the king, Ambassador."

"I would have made better use of this opportunity if I'd known it was an opportunity!"

"You're not going to sulk, are you?"

"No. I'm not." His expression lightened. She could almost see mischief taking form in his thoughts. "I've found a way to drive Scythe half insane. Where is he? Tzana, pretend to quarrel with me."

"His name is Pet!" Tzana argued, so emphatic that Ela knew she meant it.

Kien frowned. "No, he's Scythe!"

On the other side of the clearing, the huge destroyer stopped eating and began to pace. Ela was certain she saw him sweating.

✦ ✦ ✦

A light breeze from the ocean ruffled Kien's hair as he rode Scythe up Temple Hill to Ela's residence—the stone chamber carved within the cliff near the temple's ruins. He urged the destroyer through the sunny clearing and grinned.

Ela was sitting on a fallen stone behind a makeshift table near the orchard. Preparing ink and a scroll. And watching Tzana, who was playing nearby with a giggling, squealing group of little girls visiting from East Guard and Siphra. Including Tamri Het's great-granddaughter.

Tamri was "vacationing" with Ela. Still. But Kien couldn't begrudge the spry octogenarian Ela's company. They suited each other well. And Tamri's no-nonsense presence staved off any gossip that might brew if Ela and Tzana were living alone. She also chased off other would-be suitors—a practice Kien happily encouraged.

Ela glanced up and smiled. Kien couldn't mistake her expression. She was delighted to see him. Prophet or not, she did love him, he was sure of it. All the more reason to continue his pursuit.

Kien dismounted and turned Scythe loose to prune the shrubs. "Good morning, Prophet! No squabbling scholars today?"

"Not yet. Are you off on a mission, Ambassador?"

"Not yet." He sat on a broken pillar. "I'm leaving with General

Rol next week." Offering a mock half bow, he said, "Kien Lantec—judge-advocate in training."

"You'll be superb," she murmured. "But that's merely my opinion."

"Which is why I've come to visit. I want your opinion."

"About . . . ?"

Kien blurted out the question he'd feared to ask. "Should we Tracelanders be concerned about your presence? Are you planning to overthrow our government as you did in Istgard and Siphra?"

She laughed and set her still-unused reed pen in its stand. "No. Even prophets need a place to rest. For now, my place is here. To rest and teach and write. Meanwhile, if you stubborn Tracelanders listen to the Infinite—and I'm praying with all my might you do—He will be satisfied. Look."

Ela lifted an ivory tablet and pointed to the engraving on its base. *Lan Tek.* "The Lantec name in its old form. Your rebel heritage was based on more than squabbles over land rights and political differences. Love of the Infinite separated your ancestors from Istgard's gods."

Kien studied the tablet, bemused. He couldn't deny the engraving's age. Or her assumption. Well, well. Here was a lesson old Master Cam Wroth had never offered in his classes. Kien inspected the aged tablet until Ela asked, "What are you sending to Istgard for the wedding?"

"Wedding?"

"Tsir Aun and Tek Lara's wedding. They've sent word that they'll marry next month. I have little to offer but my prayers for blessings."

"I'm sure they consider your prayers for them to be a great honor." Kien envied the couple. Soon, he hoped to send Tsir Aun similar news of his own wedding to Ela.

Did Ela know how appealing she looked, sitting in the sunshine, with ink on her fingers and her hair frazzled? Probably not—which was one of her many charms. Kien leaned toward her, deliberately lowered his voice, and began to cajole softly. "Promise you'll write to me while I'm gone. Send me your favorite verses from the Books of the Infinite—I need to learn them, you know. . . ."

It was true. He did want to study these sacred writings his ancestors had cherished. They were part of his heritage. And the Infinite and Ela composed his future.

Anyway, how could she refuse a departing soldier's earnest request? "Promise?"

✦ ✦ ✦

Ela watched Kien ride away on Scythe. She must not mope and be miserable in their absence. Really, she shouldn't have promised to write him. She would long for his messages. Crave them. It was dangerous . . . foolish! Yet she'd been unable to refuse Kien.

Frustratingly irresistible man!

"Infinite? Why didn't You warn me?"

Silence answered. Ela felt the Infinite's presence as He waited and watched.

And loved. Always.

At peace with her Creator, she lifted her pen, tapped it in the ink jar, and began to write on her weighted parchment.

These are the records of Ela, prophet of Parne.

In the last year of the reign of King Tek An of Istgard, the Infinite sent His prophet of Parne a vision. . . .

ACKNOWLEDGMENTS

My dear Lord and Savior, thank you for your endless loving-kindness. I'm still amazed and blessed that you sent Ela to pester me until I listened! Applause and lunch out to Donita K. Paul, my dear friend and fellow fantasy fiction fanatic extraordinaire, who read the first few chapters as I wrote them and cheered me onward. Donita, you are a gem, thank you!

To my brilliant fightmaster-brother, Joe Barnett, for cheerfully providing emergency fencing and sword info and reviewing certain nightmare-inducing scenes. Red Robin!!!

Honors and a group hug to the Hobbit Hole critique groups: Donita K. Paul, Evangeline Denmark, Beth DeVore, Jim Hart, Beth K. Vogt, and Mary Agius. When are we meeting again?

To the Lost Genre Guild, thank you for the fun and debates, particularly Caprice Hokestadt, Pete you-know-who-you-are, Frank Creed, Forrest Schultz, Alice Roelke, Fred Warren, Noah Arsenault, and Johne Cooke, who offered suggestions and riotous puns.

Special thanks to Katharin Fiscaletti for her artistic imagination—I look forward to future works, Kat! Also thanks to Lisa Buffaloe, Anita Mellot, Ann-Louise Gremminger, Becky Cardwell, Steve Visel, Rene McLean, Robert Mullin, Linda and

Bob Mullin, Jeri Fontyn, Beka Thelen, and Anna Thelen for the fun and cheers. A wave to Scott Rogers and the Falcon 1644 team—thanks for putting up with me. Special hugs to Debbie and Star, Kristen, and Kaitlyn Coutee, who loved Pet and offered horse sense.

Last, but not least, endless gratitude to the team at Community Bible Studies. Your lessons and devotion to sharing the Lord's written Word have been—and continue to be—inspiring!

DISCUSSION QUESTIONS

1. What is Ela's first action when she realizes she is truly hearing the voice of her Creator, the Infinite? Do you think Ela's response to the Infinite's command is characteristic of a true prophet? Why or why not?

2. What do you believe is Ela's most critical personal challenge as she takes on her role as the Infinite's prophet? What would trouble you the most if you were chosen to be a prophet?

3. Ela's fragile little sister, Tzana, accompanies Ela with the Infinite's express permission. How does the Infinite ultimately reach others through Tzana's obedience and her frailty?

4. In the borderlands, the Infinite leaves Ela completely alone, shattering her physically and spiritually. What long-term effect does this temporary loss of His presence have on Ela? How might Ela's enemies benefit from her devastating experience?

5. What is your first impression of Kien Lantec? What aspects of his character emerge as he faces extreme, often dangerous

circumstances? Do you think your Creator inspires similar characteristics in you during times of testing? What traits do you want others to see in you as you confront challenges?

6. Ela often questions her worth as a prophet. Why does she see herself as a failure? Does the Infinite agree with her? Can you think of any Old Testament prophets or leaders who believed they were failures?

7. As their relationship progresses, Ela and Kien each struggle with their physical and emotional responses toward the other. What evidence, if any, did you find of genuine love in their relationship, as opposed to basic physical attraction? Do you believe that Ela is justified in believing she must confront her life as a prophet alone?

8. Did you find evidence throughout the story that the Infinite protected Ela? Did He reward her? If so, then how? Has your Creator protected you and/or rewarded you?

9. What parallels did you find between Ela and familiar Old Testament prophets? What differences?

10. Do you believe the "other-world" setting of this story helped your understanding of Old Testament prophets? Why or why not?

ABOUT THE AUTHOR

R. J. Larson is the author of numerous devotionals featured in publications such as *Women's Devotional Bible* and *Seasons of a Woman's Heart*. She lives in Colorado Springs, Colorado, with her husband and their two sons. *Prophet* marks her debut in the fantasy genre.

An excerpt from

Kien Lantec lifted his chin, pressed his fingers against his wet skin, then swept the razor up his throat—just as the Infinite's voice resonated within his thoughts.

You will go to ToronSea.

"Ow!" Jolted by the voice, Kien gasped, dropped the razor, and leaped backward as the blade clattered on the tiled floor, threatening his bare toes. Hearing from one's Creator evidently involved undreamed-of risks. Kien exhaled and thumped a sweating fist against his heart. Steady.

ToronSea? Why? He'd just returned home on military leave. His first leave! And ToronSea was at the edge of nowhere, governed by a pack of thick-skulled antisocials who were supposed to be civilized Tracelanders. Controlling himself, Kien smudged some powdered balm against the bloodied nick beneath his jaw. "Go to ToronSea?"

You will warn My faithful in ToronSea of My displeasure because they are beguiled by worshipers of Atea. Tell the one who speaks for them that he must be faithful to Me and seek My will. You must also speak to certain deceived ones who love Atea. Tell them only that I see their failings and seek their hearts. The wise will hear Me.

Worshipers of Atea. Weren't they given over to disturbing quirks like divination through watching the death throes of victims in ritual strangulations? Kien hoped the often-repeated stories were unfounded. He didn't relish being the target of a divination ritual. "But, Infinite, I'm not a prophet. I'm a—"

Are you My servant?

Defeated before he'd begun. "Yes. I am Your servant." Kien meant every word of his pledge, but he didn't have to feel

345

comfortable about it, did he? He moistened his lips. "Am I no longer training to be a military judge?"

Waiting silence answered. Kien exhaled, retrieved his razor, and tried to ask an answerable question. "Should I depart today?"

Yes.

"Will I survive?"

More Omnipotent silence. Survival, evidently, shouldn't be his first consideration. "Fine. I'll finish shaving, then organize a few details and gather my gear. Will one knapsack suffice?"

He paused. Nothing. It seemed he must answer most of his own questions. And he had plenty to ask. For example, why wasn't the Infinite sending His true prophet, Ela of Parne, to confront ToronSea? Though sending Ela into any situation where her life might be endangered was completely unacceptable to Kien. For Ela's sake, Kien would go to ToronSea himself.

Ela . . . Kien grinned into his polished metal mirror and finished shaving. He now had an ideal excuse to visit the most captivating person now living in East Guard. No doubt Ela would—

"Kien?" His mother's voice echoed up the stairwell steps to his tower room. "Keee-en!"

He hurriedly wiped his face and smoothed his tunic before crossing the room and opening the door. Ara Lantec marched up the last few spiraling stone steps and stopped on the landing. Her cool gray eyes narrowed. She folded her elegant arms and glared, her usually serene face a study of restrained maternal fury. "Your destroyer is eating my garden! My whole garden! Unless you can control that monster, your father will have him shot by archers, then butchered and stewed!"

Kien saw six months of military wages vanish, consumed by a gargantuan warhorse's gluttony. "Sorry. I'll pay for the damages."

Ara seethed. "Paying for my garden won't help me this evening. My reception is ruined!"

He wasn't about to offer advice for saving his mother's reception—a gathering of the Tracelands' most elite women: wives of members of the Grand Assembly. And their daughters, whom

Kien devoutly hoped to escape. No doubt his parents would be planning his wedding the instant he smiled at one of those spoiled girls. Kien kissed his mother's perfectly arranged dark hair, hoping to soothe her. She scowled.

Barefoot, he started down the stairs. "Don't worry. You'll be rid of me, and the destroyer, by midday. I'm leaving on an assignment."

"What? You've just returned after six months of duty."

"It's an emergency." And that emergency looked positively inviting compared to his mother's wrath—not to mention her reception. Several steps down, he hesitated and looked up. "Anyway, I thought you wanted me gone."

"No, I simply want you to kill that destroyer!"

"Oh, sure." Kien hoped she hadn't caught his sarcasm. Chaining the beast, not killing it, would have to suffice. Kien rushed down the spiraling stone steps and charged through the stairwell's open doorway, into the adjoining hall. "Scythe!"

He found the black monster-horse in Mother's formal garden, dwarfing a crimson stand of miniature spice trees, crunching down leaf after expensive leaf. The massive creature turned his rump toward Kien and flicked his long black tail.

Kien growled. "I know you heard me. Don't you dare turn away!"

Scythe swung his big head around, irritable, still chewing. Kien glared and grabbed his halter. "Not another bite! Your morning meal is finished. Move. Now. Obey."

At least destroyers heeded *Obey*—though the command never improved their attitudes. The oversized brute grumbled as Kien led him toward the stable. To gain his cooperation, Kien said, "Let me make myself presentable, then we'll visit Ela."

Scythe's big ears perked. "Ela," Kien repeated, knowing she was this beast's greatest weakness. Kien's as well. "I'm sure she has six months' worth of shrubs for you to devour."

He continued to talk of Ela as he reluctantly chained Scythe to an iron ring embedded in stone within the stable yard. "Wait. I'll return." He'd won this round. With the destroyer at least.

His mother and the Infinite were different matters entirely.

ToronSea's Ateans and their lethal divination rituals demanded his presence.

Kien hoped he would survive.

✦ ✦ ✦

Seated on a woven mat near the ancient stone ruins of the Infinite's temple, Ela Roeh shifted in place and studied her scholars.

Five young ladies sat before her, decorously clad in pastel tunics and soft mantles. Wielding reed pens over their wax writing tablets, they bowed their fashionable, curl-crowned heads in the early autumn sunlight and wrote the morning's lesson.

It was troublesome to realize her students were all near her own age. In spirit, Ela felt older than eighteen. But surely not older than her dear eightyish chaperone. Ela slid a glance toward Tamri Het, a Siphran who'd followed Ela to the Tracelands seven months past. Seated nearby, Tamri looked utterly harmless. Who would ever believe this great-grandmother was a mob-inciting revolutionary? Particularly now, as she hummed like a girl, her veils fluttering in the light breeze . . .

Hmm. Perhaps in spirit she was older than Tamri. Not that it mattered.

Old-spirited or not, all prophets of Parne died young. The Infinite had confirmed it. Ela chewed her lower lip. Surely her death would serve the Infinite's purpose. But when?

Tzana, Ela's fragile little sister, crept onto the mat, her small, prematurely aged face wrinkled with both concern and with her incurable condition. "You look sad," Tzana whispered.

Bending, Ela returned the whisper. "I'm not."

However, she was restless. Ela tucked back one of Tzana's sparse curls and willed herself to relax. Tzana huddled beneath Ela's arm and shivered until Ela snuggled her close. The little girl disliked the cooler autumn air. Ela couldn't blame her. Tzana was accustomed to Parne's warmer climate, which was more soothing to her arthritis than these damp ocean-borne breezes.

Tonight, Ela decided, she must prepare more ointment to ease Tzana's aching joints.

Another whisper lifted—this time from among her students. "Finished!" Beka Thel, Kien's sister, set down her pen and tablet with a delicate click. Beka was as clever as her brother. And equally charming. Warm brown eyes sparkling, Beka threw Ela a mischievous smile so like Kien's that Ela sighed. Kien . . .

She returned Beka's smile. But as they waited for the other four girls to finish their work, Ela scolded herself inwardly. She mustn't think of Kien. Why torment herself? Yet she thought of him constantly. Not proper musings for a prophet. It was more fitting to consider the Infinite.

Ela closed her eyes and offered silent worship to her Creator until agitation permeated her thoughts. A dark, unsteadying fear. Why?

Infinite?

Silence. Yet she perceived His Spirit hovering near. Determined, Ela closed her eyes, focused on her prayer and on the Infinite. He might not answer whenever it pleased her, but He did answer. She simply needed to persist, then accept His decisions.

Infinite, what is Your will?

Before Ela could gasp, a vision enveloped her like a cloak and sucked her spirit into a whirlwind, transporting her to Parne. Home. But not to her family. Ela trembled as she recognized her surroundings. She was standing atop the guard's stone lookout shelter on Parne's soaring wall walk. Too high! Dizzied, she fixed her thoughts on breathing and enduring the vision's torment. Infinite!

Child of dust, the Infinite murmured, *what do you see?*

Scared to look down, Ela fixed her gaze on the western horizon. On a terrifyingly huge mirage-like image, spreading from north to south. Barely able to squeak out the words, Ela whispered, "I see a giant cauldron in the sky . . . pouring boiling liquid toward Parne."

Home. About to be destroyed.

As Ela tried to gather her wits, her Creator said, *My people have forsaken Me! They burn incense to other gods, and they worship idols made by their own hands.*

"No . . ."

Disaster is about to overtake Parne, and all who live there.

"No!" All who live there? Father. Mother. And her baby brother. Where was Tzana? Ela's arms and legs felt weighted now, as if turned to stone. Impossible to reach Tzana . . . though she heard her sister calling her from a distance.

Nightmarish images came to life behind her eyelids and within her thoughts. The vision expanded with such force, with such an inundation of faces, whisperings, and terrors, that Ela screamed. Falling from the lookout—

Darkness, thicker than she'd ever known, drew her soul beneath the ground, entombing her alive. As she clawed at dank walls within her vision and inhaled the stomach-churning stench of death, the Infinite said, *Prepare yourself.*

The vision's agony closed in tight, crushing her. Desperate to save her family, and Parne, Ela fought for consciousness and failed.

If you enjoyed *Prophet*, you may also like…

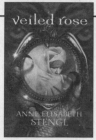
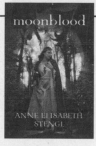